D1499164

VANDEMAI

FOLLY

A Bur Oak Book

9.13
Univ. of A KNA

Herbert Quick

Vandemark's Folly

With a new introduction
by Allan G. Bogue

University of Iowa Press Ψ Iowa City

40966

University of Iowa Press,
Iowa City 52242
Copyright 1922 by H. Quick;
copyright renewed 1949 by Ella Corey Quick;
this edition copyright © 1987 by the University of Iowa
All rights reserved
Printed in the United States of America
First paperback edition, 1987
Book and cover design by Richard Hendel
Typesetting of 1987 material by
G&S Typesetters, Inc., Austin, Texas
Printing and binding by
Versa Press, Inc., East Peoria, Illinois

No part of this book may be reproduced
or utilized in any form or by any means,
electronic or mechanical, including photocopying
and recording, without permission
in writing from the publisher.

Library of Congress Cataloging-in-Publication Data
Quick, Herbert, 1861–1925.
Vandemark's folly.
(A Bur Oak Book)
Originally published: Indianapolis: Bobbs-Merrill, 1922.
I. Title.
PS3533.U53V3   1987   813'.54   87-10800
ISBN 0-87745-182-6 (pbk.)

CONTENTS

HISTORICAL
INTRODUCTION

ALLAN G. BOGUE

In the barracks of the Red Cross at Vladivostok, the head
of a commission to conclude that agency's work in the
Far East lay close to death, his "heart missing on all the
cylinders but one for lack of circulating medium." Feebly
trying to put his affairs in order, he requested that an old
Iowa friend be asked to complete a novel lying unfinished in his desk at home in Berkeley Springs, West Virginia.[1] The year was 1920 and the man was John Herbert
Quick. But Quick survived the hemorrhaging ulcer, returned to the United States, underwent surgery, and himself completed the manuscript, which was published in
1922 as the novel *Vandemark's Folly*.

Herbert Quick, born in 1861 in a "little shanty" close
to the border between Grundy and Hardin counties in
Iowa, grew up on a farm in Grundy County. Somewhat
crippled by polio at an early age, he became a school-
teacher in his teens and remained one until—after reading law for several years in the office of an attorney in
Mason City—he gained admission to the Iowa bar. Then
followed fifteen years of legal practice in Sioux City, beginning in 1890. During this period Quick energetically
prosecuted boodlers (political grafters) and for two years
served as the reform mayor of the city. But from an early
age he had dreamed of being a writer: "I cannot remember when things that I saw and experienced did not appeal to me as the stuff of writing."[2] One of his close
friends in Sioux City would recall Quick's habit of recording stories, expressions, and phrases that he hoped to

use in fiction.[3] In 1901, at the age of forty, he published his first book, a volume of fairy tales for children. In the same year he submitted a poem to the *Century Magazine* about the prairie fires and plant and animal life on the Iowa prairie he had known as a boy; the editor accepted it with an encouraging note. These events strengthened Quick's appetite for writing, and after he had published *Double Trouble*, which he later called his "first really successful novel," he abandoned the law in 1905 and became a professional writer. Friends clucked, he recalled, and said, "Poor old Quick! The old simpleton will starve surely now! And he had a fairly good law practice!"[4]

Herbert Quick published eighteen books before his death, but journalism sustained him during the early years of his literary career. He had already written numerous stories for a Sioux City publication on behalf of the dry-farming movement, and in 1908 he became associate editor of *La Follette's Weekly Magazine*. The next year he became editor of *Farm and Fireside*, holding that position until 1916. During this period he established himself as one of the country's leading agricultural journalists and became a member of the inner circle of writers of the *Saturday Evening Post*. Meanwhile he contributed a stream of editorials to the daily press.

Herbert Quick was a Progressive Democrat whose deep affection for the agricultural heritage of the country and belief in the superiority of rural life did not blind him to the fact that there was much in rural America that was both unpleasant and inequitable. Deeply influenced as a young man by reading Henry George's *Progress and Poverty*, he was convinced that Americans must change their fundamental attitudes concerning the nation's natural resources and adapt education to the particular needs of country folk. But at the same time he was an optimistic, practical man who understood the ways of politics and who could, himself, play the public relations man, lobbyist, or politician. He once tried his hand at real estate promotion, ran on occasion for public office, and later prided himself on the fact that he had been in "the group that put the parcels post law through, and then the Federal Farm Loan Act."[5] In 1916 President Wilson appointed him to a position on the Federal Farm Loan Board, and he spent three years helping to organize the system of rural credit agencies that was perhaps Progressivism's greatest contribution to meeting the unique needs of American farmers.

While serving as a member of the Federal Farm Loan Board, he began the first of what he planned as a series of novels depicting life in the nineteenth-century Iowa that he had known. These novels were not conceived on the spur of the moment—he later claimed that he had developed the basic concept and begun to plan the volumes before he was twenty and that he had described the project to a friend in an Indianapolis park some fifteen years before the first of them, *Vandemark's Folly*, appeared.[6] Quick regarded his work on the Federal Farm Loan Board as a form of war work, of the kind that a man of his age and physical condition could most usefully perform. But his duties took him from his writing, and when the war was over he resigned to devote full time to the Iowa novels, forgoing the salary of $10,000 per year that the position would have brought him during the remaining five years of his term of appointment. However, as Quick put it to a literary critic in 1924, he was "the worst hound pup you ever saw for following off false trails."[7] The Red Cross assignment intrigued him and almost cost him his life. After he had undergone surgery at the Mayo Clinic, the Iowa novels together with his apple farm and country home in Berkeley Springs, West Virginia, became his major concerns. Eventually he completed the novel that had languished in his desk during the Siberian adventure and also published its two companions,

The Hawkeye and *The Invisible Woman,* although ill health continued to plague him, and his ulcer required surgery again in 1923. He had completed the first segment of an autobiography when, following an address delivered at the University of Missouri in May 1925, a heart attack ended his career.

While he was planning the Iowa novels, Quick visualized each of them as part of a trilogy portraying midwestern life from an ever-widening perspective. He planned to call the first novel *Vandemark Township,* the second *Monterey County,* and the third simply *Iowa.* The first book would describe immigration to the new state of Iowa and the rural pioneering experience there during the 1850s. The second would portray in detail county politics and life in the county seat. The concluding volume would concern state politics during the late nineteenth century.[8] Although this original design comprised only three novels, Quick, while working on his autobiography, began to plan a fourth novel, in which he intended to return to the Iowa farm life that he had rendered so successfully in *Vandemark's Folly* and *The Hawkeye.* The fourth book, tentatively entitled *Hell Slew,* was to be set in the twentieth century and would deal to some extent with the German-American settlement in Monterey County.[9] His death terminated this project.

Quick sold the serial rights to the first Iowa novel to *Ladies' Home Journal.* In negotiations which he then conducted with the Bobbs-Merrill Company for publication of the book, he described it and discussed its relation to the two that were to follow:

> This is the first of three novels which will cover the history of Iowa from its early settlement to recent times. The first which is finished, is the way things look and happened to a green boy settling in Iowa in the fifties. It is a cross section of the life of a boy born

in southeastern New York in 1837 and takes in life on the Erie Canal, the factory life of the day, the things people thought and did, and the great flood of immigration into the Midwest. It sees only what a boy of that sort could see struggling with life on the trail and on the prairie farm. It has the lost prairie of Iowa in it. . . .

The three [novels] will constitute a single work and will be the story of Iowa and of the whole Middle West. It will be a sort of prose epic of the greatest thing in history of its kind. I lived this life, and am the only writing man who did. Garland did not live it, nor did Hough, though the former was born in Wisconsin, and the latter in Illinois [sic]. I was of the thing, as they were not. The story I have finished is a mingling of the life of my father, of my wife's father, of our relatives and neighbors.[10]

Although Quick resisted editorial changes to his book, he was apparently more tolerant of changes that magazine editors felt obliged to make. He allowed the editors of *Ladies' Home Journal* to leave "all the guts out of the story" when they prepared it for serialization in 1921 and to change the title to *Vandemark's Folly*. When the editors of Bobbs-Merrill also balked at using the title *Vandemark Township*, he suggested the *Journal*'s title as a satisfactory compromise.[11] The titles of the later books were likewise changed in deference to editorial criticism, somewhat obscuring Quick's original grand design.

Vandemark's Folly is the recollected story of Jacobus Teunis Vandemark, born in Ulster County, New York, on Turnip Day, July 27, 1838. His widowed mother took a second husband, a rascally patent-medicine salesman, who made life a living hell for both mother and son and put the lad to work in a cotton mill at the age of six. When he was thirteen, the boy ran away to work on the

Erie Canal and lost touch with his mother. But after several years of working for a friendly canal captain, Vandemark tracked her west to Madison, Wisconsin. His stepfather satisfied the son's claim to her estate by deeding him a section of land in Iowa and outfitting him so that he could settle upon it. On the trail to Iowa, young Vandemark traded his livestock for additional animals, arriving in Monterey County as the owner of a considerable herd of cattle, the basis for his nickname "Cow." During the trip he also encountered various individuals whose destinies were to mingle with his own; most fatefully, he gave shelter to Virginia Royall, who was fleeing from the advances of her womanizing brother-in-law, Buckner Gowdy, a wealthy Kentuckian. When the young people arrived at his land, they discovered that it was Hell Slew, an intimidating marsh, soon derisively renamed Vandemark's Folly. Having confronted this crisis, Vandemark settled into the task of developing a farm. Interwoven in the book are his later relations with Virginia Royall and Buck Gowdy and accounts of the local claim club, a prairie fire, and other incidents of pioneer life in central Iowa. Having returned from brief service in the Civil War, young Jake finally trounced Buck Gowdy and saved Virginia from an Iowa blizzard by finding shelter in a straw stack, where he proposed. Not only had he won the most desirable young woman in the county, but time would show that Hell Slew was fantastically rich farmland. Looking back on these events, Uncle Jake Vandemark believed he had been a most fortunate man.

Herbert Quick undoubtedly believed that he had dealt successfully with a great theme, but it seems clear that the enthusiasm expressed in his letters to the Bobbs-Merrill staff also reflected his desire to spur them to more active advertising of the book as well as the companion novels that were to come later. Quick refused to allow the editors to claim that *Vandemark's Folly* was the best

American novel ever written, but he was willing for them to publicize the fact that he had refused to allow them to make that claim. He wrote to Hewitt H. Howland of the Bobbs-Merrill Company:

> Really the story is a better treatment of The Growth of the Soil than Hamsun's book for which he got the Nobel prize this year. It is the inside story of the greatest epoch in American history and the growth of the soil. And while we had some immoralities and departures from the Commandments as I show, I am glad to say that veritism itself could not reduce the settlement of our soil to the dead level of sordidness shown in the Norwegian tale. And we did it on a great scale and not by carrying burdens on the back as Hamsun's Isak did. The difference between the settlement of our Midwest and the newer parts of Norway is just the difference between Jake Vandemark with his train of cows, and Isak with his burdens on his back and his pair of goats, and Jacob's nice wife and the irregular relations between Isak and his woman. . . .[12]

In the margin of this letter Quick penciled the word "Conceit" and added the word "No." Yet the need for advertising copy was perhaps in Quick's mind: he ended the letter with "Anything in this?" Later he was to comment on the "simplicity and elemental character which is the great charm of Vandemark for many readers."[13] When an Iowa lady complained that there was too much sex in the book for readers of school age, Quick defended himself:

> I think the book will be read all through the future as having significance as to the moral, political, sociological, and historical development of America. I want

the readers, whether they are in school or out of it, to
know what boys were allowed to do and see on the
Erie and the other canals of that date. I want them to
know what sort of people carried on the great and
necessary work of transportation, which saved the
Union when it tended to break at the end of transportation lines. I want them to know how the people of
the United States allowed their little children to work
themselves to death in the factories of that period. So
I use actual occurrences which I have obtained from
actual participants—as the basis of my novel. I am
glad to have been able to find them. My only regret
lies in my inability to use them as well as they might
have been used. But I would not gloss one of them
over.[14]

In general, reviewers greeted *Vandemark's Folly* with
praise; some even discovered in it qualities essential to
that unachieved masterpiece, "the great American
novel."[15] *The Hawkeye,* which appeared in the next year,
apparently benefited from the favorable reception of
Vandemark's Folly, and it in turn found new readers for
the first book. Visiting Iowa to promote *Vandemark's
Folly,* Quick found himself "lionized to an embarrassing
degree," in both Iowa and Missouri; and a favorite pas-
time of those whose memories extended back into the
nineteenth century was trying to match the names of actual Iowans with Quick's characters. Benjamin Shambaugh of the Department of Political Science at the State
University of Iowa and director of the state historical society delighted Quick by repeating his conversation about
Vandemark's Folly with Samuel Sloan, the English department's specialist on the novel. "I don't know anything about novels," said Shambaugh, "but as history
this is a great and an accurate book." "I don't know anything about history," replied Sloan, "but as a novel it is a
great book."[16]

The *Nation*'s "roving critic," Carl Van Doren, wrote one of the more unfavorable reviews of *Vandemark's Folly*. According to Van Doren the book was a throwback to the historical romances of twenty years earlier, and Jacob Vandemark was drawn "very much in the manner of" Winston Churchill's David Ritchie. Both heroes, he argued, were unfortunately constrained by the romantic convention that descended from *Lorna Doone*'s ponderous hero, John Ridd. It was a pity, he suggested, because the westward movement was a great theme. Although he commended the research, liked some of the minor characters, and found the style "free and charming," he argued that

> to see wherein . . . [*Vandemark's Folly*] falls short
> of some of the greatness with which it is credited,
> one has only to think of any of the better Icelandic
> sagas. The parallel is exact. The sagas, set down with
> scrupulous exactness or with the look of scrupulous
> exactness, are the records of certain settlers who
> went from an older country to a newer. They, unlike
> *Vandemark's Folly* with its romantic conventions,
> keep their eyes forever on the immediate facts of life
> as their writers understand them. They know how to
> represent heroic deeds by letting the deeds speak for
> themselves. . . .[17]

Although he clearly distinguished between the role of the novelist and the job of the historian, Herbert Quick apparently believed that in this instance the critics should have asked, Are Cow Vandemark and his fellow characters believable? Could the events in which they participated really have happened? To these questions the author would have replied: "This man and his relatives, friends, and enemies did indeed live in frontier Iowa; they did the things described in the book." The benevolent glow that suffuses Uncle Jake's narrative may be found again and again in the stories of early settlers in county histories and in the statements of pioneers in the transactions of the old-settlers associations. Scattered throughout *Vandemark's Folly* is a generous sample of the vernacular idiom of the midwestern frontier. If Buck Gowdy seems a somewhat melodramatic villain, we should remember that in the pioneer period some Iowans did in fact own broad holdings, that some Iowans did in fact drive their horses hard, that some Iowans did in fact pursue women with ruthless enthusiasm. It is not too much to believe that one individual did all three. The initial verdict of literary historians, however, was that Quick's Iowa novels were not masterpieces, that as novels they fell short of Willa Cather's stories of pioneer life in the Middle West. At the time, Quick apparently regarded Hamlin Garland and Emerson Hough as his major rivals in interpreting the midwestern experience. Garland originally achieved success by writing realistic stories of the farm, highly pessimistic in tone. Quick believed that the midwestern pioneer had taken part in an epic experience that was personally rewarding; critics detected romantic, even melodramatic, overtones in his book.

The discursiveness for which some critics faulted *Vandemark's Folly* is an asset for the historian because it portrays the detail and color of the pioneer era. Although Quick preferred writing fiction to factual articles, he had the journalist's fetish for accuracy. In some earlier novels he had tried to convey an ideological message; in the books of the Hawkeye trilogy, he was trying to tell good stories while at the same time describing the natural environment and writing the early social history of the prairie heartland. He accentuates this point in the letters he wrote about *Vandemark's Folly*, emphasizing the research he had put into the novel; and we know that he borrowed books from the Iowa State Historical Society and read Iowa newspapers at the Library of Congress while preparing the last two volumes of the trilogy.[18] Of *Vandemark's Folly* he wrote:

> The life in New York and along the canal in the earlier portions of the book is historically accurate. My father and my mother and my grandparents, and my wife's parents and grandparents lived in York state during these years. I got the cotton-mill facts from an old man who knew from having worked in the mills. He was eighty-five years old. The canal life is from a hired man who used to come to Iowa and work in the harvest field with me on my father's Iowa farm year after year, and talked all the time of life on the canal. But in order to know exactly the mental atmosphere I studied the period as if I were going to write a history of canals in America.[19]

He admitted that characters in the book were modeled on Iowans of his acquaintance and was somewhat embarrassed when one reader correctly identified Coker F. "Father" Clarkson, member of an eminent Iowa political family. American literature provides few, if any, better descriptions of the prairie than those in *Vandemark's Folly;* they arose from Quick's recollections of the days when he and his brother picked up the eggs of prairie chickens by the hundred and when prairie fires ran unchecked from the Cedar River to the Iowa.

We cannot argue, of course, that Quick's research was as thorough as that of a historian should be, nor was he trying to do more than present a generalized picture of western immigration and prairie settlement. But the social structure, institutional fabric, and many of the local events described in *Vandemark's Folly* ring true. Arthur M. Schlesinger, Sr., believed that the novel revealed a "historian's viewpoint" in its author and, according to

Quick, invited him to contribute a volume to the twelve-volume history of civilization in America the historian was planning.[20]

Had Quick's reading included Frederick Jackson Turner's "The Significance of the Frontier in American History"? While that seminal essay may have influenced him, its basic ideas are to be found, at least in part, in *Progress and Poverty,* which he had read before Turner presented his famous paper. In any case, the idea that the frontier settlers were in a primitive state of "pre-civilization" is to be found in Quick's writing.[21] Unlike Turner, however, he was sure that the prairie frontier was a unique one, where the pioneers first met and solved the challenge of the grasslands.[22] After *The Hawkeye* appeared, he sent a gift copy to Turner. Alas, the historian's letter of response, though comforting, could not be converted to advertising that would sell copies to the "hoipolloi."[23] On the whole, Turner's version of the frontier hypothesis does not seem to have been a major influence in shaping Quick's ideas. But the contrast Quick drew between pioneering in the forest and on the grasslands was to appear, much more fully developed, in Walter Prescott Webb's highly successful book, *The Great Plains.*

Vandemark's Folly sold well for the period, but not spectacularly. Appearing early in 1922, it advanced to tenth place on one list of best-sellers during that spring, but it did not become a best-seller in the usual meaning of that phrase.[24] Correspondence between Quick and officers of the Bobbs-Merrill Company reveals some disappointment at sales during 1922.[25] Quick hinted that the publisher's advertising campaign had been ineffective.[26] Bobbs-Merrill sold reprint rights to A. L. Burt and Company for a popular edition that appeared in 1924. In 1939 Grosset and Dunlap obtained reprint rights to both *Vandemark's Folly* and *The Hawkeye.* Details concerning these later printings are apparently unavailable. At least one Iowa newspaper arranged to serialize *Vandemark's Folly* in its columns during the early 1930s.[27] One of the officers of Bobbs-Merrill wrote in January of 1922, "I rather imagine that we have in *Vandemark's Folly* the real epic of the development of Iowa."[28] Yet the faithfulness with which Quick had depicted the Iowa story may have detracted from the general appeal of the book.

Between 1940 and the late 1960s Herbert Quick found few admirers among specialists in American literature. Then, however, scholars began to find enduring merits in his work.[29] One of them, Professor Carl L. Keen, suggested that the Iowa trilogy is an outstanding illustration of the Adamic myth in American fiction, in which Cow Vandemark represents the unfallen Adam.[30] Decades earlier Clarence A. Andrews had called *Vandemark's Folly* and its companion, *The Hawkeye,* "the two best novels ever written about the Iowa farm and town scene of the nineteenth century."[31] To the historian *Vandemark's Folly* is valuable because it faithfully depicts one chapter in the epic of a nation moving westward. If the book is, in reality, only "near history," few historians have been able to match its perceptive portrayal of the pioneer experience.

NOTES

Note: This is a revised version of my article "Herbert Quick's Hawkeye Trilogy," first published in *Books at Iowa* 16 (April 1972).

1. Herbert Quick to Frederic F. Van de Water, April 28, 1924. A copy of this letter is to be found in the files of the Bobbs-Merrill Company in the Lilly Library, Indiana University, Bloomington, Indiana (hereafter cited as BMCP). Permission to quote

from unpublished letters has kindly been granted by Herbert Quick's daughter, Mrs. Margaret Q. Ball.

2. Ibid.

3. *Sioux City Tribune*, October 21, 1925.

4. Herbert Quick to Frederic F. Van de Water, April 28, 1924. BMCP.

5. Herbert Quick to Edgar R. Harlan, September 26, 1924. Edgar R. Harlan Papers, Iowa Department of History and Archives, Des Moines, Iowa (hereafter cited as ERHP).

6. Herbert Quick to H. H. Howland, December 22, 1921. BMCP. Quick's autobiography, *One Man's Life* (Indianapolis, 1925), did not carry his story beyond the early prairie years, and he destroyed most of his correspondence. A number of the letters cited in this introduction are rich in autobiographical detail; also of considerable interest is Quick's article, "I Picked My Goal at Ten—Reached It at Sixty," *American Magazine* 94 (October 1922): 50–51, 161–64. See also Carl Keen, "Herbert Quick and the American Dream," *Valleys of History* 3 (Autumn 1967): 12–16.

7. Herbert Quick to Frederic F. Van de Water, April 28, 1924. BMCP.

8. Herbert Quick to H. H. Howland, April 26, 1921. BMCP.

9. Herbert Quick to H. H. Howland, February 2 and 6, 1925. BMCP.

10. Herbert Quick to W. C. Bobbs, February 26, 1921. BMCP.

11. Herbert Quick to H. H. Howland, August 1, 1921. BMCP.

12. Herbert Quick to H. H. Howland, September 10, 1921. BMCP.

13. Herbert Quick to H. H. Howland, July 2, 1922. BMCP.

14. Herbert Quick to D. L. Chambers, March 3, 1922. BMCP.

15. See, for instance, *New York Times Book Review*, December 7, 1924, p. 8.

16. Herbert Quick to H. H. Howland, May 30, 1922. BMCP.

17. Carl Van Doren, "The Roving Critic," *Nation*, March 15, 1922, p. 319.

18. Herbert Quick to H. H. Howland, July 2, 1922. BMCP; *Des Moines Tribune*, May 11, 1925.

19. Herbert Quick to H. H. Howland, December 22, 1921. BMCP.

20. Herbert Quick to H. H. Howland, February 9, 1923. BMCP.

21. Herbert Quick to Edgar R. Harlan, September 26, 1924. ERHP.

22. Herbert Quick to Edgar R. Harlan, May 2, 1925. ERHP.

23. Herbert Quick to H. H. Howland, July 1, 1923; Quick to D. L. Chambers, August 11, 1923. BMCP.

24. The leading authority on Herbert Quick's fiction, Professor Carl L. Keen of Oshkosh State University, believes that Bobbs-Merrill sold 75,000 copies of the book during the first few months after publication. A royalty statement among the August 1922 letters in the Quick correspondence (BCMP) suggests a sale of 27,500 copies through the first half of 1922. In a letter to this writer dated July 7, 1969, Miss Lois Stewart of Bobbs-Merrill reports that the company print-and-bind records show a printing of 34,000 copies.

25. Herbert Quick to D. L. Chambers, April 21, 1922. BMCP.

26. Barton W. Curry to Herbert Quick, September 23, 1922. BMCP.

27. See the *Des Moines Tribune Capital,* October 20, 1931.

28. D. L. Chambers to Edgar R. Harlan, January 30, 1922. ERHP.

29. Roy W. Meyer, *The Middle Western Farm Novel in the Twentieth Century* (Lincoln, 1965), pp. 47–56; Carl Lee Keen, "The Fictional Writings of Herbert Quick," Ph.D. diss., Michigan State University, 1967; and Frederick Garver Morain, "Herbert Quick, Iowa Agrarian," Ph.D. diss., Yale University, 1970.

30. Carl Lee Keen, "Fictional Writings of Herbert Quick," p. 3; see p. 132 for another general interpretation of the place of *Vandemark's Folly* in the trilogy.

31. Clarence A. Andrews, *A Literary History of Iowa* (Iowa City, 1922), pp. 72–73.

VANDEMARK'S
FOLLY

INTRODUCTION

The work of writing the history cf this township—I mean Vandemark Township, Monterey County, State of Iowa—has been turned over to me. I have been asked to do this I guess because I was the first settler in the township; it was named after me; I live on my own farm —the oldest farm operated by the original settler in this part of the country; I know the history of these thirty-six square miles of land and also of the wonderful swarming of peoples which made the prairies over; and the agent of the Excelsior County History Company of Chicago, having heard of me as an authority on local history, has asked me to write this part of their new History of Monterey County for which they are now canvassing for subscribers. I can never write this as it ought to be written, and for an old farmer with no learning to try to do it may seem impudent, but sometimes a great genius may come up who will put on paper the strange and splendid story of Iowa, of Monterey County, and of Vandemark Township; and when he does write this, the greatest history ever written, he may find such adventures as mine of some use to him. Those who lived this history are already few in number, are fast passing away and will soon be gone. I lived it, and so did my neighbors and old companions and friends. So here I begin.

The above was my first introduction to this history; and just here, after I had written a nice fat pile of manuscript, this work came mighty close to coming to an end.

INTRODUCTION

I suppose every person is more or less of a fool, but at my age any man ought to be able to keep himself from being gulled by the traveling swindlers who go traipsing about the country selling lightning rods, books, and trying by every means in their power to get the name of honest and propertied men on the dotted line. Just now I began tearing up the opening pages of my History of Vandemark Township, and should have thrown them in the base-burner if it had not been for my granddaughter, Gertrude.

The agent of the Excelsior County History Company called and asked me how I was getting along with the history, and when I showed him what I have written, he changed the subject and began urging me to subscribe for a lot of copies when it is printed, and especially, to make a contract for having my picture in it. He tried to charge me two hundred seventy-five dollars for a steel engraving, and said I could keep the plate and have others made from it. Then I saw through him. He never wanted my history of the township. He just wanted to swindle me into buying a lot of copies to give away, and he wanted most to bamboozle me into having a picture made, not half so good as I can get for a few dollars a dozen at any good photographer's, and pay him the price of a good team of horses for it. He thought he could gull old Jake Vandemark! If I would pay for it, I could get printed in the book a few of my remarks on the history of the township, and my two-hundred-and-seventy-five-dollar picture. Others would write about something else, and get their pictures in. In that way this smooth scoundrel would make thousands of dollars out of people's vanity—and he expected me to be one of them! If I can put him in jail I'll do it—or I would if it were not for posting myself as a fool.

"Look here," I said, after he had told me what a splendid thing it would be to have my picture in the book so future generations could see what a big man I was. "Do you want what I know about the history of Vandemark Township in your book, or are you just out after my money?"

"Well," he said, "if, after you've written twenty or thirty pages, and haven't got any nearer Vandemark Township than a canal-boat, somewhere east of Syracuse, New York, in 1850, I'll need some money if I print the whole story—judging of its length by that. Of course, the publication of the book must be financed."

"There's the door!" I said, and pointed to it.

He went out like a shot, and Gertrude, who was on the front porch, came flying in to see what he was running from. I was just opening the stove door. In fact I had put some scraps of paper in; but there was no fire.

"Why, grandpa," she cried, "what's the matter? What's this manuscript you're destroying? Tell me about it!"

"Give it to me!" I shouted; but she sat down with it and began reading. I rushed out, and was gone an hour. When I came back, she had pasted the pages together, and was still reading them. She came to me and put her arms about my neck and kissed me; and finally coaxed me into telling her all about the disgraceful affair.

Well, the result of it all was that she has convinced me of the fact that I had better go on with the history. She says that these county-history promoters are all slippery people, but that if I can finish the history as I have begun, it may be well worth while.

"There are publishers," she said, "who do actually print such things. Maybe a real publisher will want this. I know a publisher who may be glad to get it. And, anyhow, it is a shame for all your experiences to be lost to the world. It's very interesting as far as you've got. Go on with it; and if no publisher wants to print it now, we'll give the manuscript to the Public Library in Monterey Centre, and maybe, long after both of us are dead and gone, some historian will find it and have it printed. Some time it will be found precious. Write it, grandpa, for my sake! We can make a wonderful story of it."

"We?" I said.

"You, I mean, of course," she replied; "but, if you really want me to do it, I will type it for you, and maybe do a little editing. Maybe you'll let me do a little foot-note once in a while, so my name will go into it with yours. I'd be awfully proud, grandpa."

"It'll take a lot of time," I said.

"And you can spare the time as well as not," she answered.

"You all think because I don't go into the field with a team any more," I objected, "that I don't amount to anything on the farm; but I tell you that what I do in the way of chores and planning, practically amounts to a man's work."

"Of course it does," she admitted, though between you and me it wasn't so. "But any man can do the chores, and the planning you can do still—and nobody can write the History of Vandemark Township but Jacobus Teunis Vandemark. You owe it to the West, and to the world."

So, here I begin the second time. I have been bothered up to now by feeling that I have not been making much progress; but now there will be no need for me to skip anything. I begin, just as that canvassing rascal said, a long way from Vandemark Township, and many years ago in point of time; but I am afloat with my prow toward the setting sun on that wonderful ribbon of water which led to the West. I was caught in the current. Nobody could live along the Erie Canal in those days without feeling the suck of the forests, and catching a breath now and then of the prairie winds. So all this really belongs in the history.

J. T. VANDEMARK.

VANDEMARK'S FOLLY

CHAPTER I

A FLAT DUTCH TURNIP BEGINS ITS CAREER

MY name is Jacobus Teunis Vandemark. I usually
sign J. T. Vandemark; and up to a few years ago
I thought as much as could be that my first name was
Jacob; but my granddaughter Gertrude, who is strong
on family histories, looked up my baptismal record in an
old Dutch Reformed church in Ulster County, New York,
came home and began teasing me to change to Jacobus.
At first I would not give up to what I thought just her
silly taste for a name she thought more stylish than plain
old Jacob; but she sent back to New York and got a certi-
fied copy of the record. So I had to knuckle under.
Jacobus is in law my name just as much as Teunis, and
both of them, I understand, used to be pretty common
names among the Vandemarks, Brosses, Kuyckendalls,
Westfalls and other Dutch families for generations. It
makes very little difference after all, for most of the
neighbors call me Old Jake Vandemark, and some of the
very oldest settlers still call me Cow Vandemark, because
I came into the county driving three or four yoke of
cows—which make just as good draught cattle as oxen,
being smarter but not so powerful. This nickname is gall

I

and wormwood to Gertrude, but I can't quite hold with her whims on the subject of names. She spells the old surname van der Marck—a little *v* and a little *d* with an *r* run in, the first two syllables written like separate words, and then the big *M* for Mark with a *c* before the *k*. But she will know better when she gets older and has more judgment. Just now she is all worked up over the family history on which she began laboring when she went east to Vassar and joined the Daughters of the American Revolution. She has tried to coax me to adopt "van der Marck" as my signature, but it would not jibe with the name of the township if I did; and anyhow it would seem like straining a little after style to change a name that has been a household word hereabouts since there were any households. The neighbors would never understand it, anyhow; and would think I felt above them. Nothing loses a man his standing among us farmers like putting on style.

I was born of Dutch parents in Ulster County, New York, on July 27, 1838. It is the only anniversary I can keep track of, and the only reason why I remember it is because on that day, except when it came on a Sunday, I have sown my turnips ever since 1855. Everybody knows the old rhyme:

> "On the twenty-seventh of July
> Sow you turnips, wet or dry."

And wet or dry, my parents in Ulster County, long, long ago, sowed their little red turnip on that date.

I often wonder what sort of dwelling it was, and whether the July heat was not pretty hard on my poor mother. I think of this every birthday. I guess a habit of mind has grown up which I shall never break off; the moment I begin sowing turnips I think of my mother bringing forth her only child in the heat of dog-days, and of the sweat of suffering on her forehead as she listened to my first cry. She is more familiar to me, and really dearer in this imaginary scene than in almost any real memory I have of her.

I do not remember Ulster County at all. My first memory of my mother is of a time when we lived in a little town the name and location of which I forget; but it was by a great river which must have been the Hudson I guess. She had made me a little cap with a visor and I was very proud of it and of myself. I picked up a lump of earth in the road and threw it over a stone fence, covered with vines that were red with autumn leaves—woodbine or poison-ivy I suppose. I felt very big, and ran on ahead of my mother until she called to me to stop for fear of my falling into the water. We had come down to the big river. I could hardly see the other side of it. The whole scene now grows misty and dim; but I remember a boat coming to the shore, and out of it stepped John Rucker.

Whether he was then kind or cross to me or to my mother I can not remember. Probably my mind was too young to notice any difference less than that between love and cruelty. I know I was happy; and it seems to me that the chief reason of my joy was the new cap and the fact that my heart swelled and I was proud of myself. I do not believe that I was more than three years old. All this may be partly a dream; but I think not.

John Rucker was no dream. He was my mother's

second husband; and by the time I was five years old, and had begun to go to one little school after another as we moved about, John Rucker had become the dark cloud in my life. He paid little attention to me, but I recollect that by the time we had settled ourselves at Tempe I was afraid of him. Two or three times he whipped me, but no more severely than was the custom among parents. Other little boys were whipped just as hard, and still were not afraid of their fathers. I think now that I was afraid of him because my mother was. I can not tell how he looked then, except that he was a tall stooped man with a yellowish beard all over his face and talked in a sort of whine to others, and in a sharp domineering way to my mother. To me he scarcely ever spoke at all. At Tempe he had some sort of a shop in which he put up a dark-colored liquid—a patent medicine—which he sold by traveling about the country. I remember that he used to complain of lack of money and of the expense of keeping me; and that my mother made clothes for people in the village.

Tempe was a little village near the Erie Canal somewhere between Rome and Syracuse. There was a dam and water-power in Tempe or near there, which, I think, was the overflow from a reservoir built as a water-supply for the Erie Canal—but I am not sure. I can not find Tempe on the map; but many names have been changed since those days. I think it was farther west than Canastota, but I am not sure—it was a long time ago.

2

Once, for some reason of his own, and when he had got some money in an unexpected way, Rucker took my mother and me to Oneida for an outing. My mother and I camped by the roadside while Rucker went somewhere to a place where a lot of strangers were starting a colony of Free Lovers. After he returned he told my mother that we had been invited to join the colony, and argued that it would be a good thing for us all; but my mother got very mad at him, and started to walk home leading me by the hand. She sobbed and cried as we walked along, especially after it grew late in the afternoon and Rucker had not overtaken us with the horse and democrat wagon. She seemed insulted, and broken-hearted; and was angry for the only time I remember. When we at last heard the wagon clattering along behind us in the woods, we sat down on a big rock by the side of the road, and Rucker meanly pretended not to see us until he had driven on almost out of sight. My mother would not let me call out to him; and I stood shaking my fist at the wagon as it went on past us, and feeling for the first time that I should like to kill John Rucker. Finally he stopped and made us follow on until we overtook him, my mother crying and Rucker sneering at both of us. This must have been when I was nine or ten years old. The books say that the Oneida Community was established there in 1847, when I was nine.

Long before this I had been put out by John Rucker to work in a factory in Tempe. It was a cotton mill run, I think, by the water-power I have mentioned. We lived in a log house on a side-hill across the road and above the cotton mill. We had no laws in those days against child labor or long hours. In the winter I worked by candle-light for two hours before breakfast. We went to work at five—I did this when I was six years old—

and worked until seven, when we had half an hour for breakfast. As I lived farther from the mill than most of the children who were enslaved there, my breakfast-time was very short. At half past seven we began again and worked until noon, when we had an hour for dinner. At one o'clock we took up work once more and quit at half past five for supper. At six we began our last trick and worked until eight—thirteen hours of actual labor.

I began this so young and did so much of it that I feel sure my growth was stunted by it—I never grew above five feet seven, though my mother was a good-sized woman, and she told me that my father was six feet tall— and my children are all tall. Maybe I should never have been tall anyhow, as the Dutch are usually broad rather than long. Of course this life was hard. I was very little when I began watching machines and tending spindles, and used to cry sometimes because I was so tired. I almost forgot what it was to play; and when I got home at night I staggered with sleepiness.

My mother used to undress me and put me to bed, when she was not pressed with her own work; and even then she used to come and kiss me and see that I had not kicked the quilt off before she lay down for her short sleep. I remember once or twice waking up and feeling her tears on my face, while she whispered "My poor baby!" or other loving and motherly words over me. When John Rucker went off on his peddling trips she would take me out of the factory for a few days and send me to school. The teachers understood the case, and did all they could to help me in spite of my irregular attendance; so that I learned to read after a fashion, and as for arithmetic, I seemed to understand that naturally. I was a poor writer, though; and until I was grown I never could actually write much more than my name. I could always make a stagger at a letter when I had to by printing with a pen or pencil, and when I did not see my mother all day on account of her work and mine, I used to print out a letter sometimes and leave it in a hollow apple-tree which stood before the house. We called this our post-office. I am not complaining, though, of my lack of education. I have had a right good chance in life, and have no reason to complain—except that I wish I could have had a little more time to play and to be with my mother. It was she, though, that had the hard time.

By this time I had begun to understand why John Rucker was always so cross and cruel to my mother. He was disappointed because he had supposed when he married her that she had property. My father had died while a lawsuit for the purpose of settling his father's estate was pending, and Rucker had thought, and so had my mother, that this lawsuit would soon be ended, and that she would have the property, his share of which had been left to her by my father's will. I have never known why the law stood in my mother's way, or why it was at last that Rucker gave up all hope and vented his spite on my mother and on me. I do not blame him for feeling put out, for property is property after all, but to abuse me and my mother shows what a bad man he was. Sometimes he used to call me a damned little beggar. The first time he did that my mother looked at him with a kind of lost look as if all the happiness in life were gone. After that, even when a letter came from the lawyers who were looking after the case, holding out hope, and always asking for money, and Rucker for a day or so was quite chipper and affectionate to my mother in a sickening sort of sneaking way, her spirits never rose so far as I could see. I suppose she was what might be called a broken-hearted woman.

This went on until I was thirteen years old. I was little and not very strong, and had a cough, caused, perhaps, by the hard steady work, and the lint in the air of the factory. There were a good many cases every year of the working people there going into declines and dying of consumption; so my mother had taken me out of the factory every time Rucker went away, and tried to make me play. It was so in all the factories in those days, I guess. I did not feel like playing, and had no playmates; but I used to go down by the canal and watch the boats go back and forth. Sometimes the captains of the boats would ask me if I didn't want a job driving; but I scarcely knew what they meant. I must have been a very backward child, and I surely was a scared and conquered one. I used to sit on a stump by the tow-path, and so close to it that the boys driving the mules or horses drawing the boats could almost strike me with their whips, which they often tried to do as they went by. Then I would scuttle back into the brush and hide. There just below was a lock, but I seldom went to it because all the drivers were egged on to fight each other during the delay at the locks, and the canallers would have been sure to set them on me for the fun of seeing a fight.

On the most eventful evening of my life, perhaps. I sat on this stump, watching a boat which, after passing me, was slowing down and stopping. I heard the captain swearing at some one, and saw him come ashore and start back along the tow-path toward me as if looking for something. He was a tall man whom I had seen pass at other times, and I was wondering whether he would speak to me or not, when I felt somebody's hand snatch at my collar, and a whip came down over my thin shirt with a cut which as I write I seem to feel yet. It was John Rucker, coming home when we were not expecting him, and mad at finding me out of the factory.

"I'll learn yeh to steal my time!" he was saying. "I'll learn your mother to lie to me about your workin'. A great lubber like you traipsin' around idle, and my woman bringin' a doctor's bill on me by workin' night an' day to make up your wages to me—and lyin' to her husband! I'll track you by the blood! Take that—and that—and that!"

I had never resisted him: and even now I only tried to wiggle away from him. He held me with one hand, though; and at every pause in his scolding he cut me with the whip. Weeks after the welts on my back and shoulders turned dark along the line of the whip, and greenish at the edges. I did not cry. I felt numbed with fright and rage. Suddenly, however, the tall canal-boat captain, coming back along the tow-path, put in his oar by striking the whip out of John Rucker's hand; and snatched me away from him.

"I'll have the law on you!" snarled Rucker.

"The devil you will!" said the captain.

"I'll put you through!" screamed Rucker.

The captain eased himself forward by advancing his left foot, and with his right fist he smashed Rucker somewhere about the face. Rucker went down, and the captain picked up the whip, and carefully laying Rucker on his face stripped up his shirt and revenged me, lash for lash; and counting each cut stopped when he reached ten.

"I guess that's the number," said he, taking a look at my bloody back; "but for fear of fallin' short, here's another!" And he drew the whip back, and brought it down with a quick, sharp, terrible whistle that proved its force. "Now," said he, "you've got somethin' to put me through fer!"

Then he started back toward the boat, after picking up a clevis which it seems the driver-boy had dropped. I looked at Rucker a moment wondering what to do. He was slowly getting on his feet, groaning, bloody of face and back, miserable and pitiable. But when he saw me his look of hatred drove out of my mind my first impulse to help him. I turned and ran after the captain. That worthy never looked at me; but when he reached the boat he said to some one on board: "Bill, I call you to bear witness that I refused Bubby here a chance to run away."

"Ay, ay, sir," responded a voice from the boat.

The captain took me gently by the hand and helped me over the gunwale.

"Get out o' here," he shouted, "an' go back to your lovin' father!"

I sought to obey, but he winked at me and motioned me into the little cabin forward.

"An' now, my buck," said he, "that you've stowed yourself away and got so far from home that to put you ashore would be to maroon you in the wilderness, do you want to take a job as driver? That boy I've got lives in Salina, and we'll take you on if you feel like a life on the ocean wave. Can you drive?"

"I do' know!" said I.

"Have you ever worked?" he asked.

"I've worked ever since I was six," I answered.

"Would you like to work for me?" said he.

I looked him in the face for a moment, and answered confidently, "Yes."

"It's a whack," said he. "Maybe we'd better doctor that back o' your'n a little, and git yeh heartened up for duty."

And so, before I knew it, I was whisked off into a new life.

CHAPTER II

I LAY in a bunk in one of the two little forward cabins next the stable, shivering and sobbing, a pitiful picture of misery, I suppose, as any one ever saw. I began bawling as soon as the captain commenced putting arnica on my back—partly because it smarted so, and partly because he was so very gentle about it; although all the time he was swearing at John Rucker and wishing he had skinned him alive, as he pretty nearly did. To feel a gentle hand on my shredded back, and to be babied a little bit—these things seemed to break my heart almost, though while Rucker was flogging me I bore it without a cry or a tear. The captain dressed my back, and said, "There, there, Bubby!" and went away, leaving me alone.

I could hear the ripple of the water against the side of the boat, and once in a while a gentle lift as we passed another boat; but there was nothing much in these things to cheer me up. I was leaving John Rucker behind, it was true, but I was also getting farther and farther from my mother every minute. What would she do without me? What should I do without her? I should be free of the slavery of the factory; but I did not think of that. I should have been glad to the bottom of my heart if I could have blotted out of my life all this new tragedy and gone back to the looms and spindles. The factory seemed

an awful place now that I was free, but it was familiar;
and being free was awful, too; but I never once thought
of going back. I knew I could learn to drive the horses,
and I knew I should stay with the captain who had
flogged John Rucker. I who had never thought of running away was just as much committed to the new life as
if I had planned for it for years. Inside my spirit I suppose I had been running away every time I had gone down
and watched the boats float by; and something stronger
than my conscious will floated me along, also. I fought
myself to keep from crying; but I never thought of running up on deck, jumping ashore and going home, as I
could easily have done at any time within an hour of
boarding the boat. I buried my face in the dirty pillow
with no pillow-case on it, and filled my mouth with the
patchwork quilt. It seemed as though I should die of
weeping. My breath came in long spasmodic draughts
as much deeper and bitterer than sighs as sighs are sad-
der and more pitiful than laughter. My whipped back
pained and smarted me, but that was not what made
me cry so dreadfully; I was in the depths of despair; I
was humiliated; I was suffering from injustice; I had
lost my mother—and at this thought my breath almost
refused to come at all. Presently I opened my eyes and
found the captain throwing water in my face. He never
mentioned it afterward; but I suppose I had fainted
away. Then I went to sleep, and when I awoke it was
dark and I did not know where I was, and screamed.
The captain himself quieted me for a few minutes, and I
dropped off to sleep again. He had moved me without
my knowing it, from the drivers' cabin forward to his
own. But I must not spend our time on these things.

The captain's name was Eben Sproule. He had been a farmer and sawmill man, and still had a farm between Herkimer and Little Falls on the Mohawk River. He owned his boat, and seemed to be doing very well with her. The other driver was a boy named Asa— I forget his other name. We called him Ace. He lived at Salina, or Salt Point, which is now a part of Syracuse; and was always, in his talk to me, daring the captain to discharge him, and threatening to get a job in the salt works at Salina if ever he quit the canal. He seemed to think this would spite Captain Sproule very much. I expected him to leave the boat when we reached Syracuse; but he never did, and I think he kept on driving after I quit. Our wages cost the boat twenty dollars a month—ten dollars each—and the two hands we carried must have brought the pay-roll up to about seventy a month besides our board. We always had four horses, two in the stable forward, and two pulling the boat. We plied through to Buffalo, and back to Albany, carrying farm products, hides, wool, wheat, other grain, and such things as potash, pearlash, staves, shingles, and salt from Syracuse, and sometimes a good deal of meat; and what the railway people call "way-freight" between all the places along the route. Our boat was much slower than the packets and the passenger boats which had relays of horses at stations and went pretty fast, and had good cabins for the passengers, too, and cooks and stewards, serving fine meals; while all our cooking was done by the captain or one of our hands, though sometimes we carried a cook.

Bill, the man who answered "Ay, ay, sir!" when the captain asked him to witness that he had refused me passage on the boat, was a salt-water sailor who had signed on with the boat while drunk at Albany and now said he was going to Buffalo to try sailing on the Lakes. The other man was a green Irishman called Paddy, though I suppose that was not his name. He was good only as a human derrick or crane. We used to look upon all Irishmen as jokes in those days, and I suppose they realized it. Paddy used to sing Irish comeallyes on the deck as we moved along through the country; and usually got knocked down by a low bridge at least once a day as he sang, or sat dreaming in silence. Bill despised Paddy because he was a landsman, and used to drown Paddy's Irish songs with his sailor's chanties roared out at the top of his voice. And mingled with us on the boat would be country people traveling to or from town, pedlers, parties going to the stopping-places of the passenger boats, people loading and un-loading freight, drovers with live stock for the market, and all sorts of queer characters and odd fish who haunted the canal as waterside characters infest the water-front of ports. If I could live that strange life over again I might learn more about it; but I saw very little meaning in it then. That is always the way, I guess. We must get away from a type of life or we can't see it plainly. That has been the way as to our old prairie life in Iowa. It is only within the past few years that I have begun to see a little more of what it meant. It was not long though until even I began to feel the West calling to me with a thousand voices which echoed back and forth along the Erie Canal, and swelled to a chorus at the western gateway, Buffalo.

2

Captain Sproule had carried me aft from the drivers'
cabin to his own while I was in a half-unconscious condition, and out of pure pity, I suppose; but that was the
last soft treatment I ever got from him. He came into
the cabin just as I was thinking of getting up, and
sternly ordered me forward to my own cabin. I had
nothing to carry, and it was very little trouble to move.
We were moored to the bank just then taking on or discharging freight, and Ace was in the cabin to receive
me.

"That upper bunk's your'n," he said. "No greenhorn
gits my bunk away from me!"

I stood mute. Ace glared at me defiantly.

"Can you fight?" he asked.

"I do' know," I was obliged to answer.

"Then you can't," said Ace, with bitter contempt.
"I can lick you with one hand tied behind me!"

He drew back his fist as if to strike me, and I wonder that I did not run from the cabin and jump ashore,
but I stood my ground, more from stupor and what we
Dutch call dumbness than anything else. Ace let his fist
fall and looked me over with more respect. He was a
slender boy, hard as a whip-lash, wiry and dark. He was
no taller than I, and not so heavy; but he had come to
have brass and confidence from the life he lived. As a
matter of fact, he was not so old as I, but had grown
faster; and was nothing like as strong after I had got my
muscles hardened, as was proved many a time.

"You'll make a great out of it on the canal," he said.

"What?" said I.

"A boy that can't fight," said he, "don't last long drivin'. I've had sixteen fights this month!"

A bell sounded on deck, and we heard the voice of Bill calling us to breakfast. Ace yelled to me to come on, and all hands including the captain gathered on deck forward, where we had coffee, good home-made bread bought from a farmer's wife, fried cakes, boiled potatoes, and plenty of salt pork, finishing with pie. All the cook had to do was to boil potatoes, cook eggs when we had them and make coffee; for the most of our victuals we bought as we passed through the country. The captain had a basket of potatoes or apples on the deck which he used as cash carriers. He would put a piece of money in a potato and throw it to whoever on shore had anything to sell, and the goods, if they could be safely thrown, would come whirling over to be caught by some of us on deck. We got many a nice chicken or loaf of bread or other good victuals in that way; and we lived on the fat of the land. All sorts of berries and fruit, milk, butter, eggs, cakes, pies and the like came to the canal without any care on our part; everything was cheap, and every meal was a feast. This first breakfast was a trial, but I made a noble meal of it. The sailor, Bill, pretended to believe that I had killed a man on shore and had gone to sea to escape the gallows. Ace and Paddy to frighten me, I suppose, talked about the dangers and difficulties of the driver's life; while the captain gave all of us stern looks over his meal and looked fiercely at me as if to deny that he had ever been kind. When the meal was over he ordered Ace to the towpath, and told him to take me along and show me how to drive.

"Here," he snapped at me, "is where we make a spoon or spoil a horn. Go 'long with you!"

Ace climbed on the back of one of the horses. I looked up wondering what I was to do.

"You'll walk," said Ace; "an' keep your eyes skinned."

So we started off. Each horse leaned into the collar, and slowly the hundred tons or so of dead weight started through the water. The team knew that it was of no use to surge against the load to get it started, as horses do with a wagon; but they pulled steadily and slowly, gradually getting the boat under way, and soon it was moving along with the team at a brisk walk, and with less labor than a hundredth part of the weight would have called for on land. I have always believed in inland waterways for carrying the heavy freight of this nation; because the easiest and cheapest way to transport anything is to put it in the water and float it. This lesson I learned when Ace whipped up Dolly and Jack and took our craft off toward Syracuse.

It was a hard day for me. We were passing boats all the time, and we had to make speed to keep craft which had no right to pass us from getting by, especially just before reaching a lock. To allow another boat to steal our lockage from us was a disgrace; and many of the fights between the driver boys grew out of the rights of passing by and the struggle to avoid delays at the locks. Sometimes such affairs were not settled by the boys on the tow-path—they fought off the skirmishes; the real battles were between the captains or members of the crews.

If there were rules I don't know now what they were,

and nobody paid much attention to them. Of course we let the passenger boats pass whenever they overtook us, unless we could beat them into a lock. We delayed them then by laying our boat out into the middle of the canal and quarreling until we reached the lock; under cover maybe of some pretended mistake. Our laying the boat out to shut off a passing rival was dangerous to the slow boat, for the reason that a collision meant that the strongly-built stem-end of the boat coming up from behind could crush the weaker stern of the obstructing craft. Such are some of the things I had to learn.

3

The passing of us by a packet brought me my first grief. She came up behind us with her horses at the full trot. Their boat was down the canal a hundred yards or so at the end of the tow-line; and just before the boat itself drew even with ours she was laid over by her steersman to the opposite side of the ditch, her horses were checked so as to let her line so slacken as to drop down under our boat, her horses were whipped up by a sneering boy on a tall bay steed, her team went outside ours on the tow-path, and the passage was made. They made, as was always the case, a moving loop of their line, one end hauled by the packet, and the other by the team. I was keeping my eye skinned to see how the thing was done, when the tow-line of the packet came by, tripped me up and threw me into the canal, from which I was fished out by Bill as our boat came along. There was actual danger in this unless the steersman happened to be really steering, and laid the boat off so as to miss me.

Captain Sproule gazed at me in disgust. Ace laughed loudly away out ahead on the horse. Bill said that if it had been in the middle of the ocean I never would have been shamed by being hauled up on deck. He was sorry for my sake, as I never would live this thing down.

"Go change your clothes," said the captain, "and try, not to be such a lummox next time."

I had no change of clothes, and therefore, I took the first opportunity to get out on the tow-path, wet as I was, and begin again to learn my first trade. It was a lively occupation. There were some four thousand boats on the Erie Canal at that time, or an average of ten boats to the mile. I suppose there were from six to eight thousand boys driving then on the "Grand Canal" alone, as it was called. More than half of these boys were orphans, and it was not a good place for any boy, no matter how many parents or guardians he might have. Five hundred or more convicts in the New York State Penitentiary were men who, as I learned from a missionary who came aboard to pray with us, sing hymns and exhort us to a better life, had been canal-boat drivers. The boys were at the mercy of their captains, and were often cheated out of their wages. There were stories of young boys sick with cholera, when that disease was raging, or with other diseases, being thrown off the boats and allowed to live or die as luck might determine. There were hardship, danger and oppression in the driver's life; and every sort of vice was like an open book before him as soon as he came to understand it—which, at first, I did not. If my mother knew, as I suppose she did, what sort of occupation I had entered upon, I do not see how she could have been anything but miserable as she thought of me—though she realized keenly from what I had escaped.

Back on the tow-path, I was earning the contempt of Ace by dodging every issue, like a candidate for office. I learned quickly to snub the boat by means of a rope and the numerous snubbing-posts along the canal. This was necessary in stopping, in entering locks, and in rounding some curves; and my first glimmer of courage came from the fact that I seemed to know at once how this was to be done—the line to be passed twice about the post, and so managed as to slip around it with a great deal of friction so as to bring her to.

4

I was afraid of the other drivers, however, and I was afraid of Ace. He drove me like a Simon Legree. He ordered me to fight other drivers, and when I refused, he took the fights off my hands or avoided them as the case might require. He flicked at my bare feet with his whip. When we were delayed by taking on or discharging freight, he would try to corner me and throw me into the canal. He made me do all the work of taking care of our bunks, and cuffed my ears whenever he got a chance. He made me do his share as well as my own of the labor of cleaning the stables, and feeding and caring for the horses, sitting by and giving orders with a comical exaggeration of the manner of Captain Sproule. In short, he was hazing me unmercifully—as every one on the boat knew, though some of the things he did to me I do not think the captain would have permitted if he had known about them.

I was more miserable with the cruelty and tyranny of Ace than I had been at home; for this was a constant misery, night and day, and got worse every minute. He ruled even what I ate and drank. When I took anything at meal-times, I would first glance at him, and if he looked forbidding or shook his head, I did not eat the forbidden thing. I knew on that voyage from Syracuse to Buffalo exactly what servitude means. No slave was ever more systematically cruelized*, no convict ever more brutishly abused—unless his oppressor may have been more ingenious than Ace. He took my coverlets at night. He starved me by making me afraid to eat. He worked me as hard as the amount of labor permitted. He committed abominable crimes against my privacy and the delicacy of my feelings—and all the time I could not rebel. I could only think of running away from the boat, and was nearly at the point of doing so, when he crowded me too far one day, and pushed me to the point of one of those frenzied revolts for which the Dutch are famous.

A little girl peeking at me from an orchard beside the tow-path tossed me an apple—a nice, red juicy apple. I caught it, and put it in my pocket. That evening we tied up at a landing and were delayed for an hour or so taking on freight. I slipped into the stable to eat my apple, knowing that Ace would pound me if he learned that I had kept anything from him, whether he really wanted it or not. Suddenly I grew sick with terror, as I saw him coming in at the door. He saw what I was doing, and glared at me vengefully. He actually turned white with rage at this breach of his authority, and came at me with set teeth and doubled fists.

---

*The author insists that "cruelized" is the exact word to express his meaning, and will consent to no change.—G. v. d. M.

"Give me that apple, damn yeh!" he cried. "You sneakin' skunk, you, I'll larn ye to eat my apples!"

He snatched at the apple, and was too successful; for before he reached it I opened my hand in obedience to his onslaught; and the apple rolled in the manure and litter of the stable, and was soiled and befouled.

"Throwin' my apple in the manure, will yeh!" he yelled. "I'll larn ye! Pick that apple up!"

I reached for it with trembling hand, and held it out to him.

"It ain't fit for anything but the hogs!" he yelled. "Eat it, hog!"

I looked at the filthy thing, and raised my hand to my mouth; but before I touched it with my lips a great change came over me. I trembled still more, now; but it was not with fear. I suddenly felt that if I could kill Ace, I would be willing to die. I was willing to die trying to kill him. I could not get away from him because he was between me and the door, but now suddenly I did not want to get away. I wanted to get at him. I threw the apple down.

"Pick that apple up and eat it," he said in a low tone, looking me straight in the eye, "or I'll pound you till you can't walk."

"I won't," said I.

Ace rushed at me, and as he rushed, he struck me in the face. I went down, and he piled on me, hitting me as he could. I liked the feel of his blows; it was good to realize that they did not hurt me half so much as his abuse had done. I did not know how to fight, but I grappled with him fiercely. I reached for his hair, and he tried to bite my thumb, actually getting it in his mouth, but I jerked it aside and caught his cheek in my grip, my thumb inside the cheek-pouch, and my fingers outside. I felt a hot thrill of joy as my nails sank into his cheek inside and out, and he cringed. I held him at arm's length, helpless, and with his head drawn all askew; and still keeping my unfair hold, I rolled him over, and coming on top of him, thrust the other thumb in the other side of his mouth, frenziedly trying to rip his cheeks, and pounding his head on the deck. We rolled back into the corner, where he jerked my thumbs from his mouth, now bleeding at the corners, and desperately tried to roll me. My hand came into touch with a horseshoe on the stable floor, which I picked up, and filled with joy at the consciousness that I was stronger than he, I began beating him over the face and head with it, with no thought of anything but killing him. He turned over on his face and began trying to shield his head with his arms, at which I tore like a crazy boy, beating at arms, head, hands and neck with the dull horseshoe, and screaming, "I'll kill you! I'll kill you! I'll kill you!"

In the meantime, it gradually dawned on Ace that he was licked, and he began yelling, "Enough! Enough!" which according to the rules of the game entitled him to be let alone; but I knew nothing about the rules of the game. I saw the blood spurting from one or two cuts in his scalp. I felt it warm and slimy on my hands, and I rained my blows on him, madly and blindly, but with cruel effect after all. I did not see the captain when he came in. I only felt his grip on my right arm, as he seized it and snatched the horseshoe from me. I did not hear what he said, though I heard him saying something. When he caught both my hands, I threw myself down on the cowering Ace and tried to bite him. When he lifted me up I kicked the prostrate Ace in the face as a parting remembrance. When he stood me up in the corner of the stable and asked me what in hell I was doing, I broke away from him and threw myself on the staggering Ace with all the fury of a bulldog. And when Bill came and helped the captain hold me, I was crying like a baby, and deaf to all commands. I struggled to get at Ace until they took him away; and then I collapsed and had a miserable time of it while my anger was cooling.

"I thought Ace would crowd the mourners too hard," said the captain. "Now, Jake," said he, "will you behave?"

There was no need to ask me. A baby could have held me then.

"Don't you know," said the captain, "that you ortn't to pound a feller with a horseshoe? Do you always act like this when you fight?"

"I never had a fight before," I sobbed.

"Well, you won't have another with Ace," said the captain. "You damned near killed him. And next time fight fair!"

That night I drove alone, which I had been doing now for some time, taking my regular trick; and when we tied up at some place west of Lockport, I went to my bunk expecting to find Ace ready to renew his tyrannies, and determined to resist to the death. He was lying in the lower bunk asleep, and his bandaged head looked rather pitiful. For all that my anger flamed up again as I looked at him. I shook him roughly by the shoulder. He awakened with a moan.

"Get out of that bunk!" I commanded.

"Let me alone," he whimpered, but he got out as I told him to do.

"Climb into that upper bunk," I said.

He looked at me a moment, and climbed up. I turned in, in the lower bunk, but I could not sleep. I was boss! It was Ace now who would be the underling. It was not a cold night; but pretty soon I thought of the quilts in the upper berth, and imitating Ace's cruelty, I called up to him fiercely, awakening him again. "Throw down that quilt," I said, "I want it."

"You let me alone," whimpered Ace, but the quilt was thrown down on the deck, where I let it lie. Ace lay there, breathing occasionally with a long quivering sigh— the most pitiful thing a child ever does—and we were both children, remember, put in a most unchildlike position. I dropped asleep, but soon awakened. It had grown cold, and I reached for the quilt; but something prompted me to reach up and see whether Ace was still there. He lay there asleep, and, as I could feel, cold. I picked up the quilt, threw it over him, tucked him in as my mother used to tuck me in,—thinking of her as I did it—and went back to my bunk. I was sorry I had cut Ace's head, and had already begun to forget how cruelly he had used me. I seemed to feel his blood on my hands, and got up and washed them. The thought of Ace's bandages, and the vision of wounds under them filled me with remorse—but I was boss! Finally I dropped asleep, and awoke to find that Ace had got up ahead of me. I was embarrassed by my new authority; and sorry for what I had been obliged to do to get it; but I was a new boy from that day.

It never pays to be a slave. It never benefits a man or

a people to submit to tyranny. A slave is a man forgotten of God. If only the negroes, when they were brought to this country, had refused to work, and elected to die as other races of men have done, what a splendid thing it would have been for the world. That fight against slavery was a beautiful, a joyful thing to me, with all its penalties of compassion and guilty feeling afterward. I think the best thing a man or boy can do is to find out how far and to whom he is a slave, and fight that servitude tooth and nail as I fought Ace. It would make this a different world.

CHAPTER III

THE strange thing to me about my fight with Ace was that nobody thought of such a thing as punishing me for it. I was free to fight or not as I pleased. I needed to be free more than anything else, and I wanted plenty of good food and fresh air. All these I got, for Captain Sproule, while stern and strict with us, enforced only those rules which were for the good of the boat, and these seemed like perfect liberty to me—after I whipped Ace. As for my old tyrant, he recovered his spirits very soon, and took the place of an underling quite contentedly. I suppose he had been used to it. I ruled in a manner much milder than his. I had never learned to swear—or to use harder words than gosh, and blast, and dang where the others swore the most fearful oaths as a matter of ordinary talk. I made a rule that Ace must quit swearing; and slapped him up to a peak a few times for not obeying—which was really a hard thing for him to do while driving; and when he was in a quarrel I always overlooked his cursing, because he could not fight successfully unless he had the right to work himself up into a passion by calling names and swearing.

As for myself I walked and rode erect and felt my limbs as light as feathers, as compared with their leaden weight when I lived at Tempe and worked in the factory.

Soon I took on my share of the fighting as a matter of course. I did it as a rule without anger and found that beyond a bloody nose or a scratched face, these fights did not amount to much. I was small for my age, and like most runts I was stronger than I looked, and gave many a driver boy a bad surprise. I never was whipped, though I was pummeled severely at times. When the fight grew warm enough I began to see red, and to cry like a baby, boring in and clinching in a mad sort of way; and these young roughs knew that a boy who fought and cried at the same time had to be killed before he would say enough. So I never said enough; and in my second year I found I had quite a reputation as a fighter—but I never got any joy out of it.

If I could have forgotten my wish to see my mother it would have been in many ways a pleasant life to me. I was never tired of the new and strange things I saw— new regions, new countries. I was amazed at the Montezuma Marsh, with its queer trade of selling flags for chair seats and the like—and I was almost eaten alive by the mosquitoes while passing through it. Our boat floated along through the flags, the horses on a tow-path just wide enough to enable the teams to pass, with bog on one side and canal on the other, water birds whistling and calling, frogs croaking, and water-lilies dotting every open pool. My spirits soared as I passed spots where the view was not shut off by the reeds, and I could look out over the great expanse of flags, just as my heart rose when I first looked upon the Iowa prairies. The Fairport level gave me another thrill—an embankment a hundred feet high with the canal on the top of it, a part of a seventeen-mile level, like a river on a hill-top.

We were a happy crew, here. Ace was quite recovered from our temporary difference of opinion—for I was treating him better than he expected. He used to sing merrily a song which was a real canal-chantey, one of the several I heard, the words of which ran like this:

"Come, sailors, landsmen, one and all,
And I'll sing you the dangers of the raging canawl;
For I've been at the mercy of the winds and the waves,
And I'm one of the merry fellows what expects a
    watery grave.

"We left Albiany about the break of day;
As near as I can remember, 'twas the second day of
    May;
We depended on our driver, though he was very small,
Although we knew the dangers of the raging canawl."

The rest of it I forget; but I remember that after Bill had sung one of his chanties, like "Messmates hear a brother sailor sing the dangers of the seas," or, "We sailed from the Downs and fair Plymouth town," telling how

"To our surprise,
The storms did arise,
Attended by winds and loud thunder;
Our mainmast being tall
Overboard she did fall,
'And five of our best men fell under,"

Ace would pipe up about the dangers of the raging canal; and finally this encouraged Paddy to fill in with some song like this:

"In Dublin City, where I was born,
On Stephen's Green, where I die forlorn;

'Twas there I learnèd the baking trade,
And 'twas there they called me the Roving Blade."

All the rest of the story was of a hanging. No wonder it was hard sometimes for an Irishman to reverence the law. They sang of hanging and things leading up to it from their childhood. I remember, too, how the boys of Iowa used to sing a song celebrating the deeds of the James boys of Missouri—and about the same time we had troubles with horse-thieves. There is a good deal of power in songs and verses, whether there's much truth in poetry or not.

2

I am spending too much time on this part of my life, if it were my life only which were concerned; but the Erie Canal, and the gaps through the Alleghany Mountains, are a part of the history of Vandemark Township. The west was on the road, then, floating down the Ohio, wagoning or riding on horseback through mountain passes, boating it up the Mississippi and Missouri, sailing up the Lakes, swarming along the Erie Canal. Not only was Iowa on the road, spending a year, two years, a generation, two generations on the way and getting a sort of wandering and gipsy strain in her blood, but all the West, and even a part of Canada was moving. We once had on board from Lockport west, a party of emigrants from England to Ontario. They had come by ship from England to New York, by steamboat to Albany and canal to Lockport; and for some reason had to take a deck trip from Lockport to Buffalo, paying Captain Sproule a good price for passage. Their English dialect was so broad that I could not understand it; and I abandoned to Ace the company of their little girl who was one of a family of five—father, mother, and two boys, besides the daughter. I suppose that their descendants are in Ontario yet, or scattered out on the prairies of Western Canada. Just so the people of the canals and roads are in Iowa, and in Vandemark Township.

Buffalo was a marvel to me. It was the biggest town I had ever seen, and was full of sailors, emigrants, ships, waterside characters and trade; and I could see, feel, taste, smell, and hear the West everywhere. I was by this time on the canal almost at my ease as a driver; but here I flocked by myself like Cunningham's bull, instead of mingling with the crowds of boys whom I found here passing a day or so in idleness, while the captains and hands amused themselves as sailors do in port, and the boats made contracts for east-bound freight, and took it on. Whenever I could I attached myself to Captain Sproule like a lost dog, not thinking that perhaps he would not care to be tagged around by a child like me; and thus I saw things that should not have been seen by a boy, or by any one else—things that I never forgot, and that afterward had an influence on me at a critical time in my life. There were days spent in grog-shops, there were quarrels and brawls, and some fights, drunken men calling themselves and one another horrible names and bragging of their vices, women and men living in a terrible imitation of pleasure. I have often wondered as I have seen my boys brought up cleanly and taught steady and industrious lives in a settled community, how they would look upon the things I saw and lived through, and how well they could have stood the things that were ready to drag me down to the worst vices and crimes. I moved through all this in a sort of daze, as if it did not concern me, not even thinking much less of Captain Sproule for his doings, some of which I did not even understand: for remember I was a very backward boy for my age. This was probably a good thing for me—a very good thing. There are things in the Bible which children read without knowing their meaning, and are not harmed by them. I was harmed by what I saw in the book of life now opened to me, but not so much as one might think.

3

One evening, in a water-front saloon, Captain Sproule and another man—a fellow who was a shipper of freight, as I remember—spent an hour or so with two women whose bad language and painted faces would have told their story to any older person; but to me they were just acquaintances of the captain, and that was all. After a while the four left the saloon together, and I followed, as I followed the captain everywhere.

"That young one had better be sent to bed," said the captain's friend, pointing to me.

"Better go back to the boat, Jake," said the captain, laughing in a tipsy sort of way.

"I don't know where it is," said I; "it's been towed off somewhere."

"That's so," said the captain, "I've got to hunt it up myself—or stay all night in a tavern. Wal, come along. I'll be going home early."

The other man gave a sort of sarcastic laugh. "Bring up your boys as you like, Cap'n," said he. "He'll come to it anyhow in a year or so by himself, I guess."

"I'm going home early," said the captain.

"Course you be," said the woman, seizing the captain's arm. "Come on, Bubby!"

There were more drinks where we went, and other women like those in our party. I could not understand why they behaved in so wild and immodest a manner, but thought dimly that it was the liquor. In the meantime I grew very sleepy, being worn out by a day of excitement and wonder; and sitting down in a corner of the room, I lopped over on the soft carpet and went to sleep. The last I heard was the sound of an accordion played by a negro who had been invited in, and the scuff of feet as they danced, with loud and broken speech, much of which was quite blind to me. Anyhow, I lost myself for a long time, as I felt, when some one shook me gently by the shoulder and woke me up. I thought I was at home, in my attic bed, and that it was my mother awakening me to go to work in the factory.

"Ma," I said. "Is that you, ma!"

A woman was bending over me, her breasts almost falling from the low-cut red dress she wore. She was painted and powdered like the rest, and her face looked drawn and pale over her scarlet gown. As I pronounced the name I always called my mother, I seem to remember that her expression changed from the wild and reckless look I was becoming used to, to something like what I had always seen in my mother's eyes.

"Who you driving for, Johnny?" she asked.

"Captain Sproule," said I. "Where is he?" For on looking about I saw that there was no one there but this woman and myself.

"He'll be back after a while," said she. "Poor young one! Come with me and get a good sleep."

I was numb with sleep, and staggered when I stood up; and she put her arm around me as we moved toward the door, where we were met by two men, canallers or sailors, by their looks, who stopped her with drunken greetings.

"Ketchin' em young, Sally," said one of them. "Wot will the world come to, Jack, when younkers like this get a-goin'? Drop the baby, Sally, and come along o' me!"

The woman looked at him a moment steadily.

"Let me go," said she; "I don't want anything to do with you."

"Don't, eh?" said he. "Git away, Bub, an' let your betters have way."

I clung closer to her side, and looked at him rather defiantly. He drew back his flat hand to slap me over; but the woman pulled me behind her, and faced him, with a drawn knife in her hand. He made as if to take it from her; but his companion held him back.

"Do you want six inches o' cold steel in your liver?" he asked. "Let her be. There's plenty o' others."

"My money is jest as good's any one else's," said the first. "Jest as good's any one else's;" and began wrangling with his friend.

The woman pushed me before her and we went upstairs to a bedroom, the door of which she closed and locked. She said nothing about what had taken place below, and I at once made up my mind that it had been some sort of joke.

"You oughtn't to sleep on that floor," said she. "You'll take your death o' cold. Lay down here, and have a good comfortable nap. I'll see that Captain Sproule finds you."

I started to lie down in my clothes. "Take off them clothes," said she, as if astonished. "Do you think I want my bed all dirtied up with 'em?" And she began undressing me as if I had been a baby. She was so tender and motherly about it that I permitted her to strip me to my shirt, and then turned in. The bed was soft, and sleep began to come back to me. I saw my new friend preparing for bed, and presently I awoke to find her lying by me, and holding me in her arms: I heard her sitheing,* and I was sure she was crying. This woke me up, and I lay wondering if there was anything I could do for her, but I said nothing. Pretty soon there came a loud rap at the door, and a woman asked to be let in.

"What do you want?" asked my friend, getting out of bed as if scared, and beginning to put on her clothes. I hustled out and began dressing—a very short job with me. In the meantime the woman at the door grew louder and more commanding in her demand, so much so, that before she was fully dressed, my strange friend opened the door, and there stood a great fleshy woman, wearing a lot of jewelry; red-faced, and very angry. I can't remember much that was said; but I remember that the fat woman kept saying, "What do you mean? What do you mean? I want you to understand that my guests have their rights. One man's money is as good as another's," and the like. "Whose brat is this?" she finally asked, pointing at me.

"He's driving for a man with money," said my friend sarcastically.

"Who you driving for, Johnny?" she asked; and I told her.

---

*The writer insists that "sitheing" is quite a different thing from sighing, being a long-drawn, quivering sigh. In this I think he is correct.—G. v. d. M.

"Captain Sproule is down-stairs," said she. "He's looking for you. Go on down! And as for you, Madam, you get out of my house, and don't come back until you can please my visitors—you knife-drawin' hussy!"

I went down to the room where the captain had left me; and just as he had begun making some sly blind jokes at my expense, the woman who had befriended me came down, followed by the fat virago, cursing her and ordering her out.

"Don't let 'em hurt her!" said I. "She's a good woman. She put me to bed, and was good to me. Don't let 'em hurt her!"

We all went out together, the captain asking me what I meant; and then went on walking beside the woman, whom he called Sally, and trying to understand the case. I heard her say, "Mine would be about that size if he had lived. I s'pose every woman must be a darned fool once in a while!" The rest of the case I did not understand very well; but I knew that she went to a tavern where we all spent the night, and that the captain seemed very thoughtful when we went to bed at last—the second time for me. When we finally pulled out of Buffalo for the East, Sally was on the boat—not a very uncommon thing in those days; but the captain was very good and respectful to her until we reached a little village two or three days' journey eastward, when Sally got off the boat after kissing me good-by and telling me to be good, and try to grow up and be a good man; and went off on a country road as if she knew where she was going.

"Where did Sally go?" I asked of Captain Sproule.

"Home," said he; "and may God have mercy on her soul!"

4

I looked forward more longingly than ever to the time when I should be able to drop off the boat at Tempe, and run up to see my mother; and I fixed it up with Captain Sproule so that when we made our return trip I was to be allowed to stop over a day with her, and taking a fast boat catch up with our own craft farther east. I was proud of the fact that I had two good suits of clothes, a good hat and boots, and money in my pocket. I expected to turn my money out on the table and leave it with her. I thought a good deal of my meeting with John Rucker, and hoped fervently that I should find him absent on one of his peddling trips, in which case I meant to stay over night with my mother; and I seriously pondered the matter as to whether or not I should fight Rucker if he attacked me, as I expected he might; and Ace and I had many talks as to the best way for me to fight him, if I should decide on such a course. Ace was quite sure I could best Rucker; but I did not share this confidence. A fight with a boy was quite a different thing from a battle with a man, even though he might be a coward as I was sure Rucker was.

This proposed visit became the greatest thing in my life, a great adventure, as we glided back from Buffalo, past the locks at Lockport, where there was much fighting; past lock after lock, where the lock-tenders tried to sell magic oils, balsams and liniments for man and beast, and once in a while did so; and to whom Ace became a customer for hair-oil; after using which he sought the attention of girls by the canal side, and also those who might be passengers on our boat, or members of the emigrant families which crowded the boats going west; past the hill at Palmyra, from which Joseph Smith, the Mormon prophet, claimed to have dug the gold plates of the Book of Mormon; past the Fairport level and embankment; for three days floating so untroubled along the Rochester level without a single lock; through the Montezuma Marsh again; and then in a short time would come Tempe, and maybe my great meeting with Rucker, my longed-for visit to my mother. And then Captain Sproule got a contract for a cargo of salt to Buffalo, and we turned westward again! It would be late in the fall before we returned; but I should have more money then, and should be stronger and a better fighter.

Canal-boating was fast becoming a routine thing with me; and I must leave out all my adventures on that voyage to Buffalo, and back to Tempe. I do not remember them very clearly anyhow.

One thing happened which I must describe, because it is important. We were somewhere west of Jordan, when we met a packet boat going west. It was filled with passengers, and drew near to us with the sound of singing and musical instruments. It was crowded with emigrants always hopeful and merry, bound westward. Evidently the hold had not been able to take in all the household goods of the passengers, for there was a deck-load of these things, covered with tarpaulins.

I was sitting on the deck of our boat, wondering when I should join the western movement. When I got old enough, and had money enough, I was determined to go west and seek my fortune; for I always felt that canalling was, somehow, beneath what I wanted to do and become. The packet swept past us, giving me a good deal the same glimpse into a different sort of life that a deckhand on a freighter has when he gazes at a liner ablaze with lights and echoing with music.

On the deck of the packet sat a group of people who were listening to a tall stooped man, who seemed to be addressing them on some matter of interest. There was something familiar in his appearance; and I kept my eye on him as we went by.

As the boat passed swiftly astern, I saw that it was John Rucker.

He was better dressed than I had ever seen him; his beard was trimmed, and he was the center of his group. He was talking to a hunchback—a strange-looking person with a black beard. I wondered what had made such a change in Rucker; but I was overjoyed at the thought that he was off on a peddling trip, and that I should not meet him at home.

We floated along toward Tempe in a brighter world than I had known since the time when I felt my bosom swell at the wearing of the new cap my mother had made for me, the day when I, too young to be sad, had thrown the clod over the stone fence as we went down to the great river to meet John Rucker.

5

We tied up for the night some seven miles west of Tempe, but I could not sleep. I felt that I must see my mother that night, and so I trudged along the tow-path in the light of a young moon, which as I plodded on threw my shadow along the road before me. I walked treading on my own shadow, a very different boy from the one who had come over this same route sobbing himself almost into convulsions not many months before.

I was ready to swap canal repartee with any of the canallers. It had become my world. I felt myself a good deal of a man. I could see my mother's astonished look as she opened the door, and heard me in the gruffest voice I could command asking her if she could tell me where Mrs. Rucker lived—and yet, I felt anxious. Somehow a fear that all was not right grew in me; and when I reached the path leading up to the house I turned pale, I feel sure, to see that there was no light.

I tapped at the door; but there was no response. I felt for the key in the place where we used to leave it, but no key was there.

There were no curtains, and as I looked into a room with windows at the opposite side, I saw no furniture. The house was vacant. I went to the little leanto which was used as a summer kitchen, and tried a window which I knew how to open. It yielded to my old trick, and I crawled in. As I had guessed, the place was empty. I called to my mother, and was scared, I can't tell how much, at the echo of my voice in the deserted cabin. I ventured up the stairs, though I was mortally afraid, and found nothing save the litter of removal. I felt about the closet in my mother's bedroom, to find out if any of her clothes were there, half expecting that she would be where I wanted to find her even in the vacant house. Down in a corner I felt some small article, which I soon found was a worn-out shoe. With this, the only thing left to remember her by, I crawled out of the window, shut it carefully behind me—for I had been brought up to leave things as I found them—and stood alone, the most forlorn and deserted boy in America, as I truly believe.

The moon had gone down, and it was dark. There was frost on the dead grass, and I went out under the old apple-tree and sat down. What should I do? Where was my mother? She was the only one in the world whom I cared for or who loved me. She was gone, it was night, I was alone and hungry and cold and lost. Perhaps some of the neighbors might know where John Rucker had taken my mother—this thought came to me only after I had sat there until every house was dark. The people had all gone to bed. I tried to think of some neighbor to whom my mother might have told her destination when she moved; but I could recall none of that sort. She had been too unhappy, here in Tempe, to make friends. So I sat there shivering until morning, unwilling to go away, altogether bewildered, quite at my wits' end, steeped in despair. The world seemed too hard and tough for me.

In the morning I asked at every house if the people knew Mrs. Rucker, and where she had gone, but got no help. One woman knew her, and had employed her as a seamstress; but had found the house vacant the last time she had sent her work.

"Is she a relative of yours?" she asked.

"She is my———" I remember I stopped here and looked away a long time before I could finish the reply, "She is my mother."

"And where were you, my poor boy," said she, "when she moved?"

"I was away at work," I replied.

"Well," said she, "she left word for you somewhere, you may be sure of that. Where did you stay last night?"

"I sat under a tree," said I, "in the yard—up where we used to live."

"And where did you get breakfast?" she asked.

"I wasn't hungry," I answered. "I've been hunting for my mother since daylight."

"You poor child!" said she. "Come right into the kitchen and I'll get you some breakfast. Come in, and we'll find out how you can find your mother!"

While she got me the breakfast which I needed as badly as any meal I ever ate, she questioned me as to relatives, friends, habits, and everything which a good detective would want to know in forming a theory as to how a clue might be obtained. She suggested that I find every man in the village who had a team and did hauling, and ask each one if he had moved Mr. Rucker's family.

"Why didn't she write to you?" she finally queried.

"She didn't know where I was," I replied.

"Did she ever leave word for you anywhere," asked the woman, "before you ran away?"

"We had a place we called our post-office," I answered. "An old hollow apple-tree. We used to leave letters for each other in that. It is the tree I sat under all night."

"Look there," said the woman. "You'll find her! She wouldn't have gone without leaving a trace."

Without stopping to thank her for her breakfast and her sympathy, I ran at the top of my speed for the old apple-tree. I felt in the hollow—it seemed to be filled with nothing but leaves. Just as I was giving up, I touched something stiffer than an autumn leaf, and pulling it out found a letter, all discolored by wet and mold, but addressed to me in my mother's handwriting. I tore it open and read:

"My poor, wandering boy: We are going away—I don't know where. This only I know, we are going west to settle somewhere up the Lakes. The lawsuit is ended, and we got the money your father left me, and are going west to get a new and better start in the world. If you will write me at the post-office in Buffalo, I will inquire there for mail. I wonder if you will ever get this! I wonder if I shall ever see you again! I shall find some way to send word to you. Mr. Rucker says he knows the captain of the boat you work on, and can get his address for me in Syracuse—then I will write you. I am going very far away, and if you ever see this, and never see me again, keep it always, and whenever you see it remember that I would always have died willingly for you, and that I am going to build up for you a fortune which will give you a better life than I have lived. Be a good boy always. Oh, I don't want to go, but I have to!"

It was not signed. I read it slowly, because I was not very good at reading, and turned my eyes west—where my mother had gone. I had lost her! How could any one be found who had disappeared into that region which swallowed up thousands every month? I had no clue. I did not believe that Rucker would try to help her find me. She had been kidnaped away from me. I threw myself down on the dead grass, and found the worn-out shoe I had picked up in the closet. It had every curve of her foot—that foot which had taken so many weary steps for me. I put my forehead down upon it, and lay there a long time—so long that when I roused myself and went down to the canal, I had not sat on my old stump a minute when I saw Captain Sproule's boat approaching from the west. With a heavy heart I stepped aboard, carrying the worn-out shoe and the letter, which I have yet. The boat was the only home left me. It had become my world.

CHAPTER IV

I WAS just past thirteen when I had my great wrestle with loneliness and desertion that night under the old apple-tree at Tempe; and the next three and a half years are not of much concern to the reader who is interested only in the history of Vandemark Township. I was just a growing boy, tussling, more alone than I should have been, and with no guidance or direction, with that problem of keeping soul and body together, which, after all, is the thing with which all of us are naturally obliged to cope all through our lives. I lived here and there, most of the time looking to Eben Sproule as a prop and support, as a boy must look to some one, or fall into bad and dangerous ways—and even then, maybe he will.

I was a backward boy, and this saved me from some deadfalls, I guess; and I had the Dutch hard mouth and a tendency to feel my ground and see how the land lay, which made me take so long to balk at any new vice or virtue that the impulse or temptation was sometimes past before I could get ready to embrace it. I guess there are some who may read this who have let chances for sinful joys go by while an inward debate went on in their own souls; and if they will only own up to it, found themselves

45

afterward guiltily sorry for not falling from grace. "As a man thinketh in his heart, so is he," is Scripture, and must be true if rightly understood; but I wonder if it is as bad for one of us tardy people to regret not having sinned, as it would have been if he had been quicker and done so. I hardly think it can be as bad; for many a saint must have had such experiences—which really is thinking both right and wrong, and doing right, even if he did think wrong afterward.

That first winter, I lived on Captain Sproule's farm, and had my board, washing and mending. His sister kept house for him, and his younger brother, Finley, managed the place summers, with such help in handling it as the captain had time to give when he passed the farm on his voyages. It was quite a stock farm, and here I learned something about the handling of cattle,—and in those days this meant breaking and working them. It was a hard winter, and there was so much work on the farm that I got only one month's schooling.

The teacher was a man named Lockwood. He kept telling us that we ought to read about farming, and study the business by which we expected to live; and this made a deep impression on me. Lockwood was a real teacher, and like all such worked without realizing it on stuff more lasting than steel or stone,—young, soft human beings. I did not see that there was much to study about as to driving on the canal; and when I asked him that he said that the business of taking care of the horses and feeding them was something that ought to be closely studied if I expected to be a farmer. This looked reasonable to me; and I soon got to be one of those driver boys who were noted for the sleekness and fatness of their teams, and began getting the habit of studying any task I had to do. But I was more interested in cattle than anything else, and was sorry when spring came and we unmoored the old boat and pulled down to Albany for a cargo west. This summer was like the last, except that I was now a skilled driver, larger, stronger, and more confident than before.

I used to ask leave to go on ahead on some fast boat when we drew near to the Sproule farm, so I could spend a day or two at farm work, see the family, and better than this, I am afraid—for they were pretty good to me— look the cattle over, pet and feed the calves, colts and lambs, count the little pigs and generally enjoy myself. On these packet boats, too, I could talk with travelers, and try to strike the trail of John Rucker.

I had one never-failing subject of conversation with the Sproules and all my other acquaintances—how to find my mother. We went over the whole matter a thousand times. I had no post-office address, and my mother had depended on Rucker's getting Captain Sproule's address at Syracuse—which of course he had never meant to do—and had not asked me to inquire at any place for mail. I wrote letters to her at Buffalo as she had asked me to do in her letter, but they were re-turned unclaimed. It was plain that Rucker meant to give me the slip, and had done so. He could be relied upon to balk every effort my mother might make to find me. I inquired for letters at the post-offices in Buffalo, Syracuse, Albany and Tempe at every chance, but finally gave up in despair.

2

I had only one hope, and that was to find the hump-backed man with the black beard—the man Rucker was talking to on the boat we had passed on our voyage eastward before I found my home deserted. This was a very slim chance, but it was all there was left. Captain Sproule had noticed him, and said he had seen him a great many times before. He was a land agent, who made it a business to get emigrants to go west, away up the lakes somewhere.

"If your stepfather had any money," said the captain, "you can bet that hunchback tried to bamboozle him into some land deal, and probably did. And if he did, he'll remember him and his name, and where he left the canal or the Lakes, and maybe where he located."

"I must watch for him," I said.

"We'll all watch for him," said the captain.

Paddy was not with us the next summer; but Bill was, and so was Ace, with whom I was now on the best of terms. We all agreed to keep our eyes peeled for a hunchback with a black beard. Bill said he'd spear him with a boathook as soon as he hove in sight for fear he'd get away. Ace was sure the hunchback was a witch* who had spirited off my folks; and looked upon the situation without much hope. He would agree to sing out if he saw this monster; but that was as far as he would promise to help me.

The summer went by with no news and no hunch-back; and that winter I stayed with an aunt of Captain

---

*"Witch" in American dialect is of the common gender. "Wizard" has no place in the vocabulary.—G. v. d. M.

Sproule's, taking care of her stock. I got five dollars a month, and my keep, but no schooling. She wanted me to stay the summer with her, and offered me what was almost a man's wages; which shows how strong I was getting, and how much of a farmer I was. I did stay and helped through the spring's work; but on Captain Sproule's second passing of Mrs. Fogg's farm, I joined him, not as a driver, but as a full hand. I kept thinking all the time of my mother, and felt that if I kept to the canal I surely should find some trace of her. In this I was doing what any detective would have done; for everything sooner or later passed through the Erie Canal —news, goods and passengers. But I had little hope when I thought of the flood which surged back and forth through this river of news, and of the little bit of a net with which I fished it for information.

All this time the stream of emigration and trade swelled, and swelled until it became a torrent. I thought at times that all the people in the world had gone crazy to move west. We took families, even neighborhoods, household goods, live stock, and all the time more and more people. They were talking about Ohio, Indiana, Illinois, Michigan and Wisconsin, and once in a while the word Iowa was heard; and one family astonished us by saying that they were going to Texas.

The Mormons had already made their great migration to Utah, and the Northwestern Trail across the plains to Oregon and to California took its quota of gold-seekers every year. John C. Fremont had crossed the continent to California, and caused me to read my first book, *The Life of Kit Carson.*

Bill, who never could speak in hard enough terms

about sailing on the mud-puddle Lakes, which he had never done as yet, once went to Pittsburgh, meaning to go from there down the Ohio and up the Missouri. He had heard of the Missouri River fur-trade, and big wages on the steamboats carrying emigrants from St. Louis up-stream to Nebraska, Iowa and Dakota Territory, and bringing back furs and hides. But at Pittsburgh he was turned back by news of the outbreak of cholera at New Orleans, a disease which had struck us with terror along the canal two or three years before. That summer there were medicine pedlers working on all the boats, selling a kind of stuff they called "thieves' vinegar" which was claimed to be a medicine that was used in the old country somewhere by thieves who robbed the infected houses in safety, protected by this wonderful "vinegar"; and only told how it was made to save their lives when they were about to be hanged. A man offered me a bottle of this at Rochester, for five dollars, and finally came down to fifty cents. This made me think it was of no use, and I did not buy, though just before I had been wondering whether I had not better borrow the money of Captain Sproule; so I saved my money, which was getting to be a habit of mine.

California, the Rockies, the fur-trade, the Ohio Valley, the new cities up the Lakes and the new farms in the woods back of them, and some few tales of the prairies—all these voices of the West kept calling us more loudly and plainly every year, and every year I grew stronger and more confident of myself.

The third year I had made up my mind that I would get work on a passenger boat so as to be able to see and talk with more people who were going up and down the

Lakes and the canal. I went from one to another as I met folks who were coming back from the West, and asked every one if he had known a man out west named John Rucker; but, though I found traces of two or three Ruckers in the course of the three years, it did not take long in each case to find out that it was not the man I hated so, and so much wanted to find. People used to point me out as the boy who was trying to find a man named Rucker; and two or three came to me and told me of men they had met who might be my man. I became known to many who traveled the canal as being engaged in some mysterious quest. I suppose I had an anxious and rather strange expression as I made my inquiries.

It took me two years to make up my mind to change to a passenger boat, so slow was I to alter my way of doing things. I have always been that way. My wife read *Knickerbocker's History of New York* after the children were grown up and she had more time for reading, and always told the children that she was positive their father must be descended from that ancient Dutchman* who took thirteen months to look the ground over before he began to put up that well-known church in Rotterdam of which he was the builder. After smoking over it to the tune of three hundred pounds of Virginia tobacco, after knocking his head—to jar his ideas loose, maybe— and breaking his pipe against every church in Holland and parts of France and Germany; after looking at the site of his church from every point of view—from land, from water, and from the air which he went up into by

---

*Irving's impersonation of Homer must have nodded when he named this safe, sane and staunch worthy Hermanus Van Clattercop.—G. v. d. M.

climbing other towers; this good old Dutch contractor and builder pulled off his coat and five pairs of breeches, and laid the corner-stone of the church. I think that this delay was a credit to him. Better be slow than sorry. The church was, according to my wife, a very good one; and if the man had jumped into the job on the first day of his contract it might have been a very bad one. So, when I used to take a good deal of time to turn myself before beginning any job, and my wife would say to one of the boys: "Just wait! He'll start to build that church after a while!" I always took it as a compliment. Finally I always did the thing, if after long study it seemed the right thing to do, or if some one else had not done it in the meantime; just as I finally told Captain Sproule that I expected to work on a passenger boat the next summer, and was told by him that he had sold his boat to a company, and was to be a passenger-boat captain himself the next summer; and would sign me on if I wanted to stay with him—which I did.

3

I was getting pretty stocky now, and no longer feared anything I was likely to meet. I was well-known to the general run of canallers, and had very little fighting to do; once in a while a fellow would pick a fight with me because of some spite, frequently because I refused to drink with him, or because he was egged on to do it; and this year I was licked by three toughs in Batavia. They left me senseless because I would not say "enough." I was getting a good deal of reputation as a wrestler. I liked wrestling better than fighting; and though a small-ish man always, like my fellow Iowan Farmer Burns, I have seldom found my master at this game. It is much more a matter of sleight than strength. A man must be cautious, wary, cool, his muscles always ready, as quick as a flash to meet any strain; but the main source of my success seemed to be my ability to use all the strength in every muscle of my body at any given instant, so as to overpower a much stronger opponent by pouring out on him so much power in a single burst of force that he was carried away and crushed. I have thrown over my head and to a distance of ten feet men seventy-five pounds heavier than I was. This is the only thing I ever did so well that I never met any one who could beat me.

I was of a fair complexion, with blue eyes, and my upper lip and chin were covered with a reddish fuzz over a very ruddy skin—a little like David's of old, I guess. On the passenger boats I met a great many people, and was joked a good deal about the girls, some of whom seemed to take quite a shine to me, just as they do to any fair-haired, reasonably clean-looking boy; especially if he has a little reputation; but though I sometimes found myself looking at one of them with considerable interest there was not enough time for as slow a boy as I to begin, let alone to finish any courting operations on even as long a voyage as that from Albany to Buffalo. I was really afraid of them all, and they seemed to know it, and made a good deal of fun of me.

We did not carry our horses on this boat; but stopped at relay stations for fresh teams, and after we had pulled out from one of these stations, we went flying along at from six to eight miles an hour, with a cook getting up fine meals; and we often had a "sing" as we called it when in the evening the musical passengers got together and tuned up. Many of them carried dulcimers, accordions, fiddles, flutes and various kinds of brass horns, and in those days a great many people could sing the good old hymns in the *Carmina Sacra,* and the glees and part-songs in the old *Jubilee,* with the soprano, tenor, bass and alto, and the high tenor and counter which made better music than any gathering of people are likely to make nowadays. All they needed was a leader with a tuning-fork, and off they would start, making the great canal a pretty musical place on fine summer evenings. We traveled night and day, and at night the boat, lighted up as well as we could do it then, with lanterns and lamps burning whale-oil, and with candles in the cabin, looked like a traveling banquet-hall or opera-house or tavern.

We were always crowded with immigrants when we went west; and on our eastern voyages even, our passenger traffic was mostly related to the West, its trade, and its people. Many of the men had been out west "hunting country," and sat on the decks or in the cabins until late at night, telling their fellow-travelers what they had found, exchanging news, and sometimes altering their plans to take advantage of what somebody else had found. Some had been looking for places where they could establish stores or set up in some other business. Some had gone to sell goods. Some were travelers for the purpose of preying on others. I saw a good deal of the world, that summer, some of which I understood, but not much. I understand it far better now as I look back upon it.

I noticed for the first time now that class of men with whom we became so well acquainted later. the land speculators. These, and the bankers, many of whom seemed to have a good deal of business in the West, formed a class by themselves, and looked down from a far height on the working people, the farmers, and the masses generally, who voyaged on the same boats with them. They talked of development, and the growth of the country, and the establishments of boats and the building of railways; while the rest of us thought about homes and places to make our livings. The young doctors and lawyers, and some old ones, too, who were going out to try life on the frontiers, occupied places in between these exalted folk and the rest of us. There were preachers among our passengers, but most of them were going west. On almost every voyage there would be a minister or missionary who would ask to have the privilege of holding prayer on the boat; and Captain Sproule always permitted it. The ministers, too, were among those who hunted up the singers in the crowds and organized the song services from the *Carmina Sacra*.

4

I was getting used to the life and liked it, and gradually I found my resolve to go west getting less and less strong; when late in the summer of 1854 something happened which restored it to me with tenfold strength. We had reached Buffalo, had discharged our passengers and cargo, and were about starting on our eastward voyage when I met Bill, the sailor, as he was coming out of a water-front saloon. I ran to him and called him by name; but at first he did not know me.

"This ain't little Jake, is it?" he said. "By mighty, I b'lieve it is! W'y, you little runt, how you've growed. Come in an' have a drink with your ol' friend Bill as nussed you when you was a baby!"

I asked to be excused; for I hadn't learned to drink more than a thin glass of rum and water, and that only when I got chilled. I turned the subject by asking him what he was doing; and at that he slapped his thigh and said he had great news for me.

"I've found that hump-backed bloke," he said. "He came down on the boat with us from Milwaukee. I knowed him as soon as I seen him, but I couldn't think all the v'yage what in time I wanted to find him fer. You jest put it in my mind!"

"Where is he?" I shouted. "You hain't lost him, have you?"

Bill stood for quite a while chewing tobacco, and scratching his head.

"Where is he?" I yelled.

"Belay bellering," said Bill. "I'm jest tryin' to think whuther he went on a boat east, or a railroad car, or a stage-coach, or went to a tavern. He went to a tavern, that's what he done. A drayman I know took his dunnage!"

"Come on," I cried, "and help me find the drayman!"

"I'll have to study on this," said Bill. "My mind hain't as active as usual. I need somethin' to brighten me up!"

"What do you need?" I inquired. "Can't you think where he stays?"

"A little rum," he answered, "is great for the memory. I b'lieve most any doctor'd advise a jorum of rum for a man in my fix, to restore the intellects."

I took him back into the grog-shop and bought him rum, taking a very little myself, with a great deal of blackstrap and water. Bill's symptoms were such as to drive me to despair. He sat looking at me like an old owl, and finally took my glass and sipped a little from it.

"Hain't you never goin' to grow up?" he asked; and poured out a big glass of the pure quill for me, and fiercely ordered me to drink it. By this time I was desperate; so I smashed his glass and mine; and taking him by the throat I shook him and told him that if he did not take me to the hump-backed man or to the drayman, and that right off, I'd shut off his wind for good. When he clinched with me I lifted him from the floor, turned him upside down, and lowered him head-first into an empty barrel. By this time the saloon-keeper was on the spot making all sorts of threats about having us both arrested, and quite a crowd had gathered. I lifted Bill out of the barrel and seated him in a chair, and paid for the glasses; all the time watching Bill for fear he might renew the tussle, and take me in flank; but he sat as if dazed until I had quieted matters down, when he rose and addressed the crowd.

"My little son," said he, patting me on the shoulder. "Stoutest man of his inches in the world. We'll be round here 's evenin'—give a show. C'mon, Jake!"

"Wot I said about growin' up," said he, as we went along the street, "is all took back, Jake!"

We had not gone more than a quarter of a mile when we came to a place where there was a stand for express wagons and drays; and Bill picked out from the crowd, with a good deal of difficulty, I thought, a hard-looking citizen to whom he introduced me as the stoutest man on the Erie Canal. The drayman seemed to know me. He said he had seen me wrestle. When I asked him about the hunchback he said he knew right where he was; but there was no hurry, and tried to get up a wrestling match between me and a man twice my size who made a specialty of hauling salt, and bragged that he could take a barrel of it by the chimes, and lift it into his dray. I told him that I was in a great hurry and begged to be let off; but while I was talking they had made up a purse of twenty-one shillings to be wrestled for by us two. I finally persuaded the drayman to show me the hunch-back's tavern, and promised to come back and wrestle after I had found him; to which the stake-holder agreed, but all the rest refused to consent, and the money was given back to the subscribers. The drayman, Bill and I went off together to find the tavern—which we finally did.

It was a better tavern than we were used to, and I was a little bashful when I inquired if a man with a black beard was stopping there, and was told that there were several.

"What's his name?" asked the clerk.

" 'E's a hunchback," said Bill—I had been too diffi-dent to describe him so.

"Mr. Wisner, of Southport, Wisconsin," said the clerk, "has a back that ain't quite like the common run of backs. Want to see him?"

He was in a nice room, with a fire burning and was writing at a desk which opened and shut, and was carried with him when he traveled. He wore a broadcloth, swal-low-tailed coat, a collar that came out at the sides of his neck and stood high under his ears; and his neck was covered with a black satin stock. On the bed was a tall, black beaver, stove-pipe hat. There were a great many papers on the table and the bed, and the room looked as if it had been used by crowds of people—the floor was muddy about the fireplace, and there were tracks from the door to the cheap wooden chairs which seemed to have been brought in to accommodate more visitors than could sit on the horsehair chairs and sofa that appeared to belong in the room. Mr. Wisner looked at us sharply as we came in, and shook hands first with Bill and then with me.

"Glad to see you again," said he heartily. "Glad to see you again! I want to tell you some more about Wisconsin. I haven't told you the half of its advantages."

I saw that he thought we had been there before, and was about to correct his mistake, when Bill told him that that's what we had come for.

"What you said about Wisconsin," said Bill, winking at me, "has sort of got us all worked up."

"Is it a good country for a boy to locate in?" I asked.

"A paradise for a boy!" he said, in a kind of bubbly way. "And for a poor man, it's heaven! Plenty of work. Good wages. If you want a home, it's the only God's country. What kind of land have you been farming in the past?"

Bill said that he had spent his life plowing the seas, but that all the fault I had was being a landsman. I admitted that I had farmed some near Herkimer.

"And," sneered Mr. Wisner crushingly, "how long does it take a man to clear and grub out and subdue enough land in Herkimer County to make a living on? Ten years! Twenty years! Thirty years! Why, in Herkimer County a young man doesn't buy anything when he takes up land: he sells something! He sells himself to slavery for life to the stumps and sprouts and stones! But in Wisconsin you can locate on prairie land ready for the plow; or you can have timber land, or both kinds, or openings that are not quite woods nor quite prairie—there's every kind of land there except poor land! It's a paradise, and land's cheap. I can sell you land right back of Southport, with fine market for whatever you raise, on terms that will pay themselves—pay themselves. Just go aboard the first boat, and I'll give you a letter to my partner in Southport—and your fortunes will be made in ten years!"

"The trouble is," said Bill, "that we'll be so damned lonesome out where we don't know any one. If we could locate along o' some of our ol' mates, somebody like old John Tucker,—it would be a—a paradise, eh, Jake?"

"The freest-hearted people in the world," said Mr. Wisner. "They'll travel ten miles to take a spare-rib or a piece of fresh beef to a new neighbor. Invite the stranger in to stay all night as he drives along the road. You'll never miss your old friends; and probably you'll find old neighbors most anywhere. Why, this country has moved out to Wisconsin. It won't be long till you'll have to go there to find 'em—ha, ha, ha!"

"If we could find a man out there named Tucker ____"

"An old—sort of—of relative of mine," I put in, seeing that Bill was spoiling it all, "John Rucker."

"I know him!" cried Wisner. "Kind of a tall man with a sandy beard? Good talker? Kind of plausible talker? Used to live down east of Syracuse? Pretty well fixed? Went out west three years ago? Calls himself Doctor Rucker?"

"I guess that's the man," said I; "do you know where he is now?"

"Had a wife and no children?" asked Wisner. "And was his wife a quiet, kind of sad-looking woman that never said much?"

"Yes! Yes!" said I. "If you know where they are, I'll go there by the next boat."

"Hum," said Wisner. "Whether I can tell you the exact township and section is one thing; but I can say that they went to Southport on the same boat with me, and at last accounts were there or thereabouts—there or thereabouts."

"Come on, Bill," said I, "I want to take passage on the next boat!"

Mr. Wisner kept us a long time, giving me letters to his partner; trying to find out how much money I would have when I got to Southport; warning me not to leave that neighborhood even if I found it hard to find the Rucker family; and assuring me that if it weren't for the fact that he had several families along the canal ready to move in a week or two, he would go back with me and place himself at my service.

"And it won't be long," said he, "until I can be with you. My boy, I feel like a father to the young men locating among us, and I beg of you don't make any permanent arrangements until I get back. I can save you money, and start you on the way to a life of wealth and happiness. God bless you, and give you a safe voyage!"

"Bill," said I, as we went down the stairs, "this is the best news I ever had. I'm going to find my mother! I had given up ever finding her, Bill; and I've been so lonesome—you don't know how lonesome I've been!"

"I used to have a mother," said Bill, "in London. Next time I'm there I'll stay sober for a day and have a look about for her. You never have but about one mother, do you, Jake? A mother is a great thing—when she ain't in drink."

"I wish I could have Mr. Wisner with me when I get to Southport," I said. "He'd help me. He is such a Christian man!"

"Wal," said Bill, "I ain't as sure about him as I am about mothers. He minds me of a skipper I served under once; and he starved us, and let the second officer haze us till we deserted and lost our wages. He's about twice too slick. I'd give him the go-by, Jake."

"And now for a boat," I said.

"Wal," said Bill, "I'm sailin' to-morrow mornin' on the schooner *Mahala Peters,* an' we're short-handed. Go aboard an' ship as an A. B."

I protested that I wasn't a sailor; but Bill insisted that beyond being hazed by the mate there was no reason why I shouldn't work my passage.

"If there's a crime," said he, "it's a feller like you payin' his passage. Let's get a drink or two an' go aboard."

I explained to the captain, in order that I might be honest with him, that I was no sailor, but had worked on canal boats for years, and would do my best. He swore at his luck in having to ship land-lubbers, but took me on; and before we reached Southport—now Kenosha—I was good enough so that he wanted me to ship back with him. It was on this trip that I let the cook tattoo this anchor on my forearm, and thus got the reputation among the people of the prairies of having been a sailor, and therefore a pretty rough character. As a matter of fact the sailors on the Lakes were no rougher than the canallers—and I guess not so rough.

I was sorry, many a time, on the voyage, that I had not taken passage on a steamer, as I saw boats going by us in clouds of smoke that left Buffalo after we did; but we had a good voyage, and after seeing Detroit, Mackinaw and Milwaukee, we anchored in Southport harbor so late that the captain hurried on to Chicago to tie up for the winter. I had nearly three hundred dollars in a belt strapped around my waist, and some in my pocket; and went ashore after bidding Bill good-by—I never saw the good fellow again—and began my search for John Rucker. I did not need to inquire at Mr. Wisner's office, and I now think I probably saved money by not going there; for I found out from the proprietor of the hotel that Rucker, whom he called Doc Rucker, had moved to Milwaukee early in the summer.

"Friend of yours?" he asked.

"No," I said with a good deal of emphasis; "but I want to find him—bad!"

"If you find him," said he, "and can git anything out of him, let me know and I'll make it an object to you. An' if you have any dealings with him, watch him. Nice man, and all that, and a good talker, but watch him."

"Did you ever see his wife?" I inquired.

"They stopped here a day or two before they left," said the hotel-keeper. "She looked bad. Needed a doctor, I guess—a different doctor!"

There was a cold northeaster blowing, and it was spitting snow as I went back to the docks to see if I could get a boat for Milwaukee. A steamer in the offing was

getting ready to go, and I hired a man with a skiff to put
me and my carpet-bag aboard. We went into Milwaukee
in a howling blizzard, and I was glad to find a warm bar
in the tavern nearest the dock; and a room in which to
house up while I carried on my search. I now had
found out that the stage lines and real-estate offices were
the best places to go for traces of immigrants; and I
haunted these places for a month before I got a single
clue to Rucker's movements. It almost seemed that he
had been hiding in Milwaukee, or had slipped through so
quickly as not to have made himself remembered—which
was rather odd, for there was something about his tall
stooped figure, his sandy beard, his rather whining and
fluent talk, and his effort everywhere to get himself into
the good graces of every one he met that made it easy
to identify him. His name, too, was one that seemed to
stick in people's minds.

5

At last I found a man who freighted and drove stage
between Milwaukee and Madison, who remembered
Rucker; and had given him passage to Madison sometime, as he remembered it, in May or June—or it might
have been July, but it was certainly before the Fourth of
July.

"You hauled him—and his wife?" I asked.

"Him and his wife," said the man, "and a daughter."

"A daughter!" I said in astonishment. "They have
no daughter."

"Might have been his daughter, and not her'n," said
the stage-driver. "Wife was a good deal younger than
him, an' the girl was pretty old to be her'n. Prob'ly his.
Anyhow, he said she was his daughter."

"It wasn't his daughter," I cried.

"Well, you needn't get het up about it," said he; "I hain't to blame no matter whose daughter she wasn't. She can travel with me any time she wants to. Kind of a toppy, fast-goin', tricky little rip, with a sorrel mane."

"I don't understand it," said I. "Did you notice his wife—whether she seemed to be feeling well?"

"Looked bad," said he. "Never said nothing to nobody, and especially not to the daughter. Used to go off to bed while the old man and the girl held spiritualist doin's wherever we laid over. Went into trances, the girl did, and the old man give lectures about the car of progress that always rolls on and on and on, pervided you consult the spirits. Picked up quite a little money 's we went along, too."

I sat in the barroom and thought about this for a long time. There was something wrong about it. My mother's health was failing, that was plain from what I had heard in Southport; but it did not seem to me, no matter how weak and broken she might be, that she would have allowed Rucker to pass off any stray trollop like the one described by the stage-driver as his daughter, or would have traveled with them for a minute. But, I thought, what could she do? And maybe she was trying to keep the affair within bounds as far as possible. A good woman is easily deceived, too. Perhaps she knew best, after all; and maybe she was going on and on with Rucker from one misery to another in the hope that I, her only son, and the only relative she had on earth, might follow and overtake her, and help her out of the terrible situation in which, even I, as young and immature as I was, could see that she must find herself. I had seen too much of the under side of life not to understand the probable meaning of this new and horrible thing. I remembered how insulted my mother was that time so long ago when Rucker proposed that they join the Free-Lovers at Oneida; and how she had refused to ride home with him, at first, and had walked back on that trail through the woods, leading me by the hand, until she was exhausted, and how Rucker had tantalized her by driving by us, and sneering at us when mother and I finally climbed into the democrat wagon, and rode on with him toward Tempe. I could partly see, after I had thought over it for a day or so, just what this new torture might mean to her.

I was about to start on foot for Madison, and looked up my stage-driver acquaintance to ask him about the road.

"Why don't you go on the railroad?" he asked. "The damned thing has put me out of business, and I'm no friend of it; but if you're in a hurry it's quicker'n walkin'."

I had seen the railway station in Milwaukee, and looked at the train; but it had never occurred to me that I might ride on it to Madison. Now we always expect a railway to run wherever we want to go; but then it was the exception—and the only railroad running out of Milwaukee was from there to Madison. On this I took that day my first ride in a railway car, reaching Madison some time after three. This seemed like flying to me. I had seen plenty of railway tracks and trains in New York; but I had to come to Wisconsin to patronize one.

I rode on, thinking little of this new experience, as I remember, so filled was I with the hate of John Rucker which almost made me forget my love for my mother.

Perhaps the one was only the reverse side of the other. I had made up my mind what to do. I would try hard not to kill Rucker, though I tried him and condemned him to death in my own mind several times for every one of the eighty miles I rode; but I knew that this vengeance was not for me.

I would take my mother away from him, though, in spite of everything; and she and I would move on to a new home, somewhere, living happily together for the rest of our lives.

I was happy when I thought of this home, in which, with my new-found, fresh strength, my confidence in myself, my knack of turning my hand to any sort of common work, my ability to defend her against everything and everybody—against all the Ruckers in the world—my skill in so many things that would make her old age easy and happy, I would repay her for all this long miserable time,—the cruelty of Rucker when she took me out of the factory while he was absent, the whippings she had seen him give me, the sacrifices she had made to give me the little schooling I had had, the nights she had sewed to make my life a little easier, the tears she dropped on my bed when she came and tucked me in when I was asleep, the pangs of motherhood, and the pains worse than those of motherhood which she had endured because she was poor, and married to a beast.

I would make all this up to her if I could. I went into Madison, much as a man goes to his wedding; only the woman of my dreams was my mother. But I felt as I did that night when I returned to Tempe after my first summer on the canal—full of hope and anticipation, and yet with a feeling in my heart that again something would stand in my way.

CHAPTER V

I WENT to seek my mother in my best clothes. I had bought some new things in Milwaukee, and was sure that my appearance would comfort her greatly. Instead of being ragged, poverty-stricken, and neglected-looking, I was a picture of a clean, well-clothed working boy. I had on the good corduroy suit, and because the weather was cold, I wore a new Cardigan jacket. My shirt was of red flannel, very warm and thick; and about my neck I tied a flowered silk handkerchief which had been given me by a lady who was very kind to me once during a voyage by canal, and was called "my girl" by the men on the boat. I wore good kip boots with high tops, with shields of red leather at the knees, each ornamented with a gilt moon and star—the nicest boots I ever had; and I wore my pants tucked into my boot-tops so as to keep them out of the snow and also to show these glories in leather. With clouded woolen mittens on my hands, given me as a Christmas present by Mrs. Fogg, Captain Sproule's sister, that winter I worked for her near Herkimer, and a wool cap, trimmed about with a broad band of mink fur, and a long crocheted woolen comforter about my neck, I was as well-dressed a boy for a winter's day as a body need look for. I took a look at myself in the glass, and felt that even at the first glance, my mother

68

would feel that in casting her lot with me she would be choosing not only the comfort of living with her only son but the protection of one who had proved himself a man.

I glowed with pride as I thought of our future together, and of all I would do to make her life happy and easy. I never was a better boy in my life than on that winter evening when I went up the hilly street from the tavern in Madison to the place on a high bluff overlooking a sheet of ice, stretching away almost as far as I could see, which they told me was Fourth Lake, to the house in which I was informed Doctor Rucker lived—a small frame house among stocky, low burr oak trees, on which the dead leaves still hung, giving forth a dreary hiss as the bitter north wind blew through them.

I knocked at the door, and was answered by a red-haired young woman, with a silly grin on her face, the smirk flanked on each side with cork-screw curls which hung down over her bright blue dress; which, as I could see, was pulled out at the seams under her round and shapely arms. She put out a soft and plump hand to me, but I did not take it. She looked in my face, and shrank back as if frightened.

"Where's Rucker?" I asked; but before I had finished the question he came forward from the other room, clothed in dirty black broadcloth, his patent-medicine-pedler's smile all over his face, with a soiled frilled shirt showing back of his flowered vest, which was unbuttoned except at the bottom, to show the nasty finery beneath. He had on a broad black scarf filling the space between the points of his wide-open standing collar, and sticking out on each side. I afterward recalled the impression of a gold watch-chain, and a broad ring on his finger. He was quite changed in outward appearance from the poverty-stricken skunk I had once known; but was if anything more skunk-like than ever: yet I had to look twice to be sure of him.

"I am exceedingly glad to see you in the flesh," said he, coming forward with his hand stuck out—a hand which I stared at but never touched—"exceedingly glad to see you, my young brother. I have had a spiritual vision of you. Honor us by coming in by the fire!"

"Where's my mother?" I asked, still standing in the open door.

Rucker started at the sound of my voice, which had changed from the boy's soprano into a deep bass—much deeper than it is now. It was the hoarse croak of the hobbledehoy.

The young woman had shrunk back behind him now.

"Your mother?" said he, in a sort of panther-like purr. "A spirit has been for three days seeking to speak to a lost child through my daughter. Come in, and let us see. Let us see if my daughter can not pierce the mysteries of the unseen in your case. Come in!"

The cold was blowing in at the open door, and his tone was a little like that of a man who wants to say, but does not feel it wise to do so, "Come in and shut the door after you!"

"Your daughter!" I said, trying to think of something to say that would show what I thought of him, her, and their dirty pretense; "your daughter! Hell!"

"Young man," said he, drawing himself up stiffly, "what do you mean——?"

"I mean to find my mother!" I cried. "Where is she?"

Suddenly the thought of being halted thus longer, and the fear that my mother was not there, drove me crazy. I lunged at Rucker, and with a sweep of my arms, threw him staggering across the room. The girl screamed, and ran to, and behind him. I stormed through to the kitchen, expecting to find my mother back there, working for this smooth, sly, scroundrelly pair; but the place was deserted. There were dirty pots and pans about; and a pile of unwashed dishes stacked high in the sink—and this struck me with despair. If my mother had been about, and able to work, such a thing would have been impossible. So she either was not there or was not able to work—my instinct told me that; and I ran to the foot of the stairs, and calling as I had so often done when a child, "Ma, Ma! Where are you, ma!" I waited to hear her answer.

Rucker, pale as a sheet, came up to me, his quivering mouth trying to work itself into a sneaking sort of smile.

"Why, Jacob, Jakey," he drooled, "is this you? I didn't know you. Sit down, my son, and I'll tell you the sad, sad news!"

I heard him, but I did not trust nor understand him, and I went through that house from cellar to garret, looking for her; my heart freezing within me as I saw how impossible it would be for her to live so. There were two bedrooms, both beds lying just as they had been left in the morning—and my mother always opened her beds up for an airing when she rose, and made them up right after breakfast.

The room occupied by the young woman was the

room of a slut; the clothes she had taken off the night before, or even before that, lay in a ring about the place where her feet had been when she dropped them in the dust and lint which rolled about in the corners like feathers. Her corset was thrown down in a corner; shoes and stockings littered the floor; her comb was clogged with red hair like a wire fence with dead grass after a freshet; dingy, grimy underclothing lay about. I peered into a closet, in which there were more garments on the floor than on the nails. The other bedroom was quite as unkempt; looking as if the occupant must always do his chamber work at the last moment before going to bed. They were as unclean outwardly as inwardly.

After ransacking the house up-chamber, I ran downstairs and went into the room from which Rucker had come, where I found the girl hiding behind a sofa, peeking over the back of it at me, and screaming "Go away!" All the walls in this room were hung with some thin black cloth, and it looked like the inside of a hearse. There was a stand in one corner, and a large extension table in the middle of the room, with chairs placed about it. In the corner across from the stand was a spiritualist medium's cabinet; and hanging on the walls were a guitar, a banjo and a fiddle. A bell stood in the middle of the table, and there were writing materials, slates, and other things scattered about, which theatrical people call "properties," I am told. I tore the black draperies down, and searched for a place where my mother might be— in bed I expected to find her, if at all; but she was not there. I tried the cellar, but it was nothing but a vegetable cave, dug in the earth, with no walls, and dark as a dungeon when the girl shut down the trap-door and stood on it: from which I threw her by putting my back under it and giving a surge. When I came up she was staggering to her feet, and groaning as she felt of her head for the results of some suspected cut or bump from her fall. Rucker was following me about calling me Jacob and Jakey, a good deal as a man will try to smooth down or pacify a vicious horse or mule; and after I had looked everywhere, I faced him, took him by the throat, and choked him until his tongue stuck out, and his face was purple.

"My God," said the girl, who had grown suddenly quiet, "you're killing him!"

I looked at his empurpled face, and my madness came back on me like a rush of fire through my veins—and I shut down on his throat again until I could feel the cords draw under my fingers like taut ropes.

She laid her hand rather gently on my breast, and looked me steadily in the eye.

"Fool!" she almost whispered. "Your mother's dead! Will it bring her back to life for you to stretch hemp?"

I guess that by that action she saved my life; but it has been only of late years that I have ceased to be sorry that I did not kill him. I looked back into her eyes for a moment—I remember yet that they were bright blue, with a lighter band about the edge of the sight, instead of the dark edging that most of us have; and as I understood her meaning I took my hands from Rucker's throat, and threw him from me. He lay on the floor for a minute, and as he scrambled to his feet I sank down on the nearest chair and buried my face in my hands.

It was all over, then; my long lone quest for my mother—a quest I had carried on since I was a little, scared, downtrodden child. I should never have the chance to serve her in my way as she had served me in hers—my way that would never have been anything but a very small and easy one at the most; while hers had been a way full of torment and servitude. All my strength was gone; and the girl seemed to know it; for she came over to me and patted me on the shoulder in a motherly sort of way.

"Poor boy!" she said. "Poor boy! To-morrow, come to me and I'll show you your mother's grave. I'll take you to the doctor that attended her. I know how you feel."

I had passed a sleepless night before I remembered to feel revolted at the sympathy of this hussy who had helped to bring my mother to her death—and I did not go near her. But I inquired my way from one doctor to another—there were not many in Madison then—until I found one, named Mix, who had treated my mother in her last illness. She was weak and run down, he said, and couldn't stand a run of lung fever, which had carried her off.

"Did she mention me?" I asked.

"At the very last," said Doctor Mix, "she said once or twice, 'He had to work too hard!' I don't know who she meant. Not Rucker, eh?"

I shook my head—I knew what she meant.

"And," said he, "if you can see your way clear to arrange with old Rucker to pay my bill—winter is on now, and I could use the money."

I pulled out my pocketbook and paid the bill.

"Thank you, my boy," said he, "thank you!"

"I'm glad to do it," I answered—and turned away my head.

"Anything more I can do for you?" asked Doctor Mix, much kinder than before.

"I'd be much obliged," I replied, "if you could tell me where I can find some one that'll be able to show me my mother's grave."

"I'll take you there," he said quickly.

We rode to the graveyard in his sleigh, the bells jingling too merrily by far, I thought; and then to a marble-cutter from whom I bought a headstone to be put up in the spring. I worked out an epitaph which Doctor Mix, who seemed to see through the case pretty well, put into good language, reading as follows: "Here lies the body of Mary Brouwer Vandemark, born in Ulster County, New York, in 1815; died Madison, Wisconsin, October 19, 1854. Erected to her memory by her son, Jacob T. Vandemark." So I cut the name of Rucker from our family record; but, of course, he never knew.

Then the doctor took me back to the tavern, trying to persuade me on the way to locate in Madison. He had some vacant lots he wanted to show me; and said that he and a company of friends had laid out new towns at half a dozen different places in Wisconsin, and even in Minnesota and Iowa. Before we got back he saw, though I tried to be civil, that I was not thinking about what he was saying, and so he let me think in peace; but he shook hands with me kindly at parting, and wished I could have got there in September.

"Things might have been different," said he. "You're a darned good boy; and if you'll stay here till spring I'll get you a job."

2

There was no fire in my room, and it was cold; so there was no place to sit except in the barroom, which I found deserted but for one man, when I went back and sat down to think over my future. Should I go back to the canal? I hated to do this, though all my acquaintances were there, and the work was of the sort I had learned to do best; besides, here I was in the West, and all the opportunities of the West were before me, though it looked cold and dreary just now, and no great chances seemed lying about for a boy like me. I was perplexed. I had lost my desire for revenge on Rucker; and just then I felt no ambition, and saw no light. I was ready, I suppose, to begin a life of drifting; this time with no aim, not even a remote one—for my one object in life had vanished. But something in the way of guidance always has come to me at such times; and it came now. The one man who was in the bar when I came in got up, and moving over by me, sat down in a chair by my side.

"Cold day," said he.

I agreed, and looked him over carefully. He was a tall man who wore a long black Prince Albert coat which came down below his knees, a broad felt hat, and no overcoat. He looked cold, and rather shabby; but he talked with a good deal of style, and used many big words.

"Stranger here?" he asked.

I admitted that I was.

"May I offer," said he, "the hospitalities of the city in the form of a hot whisky toddy?"

I thanked him and asked to be excused.

"Your name," he ventured, after clearing his throat, "is Vandemark."

Then I looked at him still more sharply. How did he know my name?

"I have been looking for you," said he, "for some months—some months; and I was so fortunate as to observe the fact when you made a call last evening on our fellow-citizen, Doctor Rucker. I was—ahem—consulted professionally by the late lamented Mrs. Rucker—I am a lawyer, sir—before her death, for the purpose of securing my services in looking after the interests of her son, Mr. Jacob H. Vandemark."

"Jacob T. Vandemark," said I.

"Why, damn me," said he, looking again at his book, "it *is* a 'T.' Lawyer's writing, Jacob, lawyer's writing—notoriously bad, you know."

I sat thinking about the expression, "the interests of Jacob T. Vandemark," for a long time; but the truth did not dawn on me, my mind working slowly as usual.

"What interests?" I asked finally.

"The interest," said he, "of her only child in the estate of Mrs. Rucker."

Then there recurred to my mind the words in my mother's last letter; that the money had been paid on the settlement of my father's estate, and that she and Rucker were coming out West to make a new start in life. I had never given it a moment's thought before, and should have gone away without asking anybody a single question about it, if this scaly pettifogger, as I now know him to have been, had not sidled up to me.

"The estate," said my new friend, "is small, Jacob; but right is right, and there is no reason why this man Rucker should not be made to disgorge every cent that's coming to you—every cent! I know Doctor Rucker slightly, and I hope I shall not shock you if I say that in my opinion he would steal the Lord's Supper, and wipe his condemned lousy red whiskers and his freckled claws with the table-cloth! That's the kind of pilgrim and stranger Rucker is. He will cheat you out of your eye teeth, sir, unless you are protected by the best legal talent to be had—the best to be had—the talent and the advice of the man to whom your late lamented mother went for counsel."

"Yes," said I after a while, "I think he will."

"That is why your mother," he went on, "advised with me; for even if I have to say it, I'm a living whirlwind in court. Suppose we have a drink!"

I sat with my drink before me, slowly sipping it, and trying to see through this man and the new question he had brought up. Certainly, I was entitled to my mother's property—all of it by rights, whatever the law might be—for it came through my father. Surely this lawyer must be a good man, or my mother wouldn't have consulted him. But when I mentioned to my new friend, whose name was Jackway, my claim to the whole estate he assured me that Rucker was the legal owner of his share in it—I forgot how much.

"And," said he, "I make no doubt the old scoundrel has reduced the whole estate to possession, and is this moment," lowering his voice secretively, "acting as executor *de son tort*—executor *de son tort,* sir! I wouldn't put it past him!"

I wrote this, with some other legal expressions in my note-book.

"How can I get this money away from him?" said I, coming to the point.

"Money!" said he. "How do we know it is money? It may be chattels, goods, wares or merchandise. It may be realty. It may be *choses in action*. We must require of him a complete discovery. We may have to go back to the original probate proceedings through which your mother became seized of this property to obtain the necessary information. How old are you?"

I told him that I was sixteen the twenty-seventh of the last July.

"A minor," said he; "in law an infant. A guardian *ad litem* will have to be appointed to protect your interests, and to bring suit for you. I shall be glad to serve you, sir, in the name of justice; and to confound those with whom robbery of the orphan is an occupation, sir, a daily occupation. Come up to my office with me, and we will begin proceedings to make Rucker sweat!"

3

But this was too swift for a Vandemark. In spite of his urging, I insisted that I should have to think it over. He grew almost angry at me at last, I thought; but he went away finally, after I had taken the hint he gave and bought him another drink. The next morning he was back again, urging me to proceed immediately, "so that the property might not be further sequestrated and wasted." He did not know how slow I was to think and act; and suspected that I was going to some other lawyer, I now believe; for I noticed him shadowing me, as the detectives say, every time I walked out. On the third day, while I was still studying the matter, and making no progress, Rucker himself came into the tavern, with his neck bandaged and his head on one side, and in his best clothes; and sitting on the edge of his chair between me

and the door, as if ready to take wing at any hostile movement on my part, he broached the subject of my share in
my mother's estate.

"I want to deal with you," said he in that dangerous
whine of his, "as with my own son, Jacob, my own son."

There was nothing to say to this, and I said nothing.
I only looked at him. He was studying me closely, but
had never taken pains to learn my peculiarities when I
lived with him, and had to study a total stranger, and a
person who was too old to be treated as a child, but who
at the same time must be very green in money matters. I
was a puzzle to him, and my lack of words made me still
more of a problem.

"You know, of course," he finally volunteered, "that
the estate when it was finally wound up had mostly been
eaten up by court expenses and lawyers' fees—the robbers!"

I could see he was in earnest in this last remark; but
of course lawyers' fees and court expenses were all a
mystery to me. I did not even know that lawyers and
courts had anything to do with estates. I did not know
what an estate was—so I continued to keep still.

"There was hardly anything left," said he.

I was astonished at this; and I did not believe it.
After thinking it over for a few minutes, earnestly, and
without any thought of saying anything to catch him up,
I said: "You traveled in good style coming west on the
canal. You took a steamer up the Lakes. You have been
dressing fine ever since the money came in; and you're
keeping a woman."

He made no reply, except to say that I did not understand, but would when he showed me where every cent

of the estate money had gone which he had spent, and just
how much was left. As for his daughter—he supposed
I knew—but he never finished this speech. I rose to my
feet; and he left hurriedly, saying that he would show me
a statement in the morning. "I expect to pay your board
here," said he, "for a few days, you know—until you
decide to move on—or move back."

For a week or so I refused to talk with Rucker or
Jackway; but sat around and tried to make up my mind
what to do. To hire Jackway would take all my savings;
and the schedules which Rucker brought me on legal-cap
paper I refused even to touch with my hands. I am sure,
now, that Rucker had sent Jackway to me in the first
place, never suspecting that the matter of the estate had
been so far from my mind; and thereby, by too much
craft, he lost the opportunity of stealing it all. Jackway
kept telling me of Rucker's rascalities, so as to get into
my good graces and confidence, in which he succeeded
better than he knew; and urging me to pay him a few
dollars—just a few dollars—"to begin proceedings to
stay waste and sequestration"; but I did not give him
anything because it seemed a first step into something I
had not understood.

4

I began calling on land agents, thinking I might use
what little money I had left to make a first payment on
a farm; but the land around Madison was too high in
price for me. Two or three of these real estate agents
were also lawyers; and I caught Rucker and Jackway
together, looking worried and anxious, when I came
from the office of one of them who very kindly
informed me that, if he were in my place, he would go

across the Mississippi and settle in Iowa. He had been as far west as Fort Dodge, and described to me the great prairies, unbroken by the plow, the railroads which were just ready to cross the Mississippi, the rich soil, the chance there was to get a home, and to become my own master. I began to feel an interest in Iowa.

I think these days must have been anxious ones for Rucker, greedy as he was for my little fortune, ignorant as he was of the depth of the ignorance of the silent stupid boy with whom he was dealing—and a boy, too, who had made that one remark about his way of living and traveling that seemed to show a knowledge of just what he was doing, and had done. I could see after that, that he thought me much sharper than I was. Lawyer Jackway haunted the hotel, and was spending more money—Rucker's money, I know. He had bought a new overcoat, and was drinking a good deal more than was good for him; but he wormed out of me something about my desire for a farm, and after having had a chance to see Rucker he began talking of a compromise.

"The old swindler," said he, "has all the evidence in his own hands; and he and that red-headed spiritual partner of his will swear to anything. As your legal adviser," said he, "and the legal adviser of your sainted mother, I'd advise you to take anything he is willing to give—within bounds, of course, within bounds."

So the next time Rucker sidled into the tavern, and began beslavering me about the way the money left by my mother was being eaten up by expenses and debts, I blurted out: "Well, what will you give me to clear out and let you and your red-headed woodpecker alone?"

"Now," said he, "you are talking sensibly—sensibly.

There is a little farm out near Blue Mounds that I could, by a hard struggle, let you have; but it would be more than your share—more than your share."

This was forty acres, and would have a mortgage on it. I waited a day or so, and told him I wouldn't take it. What I was afraid of was the mortgage; but I didn't give my reasons. Then he came back with a vacant lot in Madison, and then three vacant lots, which I went and looked at, and found in a swamp. Then I told him I wanted money or farm land; and he offered me a lead mine near Mineral Point. All the time he was getting more and more worried and excited; he used to tremble when he talked to me; and as the winter wore away, and the season drew nearer when he wanted to go on his travels, or deal with the properties in which I had found out by this time he was speculating with my mother's money, just as everybody was speculating then, in mines, town sites, farm lands, railway stocks and such things, he was on tenter-hooks, I could see that, to get rid of me, whom he thought he had given the slip forever. Finally he came to me one morning, just as a warm February wind had begun to thaw the snow, and said, beaming as if he had found a gold mine for me: "Jacob, I've got just what you want—a splendid farm in Iowa."

And he laid on the table the deed to my farm in Vandemark Township, a section of land in one solid block a mile square. "Of course," said he, "I can't let you have all of it—but let us say eighty acres, or even I might clean up a quarter-section, here along the east side,"—and he pointed to a plat of it pinned fast to the deed.

"The whole piece," said I, "is worth eight hundred dollars, and not a cent more—if it's all good land. That ain't enough."

"All good land!" said he—and I could see he was
surprised at the fact that I knew Iowa land was selling
at a dollar and a quarter an acre. "Why, there ain't anything but good land there. You can put a plow in one
corner of that section, and plow every foot of it without
taking the share out of the ground."

"All or nothing," said I, "and more."

Next day he came back and said he would let me have
the whole section; but that it would break him. He
wanted to be fair with me—more than fair. People had
set me against him, he said, looking at Jackway who was
drinking at the bar; but nobody could say that he was a
man who would not deal fairly with an ignorant boy.

"I've got to have a team, a wagon, a cover for the
wagon, and provisions for the trip," I said, "and a few
hundred dollars to live on for a while after I get to Iowa."

At this he threw his hands up, and left me, saying that
if I wanted to ruin him I would have to do it through
the courts. He had gone as far as he would go, and I
would never have another offer as generous as he had
made me. The next day I met on the street the red-
headed girl, who went by the name of Alice Rucker, and
was notorious as a medium. She stopped me, and asked
why I hadn't been to see her—carrying the conversation
off casually, as if we had been ordinary acquaintances.
All I could say—for I was a little embarrassed, was "I
do' know"—which was what I had told Rucker and Jackway, in answer to a thousand questions, until they were
crazy to know how to come at me.

"Let me tell you something," said she. "If you want
that Iowa farm, pa——"

"Who?" said I.

"Rucker," said she, brazening it out with me. "He'll give you the land, and your outfit. Don't let them fool you out of the team and wagon."

"Thank you for telling me," said I; "but I guess I'll have to have more."

"If you go into court he'll beat you," said she, "and I'm telling you that as a friend, even if you don't believe me."

"I'm much obliged," I said; and I believed then, and believe now, that she was sincere.

"And when you start," said she, "if you want some one to cook and take care of you, let me know. I like traveling."

I turned red at this; and halted and mumbled, until she tripped away, laughing, but looking back at me; but I remembered what she had said, and within a week I had consented that Jackway be appointed guardian *ad litem* for me in the court proceedings; and in a short time I received a good team of mares, a bay named Fanny and a sorrel named Flora, good, twelve hundred pound chunks, but thin in flesh—I would not take geldings—a wagon, nearly new, a set of wagon bows, enough heavy drilling to make a cover, some bedding, a stove, an old double-barreled shotgun, two pounds of powder and a lot of shot, harness for the team, horse-feed, and as complete an outfit as I could think of, even to the box of axle-grease swinging under the wagon-box. Rucker groaned at every addition; and finally balked when I asked him for a hundred dollars in cash. The court entered up the proper decree, I put my deeds in my pocket, and after making a feed-box for the horses to hang on the back of the wagon-box, I pulled out for Iowa three weeks too soon—for the roads were not yet settled.

5

The night before I started, I sat in the warm bar-room, half pleased and half frightened at the new world into which I was about to enter, thinking of my new wagon and the complete equipage of emigration now shown to be mine by the bills of sale and deeds in my pocket, and occasionally putting my fingers to my nose to catch the good smell of the horse which soap and water had not quite removed. This scent I had acquired by currying and combing my mares for hours, clipping their manes and fetlocks, and handling them all over to see if they were free from blemishes. The lawyer, Jackway, my guardian *ad litem,* came into the tavern in a high and mighty and popular way, saying "How de do, ward?" in a way I didn't like, went to the bar and throwing down a big piece of money began drinking one glass after another.

As he drank he grew boastful. He bragged to the men about him of his ability. Nobody ever hired Jackway to care for his interests, said he, without having his interests taken care of.

"You can go out," said he to a peaceful-looking man who stood watching him, "into the street there, and stab the first man you meet, and Jackway'll get you clear. I'm a living whirlwind! And," looking at me as I sat in the chair by the wall, "you can steal a woman's estate and I'll get it away from her heirs for you."

I wondered if he meant me. I hardly believed that he could; for all the while he had made a great to-do about protecting my interests; and I now remembered that he had taken an oath to do so. But he kept sneering at me all the evening, and just as I was leaving to go to bed, he called the crowd up to drink with him.

"This is on the estate," he hiccoughed—for he was very drunk by this time—"and I'll give you a toast."

They all lined up, slapping him on the back; and as I stood in the door, they all lifted their glasses, and Jackway gave them what he called his "toast," which ran as follows:

"Sold again
And got the tin,
And sucked another Dutchman in!"

He paid out of a fat pocketbook, staggering, and pointing at me and looking like a tipsy imp of some sort; and finally he started over toward me, saying, "Hey, Dutchman! Wait a minute an' I'll tell you how you got sucked in!"

I grew suddenly very angry; and slammed the door in his face to prevent myself from doing him harm. I had not yet seen why I ought to do him harm; and along the road to Iowa, I was all the time wondering why I got madder and madder at Jackway; and that rhyme kept running through my mind, oftener and oftener, as I drew nearer and nearer my journey's end:

"Sold again
And got the tin,
And sucked another Dutchman in!"

It was in the latter part of March. There were snow-drifts in places along the road, and when I reached a place about where Mt. Horeb now is, I had to stop and lie up for three days for a snow-storm. I was ahead of the stream of immigrants that poured over that road in the spring of 1855 in a steady tide.

As I made my start from Madison I saw Rucker and Alice standing at the door of the tavern seemingly making sure that I was really getting out of town. He dodged back into the house when I glanced at them; but she walked out into the street and stopped me, as bold as brass.

"I'm waiting," said she. "Where shall I ride?" And she put one foot on the hub and stepped up with the other into the wagon box.

"I'm just pulling out for Iowa," I said, my face as red as her hair, I suppose.

"*We're* just pulling out," said she.

"I've got to move on," said I; "be careful or you'll get your dress muddy on the wheel."

She couldn't have expected me to take her, of course; but I thought she looked kind of hurt. There seemed to be something like tears in her eyes as she put her arms around my neck.

"Kiss your little step-sister good-by," she said. "She's been a better friend of yours than you'll ever know—you big, nice, blundering greenhorn!"

She laid her lips on mine. It was the first kiss I had ever had from any one since I was a little boy; and as I half struggled against but finally returned it, it thrilled me powerfully. Afterward I was disgusted with myself for kissing this castaway; but as I drove on, leaving her standing in the middle of the road looking after me, it almost seemed as if I were leaving a friend. Perhaps she was, in her way, the nearest thing to a friend I had then in the world—strange as it seems. As for Rucker, he was rejoicing, of course, at having trimmed neatly a dumb-head of a Dutch boy—a wrong to my poor mother, the very thought of which even after all these years, makes my blood boil.

CHAPTER VI

I BECOME COW VANDEMARK

I WAS off with the spring rush of 1855 for the new lands of the West! I kept thinking as I drove along of Lawyer Jackway's sarcastic toast, "Sold again, and got the tin, and sucked another Dutchman in!" But after all I couldn't keep myself from feeling pretty proud, as I watched the play of my horses' ears as they seemed to take in each new westward view as we went over the tops of the low hills, and as I listened to the "chuck, chuck" of the wagon wheels on their well-greased skeins. Rucker and Jackway might have given me a check on the tow-path; but yet I felt hopeful that I was to make a real success of my voyage of life to a home and a place where I could be somebody. There was pleasure in looking back at my riches in the clean, hard-stuffed straw-tick, the stove, the traveling home which belonged to me.

It seems a little queer to me now to think of it as I look out of my bay-window at my great fields of corn, my pastures dotted with stock, my feedyard full of fat steers; or as I sit in the directors' room of the bank and take my part as a member of the board. But I am really not as rich now as I was then.

I was going to a country which seemed to be drawing everybody else, and must therefore be a good country—

and I had a farm. I had a great farm. It was a mile
square. It was almost like the estate that General Can-
tine had near the canal at Ithaca I thought. To my boy's
mind it looked too big for me; and sometimes I wondered
if I should not be able to rent it out to tenants and grow
rich on my income, like the Van Renssalaers of the
Manor before the Anti-Rent difficulties.

All the while I was passing outfits which were waiting
by the roadside, or making bad weather of it for some
reason or other; or I was passed by those who had less
regard for their horse flesh than I, or did not realize
that the horses had to go afoot; or those that drew lighter
loads. There were some carriages which went flourishing
along with shining covers; these were the aristocrats;
there were other slow-going rigs drawn by oxen. Usually
there would be two or more vehicles in a train. They
camped by the roadside cooking their meals; they stopped
at wayside taverns. They gave me all sorts of how-d'ye-
does as I passed. Girls waved their hands at me from
the hind-ends of rigs and said bold things—to a boy they
would not see again; but which left him blushing and
thinking up retorts for the next occasion—retorts that
never seemed to fit when the time came; and talkative
women threw remarks at me about the roads and the
weather.

Men tried half a dozen times a day to trade me out of
my bay mare Fanny, or my sorrel mare Flora—they said
I ought to match up with two of a color; and the crow-
baits offered me would have stocked a horse-ranch.
People with oxen offered me what looked like good
swaps, because they were impatient to make better time;
and as I went along so stylishly I began turning over in

my mind the question as to whether it might not be better to get to Iowa a little later in the year with cattle for a start than to rush the season with my fine mares and pull up standing like a gentleman at my own imaginary door.

2

As I went on to the westward, I began to see Blue Mound rising like a low mountain off my starboard bow, and I stopped at a farm in the foot-hills of the Mound where, because it was rainy, I paid four shillings for putting my horses in the stable. There were two other movers stopping at the same place. They had a light wagon and a yoke of good young steers, and had been out of Madison two days longer than I had been. I noticed that they left their wagon in a clump of bushes, and that while one of them—a man of fifty or more, slept in the house, the other, a young fellow of twenty or twenty-two, lay in the wagon, and that one or the other seemed always to be on guard near the vehicle. The older man had a long beard and a hooked nose, and seemed to be a still sort of person, until some one spoke of slavery; then he broke out in a fierce speech denouncing slaveholders, and the slavocracy that had the nation in its grip.

"You talk," said the farmer, "like a black Abolitionist."

"I'm so black an Abolitionist," said he, "that I'd be willing to shoulder a gun any minute if I thought I could wipe out the curse of slavery."

The farmer was terribly scandalized at this, and when the old man walked away to his wagon, he said to the young man and me that that sort of talk would make trouble and ruin the nation; and that he didn't want any more of it around his place.

"Well," said the traveler, "you won't have any more of it from us. We're just pulling out." After the farmer went away, he spoke to me about it.

"What do you think of that kind of talk?" he asked.

"I don't own any niggers," said I. "I don't ever expect to own any. I don't see how slavery can do me any good; and I think the slaves are human."

I had no very clear ideas on the subject, and had done little thinking about it; but what I said seemed to be satisfactory to the young man. He told his friend about it, and after a while the old man, whose name was Dunlap, came to me and shook my hand, saying that he was glad to meet a young fellow of my age who was of the right stripe.

"Can you shoot?" he asked.

I told him I never had had much chance to learn, but I had a good gun, and had got some game with it almost every day so far.

"What kind of a gun?" he asked.

I told him it was a double-barreled shotgun, and he looked rather disappointed. Then he asked me if I had ever thought of going to Kansas. No, I told him, I thought I should rather locate in Iowa.

"We are going to Kansas," he said. "There's work for real men in Kansas—men who believe in freedom. You had better go along with Amos Thatcher and me."

I said I didn't believe I could—I had planned to locate in Iowa. He dropped the subject by saying that I would overtake him and Thatcher on the road, and we could talk it over again. When did I think of getting

under way? I answered that I thought I should stay
hauled up to rest my horses for a half-day anyhow, so
perhaps we might camp that night together.

"A good idea," said Thatcher, smilingly, as they drove
off. "Join us; we get lonesome."

I laid by that forenoon because one of my mares had
limped a little the day before, and I was worrying for
fear she might not be perfectly sound. I hitched up after
noon and drove on, anxiously watching her to see whether
I had not been sucked in on horse flesh, as well as in the
general settlement of my mother's estate. She seemed to
be all right, however, and we were making good headway
as night drew on, and I was halted by Amos Thatcher
who said he was on the lookout for me.

"We have a station off the road a mile or so," said
he, "and you'll have a hearty welcome if you come with
me—stable for your horses, and a bed to sleep in, and
good victuals."

I couldn't think what he meant by a station; but it was
about time to make camp anyhow, and so I took him into
the wagon with me, and we drove across country by a
plain trail, through a beautiful piece of oak openings,
to a big log house in a fine grove of burr oaks, with a
log barn back of it—as nice a farmstead as I had
seen. There were fifteen or twenty cattle in the
yards, and some sheep and hogs, and many fat hens. If
this was a station, I thought, I envied the man who
owned it. As we drove up I saw a little negro boy peeping at us from the back of the house, and as we halted a
black woman ran out and seized the pickaninny by the
ear, and dragged him back out of sight. I heard a whim-
per from the little boy, which seemed suddenly smothered

by something like a hand clapped over his mouth. Mr. Dunlap's wagon was not in sight, but its owner came out at the front door and greeted me in a very friendly way.

"What makes you call this a station?" I asked of Thatcher.

Dunlap looked at him sternly.

"I forgot myself," said Thatcher, more to Dunlap than to me.

"Never mind," replied Dunlap. "If I can tell B from a bull's foot, it's all right."

Then turning to me he said, "The old lady inside has a meal of victuals ready for us. Come in and we'll let into it."

There was nothing said at the meal which explained the things that were so blind to me; but there was a good deal of talk about rifles. The farmer was named Preston, a middle-aged man who shaved all his beard except what grew under his chin, which hung down in a long black fringe over his breast like a window-lambrequin. His wife's father, who was an old Welshman named Evans, had worked in the lead mines over toward Dubuque, until Preston had married his daughter and taken up his farm in the oak openings. They had been shooting at a mark that afternoon, with Sharp's rifles carried by Dunlap and Thatcher, and the old-fashioned squirrel rifles owned on the farm. After supper they brought out these rifles and compared them. Preston insisted that the squirrel rifles were better.

"Not for real service," said Dunlap, throwing a cartridge into the breech of the Sharp, and ejecting it to show how fast it could be done.

"But I can roll a squirrel's eye right out of his head

most every time with the old-style gun," said Preston. "This is the gun that won the Battle of New Orleans."

"It wouldn't have won against the Sharp," said Thatcher; "and you know we expect to have a larger mark than a squirrel's head, when we get to Kansas."

This was the first breech-loader I had ever seen, and I looked it over with a buying eye. It didn't seem to me that it would be much better for hunting than the old-fashioned rifle, loaded with powder and a molded bullet rammed down with a patch of oiled cloth around it; for after you have shot at your game once, you either have hit it, or it runs or flies away. If you have hit it, you can generally get it, and if it goes away, you have time to reload. Besides those big cartridges must be costly, I thought, and said so to Mr. Dunlap.

"When you're hunting Border Ruffians," said he, "a little expense don't count one way or the other; and you may be willing to pay dear for a chance to reload three or four times while the other man is ramming home a new charge. Give me the new guns, the new ideas, and the old doctrine of freedom to fight for. Don't you see?"

"Why, of course," said I, "I'm for freedom. That's why I'm going out on the prairies."

"Prairies!" said old Evans. "Prairies! What do you expect to do on the prairies?"

"Farm," I answered.

"All these folks that are rushing to the prairies," said the old man, "will starve out and come back. God makes trees grow to show men where the good land is. I read history, and there's no country that's good for anything, except where men have cut the trees, niggered off the logs, grubbed out the stumps, and made fields of it—

and if there are stones, it's all the better. 'In the sweat of
thy face shalt thou eat bread,' said God to Adam, and
when you go to the prairies where it's all ready for the
plow, you are trying to dodge God's curse on our first
parents. You won't prosper. It stands to reason that any
land that is good will grow trees."

"Some of this farm was prairie," put in Preston, "and
I don't see but it's just as good as the rest."

"It was all openings," replied Evans. "The trees was
here once, and got killed by the fires, or somehow. It was
all woods once."

"You cut down trees to make land grow grass," said
Thatcher. "I should think that God must have meant
grass to be the sign of good ground."

"Isn't the sweat of your face just as plenty when you
delve in the prairies?" asked Dunlap.

"You fly in the face of God's decree, and run against
His manifest warning when you try to make a prairie
into a farm," said Evans. "You'll see!"

"Sold again, and got the tin, and sucked another
Dutchman in!" was the ditty that ran through my head
as I heard this. Old man Evans' way of looking at the
matter seemed reasonable to my cautious mind; and,
anyhow, when a man has grown old he knows many
things that he can give no good reason for. I have
always found that the well-educated fellow with a deep-
sounding and plausible philosophy that runs against the
teachings of experience, is likely, especially in farming, to
make a failure when he might have saved himself by
doing as the old settlers do, who won't answer his arguments but make a good living just the same, while the
new-fangled practises send their followers to the poor-

house. At that moment, I would have traded my Iowa farm for any good piece of land covered with trees. But Dunlap and Thatcher had something else to talk to me about. They were for the prairies, especially the prairies of Kansas.

"Kansas," said Dunlap, "will be one of the great states of the Union, one of these days. Come with us, and help make it a free state. We need a hundred thousand young farmers, who believe in liberty, and will fight for it. Come with us, take up a farm, and carry a Sharp's rifle against the Border Ruffians!"

This sounded convincing to me, but of course I couldn't make up my mind to anything of this sort without days and days of consideration; but I listened to what they said. They told me of an army of free-state emigrants that was gathering along the border to win Kansas for freedom. They, Dunlap and Thatcher, were going to Marion, Iowa, and from there by the Mormon Trail across to a place called Tabor, and from there to Lawrence, Kansas. They were New England Yankees. Thatcher had been to college, and was studying law. Dunlap had been a business man in Connecticut, and was a friend of John Brown, who was then on his way to Kansas.

"The Missouri Compromise has been repealed," said Thatcher, his eyes shining, "and the Kansas-Nebraska Bill has thrown the fertile state of Kansas into the ring to be fought for by free-state men and pro-slavery men. The Border Ruffians of Missouri are breaking the law every day by going over into Kansas, never meaning to live there only long enough to vote, and are corrupting the state government. They are corrupting it by violence and illegal voting. If slavery wins in Kansas and

Nebraska, it will control the Union forever. The great-est battle in our history is about to be fought out in Kan-sas, a battle to see whether this nation shall be a slave nation, in every state and every town, or free. Dunlap and I and thousands of others are going down there to take the state of Kansas into our own hands, peacefully if we can, by violence if we must. We are willing to die to make the United States a free nation. Come with us!"

"But we don't expect to die," urged Dunlap, seeing that this looked pretty serious to me. "We expect to live, and get farms, and make homes, and prosper, after we have shown the Border Ruffians the muzzles of those rifles. Thatcher, bring the passengers in!"

3

Thatcher went out of the room the back way.

"We call this a station," went on Dunlap, "because it's a stopping-place on the U. G. Railway."

"What's the U. G. Railway?" I asked.

"Don't you know that?" he queried.

"I'm only a canal hand," I answered, "going to a farm out on the prairie, that I was euchred into taking in settling with a scoundrel for my share of my father's property; and I'm pretty green."

Thatcher came in then, leading the little black boy by the hand, and following him was the negro woman, carrying a baby at her breast, and holding by the hand a little woolly-headed pickaninny about three years old. They were ragged and poverty-stricken, and seemed scared at everything. The woman came in bowing and scraping to me, and the two little boys hid behind her skirts and peeked around at me with big white eyes.

"Tell the gentleman," said Thatcher, "where you're going."

"We're gwine to Canayda," said she, " 'scusin' your presence."

"How are you going to get to Canada?" asked Thatcher.

"The good white folks," said she, "will keep us hid out nights till we gits thar."

"What will happen," said Thatcher, "if this young man tells any one that he's seen you?"

"The old massa," said she, "will find out, an' he'll hunt us wif houn's, an' fotch us back, and then he'll sell us down the ribber to the cotton-fiel's."

I never heard anything quite so pitiful as this speech. I had never known before what it must mean to be really hunted. The woman shrank back toward the door through which she had come, her face grew a sort of grayish color; and then ran to me and throwing herself on her knees, she took hold of my hands, and begged me for God's sake not to tell on her, not to have her carried back, not to fix it so she'd be sold down the river to work in the cotton-fields.

"I won't," I said, "I tell you I won't. I want you to get to Canada!"

"God bress yeh," she said. "I know'd yeh was a good young gemman as soon as I set eyes on yeh! I know'd yeh was quality!"

"Who do you expect to meet in Canada?" asked Thatcher.

"God willin'," said she, "I'm gwine to find Abe Felton, the pa of dese yere chillun."

"The Underground Railway," said Dunlap, "knows

where Abe is, and will send Sarah along with change of cars. You may go, Sarah. Now," he went on, as the negroes disappeared, "you have it in your power to exercise the right of an American citizen and perform the God-accursed legal duty to report these fugitives at the next town, join a posse to hunt them down under a law of the United States, get a reward for doing it, and know that you have vindicated the law—or you can stand with God and tell the law to go to hell—where it came from— and help the Underground Railway to carry these people to heaven. Which will you do?"

"I'll tell the law to go to hell," said I.

Dunlap and Thatcher looked at each other as if relieved. I have always suspected that I was taken into their secret without their ordinary precautions; and that for a while they were a little dubious for fear that they had spilt the milk of secrecy. But all my life people have told me their secrets.

They urged me hard to go with them; and talked so favorably about the soil of the prairies that I began to think well again of my Iowa farm. When I had made it plain that I had to have a longer time to think it over, they began urging me to let them have my horses on some sort of a trade; and I began to see that a part of what they had wanted all the time was a faster team as well as a free-state recruit. They urged on me the desirability of having cattle instead of horses when I reached my farm.

"Cows, yes," said I, "but not steers."

So I slept over it until morning. Then I made them the proposition that if they would arrange with Preston to trade me four cows, which I would select from his herd, and would provide for my board with Preston until I could break them to drive, and would furnish yokes and chains in place of my harness, I would let them have the team for a hundred dollars boot-money. Preston said he'd like to have me make my selection first, and when I picked out three-year-old heifers, two of which were giving milk, he said it was a whack, if it didn't take me more than a week to break them. Dunlap and Thatcher hitched up, and started off the next morning. I had become Cow Vandemark overnight, and am still Cow Vandemark in the minds of the old settlers of Vandemark Township and some who have just picked the name up.

But I did not take on my new name without a struggle, for Flora and Fanny had become dear to me since leaving Madison—my first horses. How I got my second team of horses is connected with one of the most important incidents in my life; it was a long time before I got them and it will be some time before I can tell about it. In the meantime, there were Flora and Fanny, hitched to Dunlap and Thatcher's light wagon, disappearing among the burr oaks toward the Dubuque highway. I thought of my pride as I drove away from Madison with these two steeds, and of the pretty figure I cut the morning when red-haired Alice climbed up, offered to go with me, and kissed me before she climbed down. Would she have done this if I had been driving oxen, or still worse, those animals which few thought worth anything as draught animals—cows? And then I thought of Flora's lameness the day before yesterday. Was it honest to let Dunlap and Thatcher drive off to liberate the nation with a horse that might go lame?

"Let me have a horse," said I to Preston. "I want to catch them and tell them something.

I rode up behind the Abolitionists' wagon, waving my hat and shouting. They pulled up and waited.

"What's up?" asked Dunlap. "Going with us after all? I hope so, my boy."

"No," said I, "I just wanted to say that that nigh mare was lame day before yesterday, and I——I—I didn't want you to start off with her without knowing it."

Dunlap asked about her lameness, and got out to look her over. He felt of her muscles, and carefully scrutinized her for swelling or swinney or splint or spavin or thoroughpin. Then he lifted one foot after another, and cleaned out about the frog, tapping the hoof all over for soreness. Down deep beside the frog of the foot which she had favored he found a little pebble.

"That's what it was," said he, holding the pebble up. "She'll be all right now. Thank you for telling me. It was the square thing to do."

"If you don't feel safe to go on with the team," said I, "I'll trade back."

"No," said he, "we're needed in Kansas; and," turning up an oil-cloth and showing me a dozen or so of the Sharp's rifles, "so are these. And let me tell you, boy, if I'm any judge of men, the time will come when you won't feel so bad to lose half a dozen horses, as you feel now to be traded out of Flora and Fanny, and make a hundred dollars by the trade. Get up, Flora; go long, Fanny; good-by, Jake!" And they drove off to the Border Wars. I had made my first sacrifice to the cause of the productiveness of the Vandemark Farm.

That night a wagon went away from the Preston farm with the passengers going to Canada by the U. G. Railway. The next morning I began the task of fitting yokes to my two span of heifers, and that afternoon, I gave Lily and Cherry their first lesson. I had had some experience in driving cattle on Mrs. Fogg's farm in Herkimer County, but I should have made a botch job of it if it had not been for Mr. Preston, who knew all there was to know about cattle, and while protesting that cows could not be driven, helped me drive them. In less than a week my cows were driving as prettily as any oxen. They were light and active, and overtook team after team of laboring steers every day I drove them. Furthermore, they gave me milk. I fed them well, worked them rather lightly, and by putting the new milk in a churn I bought at Mineral Point, I found that the motion of the wagon would bring the butter as well as any churning. I had cream for my coffee, butter for my bread, milk for my mush, and lived high. A good deal of fun was poked at me about my team of cows; but people were always glad to camp with me and share my fare.

Economically, our cows ought to be made to do a good deal of the work of the farms. I have always believed this; but now a German expert has proved it. I read about it the other day in a bulletin put out by the Agricultural Department; but I proved it in Vandemark Township before the man was born that wrote the bulletin. If not pushed too hard, cows will work and give almost as much milk as if not worked at all. This statement of course won't apply to the fancy cows which are high-power milk machines, and need to be packed in cotton, and kept in satin-lined stalls; but to such cows as farmers have, and always will have, it does apply.

I was sorry to leave the Prestons, they were such whole-souled, earnest people; and before I did leave them

I was a full-fledged Abolitionist so far as belief was concerned. I never did become active, however, in spiriting slaves from one station to another of the U. G. Railway.

I drove out to the highway, and turning my prow to the west, I joined again in the stream of people swarming westward. The tide had swollen in the week during which I had laid by at the Prestons'. The road was rutted, poached deep where wet and beaten hard where dry, or pulverized into dust by the stream of emigration. Here we went, oxen, cows, mules, horses; coaches, carriages, blue jeans, corduroys, rags, tatters, silks, satins, caps, tall hats, poverty, riches; speculators, missionaries, land-hunters, merchants; criminals escaping from justice; couples fleeing from the law; families seeking homes; the wrecks of homes seeking secrecy; gold-seekers bearing southwest to the Overland Trail; politicians looking for places in which to win fame and fortune; editors hunting opportunities for founding newspapers; adventurers on their way to everywhere; lawyers with a few books; Abolitionists going to the Border War; innocent-looking outfits carrying fugitive slaves; officers hunting escaped negroes; and most numerous of all, homeseekers "hunting country"—a nation on wheels, an empire in the commotion and pangs of birth. Down I went with the rest, across ferries, through Dodgeville, Mineral Point and Platteville, past a thousand vacant sites for farms toward my own farm so far from civilization, shot out of civilization by the forces of civilization itself.

I saw the old mining country from Mineral Point to Dubuque, where lead had been dug for many years, and where the men lived who dug the holes and were called Badgers, thus giving the people of Wisconsin their nickname as distinguished from the Illinois people who came up the rivers to work in the spring, and went back in the fall, and were therefore named after a migratory fish and called Suckers; and at last, I saw from its eastern bank far off to the west, the bluffy shores of Iowa, and down by the river the keen spires and brick and wood buildings of the biggest town I had seen since leaving Milwaukee, the town of Dubuque.

I camped that night in the northwestern corner of Illinois, in a regular city of movers, all waiting their turns at the ferry which crossed the Mississippi to the Land of Promise.

4

Iowa did not look much like a prairie country from where I stood. The Iowa shore towered above the town of Dubuque, clothed with woods to the top, and looking more like York State than anything I had seen since I had taken the schooner at Buffalo to come up the Lakes. I lay that night, unable to sleep. For one thing, I needed to be wakeful, lest some of the motley crowd of movers might take a fancy to my cattle. I was learning by experience how to take care of myself and mine; besides, I wanted to be awake early so as to take passage by ferryboat "before soon" as the Hoosiers say, in the morning.

That April morning was still only a gray dawn when I drove down to the ferry, without stopping for my breakfast. A few others of those who looked forward to a rush for the boat had got there ahead of me, and we waited in line. I saw that I should have to go on the second trip rather than the first, but movers can not be impatient, and the driving of cattle cures a person of being in a hurry; so I was in no great taking because of this little delay. As I sat there in my wagon, a black-bearded, scholarly-looking man stepped up and spoke to me.

"Going across?" he asked.

"As soon as the boat will take me," I said.

"Heavy loaded?" he asked. "Have you room for a passenger?"

"I guess I can accommodate you," I answered. "Climb in."

"It isn't for myself I'm asking," he said. "There's a lady here that wants to ride in a covered wagon, and sit back where she can't see the water. It makes her dizzy and scares her awfully; can you take her?"

"If she can ride back there on the bed," said I.

He peeped in, and said that this was the very place for her. She could lie down and cover up her head and never know she was crossing the river at all. In a minute, and while it was still twilight, just as the ferry-boat came to the landing, he returned with the lady. She was dressed in some brown fabric, and wore a thick veil over her face; but as she climbed in I saw that she had yellow hair and bright eyes and lips; and that she was trembling so that her hands shook as she took hold of the wagon-bow, and her voice quivered as she thanked me, in low tones. The man with the black beard pressed her hand as he left her. He offered me a dollar for her passage; but I called his attention to the fact that it would cost only two shillings more for me to cross with her than if I went alone, and refused to take more.

"There are a good many rough fellows," said he, "at these ferries, that make it unpleasant for a lady, some-times—"

"Not when she's with me," I said.

He looked at me sharply, as if surprised that I was not so green as I looked—though I was pretty verdant. Anyhow, he said, if I should be asked if any one was with me, it would save her from being scared if I would say that I was alone—she was the most timid woman in the world.

"I'll have to tell the ferryman," I said.

"Will you?" he asked. "Why?"

"I'd be cheating him if I didn't," I answered.

"All right," he said, as if provoked at me, "but don't tell any one else."

"I ain't very good at lying," I replied.

He said for me to do the best I could for the lady, and hurried off. In the meantime, the lady had crept back on my straw-bed, and pulled the quilts completely over her. She piled pillows on one side of her, and stirred the straw up on the other, so that when she lay down the bed was as smooth as if nobody was in it. It looked as it might if a heedless boy had crawled out of it after a night's sleep, and carelessly thrown the coverlet back over it. I could hardly believe I had a passenger. When I was asked for the ferriage, I paid for two, and the ferryman asked where the other was.

"Back in the bed," I said.

He looked back, and said, "Well, I owe you something for your honesty. I never'd have seen him. Sick?"

"Not very," said I. "Don't like the water."

"Some are that way," he returned, and went on collecting fares.

As we drove up from the landing, through the rutted streets of the old mining and Indian-trading town, the black-bearded man came to me as we stopped, held back by a jam of covered wagons—a wonderful sight, even to me—and as if talking to me, said to the woman, "You'd better ride on through town;" and then to me, "Are you going on through?"

"I've got to buy some supplies," said I; "but I've nothing to stop me but that."

"Tell me what you want," he said hurriedly, and looking about as if expecting some danger, "and I'll buy it for you and bring it on. Which way are you going?"

"West into Iowa," I answered.

"Go on," said he, "and I'll make it right with you. Camp somewhere west of town. I'll come along to-night or to-morrow. I'll make it right with you."

"I don't see through this," I said, with my usual indecision as to doing something I did not understand. "I thought I'd look around Dubuque a little."

"For God's sake," said the woman from the bed, "take me on—take me on!"

Her tones were so pleading, she seemed in such an agony of terror, that I suddenly made up my mind in her favor. Surely there would be no harm in carrying her on as she wished.

"All right," I said to her, but looking at him, "I'll take you on! You can count on me." And then to him, "I'll drive on until I find a good camping-place late this afternoon. You'll have to find us the best way you can."

He thanked me, and I gave him a list of the things I wanted. Then he went on up the street ahead of us, walking calmly, and looking about him as any stranger might have done. We stood for some time, waiting for the jam of teams to clear, and I gee-upped and whoa-hawed on along the street, until we came to a building on which was a big sign, "Post-Office." There was a queue of people waiting for their mail, extending out at the door, and far down the sidewalk. In this string of emigrants stood our friend, the black-bearded man. Just as we passed, a rather thin, stooped man, walking along on the other side of the street, rushed across, right in front of my lead team, and drawing a pistol, aimed at the black-bearded man, who in turn stepped out of line and drew his own weapon.

"I call upon you all to witness," said the black-bearded man, "that I act in self-defense."

A bystander seized the thin man's pistol hand, and yelled at him not to shoot or he might kill some one—of course he meant some one he did not aim at, but it sounded a little funny, and I laughed. Several joined in the laugh, and there was a good deal of confusion. At last I heard the black-bearded man say, "I'm here alone. He's accused his wife of being too thick with a dozen men. He's insanely jealous, gentlemen. I suppose his wife may have left him, but I'm here alone. I just crossed the river alone, and I'm going west. If he's got a warrant, he's welcome to have it served if he finds his wife with me. Come on, gentlemen—but take the fool's pistol away from him."

As I drove on I saw that the woman had thrown off the quilt, and was peeping out at the opening in the cover at the back, watching the black-bearded and the thin man moving off in a group of fellows, one of whom held the black-bearded man by the arm a good deal as a deputy sheriff might have done.

The roads leading west out of Dubuque were horrible,

then, being steep stony trails coming down the hollows and washed like watercourses at every rain. Teams were stalled, sometimes three and four span of animals were used to get one load to the top, and we were a good deal delayed. I was so busy trying to keep from upsetting when I drove around stalled outfits and abandoned wagons, and so occupied in finding places where I might stop and breathe my team, that I paid little attention to my queer-acting passenger; but once when we were standing I noticed that she was covered up again, and seemed to be crying. As we topped the bluffs, and drew out into the open, she sat up and began to rearrange her hair. After a few miles, we reached a point from which I could see the Iowa prairie sweeping away as far as the eye could see. I drew out by the roadside to look at it, as a man appraises one with whom he must live—as a friend or an enemy.

I shall never forget the sight. It was like a great green sea. The old growth had been burned the fall before, and the spring grass scarcely concealed the brown sod on the uplands; but all the swales were coated thick with an emerald growth full-bite high, and in the deeper, wetter hollows grew cowslips, already showing their glossy, golden flowers. The hillsides were thick with the woolly possblummies* in their furry spring coats protecting them against the frost and chill, showing purple-violet on the outside of a cup filled with golden stamens, the first fruits of the prairie flowers; on the warmer southern

---

*"Paas-bloeme" one suspects is the Rondout Valley origin of this term applied to a flower, possibly seen by the author on this occasion for the first time—the American pasque-flower, the Iowa prairie type of which is *Anemone patens*: the knightliest little flower of the Iowa uplands.—G. v. d. M.

slopes a few of the splendid bird's-foot violets of the prairie were showing the azure color which would soon make some of the hillsides as blue as the sky; and standing higher than the peering grass rose the rough-leafed stalks of green which would soon show us the yellow puccoons and sweet-williams and scarlet lilies and shooting stars, and later the yellow rosin-weeds, Indian dye-flower and goldenrod. The keen northwest wind swept before it a flock of white clouds; and under the clouds went their shadows, walking over the lovely hills like dark ships over an emerald sea.

The wild-fowl were clamoring north for the summer's campaign of nesting. Everywhere the sky was harrowed by the wedged wild geese, their voices as sweet as organ tones; and ducks quacked, whistled and whirred overhead, a true rain of birds beating up against the wind. Over every slew, on all sides, thousands of ducks of many kinds, and several sorts of geese hovered, settled, or burst up in eruptions of birds, their back-feathers shining like bronze as they turned so as to reflect the sunlight to my eyes; while so far up that they looked like specks, away above the wind it seemed, so quietly did they circle and sail, floated huge flocks of cranes—the sand-hill cranes in their slaty-gray, and the whooping cranes, white as snow with black heads and feet, each bird with a ten-foot spread of wing, piping their wild cries which fell down to me as if from another world.

It was sublime! Bird, flower, grass, cloud, wind, and the immense expanse of sunny prairie, swelling up into undulations like a woman's breasts turgid with milk for a hungry race. I forgot myself and my position in the world, my loneliness, my strange passenger, the problems of my life; my heart swelled, and my throat filled. I sat looking at it, with the tears trickling from my eyes, the uplift of my soul more than I could bear. It was not the thought of my mother that brought the tears to my eyes, but my happiness in finding the newest, strangest, most delightful, sternest, most wonderful thing in the world— the Iowa prairie—that made me think of my mother. If I only could have found her alive! If I only could have had her with me! And as I thought of this I realized that the woman of the ferry had climbed over the back of the spring-scat and was sitting beside me.

"I don't wonder," said she, "that you cry. Gosh! It scares me to death!"

CHAPTER VII

ADVENTURE ON THE OLD RIDGE ROAD

VANDEMARK TOWNSHIP and Monterey County, as any one may see by looking at the map of Iowa, had to be reached from Wisconsin by crossing the Mississippi at Dubuque and then fetching across the prairie to the journey's end; and in 1855 a traveler making that trip naturally fell in with a good many of his future neighbors and fellow-citizens pressing westward with him to the new lands.

Some were merely hunting country, and were ready to be whiffled off toward any neck of the woods which might be puffed up by a wayside acquaintance as ignorant about it as he. Some were headed toward what was called "the Fort Dodge country," which was anywhere west of the Des Moines River. Some had been out and made locations the year before and were coming on with their stuff; some were joining friends already on the ground; some had a list of Gardens of Eden in mind, and meant to look them over one after the other until a land was found flowing with milk and honey, and inhabited by roast pigs with forks sticking in their backs and carving knives between their teeth.

Very few of the tillers of the soil had farms already marked down, bought and paid for as I had; and I sometimes talked in such a way as to show that I was a little on my high heels; but they were freer to tack, go about, and run before the wind than I; for some one was sure to stick to each of them like a bur and steer him to some definite place, where he could squat and afterward take advantage of the right of preemption, while I was forced to ferret out a particular square mile of this boundless prairie, and there settle down, no matter how far it might be from water, neighbors, timber or market; and fight out my battle just as things might happen. If the woman in the wagon was "scared to death" at the sight of the prairie, I surely had cause to be afraid; but I was not. I was uplifted. I felt the same sense of freedom, and the greatness of things, that came over me when I first found myself able to take in a real eyeful in driving my canal-boat through the Montezuma Marsh, or when I first saw big waters at Buffalo. I was made for the open, I guess.

There were wagon trails in every westerly direction from all the Mississippi ferries and landings; and the roads branched from Dubuque southwestward to Marion, and on to the Mormon trail, and northwestward toward Elkader and West Union; but I had to follow the Old Ridge Road west through Dubuque, Delaware, Buchanan and Blackhawk Counties, and westward. It was called the Ridge Road because it followed the knolls and hogbacks, and thus, as far as might be, kept out of the slews.

The last bit of it so far as I know was plowed up in 1877 in the northeastern part of Grundy County. I saw this last mile of the old road on a trip I made to Waterloo, and remember it. This part of it had been established by a couple of Hardin County pioneers who got lost in the forty-mile prairie between the Iowa and Cedar Rivers about three years before I came in and showed their fitness for citizenship by filling their wagon with stakes on the way back and driving them on every sightly place as guides for others—an Iowa Llano Estacado was Grundy Prairie.

This last bit of it ran across a school section that had been left in prairie sod till then. The past came rolling back upon me as I stopped my horses and looked at it, a wonderful road, that never was a highway in law, curving about the side of a knoll, the comb between the tracks carrying its plume of tall spear grass, its barbed shafts just ripe for boys to play Indian with, which bent over the two tracks, washed deep by the rains, and blown out by the winds; and where the trail had crossed a wet place, the grass and weeds still showed the effects of the plowing and puddling of the thousands of wheels and hoofs which had poached up the black soil into bubbly mud as the road spread out into a bulb of traffic where the pioneering drivers sought for tough sod which would bear up their wheels. A plow had already begun its work on this last piece of the Old Ridge Road, and as I stood there, the farmer who was breaking it up came by with his big plow and four horses, and stopped to talk with me.

"What made that old road?" I asked.

"Vell," said he, "dot's more as I know. Somebody, I dank."

And yet, the history of Vandemark Township was in that old road that he complained of because he couldn't do a good job of breaking across it—he was one of those

German settlers, or the son of one, who invaded the state after the rest of us had opened it up.

The Old Ridge Road went through Dyersville, Manchester, Independence, Waterloo, and on to Fort Dodge —but beyond there both the road and—so far as I know —the country itself, was a vague and undefined thing. So also was the road itself beyond the Iowa River, and for that matter it got to be less and less a beaten track all the way as the wagons spread out fanwise to the various fords and ferries and as the movers stopped and settled like nesting cranes. Of course there was a fringe of well-established settlements a hundred miles or so beyond Fort Dodge, of people who, most of them, came up the Missouri River.

Our Iowa wilderness did not settle up in any uniform way, but was inundated as a field is overspread by a flood; only it was a flood which set up-stream. First the Mississippi had its old town, away off south of Iowa, near its mouth; then the people worked up to the mouth of the Missouri and made another town; then the human flood crept up the Mississippi and the Missouri, and Iowa was reached; then the Iowa valleys were occupied by the river immigration, and the tide of settlement rose until it broke over the hills on such routes as the Old Ridge Road; but these cross-country streams here and there met other trickles of population which had come up the belts of forest on the streams. I was steering right into the wilderness; but there were far islands of occupation—the heft of the earliest settlements strongly southern in character—on each of the Iowa streams which I was to cross, snuggled down in the wooded bottom lands on the Missouri, and even away beyond at Salt Lake, and farther off in Oregon and California where the folk-freshet broke on the Pacific—a wave of humanity dashing against a reef of water.

Of course, I knew very little of these things as I sat there, ignorant as I was, looking out over the grassy sea, in my prairie schooner, my four cows panting from the climb, and with the yellow-haired young woman beside me, who had been wished on me by the black-bearded man on leaving the Illinois shore. Most of it I still had to spell out through age and experience, and some reading. I only knew that I had been told that the Ridge Road would take me to Monterey County, if the weather wasn't too wet, and I didn't get drowned in a freshet at a ferry or slewed down and permanently stuck fast somewhere with all my goods.

"Gee-up," I shouted to my cows, and cracked my blacksnake over their backs; and they strained slowly into the yoke. The wagon began chuck-chucking along into the unknown.

"Stop!" said my passenger. "I've got to wait here for my—for my husband."

"I can't stop," said I, "till I get to timber and water."

"But I must wait," she pleaded. "He can't help but find us here, because it's the only way to come; but if we go on we may miss him—and—and—I've just got to stop. Let me out, if you won't stop."

I whoaed up and she made as if to climb out.

"He may not get out of Dubuque to-day," I said. "He said so. And for you to wait here alone, with all these movers going by, and with no place to stay to-night will be a pretty pokerish thing to do."

Finally we agreed that I should drive on to water and

timber, unless the road should fork; in which case we were to wait at the forks no matter what sort of camp it might be.

The Ridge Road followed pretty closely the route afterward taken by the Illinois Central Railroad; but the railroad takes the easiest grades, while the Ridge Road kept to the high ground; so that at some places it lay a long way north or south of the railway route on which trains were running as far as Manchester within about two years. It veered off toward the head waters of White Water Creek on that first day's journey; and near a new farm, where they kept a tavern, we stopped because there was water in the well, and hay and firewood for sale. It was still early. The yellow-haired woman, whose name I did not know, alighted, and when I found that they would keep her for the night, went toward the farm-house without thanking me—but she was too much worried about something to think of that, I guess; but she turned and came back.

"Which way is Monterey Centre?" she asked.

"Away off to the westward," I answered.

"Is it far?"

"A long ways," I said.

"Is it on this awful prairie?" she inquired.

"Yes," said I, "I guess it is. It's farther away from timber than this I calculate."

"My lord," she burst out. "I'll simpy die of the horrors!"

She looked over the trail toward Dubuque, and then slowly went into the house.

So, then, these two with all their strange actions were

going to Monterey County! They would be neighbors of mine, maybe; but probably not. They looked like town people; and I knew already the distance that separated farmers from the dwellers in the towns—a difference that as I read history, runs away back through all the past. They were far removed from what I should be— something that I realized more and more all through my life—the difference between those who live on the farms and those who live on the farmers.

There was a two-seated covered carriage standing before the house, and across the road were two mover-wagons, with a nice camp-fire blazing, and half a dozen men and women and a lot of children about it cooking a meal of victuals. I pulled over near them and turned my cows out, tied down head and foot so they could bait and not stray too far. I noticed that their cows, which were driven after the wagon, had found too fast for them the pace set by the horse teams, had got very foot-sore, and were lying down and not feeding—for I drove them up to see what was the matter with them.

2

Before starting-time in the morning, I had swapped two of my driving cows for four of their lame ones, and hauled up by the side of the road until I could break my new animals to the yoke and allow them to recuperate. I am a cattleman by nature, and was more greedy for stock than anxious to make time—maybe that's another reason for being called Cow Vandemark. The neighbors used to say that I laid the foundation of my present competence by trading one sound cow for two lame ones every few miles along the Ridge Road, coming into the state, and then feeding my stock on speculators' grass in the summer and straw that my neighbors would otherwise have burned up in the winter. What was a week's time to me? I had a lifetime in Iowa before me.

"Whose rig is that?" I asked, pointing to the carriage.

"Belongs to a man name of Gowdy," the mover told me. "Got a hell-slew of wuthless land in Monterey County an' is going out to settle on it."

"How do you know it's worthless?" I inquired pretty sharply; for a man must stand up for his own place whether he's ever seen it or not.

"They say so," said he.

"Why?" I asked.

"Out in the middle of the Monterey Prairie," he said. "You can't live in this country 'less you settle near the timber."

"Instead of stopping at this farm," I said, "I should think he'd have gone on to the next settlement. Horses lame?"

"Best horses I've seen on the road," was the answer. "Kentucky horses. Gowdy comes from Kentucky. Stopped because his wife is had sick."

"Where's he?" I asked.

"Out shooting geese," said he. "Don't seem to fret his gizzard about his wife; but they say she's struck with death."

All the while I was cooking my supper I was thinking of this woman, "struck with death," and her husband out shooting geese, while she struggled with our last great antagonist alone. One of the women came over from the other camp with her husband, and I spoke to her about it.

"This man," said she, "jest acts out what all the men

feel. A womern is nothing but a thing to want as long as she is young and can work. But this womern hain't quite alone. She's got a little sister with her that knows a hull lot better how to do for her than any darned man would!"

It grew dark and cold—a keen, still, frosty spring evening which filled the sky with stars and bespoke a sunny day for to-morrow, with settled warmer weather. The geese and ducks were still calling from the sky, and not far away the prairie wolves were howling about one of the many carcasses of dead animals which the stream of immigration had already dropped by the wayside. I was dead sleepy, and was about to turn in, when my black-bearded man last seen in Dubuque with a constable holding him by the arm, came driving up, and went about among the various wagons as if looking for something. I knew he was seeking me, and spoke to him.

"Oh!" he said, as if all at once easier in his mind. "Where's my——"

"She's in the house," I said; "this is a kind of a tavern."

"Good!" said he. "I'm much obliged to you. Here's your supplies. I had to buy this light wagon and a team of horses in Dubuque, and it took a little time, it took a little time."

I now noticed that he had a way of repeating his words, and giving them a sort of friendly note as if he were taking you into his confidence. When I offered to pay him for the supplies, he refused. "I'm in debt to you. I don't remember what they cost—got them with some things for myself; a trifle, a trifle. Glad to do more for you—no trouble at all, none whatever."

"Didn't you have any trouble in Dubuque?" I asked, thinking of the man who had threatened to shoot him in front of the post-office, and how the black-bearded man had called upon the bystanders to bear witness that he was about to shoot in self-defense. He gave me a sharp look; but it was too dark to make it worth anything to him.

"No trouble at all," he said. "What d'ye mean?"

Before I could answer there came up a man carrying a shotgun in one hand, and a wild goose over his shoulder. Following him was a darky with a goose over each shoulder. I threw some dry sticks on my fire, and it flamed up showing me the faces of the group. Buckner Gowdy, or as everybody in Monterey County always called him, Buck Gowdy, stood before us smiling, powerful, six feet high, but so big of shoulder that he seemed a little stooped, perfectly at ease, behaving as if he had always known all of us. He wore a little black mustache which curled up at the corners of his mouth like the tail feathers of a drake. His clothes were soaked and gaumed up with mud from his tramping and crawling through the marshes; but otherwise he looked as fresh as if he had just risen from his bed, while the negro seemed ready to drop.

When Buck Gowdy spoke, it was always with a little laugh, and that slight stoop toward you as if there was something between him and you that was a sort of secret —the kind of laugh a man gives who has had many a joke with you and depends on your knowing what it is that pleases him. His eyes were brown, and a little close together; and his head was covered with a mass of wavy dark hair. His voice was rich and deep, and pitched low as if he were telling you something he did not want everybody to hear. He swore constantly, and used nasty language; but he had a way with him which I have seen him use to ministers of the gospel without their seeming to take notice of the improper things he said. There was something intimate in his treatment of every one he spoke to; and he was in the habit of saying things, especially to women, that had all sorts of double meanings—meanings that you couldn't take offense at without putting yourself on some low level which he could always vow was far from his mind. And there was a vibration in his low voice which always seemed to mean that he felt much more than he said.

"My name's Gowdy," he said; "all you people going west for your health?"

"I," said the black-bearded man, "am Doctor Bliven; and I'm going west, I'm going west, not only for my health, but for that of the community."

"Glad to make your acquaintance," said Gowdy; "and may I crave the acquaintance of our young Argonaut here?"

"Let me present Mr.—" said Doctor Bliven, "Mr.—— Mr.——"

"Vandemark," said I.

"Let me present Mr. Vandemark," said the doctor, "a very obliging young man to whom I am already under many obligations, many obligations."

Buckner Gowdy took my hand, bringing his body close to me, and looking me in the eyes boldly and in a way which was quite fascinating to me.

"I hope, Mr. Vandemark," said he, "that you and

Doctor Bliven are going to settle in the neighborhood to which I am exiled. Where are you two bound for?"

"I expect to open a drug store and begin the practise of medicine," said the doctor, "at the thriving town of Monterey Centre."

"I've got some land in Monterey County," said I; "but I don't know where in the county it is."

Doctor Bliven started; and Buckner Gowdy shook my hand again, and then the doctor's.

"A sort of previous neighborhood reunion," said he. "I expect one of these days to be one of the old residenters of Monterey County myself. I am a fellow-sufferer with you, Mr. Vandemark—I also have land there. Won't you and the doctor join me in a night-cap in honor of our neighborship; and drink to better acquaintance? And let's invite our fellow wayfarers, too. I have some game for them."

He looked across to the other camp, and we went over to it, Gowdy giving the third goose and the gun to the negro who had hard work to manage them. I had a roadside acquaintance with the movers, but did not know their names. In a jiffy Gowdy had all of them, and had found out that they expected to locate near Waverly. In five minutes he had begun discussing with a pretty young woman the best way to cook a goose; and soon wandered away with her on some pretense, and we could hear his subdued, vibratory voice and low laugh from the surrounding darkness, and from time to time her nervous giggle. Suddenly I remembered his wife, certainly very sick in the house, and the talk that she was "struck with death"—and he out shooting geese, and now gallivanting around with a strange girl in the dark.

There must be some mistake—this man with the bold eyes and the warm and friendly handclasp, with the fascinating manners and the neighborly ideas, could not possibly be a person who would do such things. But even as I thought this, and made up my mind that, after all, I would join him and the queer-behaving doctor in a friendly drink, a woman came flying out of the house and across the road, calling out, asking if any one knew where Mr. Gowdy was, that his wife was dying.

He and the girl came to the fire quickly, and as they came into view I saw a movement of his arm as if he was taking it from around her waist.

"I'm here," said he—and his voice sounded harder, somehow. "What's the matter?"

"Your wife," said the woman, "—she's taken very bad, Mr. Gowdy."

He started toward the house without a word; but before he went out of sight he turned and looked for a moment with a sort of half-smile at the girl. For a while we were all as still as death. Finally Doctor Bliven remarked that lots of folks were foolish about sick people, and that more patients were scared to death by those about them than died of disease. The girl said that that certainly was so. Doctor Bliven then volunteered the assertion that Mr. Gowdy seemed to be a fine fellow, and a gentleman if he ever saw one. Just then the woman came from across the road again and asked for "the man who was a doctor."

"I'm a doctor," said Bliven. "Somebody wants me?"

She said that Mr. Gowdy would like to have him come into the house—and he went hurriedly, after taking a medicine-case from his democrat wagon. I saw my yellow-haired passenger of the Dubuque ferry meet him before the door, throw her arms about him and kiss him. He returned her greeting, and they went through the door together into the house.

3

I turned in, and slept several hours very soundly, and then suddenly found myself wide awake. I got up, and as I did almost every night, went out to look after my cattle. I found all but one of them, and fetched a compass about the barns and stables, searching until I found her. As I passed in front of the door I heard moanings and cryings from a bench against the side of the house, and stopped. It was dawn, and I could see that it was either a small woman or a large child, huddled down on the bench crying terribly, with those peculiar wrenching spasms that come only when you have struggled long, and then quite given up to misery. I went toward her, then stepped back, then drew closer, trying to decide whether I should go away and leave her, or speak to her; and arguing with myself as to what I could possibly say to her. She seemed to be trying to choke down her weeping, burying her head in her hands, holding back her sobs, wrestling with herself. Finally she fell forward on her face upon the bench, her hands spread abroad and hanging down, her face on the hard cold wood—and all her moanings ceased. It seemed to me that she had suddenly dropped dead; for I could not hear from her a single sigh or gasp or breath, though I stepped closer and listened—not a sign of life did she give. So I put my arm under her and raised her up, only to see that her face was ghastly white, and that she seemed quite dead. I picked her up, and found that, though she was slight and girl-ish, she was more woman than child, and carried her over to the well where there was cold water in the trough, from which I sprinkled a few icy drops in her face—and she gasped and looked at me as if dazed.

"You fainted away," I said, "and I brought you to."

"I wish you hadn't!" she cried. "I wish you had let me die!"

"What's the matter, little girl?" I asked, seating her on the bench once more. "Is there anything I can do?"

"Oh! oh! oh! oh!" she cried, maybe a dozen times—and nothing more, until finally she burst out: "She was all I had in the world. My God, what will become of me!" And she sprang up, and would have run off, I believe, if Buckner Gowdy had not overtaken her, and coaxingly led her back into the house.

We come now into a new state of things in the history of Vandemark Township.

We meet not only the things that made it, but the actors in the play.

Buckner Gowdy, Doctor Bliven, their associates, and others not yet mentioned will be found helping to make or mar the story all through the future; for an Iowa community was like a growing child in this, that its character in maturity was fixed by its beginnings.

I know communities in Iowa that went into evil ways, and were blighted through the poison distilled into their veins by a few of the earliest settlers; I know others that began with a few strong, honest, thinking, reading, praying families, and soon began sending out streams of good influence which had a strange power for better things;

I knew other settlements in which there was a feud from the beginning between the bad and the good; and in some of them the blight of the bad finally overwhelmed the good, while in others the forces of righteousness at last grappled with the devil's gang, and, sometimes in violence, redeemed the neighborhood to a place in the light.

In one of these classes Monterey County, and even Vandemark Township, took its place. Buckner Gowdy and Doctor Bliven, the little girl who fainted away on the wooden bench in the night, and the yellow-haired woman who stole a ride with me across the Dubuque ferry had their part in the building up of our great community —and others worked with them, some for the good and some for the bad.

Now I come to people whose histories I know by the absorption of a lifetime's experience. I know that it was Mrs. Bliven's husband—we always called her that, of course—who expected to arrest the pair of them as they crossed the Dubuque ferry; and that I was made a cat's-paw in slipping her past her pursuers and saving Bliven from arrest. I know that Buckner Gowdy was a wild and turbulent rakehell in Kentucky and after many bad scrapes was forced to run away from the state, and was given his huge plantation of "worthless" land—as he called it—in Iowa; that he had married his wife, who was a poor girl of good family named Ann Royall, because he couldn't get her except by marrying her.

I know that her younger sister, Virginia Royall, came with them to Iowa, because she had no other relative or friend in the world except Mrs. Gowdy. I pretty nearly know that Virginia would have killed herself that night on the prairie by the Old Ridge Road, because of a sudden feeling of terror, at the situation in which she was left, at the prairies and the wild desolate road, at Buck Gowdy, at life in general—if she had had any means with which to destroy her life. I know that Buck Gowdy took her into the house and comforted her by telling her that he would care for her, and send her back to Kentucky.

A funeral by the wayside! This was my first experience with a kind of tragedy which was not quite so common as you might think. Buckner Gowdy instead of giving his wife a grave by the road, as many did, sent the man of the house back to Dubuque for a hearse, the women laid out the corpse, and after a whole day of waiting, the hearse came, and went back over the road down the Indian trail through the bluffs to some graveyard in the old town by the river. Virginia Royall sat in the back seat of the carriage with Buckner Gowdy, and the darky, Pinckney Johnson—we all knew him afterward—drove solemnly along wearing white gloves which he had found somewhere. Virginia shrank away over to her own side of the seat as if trying to get as far from Buckner Gowdy as possible.

The movers moved on, leaving me four of their cows instead of two of mine, and I went diligently to work breaking them to the yoke. New prairie schooners came all the time into view from the East, and others went over the sky-line into the West.

4

And that day the Fewkes family hove into sight in a light democrat wagon drawn by a good-sized apology

for a horse, poor as a crow, and carrying sail in the most
ferocious way of any beast I ever saw. He had had a
bad case of poll-evil and his head was poked forward as
if he was just about to bite something, and his ears were
leered back tight to his head with an expression of the
most terrible anger—I have known people who went
through the world in a good deal the same way for much
the same reasons.

Old Man Fewkes was driving, and sitting by him was
Mrs. Fewkes in a faded calico dress, her shoulders
wrapped in what was left of a shawl. Fewkes was letting old Tom take his own way, which he did by rushing
with all vengeance through every bad spot and then stopping to rest as soon as he reached a good bit of road.
The old man was thin and light-boned, with a high beak
of a nose which ought to have indicated strength of character, I suppose; but the other feature that also tells a
good deal, the chin, was hidden by a gray beard which
hung in long curving locks over his breast and saved him
the expense of a collar or cravat. His hands were like
claws—I never saw such hands doing much of the hard
work of the world—and, like his face, were covered with
great patches which, if they had not been so big would
have been freckles. His wife was a perfect picture of
those women who had the life drailed out of them
by a yielding to the whiffling winds of influence that
carried the dead leaves of humanity hither and yon in
the advance of the frontier. She sat stooped over on
the stiff broad seat, with her shoulders drawn down as
no shoulders but hers could be drawn. It was her one
outstanding point that she had no collar-bones. It
doesn't seem possible that this could be so; but she could

bring her shoulders together in front until they touched. She was rather proud of this—I suppose every one must have something to be proud of.

I guess the old man's chin must have been pretty weak; for the boys, who were seated on the back seat, both had high noses and no chins to speak of. The oldest was over twenty, I suppose, and was named Celebrate. His mother explained to me that he was born on the Fourth of July, and they called him at first Celebrate Independence Fewkes; but finally changed it to Celebrate Fourth—I am telling you this so as to give you an idea as to what sort of folks they were. Celebrate was tall and well-built, and could be a good hand if he tried; which he would do once in a while for half a day or so if flattered. The second son was named Surajah Dowlah Fewkes—the name was pronounced Surrager by everybody. Old Man Fewkes said they named him this because a well-read man had told them it might give him force of character; but it failed. He was a harmless little chap, and there was nothing bad about him except that he was addicted to inventions. When they came into camp that day he was explaining to Celebrate a plan for catching wild geese with fish-hooks baited with corn, and that evening came to me to see if he couldn't borrow a long fish-line.

"I can ketch meat for a dozen outfits with it," he said, "if I can borrow a fish-hook."

Walking along behind the wagon came the fifth member of the family, Rowena, a girl of seventeen. She went several rods behind the wagon, and as they rushed and plodded along according to old Tom's temper, I noticed that she rambled over the prairie a good deal picking flowers; and you would hardly have thought to look at her that she belonged to the Fewkes outfit at all. I guess that was the way she wanted it to look. She was as vigorous as the others were limpsey and boneless; and there was in her something akin to the golden plovers that were running in hundreds that morning over the prairies—I haven't seen one for twenty-five years! That is, she skimmed over the little knolls rather than walked, as if made of something lighter than ordinary human clay. Her dress was ragged, faded, and showed through the tears in it a tattered quilted petticoat, and she wore no bonnet or hat; but carried in her hand a boy's cap—which, according to the notions harbored by us then, it would have been immodest for her to wear. Her hair was brown and blown all about her head, and her face was tanned to a rich brown—a very bad complexion then, but just the thing the society girl of to-day likes to show when she returns from the seashore.

When her family had halted, she did not come to them at once, but made a circuit or two about the camp, like a shy bird coming to its nest, or as if she hated to do it; and when she did come it was in a sort of defiant way, swinging herself and tossing her head, and looking at every one as bold as brass. I was staring at the astonishing horse, the queer wagon, and the whole outfit with more curiosity than manners, I reckon, when she came into the circle, and caught my unmannerly eye.

"Well," she said, her face reddening under the tan, "if you see anything green throw your hat at it! Sellin' gawp-seed, or what is your business?"

"I beg your pardon," "I meant no offense," and even "Excuse me" were things I had never learned to say. I had learned to fight any one who took offense at me; and if they didn't like my style they could lump it—such was my code of manners, and the code of my class. To beg pardon was to knuckle under—and it took something more than I was master of in the way of putting on style to ask to be excused, even if the element of back-down were eliminated. Remember, I had been "educated" on the canal. So I tried to look her out of countenance, grew red, retreated, and went about some sort of needless work without a word—completely defeated. I thought she seemed rather to like this; and that evening I went over and offered Mrs. Fewkes some butter and milk, of which I had a plenty.

I was soon on good terms with the Fewkes family. Old Man Fewkes told me he was going to Negosha—a region of which I had never heard. It was away off to the westward, he said; and years afterward I made up my mind that the name was made up of the two words Nebraska and Dakota—not very well joined together. Mrs. Fewkes was not strong for Negosha; and when Fewkes offered to go to Texas, she objected because it was so far.

"Why," said the old man indignantly, "it hain't only a matter of fifteen hundred mile! An' the trees is in constant varder!"

He still harped on Negosha, though, and during the evening while we were fattening up on my bread and meat, which I had on a broad hint added to our meal, he told me that what he really wanted was an estate where he could have an artificial lake and keep some deer and plenty of ducks and geese. Swans, too, he said could be raised at a profit, and sold to other well-to-do people.

He said that by good farming he could get along with only a few hundred acres of plow land. Mrs. Fewkes grew more indulgent to these ideas as the food satisfied her hungry stomach. Celebrate believed that if he could once get out among 'em he could do well as a hunter and trapper; while Surajah kept listening to the honking of the wild geese and planning to catch enough of them with baited hooks to feed the whole family all the way to Negosha, and provide plenty of money by selling the surplus to the emigrants. Rowena sat in her ragged dress, her burst shoes drawn in under her skirt, looking at her family with an expression of unconcealed scorn. When she got a chance to speak to me, she did so in a very friendly manner.

"Did you ever see," said she, "such a set of darned infarnal fools as we are?"

Before the evening was over, however, and she had hidden herself away in her clothes under a thin and ragged comforter in their wagon, she had joined in the discussion of their castle in Spain in a way that showed her to be a legitimate Fewkes. She spoke for a white saddle horse, a beautiful side-saddle, a long blue riding-habit with shot in the seam, and a man to keep the horse in order. She wanted to be able to rub the horse with a white silk handkerchief without soiling it. Ah, well! dreams hovered over all our camps then. The howling of the wolves couldn't drive them away. Poor Rowena!

CHAPTER VIII

I STILL had some corn for my cattle, of the original supply which I had got from Rucker in Madison. Hay was fifteen dollars a ton, and all it cost the producer was a year's foresight and the labor of putting it up; for there were millions of acres of wild grass going to waste which made the sweet-smelling hay that old horsemen still prefer to tame hay. It hadn't quite the feeding value, pound for pound, that the best timothy and clover has; but it was a wonderful hay that could be put up in the clear weather of the fall when the ground is dry and warm, and cured so as to be free from dust. My teams never got the heaves when I fed prairie hay. It graveled me like sixty to pay such a price, but I had to do it because the season was just between hay and grass. Sometimes I thought of waiting over until the summer of 1856 to make hay for sale to the movers; but having made my start for my farm I could not bring myself to give up reaching it that spring. So I only waited occasionally to break in or rest up the foot-sore and lame cattle for which I traded from time to time.

The Fewkes family went on after I had given them some butter, some side pork and a milking of milk. While I was baking pancakes that last morning, Rowena came to my fire, and snatching the spider away from me took

136

the job off my hands, baking the cakes while I ate. She was a pretty girl, slim and well developed, and she had a fetching way with her eyes after friendly relations were established with her—which was pretty hard because she seemed to feel that every one looked down on her, and was quick to take offense.

"Got any saleratus?" she asked.

"No," said I. "Why?"

She stepped over to the Fewkes wagon and brought back a small packet of saleratus, a part of which she stirred into the batter.

"It's gettin' warm enough so your milk'll sour on you," said she. "This did. Don't you know enough to use saleratus to sweeten the sour milk? You better keep this an' buy some at the next store."

"I wish I had somebody along that could cook," said I.

"Can't you cook?" she asked. "I can."

I told her, then, all about my experience on the canal; and how we used to carry a cook on the boat sometimes, and sometimes cooked for ourselves. I induced her to sit by me on the spring seat which I had set down on the ground, and join me in my meal while I told her of my adventures. She seemed to forget her ragged and unwashed dress, while she listened to the story of my voyages from Buffalo to Albany, and my side trips to such places as Oswego. This canal life seemed powerfully thrilling to the poor girl. She could only tell of living a year or so at a time on some run-down or never run-up farm in Indiana or Illinois, always in a log cabin in a clearing; or of her brothers and sisters who had been "bound out" because the family was so large; and now of this last voyage in search of an estate in Negosha.

"I can make bread," said she, after a silence. "Kin you?"

When I told her I couldn't she told me how. It was the old-fashioned salt-rising bread, the receipt for which she gave me; and when I asked her to write it down I found that she was even a poorer scribe than I was. We were two mighty ignorant young folks, but we got it down, and that night I set emptins* for the first time, and I kept trying, and advising with the women-folks, until I could make as good salt-rising bread as any one. When we had finished this her father was calling her to come, as they were starting on toward Negosha; and I gave Rowena money enough to buy her a calico dress pattern at the next settlement. She tried to resist, and her eyes filled with tears as she took the money and chokingly tried to thank me for it. She climbed into the wagon and rode on for a while, but got out and came back to me while old Tom went on in those mad rushes of his, and circling within a few yards of me she said, "You're right good," and darted off over the prairie at a wide angle to the road.

I watched her with a buying eye, as she circled like a pointer pup and finally caught up with the wagon, a full mile on to the westward. I had wondered once if

---

*Our author resists firmly all arguments in favor of the generally accepted dictionary spelling, "emptyings." He says that the term can not possibly come from any such idea as things which are emptied, or emptied out. The editor is reconciled to this view in the light of James Russell Lowell's discussion of "emptins" in which he says: "Nor can I divine the original." Mr. Lowell surely must have considered "emptyings"—and rejected it.—G. v. d. M.

she had not deserted the Fewkes party forever. I had even, such is the imagination of boyhood, made plans and lived them through in my mind, which put Rowena on the nigh end of the spring seat, and made her a partner with me in opening up the new farm. But she waved her hand as she joined her family—or I thought so at least, and waved back—and was gone.

The Gowdy outfit did not return until after I had about cured the lameness of my newly-acquired cows and set out on my way over the Old Ridge Road for the West. The spring was by this time broadening into the loveliest of all times on the prairies (when the weather is fine), the days of the full blowth of the upland bird's-foot violets. Some southern slopes were so blue with them that you could hardly tell the distant hill from the sky, except for the greening of the peeping grass. The poss-blummies were still blowing, but only the later ones. The others were aging into tassels of down.

The Canada geese, except for the nesters, had swept on in that marvelous ranked army which ends the migration, spreading from the east to the west some warm morning when the wind is south, and extending from a hundred feet in the air to ten thousand, all moved by a common impulse like myself and my fellow-migrants, pressing northward though, instead of westward, with the piping of a thousand organs, their wings whirring, their eyes glistening as if with some mysterious hope, their black webbed feet folded and stretched out behind, their necks strained out eagerly to the north, and held a little high I thought as if to peer over the horizon to catch a glimpse of their promised land of blue lakes, tall reeds, and broad fields of water-celery and wild rice, with dry nests downy with the harvests of their gray breasts; and fluffy goslings swimming in orderly classes after their teachers. And up from the South following these old honkers came the snow geese, the Wilson geese, and all the other little geese (we ignorantly called all of them "brants"), with their wild flutings like the high notes of clarinets—and the ponds became speckled with teal and coot.

The prairie chickens now became the musicians of the morning and evening on the uplands, with their wild and intense and almost insane chorus, repeated over and over until it seemed as if the meaning of it must be forced upon every mind like a figure in music played with greatening power by a violinist so that the heart finally almost breaks with it—"Ka-a-a-a-a-a, ka, ka, ka, ka! *Ka-a-a-a-a-a-a,* ka, ka, ka, ka, ka, ka, ka! KA-A-A-A-A-A-A, ka, ka, ka, ka, ka, ka, ka, ka!"—Oh, there is no way to tell it! —And then the cock filled in the harmony with his lovely contribution: facing the courted hen, he swelled out the great orange globes at the sides of his head, fluffed out his feathers, strutted forward a few steps, and tolled his deep-toned bell, with all the skill of a ventriloquist, making it seem far away when he was on a near-by knoll, like a velvet gong sounded with no stroke of the hammer, as if it spoke from some inward vibration set up by a mysterious current—a liquid "Do, re, me," here full and distinct, there afar off, the whole air tremulous with it, the harmony to the ceaseless fugue in the soprano clef of the rest of the flock—nobody will ever hear it again! Nobody ever drew from it, and from the howling of the wolves, the honking of the geese, the calls of the ducks, the strange cries of the cranes as they soared with motionless

wings high overhead, or rowed their way on with long
slow strokes of their great wings, or danced their strange
reels and cotillions in the twilight; and from the myriad
voices of curlew, plover, gopher, bob-o-link, meadow-
lark, dick-cissel, killdeer and the rest—day-sounds and
night-sounds, dawn-sounds and dusk-sounds—more in-
spiration than did the stolid Dutch boy plodding west
across Iowa that spring of 1855, with his fortune in his
teams of cows, in the covered wagon they drew, and the
deed to his farm in a flat packet of treasures in a little
iron-bound trunk—among them a rain-stained letter and
a worn-out woman's shoe.

2

I got the saleratus at Dyersville, and just as I came
out of the little store which was, as I remember it, the
only one there, I saw the Gowdy carriage come down the
short street, the horses making an effort to prance under
the skilful management of Pinck Johnson, who occupied
the front seat alone, while Virginia Royall sat in the
back seat with Buckner Gowdy, her arm about the upright
of the cover, her left foot over the side as it might be in
case of a person who was ready to jump out to escape
the danger of a runaway, an overturn, or some other peril.

Gowdy did not recognize me, or if he did he did not
speak to me. He got out of the carriage and went first
into the store, coming out presently with some packages
in his hand which he tossed to the darky, and then he
joined the crowd of men in front of the saloon across the
way. Soon I saw him go into the gin-mill, the crowd following him, and the noise of voices grew louder. I had
had enough experience with such things to know pretty

well what was going on; the stink of spilled drinks, and profanity and indecency—there was nothing in them to toll me in from the flowery prairie.

As I passed the carriage Virginia nodded to me; and looking at her I saw that she was pale and tremulous, with a look in her eyes like that of a crazy man I once knew who imagined that he was being followed by enemies who meant to kill him. There is no word for it but a hunted look.

She came to my wagon, pretty soon, and surprised me by touching my arm as I was about to start on so as to make a few more miles before camping. I had got my team straightened out, and ready to start, when I felt her hand on my arm, and on turning saw her standing close to me, and speaking almost in a whisper.

"Do you know any one," she asked, "good people— along the road ahead—people we'll overtake—that would be friends to a girl that needs help?"

"Be friends," I blundered, "be friends? How be friends?"

"Give her work," she said; "take her in; take care of her. This girl needs friends—other girls—women— some one to take the place of a mother and sisters. Yes, and she needs friends to take the place of a father and brothers. A girl needs friends—friends all the time—as you were to me back there in the night."

I wondered if she meant herself; and after thinking over it for two or three days I made up my mind that she did; and then I was provoked at myself for not understanding: but what could I have done or said if I had understood? I remembered, though, how she had

skithered* back to the carriage as she saw Pinck Johnson
coming out of the saloon with Buck Gowdy; and had then
clambered out again and gone into the little hotel where
they seemed to have decided to stay all night; while I
went on over roads which were getting more and more
miry as I went west. I had only been able to tell her of
the Fewkes family—Old Man Fewkes, with his bird's
claws and a beard where a chin should have been, Surajah
Dowlah Fewkes with no thought except for silly inventions, Celebrate Fourth Fewkes with no ideas at all—

"But isn't there a man among them?" she had asked.

"A man!" I repeated.

"A man that knows how to shoot a pistol, or use a
knife," she explained; "and who would shoot or stab for
a weak girl with nobody to take care of her."

I shook my head. Not one of these was a real man
in the Kentucky, or other proper sense: and Ma Fewkes
with her boneless shoulders was not one of those women
of whom I had seen many in my life, who could be more
terrible to a wrong-doer than an army with bowie-knives.

"There's only two in the outfit," I went on, "that
have got any sprawl to them; and they are old Tom their
bunged-up horse, and Rowena Fewkes."

"Who is she?" inquired Virginia Royall.

"A girl about your age," said I. "She's ragged and
dirty, but she has a little gumption."

---

*A family word, to the study of which one would like to
direct the attention of the philologists, since traces of it are found
in the conversation of folk of unsophisticated vocabulary outside the Clan van de Marck. Doubtless it is of Yankee origin,
and hence old English. It may, of course, be derived according to Alice-in-Wonderland principles from "skip" and
"hither" or "thither" or all three; but the claim is here made
that it comes, like monkeys and men, from a common linguistic
ancestor.—G. v. d. M.

And then she had skipped away, as I finally concluded, to keep Gowdy from seeing her in conversation with me.

3

I pulled out for Manchester with Nathaniel Vincent Creede, whom everybody calls just "N. V.," riding in the spring seat with me, and his carpet-bag and his law library in the back of the wagon.

His library consisted of *Blackstone's Commentaries*—I saw them in his present library in Monterey Centre only yesterday—*Chitty on Pleading,* the *Code of Iowa of* 1850, the *Session Laws* of the state so far as it had any session laws, and a few thin books bound in yellow and pink boards. Even these few books made a pretty heavy bundle for a man to carry in one hand while he lugged all his other worldly goods in the other.

"Books are damned heavy, Mr. Vandemark," said he; "law books are particularly heavy. My library is small; but there is an adage in our profession which warns us to beware of the man of one book. He's always likely to know what's in the damned thing, you know, Mr. Vandemark; and the truth being a seamless web, if a lawyer knows all about the law in one book, he's prone to make a hell of a straight guess at what's in the rest of 'em. Hence beware of the man of one book. I may safely lay claim to being that man—in a figurative way; though there are half a dozen volumes or so back there— the small pedestal on which I stand reaching up toward a place on the Supreme Bench of the United States."

He had had a drink or two with Buckner Gowdy back there in the saloon, and this had taken the brakes off his tongue—if there were any provided in his temperament. So, aside from Buck Gowdy, I was the first of his fellow-citizens of Monterey County to become acquainted with N. V. Creede. He reminded me at first of Lawyer Jackway of Madison, the guardian *ad litem* who had sung the song that still recurred to me occasionally—

> "Sold again,
> And got the tin,
> And sucked another Dutchman in!"

But N. V. looked a little like Jackway from the fact only that he wore a long frock coat, originally black, a white shirt, and a black cravat. He was very tall, and very erect, even while carrying those books and that bag. He was smooth-shaven, and was the first man I ever saw who shaved every day, and could do the trick without a looking-glass. His eyes were black and very piercing; and his voice rolled like thunder when he grew earnest—which he was likely to do whenever he spoke. He would begin to discuss my cows, the principles of farming, the sky, the birds of passage, the flowers, the sucking in of the Dutchman—which I told him all about before we had gone five miles—the mire-holes in the slews, anything at all—and rising from a joke or a flighty notion which he earnestly advocated, he would lower his voice and elevate his language and utter a little gem of an oration. After which he would be still and solemn for a while—to let it sink in I thought.

N. V. was at that time twenty-seven years old. He came from Evansville, Indiana, by the Ohio from Evansville to St. Louis, and thence up the Mississippi. From

Dubuque he had partly walked and partly ridden with people who were willing to give him a lift.

"I am like unto the Apostle Peter," he said when he asked for the chance to ride with me, "silver and gold have I none; but such as I have I give unto thee."

"What do you mean?" I asked; for it is just as well always to be sure beforehand when it comes to pay— though, of course, I should have been glad to have him with me without money and without price.

"In the golden future of Iowa," he said, "you will occasionally want legal advice. I will accept transportation in your very safe, but undeniably slow equipage as a retainer."

"Captain Sproule used to say," I said, "that what you pay the lawyer is the least of the matter when you go to law."

"Wise Captain Sproule," replied N. V.; "and my rule shall be to keep my first client, Mr. Jacob T. Vandemark, out of the courts; and in addition to my prospective legal services, I can wield the goad-stick and manipulate the blacksnake. Moreover, when these feet of mine get their blisters healed, I can help drive the cattle; and I can gather firewood, kindle fires, and perhaps I may suggest that my conversation may not be entirely unprofitable."

I told him I would take him in as a passenger; and there our life-long friendship began. His conversation was not unprofitable. He had the vision of the future of Iowa which I had until then lacked. He could see on every quarter-section a prosperous farm, and he knew what the building of the railways must mean. As we forded the Maquoketa he laughed at the settlers working at the timber, grubbing out stumps, burning off the logs, struggling with roots.

"Your ancestors, the Dutch," said he, "have been held up to ridicule because they refused to establish a town until they found a place where dykes had to be built to keep out the sea, though there were plenty of dry places available. These settlers are acting just as foolishly. They have been used to grubbing, and they go where grubbing has to be done. Two miles either way is better land ready for the plow! Why can't every one be wise like us?"

"They have to have wood for houses, stables, and fuel," I said. "I hope my land has timber on it."

"The railroads are coming," said he, "and they will bring you coal and wood and everything you want. They are racing for the crossings of the Mississippi. Soon they will reach the Missouri—and some day they will cross the continent to the Pacific. No more Erie Canals; no more Aaron Burr conspiracies for the control of the mouth of the Mississippi. Towns! Cities! Counties! States! We are pioneers; but civilization is treading on our heels. I feel it galling my kibes*—and what are a few blisters to me! I see in my own adopted city of Lithopolis, Iowa, a future Sparta or Athens or Rome, or anyhow, a Louisville or Cincinnati or Dubuque—a place in which to achieve greatness—or anyhow, a chance to deal in town lots, defend criminals, or prosecute them, and where the unsettled will have to be settled in the courts as well as on the farm. On to Lithopolis! G'lang, Whiteface, g'lang!"

"I thought you were going to Monterey Centre," I said.

---

*The editor acknowledges the invaluable assistance of Honorable N. V. Creede in the editing of the proofs of this and a few other passages.—G. v. d. M.

"Not if the court knows itself," he said, "and it thinks it does. Lithopolis is the permanent town in Monterey County, and Monterey Centre is the mushroom."

4

Monterey County, like all the eastern counties of Iowa, all the counties along the Missouri, and every other county which was crossed by a considerable river, was dotted with paper towns. We passed many of these staked-out sites on the Old Ridge Road; and we heard of them from buyers of and dealers in their lots.

Lithopolis was laid out by Judge Horace Stone, the great outsider in the affairs of the county until he died. He platted a town in Howard County when the town-lot fever first broke out, at a place called Stone's Ferry, and named it Lithopolis, because his name was Stone, and for the additional reason that there was a stone quarry there. I've been told that the word means Stone City. The people insisted upon calling it Stone's Ferry and would not have the name Lithopolis. Judge Stone raved and tore, but he was voted down, and pulled up stakes in disgust, sold out his interests and went on to Monterey County, where he could establish a new city and name it Lithopolis. He seemed to care more for the name than anything else, and never seemed to see how funny it was that he felt it possible to make a city wherever he decreed. This was a part of the spirit of the time. The prairies were infested with Romuluses and Remuses, flourishing, not on the milk of the wolves, but seemingly on their howls, of which they often gave a pretty fair imitation.

"But Monterey Centre is the county-seat," I suggested.

"It just thinks it's going to be," said N. V. "The fact is that Monterey County is not organized, but is attached to the county south of it for judicial purposes. Let me whisper in your ear that it will soon be organized, and that the county-seat will not be Monterey Centre, but Lithopolis—that classic municipality whose sonorous name will be the admiration of all true Americans and the despair of the spelling classes in our schools. Lithopolis! It has the cadence of Alexander, and Alcibiades, and Numa Pompilius, and Belisarius—it reeks of greatness! Monterey Centre—ever been there? Ever seen that poverty-stricken, semi-hamlet, squatting on the open prairie, and inhabited by a parcel of dreaming Nimshies?"

"No," said I; "have you?"

"No," he replied. "What difference does it make? He that goeth up against Lithopolis and them that dwell therein, the same is a dreaming Nimshi."

The beginnings of faction were in our town-sites; for most of them were in no sense towns, or even villages. There was a future county-seat fight in the rivalry between Monterey Centre and Lithopolis—and not only these, but in the rival rivalries of Cole's Grove, Imperial City, Rocksylvania, New Baltimore, Cathedral Rock, Waynesville and I know not how many more projects, all ambitiously laid out in the still-unorganized county of Monterey, and all but one or two now quite lost to all human memory or thought, except as some diligent abstractor of titles or real-estate lawyer discovers something of them in the chain of title of a farm; the spires and gables of the 'fifties realized only in the towering silo, the spinning windmill, or the vine-clad porch of a substantial farm-house. But in the heyday of their new-driven corner stakes, what wars were waged for the power to draw people into them; and especially, how the county-seat fights raged like prairie fires set out by those Nimrods who sought to make up in the founding of cities for what they lacked as hunters, in comparison with the establisher of Babel and Erech and Accad and Calneh in the land of Shinar.

Between the Maquoketa and Independence I lost N. V. Creede, merely because I traded for some more lame cows and a young Alderney bull, and had to stop to break them. He stayed with me two days, and then caught a ride with one of Judge Horace Stone's teams which was making a quick trip to Lithopolis.

"Good-by, Mr. Vandemark," said he at parting, "and good luck. I am sorry not to be able to remunerate you for your hospitality, which I shall always remember for its improving conversation, its pancakes, its pork and beans, and its milk and butter, rather than for its breathless speed. And take the advice of your man of the law in parting: in your voyages over the inland waterways of life, look not upon the flush when it is red—not even the straight one; for had I not done that on a damned steamboat coming up from St. Louis I should not have been thus in my old age forsaken. And let me tell you, one day my coachman will pull up at the door of your farm-house and take you and your wife and children in my coach and four for a drive—perhaps to see the laying of the corner-stone of the United States court-house in Lithopolis. I go from your ken, but I shall return—good-by."

I was sorry to see him go. It was lonesome without him; and I was troubled by my live stock. I soon saw that I was getting so many cattle that without help in driving them I should be obliged to leave and come back for some of them. I found a farmer named Westervelt who lived by the roadside, and had come to Iowa from Herkimer County, in York State. He even knew some of the relatives of Captain Sproule; so in view of the fact that he seemed honest, I left my cattle with him, all but four cows, and promised to return for them not later than the middle of July. I made him give me a receipt for them, setting forth just what the bargain was, and I paid him then and there for looking out for them— and N. V. Creede said afterward that the thing was a perfectly good legal document, though badly spelled.

"It calls," said he, "for an application of the doctrine of *idem sonans*—but it will serve, it will serve."

I marveled that the Gowdy carriage still was astern of me after all this time; and speculated as to whether there was not some other road between Dyersville and Independence, by which they had passed me; but a few miles east of Independence they came up behind me as I lay bogged down in a slew, and drove by on the green tough sod by the roadside. I had just hitched the cows to the end of the tongue, by means of the chain, when they trotted by, and sweeping down near me halted. Virginia still sat as if she had never moved, her hand gripping the iron support of the carriage top, her foot outside the box as if she was ready to spring out. Buck Gowdy leaped out and came down to me.

"In trouble, Mr. Vandemark?" he inquired. "Can we be of any assistance?"

"I guess I can make it," I said, scraping the mud off my trousers and boots. "Gee-up there, Liney!"

My cows settled slowly into the yoke, and standing, as they did now, on firm ground, they deliberately snaked the wagon, hub-deep as it was, out of the mire, and stopped at the word on the western side of the mud-hole.

"Good work, Mr. Vandemark!" he said. "Those knowledgy folk back along the road who said you were trading yourself out of your patrimony ought to see you put the thing through. If you ever need work, come to my place out in the new Earthly Eden."

"I'll have plenty of work of my own," I said; "but maybe, sometime, I may need to earn a little money. I'll remember."

I stopped at Independence that night; and so did the Gowdy party. I was on the road before them in the morning, but they soon passed me, Virginia looking wishfully at me as they went by, and Buck Gowdy waving his hand in a way that made me think he must be a little tight—and then they drove on out of sight, and I pursued my slow way wondering why Virginia Royall had asked me so anxiously if I knew any good people who would take in and shelter a friendless girl—and not only take her in, but fight for her. I could not understand what she had said in any other way.

I had a hard time that day. The road was already cut up and at the crossings of the swales the sod on which we relied to bear up our wheels was destroyed by the host of teams that had gone on before me. That endless stream across the Dubuque ferry was flowing on ahead of me; and the fast-going part of it was passing me every hour like swift schooners outstripping a slow, round-bellied Dutch square-rigger.

The mire-holes were getting deeper and deeper; for

the weather was showery. I helped many teams out of their troubles, and was helped by some; though my load was not overly heavy, and I had four true-pulling heavy cows that, when mated with the Alderney bull I had left behind me with Mr. Westervelt, gave me the best stock of cattle—they and my other cows—in Monterey County, until Judge Horace Stone began bringing in his pure-bred Shorthorns; and even then, by grading up with Shorthorn blood I was thought by many to have as good cattle as he had. So I got out of most of my troubles on the Old Ridge Road with my cows, as I did later with them and their descendants when the wheat crop failed us in the 'seventies; but I had a hard time that day. It grew better in the afternoon; and as night drew on I could see the road for miles ahead of me a solitary stretch of highway, without a team; but far off, coming over a hill toward me, I saw a figure that looked strange and mysterious to me, somehow.

5

It seemed to be a woman or girl, for I could see even at that distance her skirts blown out by the brisk prairie wind. She came over the hill as if running, and at its summit she appeared to stop as if looking for something afar off. At that distance I could not tell whether she gazed backward, forward, to the left or the right, but it impressed me that she stood gazing backward over the route to the west along which she had come. Then, it was plain, she began running down the gentle declivity toward me, and once she fell and either lay or sat on the ground for some time. Presently, though, she got up, and began coming on more slowly, sometimes as if running, most of the time going from side to side of the road as if staggering—and finally she went out of my sight, dropping into a wide valley, to the bottom of which I could not see. It was strange, as it appeared to me; this lone woman, the prairie, night, and the sense of trouble; but, I thought, like most queer things, it would have some quite simple explanation if one could see it close by.

I made camp a few hundred yards from the road by a creek, along the banks of which grew many willows, and some little groves of box-elders and popples, which latter in this favorable locality grew eight or ten feet tall, and were already breaking out their soft greenish catkins and tender, quivering, pointed leaves: in one of these clumps I hid my wagon, and in the midst of it I kindled my camp-fire. It seemed already a little odd to find myself where I could not look out afar over the prairie.

The little creek ran bank-full, but clear, and not muddy as our streams now always are after a rain. One of the losses of Iowa through civilization has been the disappearance of our lovely little brooks. Then every few miles there ran a rivulet as clear as crystal, its bottom checkered at the riffles into a brilliant pattern like plaid delaine by the shining of the clean red, white and yellow granite pebbles through the crossed ripples from the banks. Now these watercourses are robbed of their flow by the absorption of the rich plowed fields, are all silted up, and in summer are dry; and in spring and fall they are muddy bankless wrinkles in the fields, poached full by the hoofs of cattle and the snouts of hogs; and through many a swale, you would now be surprised to know, in 1855 there ran a brook two feet wide in a thousand little loops, with beautiful dark quiet pools at the turns, some of them mantled with white water-lilies, and some with yellow. Over-hanging banks of rooty turf, had these creeks, under which the larger and soberer fishes lurked in dignified caution like bank presidents, too wise for any common bait, but eager for the big good things. The narrower reaches were all overshadowed by the long grass until you had to part the greenery to see the water. Now such a valley is a forest of corn unbroken by any vestige of brook, creek, rivulet or rill.

That night at a spot which is now plow-land, I have no doubt, I listened to the frogs and prairie-chickens while I caught a mess of chubs, shiners, punkin-seeds and bullheads in a little pond not ten feet broad, within a hundred yards of my wagon, and then rolled them in flour and fried them in butter over my fire, wondering all the time about the woman I had seen coming eastward on the road ahead of me.

I was still in sight of the road, and the twilight was settling down gradually; the air was so clear that even in the absence of a moon, it was long after sunset before it was dark; so I could sit in my dwarf forest, and keep watch of the road to the west to see whether that woman was really a lonely wanderer against the stream of travel, or only a stray from some mover's wagon camped ahead of me along the road.

A pack of wolves just off the road and to the west at that moment began their devilish concert over some wayside carcass—just at the moment when she came in sight. She appeared in the road where it came into my view twenty rods or so beyond the creek, and on the other side of it.

I heard her scream when the first howls of the wolves broke the silence; and then she came running, stumbling, falling, partly toward me and partly toward a point up-stream, where I thought she must mean to cross the brook —a thing which was very easy for one on foot, since it called only for a little jump from one bank to the other. She seemed to be carrying something which when she fell would fly out of her hand, and which in spite of her panic she would pick up before she ran on again.

She came on uncertainly, but always running away from the howls of the wolves, and just before she reached the little creek, she stopped and looked back, as if for a sight of pursuers—and there were pursuers. Perhaps a hundred yards back of her I saw four or five slinking dark forms; for the cowardly prairie wolf becomes bold when fled from, and partly out of curiosity, and perhaps looking forward to a feast on some dead or dying animal, they were stalking the girl, silent, shadowy, evil, and maybe dangerous. She saw them too—and with another scream she plunged on through the knee-high grass, fell splashing into the icy water of the creek, and I lost sight of her.

My first thought was that she was in danger of drowning, notwithstanding the littleness of the brook; and I ran to the point from which I had heard her plunge into the water, expecting to have to draw her out on the bank; but I found only a place where the grass was wallowed down as she had crawled out, and lying on the ground was the satchel she had been carrying. Dark as it was I could see her trail through the grass as she had made her way on; and I followed it with her sachel in my hand, with some foolish notion of opening a conversation with her by giving it back to her.

A short distance farther, on the upland, were my four cows, tied head and foot so they could graze, lying down to rest; and staggering on toward them went the woman's form, zigzagging in bewilderment. She came all at once upon the dozing cows, which suddenly gathered themselves together in fright, hampered by their hobbling ropes, and one of them sent forth that dreadful bellow of a scared cow, worse than a lion's roar. The woman uttered another piercing cry, louder and shriller than any she had given yet; she turned and ran back to me, saw my dark form before her, and fell in a heap in the grass, helpless, unnerved, quivering, quite done for.

"Don't be afraid," said I; "I won't let them hurt you —I won't let anything hurt you!"

I didn't go very near her at first, and I did not touch her. I stood there repeating that the wolves would not hurt her, that it was only a gentle cow which had made that awful noise, that I was only a boy on my way to my farm, and not afraid of wolves at all, or of anything else. I kept repeating these simple words of reassurance over and over, standing maybe a rod from her; and from that distance stepping closer and closer until I stood over her, and found that she was moaning and catching her breath, her face in her arms, stretched out on the cold ground, wet and miserable, all alone on the boundless prairie except for a foolish boy who did not know what to do with her or with himself, but was repeating the promise that he would not let anything hurt her. She has told me since that if I had touched her she would have died. It was a long time before she said anything.

"The wolves!" she cried. "The wolves!"

"They are gone," I said. "They are all gone—and I've got a gun."

"Oh! Oh!" she cried: "Keep them away! Keep them away!"

She kept saying this over and over, sitting on the ground and staring out into the darkness, starting at every rustle of the wind, afraid of everything. It was a long time before she uttered a word except exclamations of terror, and every once in a while she broke down in convulsive sobbings. I thought there was something familiar in her voice; but I could not see well enough to recognize her features, though it was plain that she was a young girl.

"The wolves are gone," I said; "I have scared them off."

"Don't let them come back," she sobbed. "Don't let them come back!"

"I've got a little camp-fire over yonder," I said; "and if we go to it, I'll build it up bright, and that will scare them most to death. They're cowards, the wolves— a camp-fire will make 'em run. Let's go to the fire."

She made an effort to get up, but fell back to the ground in a heap. I was just at that age when every boy is afraid of girls; and while I had had my dreams of rescuing damsels from danger and serving them in other heroic ways as all boys do, when the pinch came I did not know what to do; she put up her hand, though, and I took it and helped her to her feet; but she could not walk. Summoning up my courage I picked her up and carried her toward the fire. She said nothing, except, of course, that she was too heavy for me to carry; but she clung to me convulsively. I could feel her heart beating furiously against me, and she was twitching and quivering in every limb.

"You are the boy who took care of me back there when my sister died," said she as I carried her along.

"Are you Mrs. Gowdy's sister?" I asked.

"I am Virginia Royall," she said.

6

She was very wet and very cold. I set her down on the spring seat where she could lean back, and wrapped her in a buffalo robe, building up the fire until it warmed her.

"I'm glad it's you!" she said.

Presently I had hot coffee for her, and some warm milk, with the fish and good bread and butter, and a few slices of crisp pork which I had fried, and browned warmed-up potatoes. There was smear-case too, milk gravy and sauce made of English currants. She began picking at the food, saying that she could not eat; and I noticed that her lips were pale, while her face was crimson as if with fever. She had had nothing to eat for twenty-four hours except some crackers and cheese which she had hidden in her satchel before running away; so in spite of the fact that she was in a bad way from all she had gone through, she did eat a fair meal of victuals.

I thought she ought to be talked to so as to take her mind from her fright; but I could think of nothing but my way of cooking the victuals, and how much I wished I could give her a better meal—just the same sort of talk a woman is always laughed at for—but she did not say much to me. I suppose her strange predicament began returning to her mind.

I had already made up my mind that she should sleep in the wagon, while I rolled up in the buffalo robe by the fire; but it seemed a very bad and unsafe thing to allow her to go to bed wet as she was. I was afraid to mention it to her, however, until finally I saw her shiver as the fire died down. I tried to persuade her to use the covered wagon as a bedroom, and to let me dry her clothes by the fire; but she hung back, saying little except that she was not very wet, and hesitating and seeming embarrassed; but after I had heated the bed-clothes by the fire, and made up the bed as nicely as I could, I got her into the wagon and handed her the satchel which I had clung to while bringing her back; and although she had never consented to my plan she finally poked her clothes out from under the cover at the side of the wagon, in a sort of damp wad, and I went to work getting them in condition to wear again.

I blushed as I unfolded the wet dress, the underwear, and the petticoats, and spread them over a drying rack of willow wands which I had put up by the fire. I had never seen such things before; and it seemed as if it would be very hard for me to meet Virginia in the open day afterward—and yet as I watched by the clothes I had a feeling of exaltation like that which young knights may have had as they watched through the darkness by their armor for the ceremony of knighthood; except that no such knight could have had all my thoughts and feelings.

Perhaps the Greek boy who once intruded upon a goddess in her temple had an experience more like mine; though in my case the goddess had taken part in the ceremony and consented to it. There would be something between us forever, I felt, different from anything that had ever taken place between a boy and girl in all the world (it always begins in that way), something of which I could never speak to her or to any one, something which would make her different to me, in a strange, intimate, unspeakable way, whether I ever saw her again or not. Oh, the lost enchantment of youth, which makes an idol of a discarded pair of corsets, and locates a dreat land about the combings of a woman's hair; and lives a century of bliss in a day of embarrassed silence!

It must have been three o'clock, for the rooster of the half-dozen fowls which I had traded for had just crowed, when Virginia called to me from the wagon.

"That man," said she in a scared voice, "is hunting for me."

"Yes," said I, only guessing whom she meant.

"If he takes me I shall kill myself!"

"He will never take you from me," I said.

"What can you do?"

"I have had a thousand fights," I said; "and I have never been whipped!"

I afterward thought of one or two cases in which bigger boys had bested me, though I had never cried "Enough!" and it seemed to me that it was not quite honest to leave her thinking such a thing of me when it was not quite so. And it looked a little like bragging; but it appeared to quiet her, and I let it go. From the mention she had made back there at Dyersville of men who could fight, using pistol or knife, she apparently was accustomed to men who carried and used weapons; but, thought I, I had never owned, much less carried, any weapons except my two hard fists. Queer enough to say I never thought of the strangeness of a boy's making his way into a new land with a strange girl suddenly thrown on his hands as a new and precious piece of baggage to be secreted, smuggled, cared for and defended.

CHAPTER IX

THE GROVE OF DESTINY

WHEN I had got up in the morning and rounded up my cows I started a fire and began whistling. I was not in the habit of whistling much; but I wanted her to wake up and dress so I could get the makings of the breakfast out of the wagon. After I had the fire going and had whistled all the tunes I knew—*Lorena, The Gipsy's Warning, I'd Offer Thee This Hand of Mine,* and *Joe Bowers,* I tapped on the side of the wagon, and said "Virginia!"

She gave a scream, and almost at once I heard her voice calling in terror from the back of the wagon; and on running around to the place I found that she had stuck her head out of the opening of the wagon cover and was calling for help and protection.

"Don't be afraid," said I. "There's nobody here but me."

"Somebody called me 'Virginia,'" she cried, her face pale and her whole form trembling. "Nobody but that man in all this country would call me that."

She hardly ever called Gowdy by any other name but "that man," so far as I have heard. Something had taken place which struck her with a sort of dumbness; and I really believe she could not then have spoken the

name Gowdy if she had tried. What it was that happened she never told any one, unless it was Grandma
Thorndyke, who was always dumb regarding the sort of
thing which all the neighbors thought took place. To
Grandma Thorndyke sex must have seemed the original
curse imposed on our first parents; eggs and link sau-
sages were repulsive because they suggested the insides of
animals and vital processes; and a perfect human race
would have been to her made up of beings nourished by
the odors of flowers, and perpetuated by the planting of
the parings of finger-nails in antiseptic earth—or something of the sort. My live-stock business always had
to her its seamy side and its underworld which she always turned her face away from—though I never saw a
woman who could take a new-born pig, calf, colt or fowl,
once it was really brought forth so it could be spoken of,
and raise it from the dead, almost, as she could. But
every trace of the facts up to that time had to be concealed, and if not they were ignored by Grandma Thorndyke. New England all over!

If Gowdy was actually guilty of the sort of affront
to little Virginia for which the public thought him re-
sponsible, I do not see how the girl could ever have told
it to grandma. I do not see how grandma could ever
have been made to understand it. I suspect that the
worst that grandma ever believed, was that Gowdy swore
or used what she called vulgar language in Virginia's
presence. Knowing him as we all did afterward, we
suspected that he attempted to treat her as he treated all
women—and as I believe he could not help treating them.
It seems impossible of belief—his wife's orphan sister,
the recent death of Ann Gowdy, the girl's helplessness

and she only a little girl; but Buck Gowdy was Buck
Gowdy, and that escape of his wife's sister and her flight
over the prairie was the indelible black mark against him
which was pointed at from time to time forever after
whenever the people were ready to forgive those daily
misdoings to which a frontier people were not so critical
as perhaps they should have been. Indeed he gained a
certain popularity from his boast that all the time he
needed to gain control over any woman was half an hour
alone with her—but of that later, if at all.

"That was me that called you 'Virginia,'" said I. "I
want to get into the wagon to get things for breakfast—
after you get up."

"I never thought of your calling me Virginia," she
answered—and I had no idea what was in her mind. I
saw no reason why I shouldn't call her by her first name.
"Miss" Royall would have been my name for the wife
of a man named Royall. It was not until long afterward
that I found out how different my manners were from
those to which she was accustomed.

I never thought of such a thing as varying from my
course of conduct on her account; and just as would
have been the case if my outfit had been a boat for which
time and tide would not wait, I yoked up, after the breakfast was done, and prepared to negotiate the miry crossing of the creek and pull out for Monterey County,
which I hoped to reach in time to break some land and
plant a small crop. We did not discuss the matter of her
going with me—I think we both took that for granted.
She stood on a little knoll while I was making ready to
start, gazing westward, and when the sound of crack-
ing whips and the shouts of teamsters told of the ap-

proach of movers from the East, even though we were
some distance off the trail, she crept into the wagon so as
to be out of sight.   She had eaten little, and seemed
weak and spent; and when we started, I arranged the
bed in the wagon for her to lie upon, just as I had done
for Doctor Bliven's woman, and she seemed to hide
rather than anything else as she crept into it.   So on we
went, the wagon jolting roughly at times, and at times
running smoothly enough as we reached dry roads worn
smooth by travel.

Sometimes as I looked back, I could see her face with
the eyes fixed upon me questioningly; and then she
would ask me if I could see any one coming toward us
on the road ahead.

"Nobody," I would say; or, "A covered wagon going
the wrong way," or whatever I saw.   "Don't be afraid,"
I would add; "stand on your rights.   This is a free
country.   You've got the right to go east or west with
any one you choose, and nobody can say anything against
it.   And you've got a friend now, you know."

"Is anybody in sight?" she asked again, after a long
silence.

I looked far ahead from the top of a swell in the
prairie and then back.   I told her that there was no one
ahead so far as I could see except teams that we could
not overtake, and nobody back of us but outfits even
slower than mine.   So she came forward, and I helped her
over the back of the seat to a place by my side.   For the
first time I could get a good look at her undisturbed—if
a bashful boy like me could be undisturbed journeying
over the open prairie with a girl by his side—a girl altogether in his hands.

First I noticed that her hair, though dark brown, gave out gleams of bright dark fire as the sun shone through it in certain ways. I kept glancing at that shifting gleam whenever we turned the slow team so that her hair caught the sun. I have seen the same flame in the mane of a black horse bred from a sorrel dam or sire. As a stock breeder I have learned that in such cases there is in the heredity the genetic unit of red hair overlaid with black pigment. It is the same in people. Virginia's father had red hair, and her sister Ann Gowdy had hair which was a dark auburn. I was fascinated by that smoldering fire in the girl's hair; and in looking at it I finally grew bolder, as I saw that she did not seem to suspect my scrutiny, and I saw that her brows and lashes were black, and her eyes very, very blue—not the buttermilk blue of the Dutchman's eyes, like mine, with brows and lashes lighter than the sallow Dutch skin, but deep larkspur blue, with a dark edging to the pupil— eyes that sometimes, in a dim light, or when the pupils are dilated, seem black to a person who does not look closely. Her skin, too, showed her ruddy breed—for though it was tanned by her long journey in the sun and wind, there glowed in it, even through her paleness, a tinge of red blood—and her nose was freckled. Glimpses of her neck and bosom revealed a skin of the thinnest, whitest texture—quite milk-white, with pink showing through on account of the heat. She had little strong brown hands, and the foot which she put on the dashboard was a very trim and graceful foot like that of a thoroughbred mare, built for flight rather than work, and it swelled beautifully in its grass-stained white stocking above her slender ankle to the modest skirt.

A great hatred for Buck Gowdy surged through me as I felt her beside me in the seat and studied one after the other her powerful attractions—the hatred, not for the man who misuses the defenseless girl left in his power by cruel fate; but the lust for conquest over the man who had this girl in his hands and who, as she feared, was searching for her. I mention these things because, while they do not excuse some things that happened, they do show that, as a boy who had lived the uncontrolled and, by association, the evil life which I had lived, I was put in a very hard place.

2

After a while Virginia looked back, and clutched my arm convulsively.

"There's a carriage overtaking us!" she whispered. "Don't stop! Help me to climb back and cover myself up!"

She was quite out of sight when the carriage turned out to pass, drove on ahead, and then halted partly across the road so as to show that the occupants wanted word with me. I brought my wagon to a stop beside them.

"We are looking," said the man in the carriage, "for a young girl traveling alone on foot over the prairie."

The man was clearly a preacher. He wore a tall beaver hat, though the day was warm, and a suit of ministerial black. His collar stood out in points on each side of his chin, and his throat rested on a heavy stock-cravat which went twice around his neck and was tied in a stout square knot under his chin on the second turn. Under this black choker was a shirt of snowy white, as was his collar, while his coat and trousers looked worn and threadbare. His face was smooth-shaven, and his hair once black was now turning iron-gray. He was then about sixty years old.

"A girl," said I deceitfully, "traveling afoot and alone on the prairie? Going which way?"

The woman in the carriage now leaned forward and took part in the conversation. She was Grandma Thorndyke, of whom I have formerly made mention. Her hair was white, even then. I think she was a little older than her husband; but if so she never admitted it. He was a slight small man, but wiry and strong; while she was taller than he and very spare and grave. She wore steel-bowed spectacles, and looked through you when she spoke. I am sure that if she had ever done so awful a thing as to have put on a man's clothes no one would have seen through her disguise from her form, or even by her voice, which was a ringing tenor and was always heard clear and strong carrying the soprano in the First Congregational Church of Monterey Centre after Elder Thorndyke had succeeded in getting it built.

"Her name is Royall," said Grandma Thorndyke—I may as well begin calling her that now as ever— "Genevieve Royall. When last seen she was walking eastward on this road, where she is subject to all sorts of dangers from wild weather and wild beasts. A man on horseback named Gowdy, with a negro, came into Independence looking for her this morning after searching everywhere along the road from some place west back to the settlement. She is sixteen years old. There wouldn't be any other girl traveling alone and without provision. Have you passed such a person?"

"No, I hain't," said I. The name "Genevieve" helped me a little in this deceit.

"You haven't heard any of the people on the road speak of this wandering girl, have you?" asked Elder Thorndyke.

"No," I answered; "and I guess if any of them had seen her they'd have mentioned it, wouldn't they?"

"And you haven't seen any lone girl or woman at all, even at a distance?" inquired Grandma Thorndyke.

"If she passed me," I said, turning and twisting to keep from telling an outright lie, "it was while I was camped last night. I camped quite a little ways from the track."

"She has wandered off upon the trackless prairie!" exclaimed Grandma Thorndyke. "God help her!"

"He will protect her," said the elder piously.

"Maybe she met some one going west," I suggested, rather truthfully, I thought, "that took her in. She may be going back west with some one."

"Mr. Gowdy told us back in Independence," returned Elder Thorndyke, "that he had inquired of every outfit he met from the time she left him clear back to that place; and he overtook the only two teams on that whole stretch of road that were going east. It is hard to understand. It's a mystery."

"Was he going on east?" I asked—and I thought I heard a stir in the bed back of me as I waited for the answer.

"No," said the elder, "he is coming back this way, hunting high and low for her. I have no doubt he will find her. She can not have reached a point much farther east than this. She is sure to be found somewhere be-

tween here and Independence—or within a short distance
of here. There is nothing dangerous in the weather, the
wild animals, or anything, but the bewilderment of being
lost and the lack of food. God will not allow her to be
lost."

"I guess not," said I, thinking of the fate which led
me to my last night's camp, and of Gowdy's search having missed me as he rode by in the night.

They drove on, leaving us standing by the roadside.
Virginia crept forward and peeked over the back of the
seat after them until they disappeared over a hillock.
Then she began begging me to go where Gowdy could
not find us. He would soon come along, she said, with
that tool of his, Pinck Johnson, searching high and low
for her as that man had said. Everybody would help
him but me. I was all the friend she had. Even those
two good people who were inquiring were helping
Gowdy. I must drive where he could not find us. I
must!

"He can't take you from me," I declared, "unless you
want to go!"

"What can you do?" she urged wildly. "You are
too young to stand in his way. Nobody can stand in his
way. Nobody ever did! And they are two to one. Let
us hide! Let us hide!"

"I can stand in anybody's way," I said, "if I want
to."

I was not really afraid of them if worst came to
worst, but I did see that it was two to one; so I thought
of evading the search, but the hiding of a team of four
cows and a covered wagon on the open Iowa prairie was
no easy trick. If I turned off the road my tracks would

show for half a mile. If once the problem of hiding my tracks was solved, the rest would be easy. I could keep in the hollows for a few miles until out of sight of the Ridge Road, and Gowdy might rake the wayside to his heart's content and never find us except by accident; but I saw no way of getting off the traveled way without advertising my flight. Of course Gowdy would follow up every fresh track because it was almost the only thing he could do with any prospect of striking the girl's trail. I thought these things over as I drove on westward. I quieted her by saying that I had to think it out.

It was a hot afternoon by this time, and looked like a stormy evening. The clouds were rolling up in the north and west in lofty thunderheads, pearl-white in the hot sun, with great blue valleys and gorges below, filled with shadows. Virginia, in a fever of terror, spent a part of her time looking out at the hind-end of the wagon-cover for Gowdy and Pinck Johnson, and a part of it leaning over the back of the seat pleading with me to leave the road and hide her. Presently the clouds touched the sun, and in a moment the day grew dark. Far down near the horizon I could see the black fringe of the falling rain under the tumbling clouds, and in a quarter of an hour the wind began to blow from the storm, which had been mounting the sky fast enough to startle one. The storm-cloud was now ripped and torn by lightning, and deep rumbling peals of thunder came to our ears all the time louder and nearer. The wind blew sharper, and whistled shrilly through the rigging of my prairie schooner, there came a few drops of rain, then a scud of finer spray: and then the whole plain to the northwest turned white with a driving sheet of water which came on, swept over us, and blotted everything from sight in a great commingling of wind, water, fire and thunder.

Virginia cowered on the bed, throwing the quilt over her. My cattle turned their rumps to the storm and stood heads down, the water running from their noses, tails and bellies, and from the bows and yokes. I had stopped them in such a way as to keep us as dry as possible, and tried to cheer the girl up by saying that this wasn't bad, and that it would soon be over. In half an hour the rain ceased, and in an hour the sun was shining again, and across the eastern heavens there was displayed a beautiful double rainbow, and a faint trace of a third.

"That means hope," I said.

She looked at the wonderful rainbow and smiled a little half-smile.

"It doesn't mean hope," said she, "unless you can think out some way of throwing that man off our track."

"Oh," I answered, with the brag that a man likes to use when a helpless woman throws herself on his resources, "I'll find some way if I make up my mind I don't want to fight them."

"You mustn't think of that," said she. "You are too smart to be so foolish. See how well you answered the questions of that man and woman."

"And I didn't lie, either," said I, after getting under way again.

"Wouldn't you lie," said she, "for me?"

It was, I suppose, only a little womanly probe into

character; but it thrilled me in a way the poor girl could not have supposed possible.

"I would do anything for you," said I boldly; "but I'd a lot rather fight than lie."

3

The cloud-burst had flooded the swales, and across the hollows ran broad sheets of racing water. I had crossed two or three of these, wondering whether I should be able to ford the next real watercourse, when we came to a broad bottom down the middle of which ran a swift shallow stream which rose over the young grass. For a few rods the road ran directly down this casual river of flood water, and as I looked back it all at once came into my mind that I might follow this flood and leave no track; so instead of swinging back into the road I took instantly the important resolution to leave the Ridge. By voice and whip I turned my cattle down the stream to the south, and for a mile I drove in water half-hub deep.

Looking back I saw that I left no trace except where two lines of open water showed through the grass on the high spots where cattle and wheels had passed, and I knew that in an hour the flood would run itself off and wipe out even this trace. I felt a sense of triumph, and mingled with this was a queer thrill that set my hands trembling at the consciousness that the prairie had closed about me and this girl with the milk-white neck and the fire in her hair who had asked me if I would not even lie "for her."

We wound down the flooded swale, we left the Ridge Road quite out of sight, we finally drew up out of

the hollow and took to the ridges and hog-backs making
a new Ridge Road for ourselves. Nowhere in sight was
there the slightest trace of humanity or human settlement. We were alone. Still bearing south I turned
westwardly, after rolling up the covers to let in the drying wind. I kept looking back to see if we were followed;
for now I was suddenly possessed of the impulse to hide,
like a thief making for cover with stolen goods. Virginia, wearied out with the journey, the strain of her
escape, and the nervous tension, was lying on the couch,
often asking me if I saw any one coming up from behind.

The country was getting more rolling and broken as
we made our way down toward the Cedar River, or
some large creek making into it—but, of course, journeying without a map or chart I knew nothing about the lay
of the land or the watercourses. I knew, though, that I
was getting into the breaks of a stream. Finally, in the
gathering dusk I saw ahead of me the rounded crowns of
trees; and pretty soon we entered one of those beautiful
groves of hardwood timber that were found at wide dis-
tances along the larger prairie streams—I remember
many of them and their names, Buck Grove, Cole's
Grove, Fifteen Mile Grove, Hickory Grove, Crabapple
Grove, Marble's Grove, but I never knew the name of
this, the shelter toward which we had been making. I
drove in between scattered burr oaks like those of the
Wisconsin oak openings, and stopped my cattle in an
open space densely sheltered by thickets of crabapple,
plum and black-haw, and canopied by two spreading
elms. Virginia started up, ran to the front of the wagon
and looked about.

"Where are we?" she asked.

"This is our hiding-place," I replied.

"But that man—won't he follow our tracks?"

"We didn't leave any tracks," I said.

"How could we come without leaving tracks?" she queried, standing close to me and looking up into my face.

"Did you notice," said I, "that for miles we drove in the water—back there on the prairie after the rain?"

"Yes."

"We drove in the water when we left the road, and we left no tracks. Not even an Indian could track us. We can't be tracked. We've lost Gowdy—forever."

I thought at first that she was going to throw her arms about my neck; but instead she took both my hands and pressed them in a long clasp. It was the first time she had touched me, or shown emotion toward me—emotion of the sort for which I was now eagerly longing. I did not return her pressure. I merely let her hold my hands until she dropped them. I wanted to do a dozen things, but there is nothing stronger than the unbroken barriers of a boy's modesty—barriers strong as steel, which once broken down become as though they never were; while a woman even in her virgin innocence, is always offering unconscious invitation, always revealing ways of seeming approach, always giving to the stalled boy arguments against his bashfulness—arguments which may prove absurd or not when he acts upon them. It is the way of a maid with a man, Nature's way—but a perilous way for such a time and such a situation.

That night we sat about the tiny camp-fire and talked. She told me of her life in Kentucky, of her grief at the loss of her sister, of many simple things; and I told her of my farm—a mile square—of my plans, of my life on the canal—which seemed to impress her as it had Rowena Fewkes as a very adventurous career. I was sure she was beginning to like me; but of one thing I did not tell her. I did not mention my long unavailing search for my mother, nor the worn shoe and the sad farewell letter in the little iron-bound trunk in the wagon. I searched for tales which would make of me a man; but when it grew dark I put out the fire. I was not afraid of Buck Gowdy's finding us; but I did not want any one to discover us. And that night I drew out the loads of chicken shot from my gun and reloaded it with buckshot.

I could not sleep. After Virginia had lain down in the wagon, I walked about silently so as not to rouse her, prowling like a wolf. I crept to the side of the wagon and listened for her breathing; and when I heard it my hands trembled, and my heart pounded in my breast. All the things through which I had lived without partaking of them came back into my mind. I thought of what I heard every day on the canal—that all women were alike; that they existed only for that sort of companionship with men with which my eyes were so ignorantly familiar; that all their protestations and refusals were for effect only; that a man need only to be a man, to know what he wanted, and conquer it. And I felt rising in me like a tide the feeling that I was now a man. The reader who has believed of me that I passed through that canal life unspotted by its vileness has asked too much of me. The thing was not possible. I now thought of the irregular companionships of that old time as inexplicable no longer. They were the things for which men lived—the inevitable things for every real man. Only this which agitated me so terribly was different from them—no matter what happened, it would be pure and blameless—for it would be us!

4

I suppose it may have been midnight or after, when I heard a far-off splashing sound in the creek far above us. At first I thought of buffalo—though there were none in Iowa so far as I knew at that time—and only a few deer or bear; but finally, as the sound, which was clearly that of much wading, drew even with my camp, I began to hear the voices of men—low voices, as if even in that wilderness the speakers were afraid of being overheard.

"I'm always lookin'," said one, "to find some of these damned movers campin' in here when we come in with a raise."

"If I find any," said another, "they will be nepoed, damned quick."

This, I knew—I had heard plenty of it—was the lingo of thieves and what the story-writers call bandits—though we never knew until years afterward that we had in Iowa a distinct class which we should have called bandits, but knew it not. They stole horses, dealt in counterfeit money, and had scattered all over the West from Ohio to the limits of civilization a great number of "stations" as they called them where any man "of the right stripe" might hide either himself or his unlawful or stolen goods. "A raise" was stolen property. "A sight" was a prospect for a robbery, and to commit it was, to "raise the sight," or if it was a burglary or a highway robbery, the man robbed was "raked down."

A man killed was "nepoed"—a word which many new settlers in Wisconsin got from the Indians.*

In a country in which horses constitute the means of communication, the motive power for the farm and the most easily marketable form of property, the stealing of horses was the commonest sort of crime; and where the population was so sparse and unorganized, and unprovided with means of sending news abroad, horse-stealing, offering as it did to the criminally inclined a ready way of making an easy living, gradually grew into an occupation which flourished, extended into other forms of crime, had its connections with citizens who were supposed to be honest, entered our politics, and finally was the cause of a terrible crisis in the affairs of Monterey County, and, indeed, of other counties in Iowa as well as in Illinois.

I softly reached for my shotgun, and then lay very quiet, hoping that the band would pass our camp by. There were three men as I made them out, each riding one horse and leading another. They had evidently made their way into the creek at some point higher up, and were wading down-stream so as to leave no trail. Cursing as their mounts plunged into the deep holes in the high water, calling one another and their steeds the vilest of names seemingly as a matter of ordinary conversation, they went on down-stream and out of hearing. It did not take long for even my slow mind to see that they had come to this grove as I had done, for the

---

*This bit of frontier argot was rather common in the West in the 'fifties. The reappearance in the same sense of "napoo" for death in the armies of the Allies in France is a little surprising.—G. v. d. M.

purpose of hiding, nor to realize that it might be very unsafe for us to be detected in any discovery of these men in possession of whatever property they might have seized. It did not seem probable that we should be "nepoed"—but, after all, why not? Dead men tell no tales, cattle as well as merchandise were salable; and as for Virginia, I could hardly bring myself to look in the face the dangers to which she might be exposed in this worst case which I found myself conjuring up.

I listened intently for any sound of the newcomers, but everything was as silent as it had been before they had passed like evil spirits of the night; and from this fact I guessed that they had made camp farther down-stream among the trees. I stepped to the back of the wagon, and putting in my hand I touched the girl's hair. She took my hand in hers, and then dropped it.

"What is it?" she whispered.

"Don't be scared," I said, "but be very still. Some men just went by, and I'm afraid they are bad."

"Is it that man?" she asked.

"No," said I, "strangers—bad characters. I want them to go on without knowing we're here."

She seemed rather relieved at that, and told me that she was not frightened. Then she asked me where they went. I told her, and said that when it got lighter I meant to creep after them and see if they were still in the grove.

"Don't leave me," said she. "I reckon I'm a little frightened, after all, and it's very lonesome in here all alone. Please get into the wagon with me!"

I said nothing. Instead I sat for some time on the wagon-tongue and asked myself what I should do, and what she meant by this invitation. At last I started up, and trembling like a man climbing the gallows, I climbed into the wagon. There, sitting in the spring seat in the gown she had worn yesterday, with her little shoes on the dashboard, sat Virginia trying to wrap herself in the buffalo-robe.

I folded it around her and took my seat by her side. With scarcely a whisper between us we sat there and watched the stars wheel over to the west and down to their settings. At last I felt her leaning over against my shoulder, and found that she was asleep; and softly putting my arms about her outside the warm buffalo-robe, I held her sleeping like a baby until the shrill roundelays of the meadow-larks told me it was morning.

Then after taking away my arms I awakened her.

CHAPTER X

VIRGINIA opened her eyes and smiled at me. I think this was the first time that she had given me more than just a trace of a smile; but now she smiled, a very sweet winning smile; and getting spryly out of the wagon she said that she had been a lazy and useless passenger all the time she had been with me, and that from then on she was going to do the cooking. I told her that I wasn't going to let her do it, that I was strong and liked to cook; and I stammered and blundered when I tried to hint that I liked cooking for her. She looked very dense at this and insisted that I should build the fire, and show her where the things were; and when I had done so she pinned back her skirts and went about the work in a way that threw me into a high fever.

"You may bring the new milk," said she, "and by that time I'll have a fine breakfast for you."

When the milk was brought, breakfast was still a little behindhand, but she would not let me help. Anyhow, I felt in spite of my talk that I wanted to do some other sort of service for her: I wanted to show off, to prove myself a protector, to fight for her, to knock down or drive off her foes and mine; and as I saw the light smoke curling up through the tree-tops I asked myself where those men were who had made their way past us

181

in such a dark and secret sort of way and with so much bad talk back there in the middle of the night. I wondered if they had camped where they could see the smoke of our fire, or hear our voices or the other sounds we made.

I almost wished that they might. I had now in a dim, determined, stubborn way claimed this girl in my heart for my own; and I felt without really thinking of it, that I could best foreclose my lien by defeating all comers before I dragged her yielding to my cave. It is the way of all male animals—except spiders, perhaps, and bees—and a male animal was all that I was that morning. I picked up my gun and told her that I must find out where those men were before breakfast.

"No, no!" said she anxiously, "don't leave me! They might shoot you—and—then—"

I smiled disdainfully.

"If there's any shooting to be done, I'll shoot first. I won't let them see me, though; but I must find out what they are up to. Wait and keep quiet. I'll soon be back."

I knew that I should find their horses' hoof-marks at whatever place they had left the stream; and I followed the brook silently, craftily and slowly, like a hunter trailing a wild beast, examining the bank of soft black rooty earth for their tracks. Once or twice I passed across open spaces in the grove. Here I crept on my belly through the brush and weeds shoving my gun along ahead of my body.

My heart beat high. I never for a moment doubted the desperate character of the men, and in this I think I showed good judgment; for what honest horsemen

would have left the Ridge Road, or if any honest
purpose had drawn them away, what honest men would
have forced their horses to wade in the channel of a swollen stream in the middle of the night? They must have
been trying to travel without leaving tracks, just as I had
done. Their talk showed them to be bad characters, and
their fox-like actions proved the case against them. So I
crawled forward believing fully that I should be in
danger if they once found out that I had uncovered their
lurking-place. I carefully kept from making any thrash-
ing or swishing of boughs, any crackling of twigs, or
from walking with a heavy footfall; and I wondered more
and more as I neared what I knew must be the other
end of the grove, why they had not left the water and
made camp. For what other purpose had they come
to this patch of woods?

At last I heard the stamping of horses, and I lay
still for a while and peered all about me for signs of the
animals or their possessors. I moved slowly, then,
so as to bring first this open space in line with my eyes,
and then that, until, crawling like a lizard, I found my
men. They were lying on the ground, wrapped in
blankets, all asleep, very near the other end of the grove.
In the last open spot of the timber, screened from view
from the prairie by clumps of willows and other bushes,
were six horses, picketed for grazing. There were two
grays, a black, two bays and a chestnut sorrel—the latter
clearly a race-horse. They were all good horses. There
were rifles leaning against the trees within reach of the
sleeping men; and from under the coat which one of them
was using for a pillow there stuck out the butt of a navy
revolver.

Something—perhaps it was that consciousness which horses have of the approach of other beings, scent, hearing, or a sense of their own which we can not understand —made the chestnut race-horse lift his head and nicker. One of the men rose silently to a sitting posture, and reached for his rifle. For a moment he seemed to be looking right at me; but his eyes passed on, and he carefully examined every bit of foliage and every ant-hill and grass-mound, and all the time he strained his ears for sounds. I held my breath. At last he lay down again; but in a few minutes he got up, and woke the others.

This was my first sight of Bowie Bushyager. Everybody in Monterey County, and lots of other people will remember what the name of Bowie Bushyager once meant; but it meant very little more than that of his brother, Pitt Bushyager, who got up, grumbling and cursing when Bowie shook him awake. Bowie was say twenty-eight then, and a fine specimen of a man in build and size. He was six feet high, had a black beard which curled about his face, and except for his complexion, which was almost that of an Indian, his dead-black eye into which you could see no farther than into a bullet, and for the pitting of his face by smallpox, he would have been handsome.

"Shut up!" said he to his brother Pitt. "It's time we're gittin' our grub and pullin' out."

Pitt was even taller than Bowie, and under twenty-five in years. His face was smooth-shaven except for a short, curly black mustache and a little goatee under his mouth. His eyes were larger than Bowie's and deep brown, his hair curled down over his rolling collar, and he moved with an air of ease and grace that were in contrast with the slow power of Bowie. There was no doubt of it—Pitt Bushyager was handsome in a rough, daredevil sort of way.

I am describing them, not from the memory of that morning, but because I knew them well afterward. I knew all the Bushyager boys, and their father and mother and sisters; and in spite of everything, I rather liked both Pitt and Claib. Bowie was a forbidding fellow, and Asher, who was between Bowie and Pitt in age, while he was as big and strong as any of them, was the gentlest man I ever saw in his manners. He did more of the planning than Bowie did. Claiborne Bushyager was about my own age; while Forrest was older than Bowie. He was always able to convince people that he was not a member of the gang, and now, an old white-haired, soft-spoken man, still owns the original Bushyager farm, with two hundred acres added, where I must confess he has always made enough money by good farming to account for all the property he has.

These men were an important factor in the history of Monterey County for many years, and I knew all of them well; but had they known that I saw them that morning in the grove I guess I should not have lived to write this history; though it was years before the people came to believing such things of them. The third man in the grove I never saw again. Judging from what we learned afterward, I think it is safe to say that this Unknown was one of the celebrated Bunker gang of bandits, whose headquarters were on the Iowa River somewhere between Eldora and Steamboat Rock, in Hardin County. He was a small man with light hair and eyes, and kept both the Bushyagers on one side of him all the time I had them in view. When he spoke it was almost in a whisper, and he kept darting sharp glances from side to side all the time, and especially at the Bushyagers. When they left he rode the black horse and led one of the grays. I know, because I crept back to my own camp, took my breakfast with Virginia, and then spied on the Bushyagers until dinner-time. After dinner I still found them there arguing about the policy of starting on or waiting until night. Bowie wanted to start; but finally the little light-haired man had his way; and they melted away across the knolls to the west just after sunset. I returned with all the air of having driven them off, and ate my third meal cooked by Virginia Royall.

2

I do not know how long we camped in this lonely little forest; for I lost reckoning as to time. Once in a while Virginia would ask me when I thought it would be safe to go on our way; and I always told her that it would be better to wait.

I had forgotten my farm. When I was with her, I could not overcome my bashfulness, my lack of experience, my ignorance of every manner of approach except that of the canallers to the water-side women, with which I suddenly found myself as familiar through memory as with the route from my plate to my mouth; that way I had fully made up my mind to adopt; but something held me back.

I now began leaving the camp and from some lurking-place in the distance watching her as a cat watches a bird. I lived over in my mind a thousand times the attack I would make upon her defense, and her yielding after a show of resistance. I became convinced at last that she would not make even a show of resistance; that she was probably wondering what I was waiting for, and making up her mind that, after all, I was not much of a man.

I saw her one evening, after looking about to see if she was observed, take off her stockings and go wading in the deep cool water of the creek—and I lay awake at night wondering whether, after all, she had not known that I was watching her, and had so acted for my benefit—and then I left my tossed couch and creeping to the side of the wagon listened, trembling in every limb, with my ear to the canvas until I was able to make out her regular breathing only a few inches from my ear. And when in going away—as I always did, finally—I made a little noise which awakened her, she called and asked me if I had heard anything, I said no, and pacified her by saying that I had been awake and watching all the time. Then I despised myself for saying nothing more.

I constantly found myself despising my own decency. I felt the girl in my arms a thousand times as I had felt her for those delicious hours the night she had invited me to share the wagon with her, and we had sat in the spring seat wrapped in the buffalo-robe, as she slept with her head on my shoulder. I tormented myself by asking if she had really slept, or only pretended to sleep. Once away from her, once freed from the innocent look in her eyes, I saw in her behavior that night every advance which any real man might have looked for, as a signal to action. Why had I not used my opportunity to make her love me—to force from her the confession of her love? Had I not failed, not only in doing what I

would have given everything I possessed or ever hoped
to possess to have been able to do; but also had I not
failed in that immemorial duty which man owes to woman,
and which she had expected of me? Would she not laugh
at me with some more forceful man when she had found
him? Was she not scorning me even now?

I had heard women talk of greenhorns and backwoods
boys in those days when I had lived a life in which wom-
en played an important, a disturbing, and a baleful part
for every one but the boy who lived his strange life on the
tow-path or in the rude cabin; and now these outcast
women came back to me and through the very memories
of them poisoned and corrupted my nature. They peopled
my dreams, with their loud voices, their drunkenness,
their oaths, their obscenities, their lures, their tricks,
their awful counterfeit of love; and, a figure apart from
them in these dreams, partaking of their nature only so
far as I desired to have it so, walked Virginia Royall,
who had come to me across the prairie to escape a life
with Buckner Gowdy. But to the meaning of this fact I
shut the eye of my mind. I was I, and Gowdy was
Gowdy. It was no time for thought. Every moment I
pressed closer and closer to that action which I was sure
would have been taken by Eben Sproule, or Bill the
Sailor—the only real friends I had ever possessed.

We used to go fishing along the creek; and ate many
a savory mess of bullheads, sunfish and shiners, which I
prepared and cooked. We had butter, and the cows, eased
of the labors of travel, grew sleek and round, and gave us
plenty of milk. I saved for Virginia all the eggs laid by
my hens, except those used by her in the cooking. She
gave me the daintiest of meals; and I taught her to make

bread. To see her molding it with her strong small hands, was enough to have made me insane if I had had any sense left. She showed me how to make vinegar pies; and I failed in my pies made of the purple-flowered prairie oxalis; but she triumphed over me by using the deliciously acid leaves as a flavoring for sandwiches—we were getting our first experience as prairie-dwellers in being deprived of the common vegetable foods of the garden and forest. One day I cooked a delicious mess of cowslip greens with a ham-bone. She seemed to be happy; and I should have been if I had not made myself so miserable. I remember almost every moment of this time—so long ago.

One day as we were fishing we were obliged to clamber along the bank where a tree crowded us so far over the water that Virginia, in stooping to pass under the body of the tree, was about to fall; and I jumped down into the stream and caught her in my arms as she was losing her hold. I found her arms about my neck as she clung to me; and, standing in the water, I turned her about in my arms, rather roughly of necessity, caught one arm about her waist and the other under the hollows of her knees and held her so.

"Don't let me fall," she begged.

"I won't," I said—and I could say no more.

"You've got your feet all wet," said she.

"I don't care," I said—and stopped.

"How clumsy of me!" she exclaimed.

"It was a hard place to get around," said I.

"I hope you didn't lose the fish," said she.

"No," said I, "I dropped the string of them in the grass."

Now this conversation lasted a second, from one way of looking at it, and a very long time from another; and all the time I was standing there, knee-deep in the water, with Virginia's arms about my neck, her cheek almost against mine, one of my arms about her waist and the other under the hollows of her knees—and I had made no movement for putting her ashore.

"You're very strong," said she, "or you would have dropped me in the water."

"Oh," said I, "that's nothing"—and I pressed her closer.

"How will you get me back on land?" she asked; and really it was a subject which one might have expected to come up sooner or later.

I turned about with her and looked down-stream; then I turned back and looked up-stream; then I looked across to the opposite bank, at least six feet away; then I carried her up-stream for a few yards; then I started back down-stream.

"There's no good place there," said I—and I looked a long, long look into her eyes which happened to be scanning my face just then. She blushed rosily.

"Any place will do," she said. "Let me down right here where I can get the fish!"

And slowly, reluctantly, with great pains that she should not be scratched by briars, bitten by snakes, brushed by poison-ivy, muddied by the wet bank, or threatened with another fall, I put her down. She looked diligently in the grass for the fish, picked them up, and ran off to camp. After she had disappeared, I heard the bushes rustle, and looked up as I sat on the bank wringing the water from my socks and pouring it from my boots.

"Thank you for keeping me dry," said she. "You did it very nicely. And now you must stay in the wagon while I dry your socks and boots for you—you poor wet boy!"

3

She had not objected to my holding her so long; she rather seemed to like it; she seemed willing to go on camping here as long as I wished; she was wondering why I was so backward and so bashful; she was in my hands; why hold back? Why not use my power? If I did not I should make myself forever ridiculous to all men and to all women—who, according to my experience, were never in higher feather than when ridiculing some greenhorn of a boy. This thing must end. My affair with Virginia must be brought to a crisis and pushed to a decision. At once!

I wandered off again and from my vantage-point I began to watch her and gather courage from watching her. I could still feel her in my arms—so much more of a woman than I had at first suspected from seeing her about the camp. I could see her in my mind's eye wading the stream like a beautiful ghost. I could think of nothing but her all the time,—of her and the wild life of boats and backwoods harbors.

And at last I grew suddenly calm. I began to laugh at myself for my lack of decision. I would carefully consider the matter, and that night I would act.

I took my gun and wandered off across the prairie after a few birds for our larder. There were upland plover in great plenty; and before I had been away from the camp fifteen minutes I had several in my pockets. It was early in the afternoon; but instead of walking back

to camp at once I sat down on a mound at the mouth of
the old den of a wolf or badger and laid my plans; much
as a wolf or badger might have done.

Then I went back. The sun was shining with slanting mid-afternoon rays down among the trees by the
creek. I looked for Virginia; but she was not about the
wagon, neither sitting in the spring seat, nor on her box
by the fire, nor under her favorite crabapple-tree. I
looked boldly in the wagon, without the timid tapping
which I had always used to announce my presence—for
what did I care now for her privacy?—but she was not
there. I began searching for her along the creek in the
secluded nooks which abounded, and at last I heard her
voice.

I was startled. To whom could she be speaking? I
would have nobody about, now. I would show him,
whoever he was! This grove was mine as long as I
wanted to stay there with my girl. The blood rose to my
head as I went quietly forward until I could see Virginia.

She was alone! She had taken a blanket from the
wagon and spread it on the ground upon the grass under
a spreading elm, and scattered about on it were articles
of clothing which she had taken from her satchel—that
satchel to which the poor child had clung so tightly while
she had come to my camp across the prairie on the Ridge
Road that night—which now seemed so long ago.
There was a dress on which she had been sewing; for the
needle was stuck in the blanket with the thread still in the
garment; but she was not working. She had in her lap as
she sat cross-legged on the blanket, a little wax doll to
which she was babbling and talking as little girls do.
She had taken off its dress, and was carefully wiping its

face, telling it to shut its eyes, saying that mama wouldn't hurt it, asking it if she wasn't a bad mama to keep it shut up all the time in that dark satchel, asking it if it wasn't afraid in the dark, assuring it that mama wouldn't let anybody hurt it—and all this in the sweetest sort of baby-talk. And then she put its dress on, gently smoothed its hair, held it for a while against her bosom as she swayed from side to side telling it to go to sleep, hummed gently a cradle song, and put it back in the satchel as a mother might put her sleeping baby in its cradle.

I crept silently away.

It was dark when I returned to camp, and she had supper ready and was anxiously awaiting me. She ran to me and took my hand affectionately.

"What kept you so long?" she asked earnestly. "I have been anxious. I thought something must have happened to you!"

And as we approached the fire, she looked in my face, and cried out in astonishment.

"Something has happened to you. You are as white as a sheet. What is it? Are you sick? What shall I do if you get sick!"

"No," I said, "I am not sick. I am all right—now."

"But something has happened," she insisted. "You are weak as well as pale. Let me do something for you. What was it?"

"A snake," I said, for an excuse. "A rattlesnake. It struck at me and missed. It almost struck me. I'll be all right now."

The longer I live the surer I am that I told her very nearly the truth.

That night we sat up late and talked. She was only a dear little child, now, with a bit of the mother in her. She was really affectionate to me, more so than ever before, and sometimes I turned cold as I thought of how her affection might have been twisted into deviltry had it not been so strangely brought home to me that she was a child, with a good deal of the mother in her. I turned cold as I thought of her playing with her doll while I had been out on the prairie laying poison plots against her innocence, her defenselessness, her trust in me.

Why, she was like my mother! I had not thought of my mother for days. When she had been young like Virginia, she must have been as beautiful; and she had played with dolls; but never except while she was an innocent child, as Virginia now was.

For the first time I talked of mother to Virginia. I told her of my mother's goodness to me while Rucker was putting me out to work in the factory—and Virginia grew hot with anger at Rucker, and very pitiful of the poor little boy going to work before daylight and coming home after dark. I told her of my running away, and of my life on the canal, with all the beautiful things I had seen and the interesting things I had done, leaving out the fighting and the bad things. I told her of how I had lost my mother, and my years of search for her, ending at that unmarked grave by the lake. Virginia's eyes shone with tears and she softly pressed my hand.

I took from my little iron-bound trunk that letter which I had found in the old hollow apple-tree, and we read it over together by the flickering light of a small fire which I kindled for the purpose; and from the very bottom of the trunk, wrapped in a white handkerchief which I had bought for this use, I took that old worn-out shoe which I had found that dark day at Tempe—and I began telling Virginia how it was that it was so run over, and worn in such a peculiar way.

My mother had worked so hard for me that she had had a good deal of trouble with her feet—and such a flood of sorrow came over me that I broke down and cried. I cried for my mother, and for joy at being able to think of her again, and for guilt, and with such a mingling of feeling that finally I started to rush off into the darkness—but Virginia clung to me and wiped away my tears and would not let me go. She said she was afraid to be left alone, and wanted me with her—and that I was a good boy. She didn't wonder that my mother wanted to work for me—it must have been almost the only comfort she had.

"If she had only lived," I said, "so I could have made a home for her!"

"She knows all about that," said Virginia; "and when she sees you making a home for some one else, how happy it will make her!"

Virginia was the older of the two, now, the utterer of words of comfort; and I was the child. The moon rose late, but before we retired it flooded the grove with light. The wolves howled on the prairie, and the screech-owls cried pitifully in the grove; but I was happy. I told Virginia that we must break camp in the morning and move on. I must get to my land, and begin making that home. She sighed; but she did not protest. She would always remember this sojourn in the grove, she said; she had felt so safe! She hardly knew what she would do when we reached the next settlement; but she must think out

some way to get back to Kentucky. When the time came
for her to retire, I carried her to the wagon and lifted her
in—and then went to my own bed to sleep the first sound
sweet sleep I had enjoyed for days. The air had been
purified by the storm.

CHAPTER XI

IN DEFENSE OF THE PROPRIETIES

VIRGINIA and I arrived in Waterloo about two days after we left the Grove of Destiny, as my granddaughter Gertrude insists on calling the place at which we camped after we left Independence. We went in a sort of rather-guess way back to the Ridge Road, very happy, talking to each other about ourselves all the while, and admiring everything we saw along the way.

The wild sweet-williams were in bloom, now, and scattered among them were the brilliant orange-colored puccoons; and the grass even on the knolls was long enough to wave in the wind like a rippling sea. It was a cool and sunny spell of weather, with fleecy clouds chasing one another up from the northwest like great ships under full sail running wing-and-wing before the northwest wind which blew strong day and night. It was a new sort of weather to me—the typical high-barometer weather of the prairies after a violent "low." The driving clouds on the first day were sometimes heavy enough to spill over a scud of rain (which often caught Virginia like a cold splash from a hose), and were whisked off to the southeast in a few minutes, followed by a brilliant burst of sunshine—and all the time the shadows of the clouds raced over the prairie in big and little bluish patches speeding forever onward over a groundwork of green and gold dotted with the white and purple and yellow of the flowers.

We were now on terms of simple trust and confidence. We played. We bet each other great sums of money as to whether or not the rain-scud coming up in the west would pass over us, or miss us, or whether or not the shadow of a certain cloud would pass to the right or the left. People with horse teams who were all the time passing us often heard us laughing, and looked at us and smiled, waving their hands, as Virginia would cry out, "I won that time!" or "You drove slow, just to beat me!" or "Well, I lost, but you owe me twenty-five thousand dollars yet!"

Once an outfit with roan horses and a light wagon stopped and hailed us. The woman, sitting by her husband, had been pointing at us and talking to him.

"Right purty day," he said.

"Most of the time," I answered; for it had just sloshed a few barrels of water from one of those flying clouds and forced us to cover ourselves up.

"Where's your folks?" he asked.

"We ain't too old to travel alone," I replied; "but we'll catch up with the young folks at Waterloo!"

He laughed and whipped up his team.

"Go it while you're young!" he shouted as he went out of hearing.

We were rather an unusual couple, as any one could see; though most people doubtless supposed that there were others of our party riding back under the cover. Virginia had not mentioned Buckner Gowdy since we camped in the Grove of Destiny; and not once had she looked with her old look of terror at an approaching or

overtaking team, or scuttled back into the load to keep
from being seen. I guess she had come to believe in the
sufficiency of my protection.

2

Waterloo was a town of seven or eight years of age—
a little straggling village on the Red Cedar River, as it
was then called, building its future on the growth of the
country and the water-power of the stream. It was
crowded with seekers after "country," and its land dealers and bankers were looking for customers. It seemed
to be a strong town in money, and I had a young man
pointed out to me who was said to command unlimited
capital and who was associated with banks and land
companies in Cedar Rapids and Sioux City,—I suppose
he was a Greene, a Weare, a Graves, a Johnson or a
Lusch. Many were talking of the Fort Dodge country,
and of the new United States Land Office which was
just then on the point of opening at Fort Dodge. They
tried to send me to several places where land could be
bought cheaply, in the counties between the Cedar and
the Iowa Rivers, and as far west as Webster County;
but when I told them that I had bought land they at
once lost interest in me.

We camped down by the river among the trees, and
it was late before we were free to sleep, on account of
the visits we received from movers and land men; but
finally the camp-fires died down, the songs ceased, the
music of accordions and fiddles was heard no more, and
the camp of emigrants became silent.

Virginia bade me good night, and I rolled up in my
blankets under the wagon. I began wondering, after the

questions which had been asked as to our relationship, just what was to be the end of this strange journey of the big boy and the friendless girl. We were under some queer sort of suspicion—that was clear. Two or three wives among the emigrants had tried to get a word with Virginia in private; and some of the men had grinned and winked at me in a way that I should have been glad to notice according to my old canal habits; but I had sense enough to see that that would never do.

Virginia was now as free from care as if she had been traveling with her brother; and what could I say? What did I want to say? By morning I had made up my mind that I would take her to my farm and care for her there, regardless of consequences—and I admit that I was not clear as to the proprieties. Every one was a stranger to every one else in this country. Whose business was it anyhow? Doctor Bliven and his companion—I had worked out a pretty clear understanding of their case by this time—were settling in the new West and leaving their past behind them. Who could have anything to say against it if I took this girl with me to my farm, cared for her, protected her; and gave her the home that nobody else seemed ready to give?

"Do you ever go to church?" asked Virginia. "It's Sunday."

"Is there preaching here to-day?" I asked.

"Don't you hear the bell?" she inquired.

"Let's go!" said I.

We were late; and the heads of the people were bowed in prayer as we went in; so we stood by the door until the prayer was over. The preacher was Elder Thorndyke. I was surprised at seeing him because he

had told me that he and his wife were going to Monterey
Centre; but there he was, laboring with his text, speaking in a halting manner, and once in a while bogging
down in a dead stop out of which he could not pull himself without giving a sort of honk like a wild goose. It
was his way. I never sat under a preacher who had better reasoning powers or a worse way of reasoning.
Down in front of him sat Grandma Thorndyke, listening
intently, and smiling up to him whenever he got in hub-
deep; but at the same time her hands were clenched into
fists in her well-darned black-silk gloves.

I did not know all this then, for her back was toward
us; but I saw it so often afterward! It was that honking
habit of the elder's which had driven them, she often told
me, from New England to Ohio, then to Illinois, and finally out to Monterey Centre. The new country caught
the halt like Elder Thorndyke, the lame like the
Fewkeses, the outcast like the Bushyagers and the Blivens, the blind like me, the far-seeing like N. V. Creede,
the prophets like old Dunlap the Abolitionist and Amos
Thatcher, and the great drift of those who felt a drawing toward the frontier like iron filings to a magnet, or
came with the wind of emigration like tumble-weeds before the autumn blast.

I remembered that when Virginia was with me back
there by the side of the road that first day, Elder
Thorndyke and his wife had come by inquiring for
her; and I did not quite relish the idea of being
found here with her after all these long days; so when
church was out I took Virginia by the hand and tried to
get out as quickly as possible; but when we reached the
door, there were Elder Thorndyke and grandma shaking

hands with the people, and trying to be pastoral; though it was clear that they were as much strangers as we. The elder was filling the vacant pulpit that day by mere chance, as he told me; but I guess he was really candidating a little after all. It would have been a bad thing for Monterey Centre if he had received the call.

They greeted Virginia and me with warm handclasps and hearty inquiries after our welfare; and we were passing on, when Grandma Thorndyke headed us off and looked me fairly in the face.

"Why," said she, "you're that boy! Wait a minute."

She stepped over and spoke to her husband, who seemed quite in the dark as to what she was talking about. She pointed to us—and then, in despair, she came back to us and asked us if we wouldn't wait until the people were gone, as she wanted us to meet her husband.

"Oh, yes," said Virginia, "we'll be very glad to."

"Let us walk along together," said grandma, after the elder had joined us. "Ah—this is my husband, Mr. Thorndyke, Miss———"

"Royall," said Virginia, "Virginia Royall. And this is Jacob Vandemark."

"Where do you live?" asked grandma.

"I'm going out to my farm in Monterey County," I said; "and Virginia is—is—riding with me a while."

"We are camping," said Virginia, smiling, "down by the river. Won't you come to dinner with us?"

3

Grandma ran to some people who were waiting, I suppose, to take them to the regular minister's Sunday dinner, and seemed to be making some sort of plea to be excused. What it could have been I have no idea; but I suspect it must have been because of the necessity of saving souls; some plea of duty; anyhow she soon returned, and with her and the elder we walked in silence down to the grove where our wagon stood among the trees, with my cows farther up-stream picketed in the grass.

"Just make yourselves comfortable," said I; "while I get dinner."

"And," said the elder, "I'll help, if I may."

"You're company," I said.

"Please let me," he begged; "and while we work we'll talk."

In the meantime Grandma Thorndyke was turning Virginia inside out like a stocking, and looking for the seamy side. She carefully avoided asking her about our whereabouts for the last few days, but she scrutinized Virginia's soul and must have found it as white as snow. She found out how old she was, how friendless she was, how—but I rather think not why—Virginia had run away from Buck Gowdy; and all that could be learned about me which could be learned without entering into details of our hiding from the world together all those days alone on the trackless prairie. That subject she avoided, though of course she must have had her own ideas about it. And after that, she came and helped me with the dinner, talking all the time in such a way as to draw me out as to my past. I told her of my life on the canal—and she looked distrustfully at me. I told her of my farm, and of how I got it; and that brought out the story of my long hunt for my mother, and of my finding of her unmarked grave. Of my relations with Virginia she seemed to want no information. By the time our dinner was over—one of my plentiful wholesome meals, with some lettuce and radishes and young onions I had bought the night before—we were chatting together like old friends.

"That was a better dinner," said the elder, "than we'd have had at Mr. Smith's."

"But Jacob, here," said grandma, "is not a deacon of the church."

"That doesn't lessen my enjoyment of the dinner," said the elder.

"No," said Grandma Thorndyke dryly, "I suppose not. But now let us talk seriously. This child"—taking Virginia's hand—"is the girl they were searching for back there along the road."

"Ah," said the elder.

"She had perfectly good reasons for running away," went on Grandma Thorndyke, "and she is not going back to that man. He has no claim upon her. He is not her guardian. He is only the man who married her sister—and as I firmly believe, killed her!"

"I wouldn't say that," said the elder.

"Now I calculate," said Grandma Thorndyke, "and unless I am corrected I shall so report—and I dare any one to correct me!—that this child"—squeezing Virginia's hand—"had taken refuge at some dwelling along the road, and that this morning—not later than this morning—as Jacob drove along into Waterloo he overtook Virginia walking into town where she was going to seek a position of some kind. So that you two children were together not longer than from seven this morning until just before church. You ought not to travel on the Sabbath!"

"No, ma'am," said I; for she was attacking me.

"Now we are poor," went on Grandma Thorndyke, "but we never have starved a winter yet; and we want a child like you to comfort us, and to help us—and we mustn't leave you as you are any longer. You must ride on with Mr. Thorndyke and me."

This to Virginia—who stretched out her hands to me, and then buried her face in them in Grandma Thorndyke's lap. She was crying so that she did not hear me when I asked:

"Why can't we go on as we are? I've got a farm. I'll take care of her!"

"Children!" snorted grandma. "Babes in the wood!"

I think she told the elder in some way without words to take me off to one side and talk to me; for he hummed and hawed, and asked me if I wouldn't show him my horses. I told him that I was driving cows, and went with him to see them. I now had six again, besides those I had left with Mr. Westervelt back along the road toward Dubuque; and it took me quite a while to explain to him how I had traded and traded along the road, first my two horses for my first cows, and then always giving one sound cow for two lame ones, until I had great riches for those days in cattle.

He thought this wonderful, and said that I was a second Job; and had every faculty for acquiring riches. I had actually made property while moving, an operation that was so expensive that it bankrupted many people. It was astonishing, he insisted; and began looking upon me with more respect—making property being the thing in which he was weakest, except for laying up treasures in Heaven. He was surprised, too, to learn that cows could be made draught animals. He had always thought of them as good for nothing but giving milk. In fact I found myself so much wiser than he was in the things we had been discussing that when he began to talk to me about Virginia and the impossibility of our going together as we had been doing, it marked quite a change in our relationship—he having been the scholar and I the teacher.

"Quite a strange meeting," said he, "between you and Miss Royall."

"Yes," said I, thinking it over, from that first wolf-hunted approach to my camp to our yesterday of clouds and sunshine; "I never had anything like it happen to me."

"Mrs. Thorndyke," said he, "is a mighty smart woman. She knows what'll do, and what won't do better than—than any of us."

I wasn't ready to admit this, and therefore said nothing.

"Don't you think so?" he asked.

"I do' know," I said, a little sullenly.

"A girl," said he, "has a pretty hard time in life if she loses her reputation."

Again I made no reply.

"You are just two thoughtless children," said he; "aren't you now?"

"She's nothing," said I, "but a little innocent child!"

"Now that's so," said he, "that's so; but after all she's old enough so that evil things might be thought of her—evil things might be said; and there'd be no answer to them, no answer. Why, she's a woman grown—a woman grown; and as for you, you're getting a beard. This won't do, you know; it is all right if there were just you and Miss Royall and my wife and me in the world; but you wouldn't think for a minute of traveling with this little girl the way you have been—the way you speak of doing, I mean—if you knew that in the future, when she must make her way in the world with nothing but her friends, this little boy-and-girl experience might take her friends from her; and when she will have nothing but her good name you don't want, and would not for the world have anything thoughtlessly done now, that might take her good name from her. You are too young to understand this as you will some day——"

"The trouble with me," I blurted out, "is that I've never had much to do with good women—only with my mother and Mrs. Fogg—and they could never have anything said against them—neither of them!"

"Where have you lived all your life?" he asked.

Then I told him of the way I had picked up my hat and come up instead of being brought up, of the women along the canal, of her who called herself Alice Rucker, of the woman who stole across the river with me—but I didn't mention her name—of as much as I could think of in my past history; and all the time Elder Thorndyke gazed at me with increasing interest, and with something the look we have in listening to tales of midnight murder and groaning ghosts. I must have been an astonishing sort of mystery to him. Certainly I was a castaway and an outcast to his ministerial mind; and boy as I was, he seemed to feel for me a sort of awed respect mixed up a little with horror.

"Heavenly Father!" he blurted out. "You have escaped as by the skin of your teeth."

"I do' know," said I.

"But don't you understand," he insisted, "that this trip has got to end here? Suppose your mother, when she was a child in fact, but a woman grown also, like Miss Royall, had been placed as she is with a boy of your age and one who had lived your life————"

"No," said I, "it won't do. You can have her!"

4

I really felt as if I was giving up something that had belonged to me. I felt the pangs of renunciation.

We walked back to the wagon in silence, and found Virginia and Grandma Thorndyke sitting on the spring seat with grandma's arm about the girl, with a handkerchief in her hand, just as if she had been wiping the tears from Virginia's eyes; but the girl was laughing and talking in a manner more lively than I had ever seen her exhibit. She was as happy, apparently, as I was gloomy and downcast.

I wanted the Thorndykes to go away so that I could have a farewell talk with Virginia; but they stayed on and stayed on, and finally, after dark, grandma rose with a look at Virginia which she seemed to understand, and they took my girl's satchel and all walked off together toward the tavern.

I sat down and buried my face in my hands, Virginia's good-by had been so light, so much like the parting of two mere strangers. And after all what was I to her but a stranger? She was of a different sort from me. She had lived in cities. She had a good education

—at least I thought so. She was like the Thorndykes—
city folks, educated people, who could have no use for a
clodhopper like me, a canal hand, a rough character.
And just as I had plunged myself into the deepest despair, I heard a light footfall, and Virginia knelt down
before me on the ground and pulled my hands from my
eyes.

"Don't cry," said she. "We'll see each other again.
I came back to bid you good-by, and to say that you've
been so good to me that I can't think of it without tears!
Good-by, Jacob!"

She lifted my face between her two hands, kissed me
the least little bit, and ran off. Back in the darkness I
saw the tall figure of Grandma Thorndyke, who seemed
to be looking steadily off into the distance. Virginia
locked arms with her and they went away leaving me
with my cows and my empty wagon—filled with the goods
in which I took so much pride when I left Madison.

With the first rift of light in the east I rose from my
sleepless bed under the wagon—I would not profane her
couch inside by occupying it—and yoked up my cattle.
Before noon I was in Cedar Falls; and from there west I
found the Ridge Road growing less and less a beaten
track owing to decreasing travel, but plainly marked by
stakes which those two pioneers had driven along the
way as I have said for the guidance of others in finding a
road which they had missed themselves.

We were developing citizenship and the spirit of
America. Those wagon loads of stakes cut on the Cedar
River in 1854 and driven in the prairie sod as guides for
whoever might follow showed forth the true spirit of the
American pioneer.

But I was in no frame of mind to realize this. I was drawing nearer and nearer my farm, but for a day or so this gave me no pleasure. My mind was on other things. I was lonelier than I had been since I found Rucker in Madison. I talked to no one—I merely followed the stakes—until one morning I pulled into a strange cluster of houses out on the green prairie, the beginning of a village. I drew up in front of its blacksmith shop and asked the name of the place. The smith lifted his face from the sole of the horse he was shoeing and replied, "Monterey Centre."

I looked around at my own county, stretching away in green waves on all sides of the brand-new village; which was so small that it did not interfere with the view. I had reached my own county! I had been a part of it on this whole wonderful journey, getting acquainted with its people, picking up the threads of its future, now its history.

Prior to this time I had been courting the country; now I was to be united with it in that holy wedlock which binds the farmer to the soil he tills. Out of this black loam was to come my own flesh and blood, and the bodies, and I believe, in some measure, the souls of my children. Some dim conception of this made me draw in a deep, deep breath of the fresh prairie air.

CHAPTER XII

THAT last night before I reached my "home town" of Monterey Centre, I had camped within two or three miles of the settlement. I forgot all that day to inquire where I was: so absent-minded was I with all my botheration because of losing Virginia. I was thinking all the time of seeing her again, wondering if I should ever see her alone or to speak to her, ashamed of my behavior toward her—in my thoughts at least—vexed because I had felt toward her, except for the last two or three days, things that made it impossible to get really acquainted and friendly with her. I was absorbed in the attempt to figure out the meaning of her friendly acts when we parted, especially her coming back, as I was sure she had, against the will of Grandma Thorndyke; and that kiss she had given me was a much greater problem than making time on my journey: I lived it over and over again a thousand times and asked myself what I ought to have done when she kissed me, and never feeling satisfied with myself for not doing more of something or other, I knew not what. It was well for me that my teams were way-wised so that they drove themselves. I could have made Monterey Centre easily that night; for it was only about eight o'clock by the sun next morning when I pulled up at the blacksmith shop, and was told by Jim Boyd, the smith, that I was in Monterey Centre.

And now I did not know what to do. I did not know where my land was, nor how to find out. Monterey Prairie was as blank as the sea, except for a few settlers' houses scattered about within a mile or two of the village. I sat scratching my head and gazing about me like a lunkhead while Boyd finished shoeing a horse, and had begun sharpening the lay of a breaking-plow—when up rode Pitt Bushyager on one of the horses he and his gang had had in the Grove of Destiny back beyond Waterloo.

I must have started when I saw him; for he glanced at me sharply and suspiciously, and his dog-like brown eyes darted about for a moment, as if the dog in him had scented game: then he looked at my jaded cows, at my muddy wagon, its once-white cover now weather-beaten and ragged, and at myself, a buttermilk-eyed, tow-headed Dutch boy with a face covered with down like a month-old gosling; and his eyes grew warm and friendly, as they usually looked, and his curly black mustache parted from his little black goatee with a winning smile. After he had turned his horse over to the smith, he came over and talked with me. He said he had seen cows broken to drive by the Pukes—as we used to call the Missourians—but never except by those who were so "pore" that they couldn't get horses, and he could see by my nice outfit, and the number of cows I had, that I could buy and sell some of the folks that drove horses. What was my idea in driving cows?

"They are faster than oxen," I said, "and they'll make a start in stock for me when I get on my farm; and they give milk when you're traveling. I traded my horses for my first cows, and I've been trading one sound cow for two lame ones all along the road. I've got some more back along the way."

"Right peart notion," said he. "I reckon you'll do for Iowa. Where you goin'?"

Then I explained about my farm, and my problem in finding it.

"Oh, that's easy!" said he. "Oh, Mr. Burns!" he called to a man standing in a doorway across the street. "Come over here, if you can make it suit. He's a land-locater," he explained to me. "Makes it a business to help newcomers like you to get located. Nice man, too."

By this time Henderson L. Burns had started across the street. He was dressed stylishly, and came with a sort of prance, his head up and his nostrils flaring like a Jersey bull's, looking as popular as a man could appear. We always called him "Henderson L." to set him apart from Hiram L. Burns, a lawyer that tried to practise here for a few years, and didn't make much of an out of it.

"Mr. Burns," said Pitt Bushyager, "this is Mr.——"

"Vandemark," said I: "Jacob Vandemark"—you see I did not know then that my correct name is Jacobus.

"Mine's Bushyager," said he, "Pitt Bushyager. Got a raft of brothers and sisters—so you'll know us better after a while. Mr. Burns, this is Mr. Vandemark."

"Glad to meet you, Mr. Vandemark," said Henderson L., flaring his nostrils, and shaking my hand till it ached. "Hope you're locating in Monterey County. Father with you?"

"No," said I, "I am alone in the world—and this outfit is all I've got."

"Nice outfit," said he. "Good start for a young fellow; and let me give you a word of advice. Settle in Monterey County, as close to Monterey Centre as you can get. People that drive through, hunting for the earthly paradise, are making a great mistake; for this is the garden spot of the garden of the world. This is practically, and will without a shadow of doubt be permanently the county-seat of the best county in Iowa, and that means the best in the known world. We are just the right distance from the river to make this the location of the best town in the state, and probably eventually the state capital. Land will increase in value by leaps and bounds. No stumps, no stones, just the right amount of rainfall—the garden spot of the West, Mr. Vandemark, the garden spot——"

"This boy," said Pitt Bushyager, "has land already entered. I told him you'd be able to show it to him."

"Land already entered?" he queried. "I don't seem to remember the name of Vandemark on the records. Sure it's in this county?"

I went back to the little flat package in the iron-bound trunk, found my deed, and gave it to him. He examined it closely.

"Not recorded," said he. "Out near Hell Slew, somewhere. Better let me take you over to the recorder's office, and have him send it in for record. Name of John Rucker on the records. I think the taxes haven't been paid for a couple of years. Better have him send and get a statement. I'll take you to the land. That's my business—guarantee it's the right place, find the corners, and put you right as a trivet all for twenty-five dollars."

"To-day?" I asked. "I want to get to breaking."

"Start as soon as we get through here," said he as we entered the little board shack which bore the sign, "County Offices." "No time to lose if you're going to plant anything this year. Le'me have that deed. This is Mr. Vandemark, Bill."

I don't remember what "Bill's" full name was, for he went back to the other county as soon as the government of Monterey was settled. He took my deed, wrote a memorandum of filing on the back of it, and tossed it into a basket as if it amounted to nothing, after giving me a receipt for it. Henderson L. had some trouble to get me to leave the deed, and the men about the little substitute for a court-house thought it mighty funny, I guess; but I never could see anything funny about being prudent. Then he got his horse, hitched to a buckboard buggy, and wanted me to ride out to the land with him; but I would not leave my cows and outfit. Henderson L. said he couldn't bother to wait for cows; but when he saw my shotgun, and the twenty-five dollars which I offered him, he said if I would furnish the gun and ammunition he would kill time along the road, so that the whole outfit could be kept together. He even waited while I dickered with Jim Boyd for a breaking plow, which I admitted I should need the first thing, as soon as Jim mentioned it to me.*

"This is Mr. Thorkelson," said he as he rejoined me after two or three false starts. "He's going to be a neigh-

---

*The date on the deed shows this to have been May 25, 1855—the day the author first saw what has since become Vandemark Township. Although its history is so far written, the township was not yet legally in existence.—G. v. d. M.

bor of yours. I'm going to locate him on a quarter out your way—Mr. Vandemark, Mr. Thorkelson."

Magnus Thorkelson gave me his hand bashfully. He was then about twenty-five; and had on the flat cap and peasant's clothes that he wore on the way over from Norway. He had red hair and a face spotted with freckles; and growing on his chin and upper lip was a fiery red beard. He was so tall that Henderson L. tried to tell him not to come to the Fourth of July celebration, or folks might think he was the fireworks; but Magnus only smiled. I don't believe he understood: for at that time his English was not very extensive; but after all, he is as silent now as he was then. We looked down on all kinds of "old countrymen" then, and thought them much below us; but Magnus and I got to be friends as we drove the cows across the prairie, and we have been friends ever since. It was not until years after that I saw what a really remarkable man Magnus was, physically, and mentally—he was so mild, so silent, so gentle. He carried a carpetbag full of belongings in one hand, which he put in the wagon, and a fiddle in its case in the other. It was a long time, too, before I began to feel how much better his fiddling was than any I had ever heard. It didn't seem to have as much tune to it as the old-style fiddling, and he would hardly ever play for dances; but his fiddle just seemed to sing. He became a part of the history of Vandemark Township; and was the first fruits of the Scandinavian movement to our county so far as I know.

2

As we turned back over the way I had come for about half a mile, we met coming into town, the well-known spanking team of horses of Buckner Gowdy; but now it was hitched to a light buggy, but was still driven by Pinck Johnson, who had the horses on a keen gallop as if running after a doctor for snake-bite or apoplexy. It was the way Gowdy always went careering over the prairies, killing horses by the score, and laughingly answering criticisms by saying that there would be horses left in the world after he was gone. He said he hadn't time to waste on saving horses; but he always had one or two teams that he took good care of; and once in a while Pinck Johnson went back, to Kentucky, it was said, and brought on a fresh supply. As they came near to us the negro pulled up, and halted just after they had passed us. We stopped, and Gowdy came back to my wagon.

"How do you do, Mr. Vandemark," he said. "I am glad to see that you survived all the dangers of the voyage."

"How-de-do," I answered, looking as blank as I could; for Virginia was on my mind as soon as I saw him. "I come slow, but I'm here."

All through this talk, Gowdy watched my face as if to catch me telling something crooked; and I made up my mind to give him just enough of the truth to cover what he was sure to find out whether I told him or not.

"Did you pick up any passengers as you came along?" he asked, with a sharp look.

"Yes," I said. "I had a lawyer with me for a day or two—Mr. Creede."

"Heard of him," said Gowdy. "Locating over at our new town of Lithopolis, isn't he? See anybody you knew on the way?"

"Yes," I said. "I saw your sister-in-law in Waterloo.

She was with a minister and his wife—a Mr. and Mrs. Thorndyke—or something like that."

"Yes," said Gowdy, trying to be calm. "Friends of ours—of hers."

"They're here in the city," said Henderson L. "He's going to be the new preacher."

"I know," said Gowdy. "I know. Able man, too. How did it happen that I didn't see your outfit, Mr. Vandemark? I went back over the road after I passed you there at the mud-hole, and returned, and wondered why I didn't see you. Thought you had turned off and given Monterey County up. Odd I didn't see you." And all the time he was looking at me like a lawyer cross-examining a witness.

"Oh," said I, "I went off the road a few miles to break in some cattle I had traded for, and to let them get over their sore-footedness, and to leave some that I couldn't bring along. I had so many that I couldn't make time. I'm going back for them as soon as I can get around to it. You must have missed me that way."

"Trust Mr. Vandemark," said he, "to follow off any cattle track that shows itself. He is destined to be the cattle king of the prairies, Mr. Burns. I'm needing all the men I can get, Mr. Vandemark, putting up my house and barns and breaking prairie. I wonder if you wouldn't like to turn an honest penny by coming over and working for me for a while?"

He had been astonished and startled at the word that Virginia, after escaping from him, had found friends, and tried to pass the matter off as something of which he knew; but now he was quite his smiling, confidential self again, talking as if his offering me work was a favor he was begging in a warm and friendly sort of manner. I explained that I myself was getting my farm in condition to live upon, but might be glad to come to him later; and we drove on—I all the time sweating like a butcher under the strain of this getting so close to my great secret—and Virginia's.

Would it not all have to come out finally? What would Gowdy do to get Virginia back? Would he try at all? Did he have any legal right to her control and custody? I trusted completely in Grandma Thorndyke's protection of her—an army with banners would not have given me more confidence; for I could not imagine any one making her do anything she thought wrong, and ten armies with all the banners in the world could not have forced her to allow anything improper—and she had said that she and the elder were going to take care of the poor friendless girl—yet, I looked back at the Gowdy buggy flying on toward the village, in two minds as to whether or not I ought to go back and do—something. If I could have seen what that something might have been, I should probably have gone back; but I could not think just where I came into the play here.

So I went on toward the goal of all my ambitions, my square mile of Iowa land, steered by Henderson L. Burns, who, between shooting prairie chickens, upland plover and sickle-billed curlew, guided me toward my goal by pointing out lone boulders, and the mounds in front of the dens of prairie wolves and badgers. We went on for six miles, and finally came to a place where the land slopes down in what is a pretty steep hill for Iowa, to a level bottom more than a mile across, at the farther side of which the land again rises to the general level of the country in another slope, matching the one on the brow of which we halted. The general course of the two hills is easterly and westerly, and we stood on the southern side of the broad flat valley.

3

As I write, I can look out over it. The drainage of the flat now runs off through a great open ditch which I combined with my neighbors to have dredged through by a floating dredge in 1897. The barge set in two miles above me, and after it had dug itself down so as to get water in which to float, it worked its way down to the river eight miles away. The line of this ditch is now marked by a fringe of trees; but in 1855, nothing broke the surface of the sea of grass except a few clumps of plum trees and willows at the foot of the opposite slope, and here and there along the line of the present ditch, there were ponds of open water, patches of cattails, and the tent-like roofs of muskrat-houses. I had learned enough of the prairies to see that this would be a miry place to cross, if a crossing had to be made; so I waited for Henderson L. to come up and tell me how to steer my course.

"This is Hell Slew," said he as he came up. "But I guess we won't have to cross. Le's see; le's see! Yes, here we are."

He looked at his memorandum of the description of my land, looked about him, drove off a mile south and came back, finally put his horse down the hill to the base of it, and out a hundred yards in the waving grass that made early hay for the town for fifteen years, he

found the corner stake driven by the government survey-
ors, and beckoned for me to come down.

"This is the southeast corner of your land," said he.
"Looks like a mighty good place for a man with as good a
shotgun as that—ducks and geese the year round!"

"Where are the other corners?" I asked.

"That's to be determined," he answered.

To determine it, he tied his handkerchief about the
felly of his buggy wheel, held a pocket compass in his
left hand to drive by, picked out a tall rosin-weed to mark
the course for me, and counted the times the handkerchief went round as the buggy traveled on. He knew
how many turns made a mile. The horse's hoofs sucked
in the wet sod as we got farther out into the marsh, and
then the ground rose a little and we went up over a head-
land that juts out into the marsh; then we went down
into the slew again, and finally stopped in a miry place
where there was a flowing spring with tall yellow lady's-
slippers and catkined willows growing around it. After
a few minutes of looking about, Burns found my southwest corner. We made back to the edge of the slope, and
Henderson L. looked off to the north in despair.

"My boy," said he, "I've actually located your two
south corners, and you can run the south line yourself
from these stakes. The north line is three hundred and
twenty rods north of and parallel to it—and the east and
west lines will run themselves when you locate the north
corners—but I'll have to wait till the ground freezes, or
get Darius Green to help me—and the great tide of
immigration hain't brought him to this neck of the woods
yet."

"But where's my land?" I queried: for I did not understand all this hocus-pocus of locating any given spot in the Iowa prairies in 1855. "Where's my land?"

"The heft of it," said he, "is right down there in Hell Slew. It's all pretty wet; but I think you've got the wettest part of it; the best duck ponds, and the biggest muskrat-houses. This slew is the only blot in the 'scutcheon of this pearl of counties, Mr. Vandemark—the only blot; and you've got the blackest of it."

I leaned back against the buggy, completely unnerved. Magnus put out his hand as if to grasp mine, but I did not take it. There went through my head that rhyme of Jackway's that he hiccoughed out as he drank with his cronies —on my money—that day last winter back in Madison: "Sold again, and got the tin, and sucked another Dutchman in!" This huge marsh was what John Rucker, after killing my mother, had deeded me for my inheritance!

In that last word I had from her, the poor stained letter she left in the apple-tree—perhaps it was her tears, and not the rain that had stained it so—she had said: "I am going very far away, and if you ever see this, keep it always, and whenever you see it remember that I would always have died willingly for you, and that I am going to build up for you a fortune which will give you a better life than I have lived." And this was the fortune which she had built up for me! I hated myself for having been gulled—it seemed as if I had allowed my mother to be cheated more than myself. Good land, I thought, was selling in Monterey County for two dollars an acre. The next summer when I bought an eighty across the road so as to have more plow-land, I paid three dollars and a half an acre, and sorrowed over it afterward: for in 1857 I could have got all I wanted of the best land—if I had

had the money, which I had not—at a dollar and a quarter. At the going price then, in 1855, this section of land, if it had been good land, would have been worth only twelve or thirteen hundred dollars. At that rate, what was this swamp worth? Nothing!

I can still feel sorry for that poor boy, myself, green as grass, and without a friend in the world to whom he could go for advice, halted in his one-sided battle with the world, out there on the bare prairie, looking out on what he thought was the scene of his ruin, and thinking that every man's hand had been against him, and would always be. Where were now all my dreams of fat cattle, sleek horses, waddling hogs, and the fine house in which I had had so many visions of spending my life, with a more or less clearly-seen wife—especially during those days after Rowena Fewkes had told me how well she could cook, and proved it by getting me my breakfast; and the later days of my stay in the Grove of Destiny with Virginia Royall. Any open prairie farm, with no house, nothing with which to make a house, and no home but a wagon, and no companions but my cows would have been rather forbidding at first glance; but this—I was certain I was ruined; I suppose I must have looked a little bad, for Henderson T. laid his hand on my shoulder.

"Don't cave in, my boy," said he. "You're young—and there's oceans of good land to be had. Keep a stiff upper lip!"

"I'll kill him!" I shouted. "I'll kill John Rucker!"

"Don't, till you catch him," said Burns. "And what good would it do anyhow?"

"Is there any plow-land on it?" I asked, after getting control of myself.

"Some," said Henderson L. cheerfully. "Don't you remember that we drove up over a spur of the hill back there? Well, all the dry land north of our track is yours. Finest building-spot in the world, Jake. We'll make a farm of this yet. Come back and I'll show you."

4

So we went back and looked over all the dry ground I possessed, and agreed that there were about forty acres of it, and as Burns insisted, sixty in a dry season; and he stuck to it that a lot of that slew was as good pasture especially in a dry time as any one could ask for. This would be fine for a man as fond of cows as I was, though, of course, cows could range at will all over the country. It was fine hay land, he said, too, except in the wettest places; but it was true also, that any one could make hay anywhere.

I paid Henderson L., bade good-by to Magnus Thorkelson, drove my outfit up on the "building-spot," and camped right where my biggest silo now stands. I sat there all the afternoon, not even unhitching my teams, listening as the afternoon drew on toward night, to the bitterns crying "plum pudd'n'" from the marsh, to the queer calls of the water-rail, and to the long-drawn "whe-e-ep—whe-e-e-ew!" of the curlews, as they alighted on the prairie and stretched their wings up over their backs.

I could never be much of a man, I thought, on a forty-acre farm, nor build much of a house. I had come all the way from York State for this! The bubble had grown brighter and brighter as I had made my strange way across the new lands, putting on

more and more of the colors of the rainbow, and now, all
had ended in this spot of water on the floor of the earth.
I compared myself with the Fewkeses, as I remembered
how I had told Virginia just how the rooms of the house
should be arranged, and allowed her to change the
arrangement whenever she desired, and even to put great
white columns in front as she said they did in Kentucky.
We had agreed as to just what trees should be set out,
and what flowers should be planted in the blue-grass
lawn.

All this was gone glimmering now—and yet as I
sit here, there are the trees, and there are the flowers,
very much as planned, in the soft blue-grass lawn; about
the only thing lacking being the white columns.

I was lying on the ground, looking out across the
marsh, and as my misfortunes all rolled back over my
mind I turned on my face and cried like a baby. Finally,
I felt a large light hand laid softly on my head. I looked
up and saw Magnus Thorkelson bending over me.

"Forty acres," said he, "bane pretty big farm in Norvay. My fadder on twenty acres, raise ten shildren. Not
so gude land like dis. Vun of dem shildern bane college
professor, and vun a big man in leggislatur. Forty acre
bane gude farm, for gude farmer."

I turned over, wiped my sleeve across my eyes, and
sat up.

"I guess I dropped asleep," I said.

"Yass," he said. "You bane sleep long time. I came
back to ask if I stay vith you. I halp you. You halp me.
Ve halp each udder. Ve be neighbors alvays. I get farm
next you. I halp you build house, an' you halp me.
Maybe ve lif togedder till you git vooman, or I git voo-

man—if American vooman marry Norwegian man. I stay?"

I took his hand and pressed it. After a few days' studying over it, I made up my mind that in the kindness of his heart he had come back just to comfort me. And all that he had said we would do, we did. Before long we had a warm dugout barn built in the eastern slope of the hillside, partly sheltered from the northwestern winds, and Magnus and I slept in one end of it on the sweet hay we cut in the marsh while the cows ranged on the prairie. Together we broke prairie, first on his land, then on mine. Together we hauled lumber from the river for my first little house.

If we first settlers in Iowa had possessed the sense the Lord gives to most, we could have built better and warmer, and prettier houses than the ones we put up, of the prairie sod which we ripped up in long black ribbons of earth; but we all were from lands of forests, and it took a generation to teach our prairie pioneers that a sod house is a good house. I never saw any until the last of Iowa was settling up, out in the northwestern part of the state, in Lyon, Sioux and Clay Counties.

All that summer, every wagon and draught animal in Monterey County was engaged in hauling lumber—some of it such poor stuff as basswood sawed in little sawmills along the rivers; and it was not until in the 'eighties that the popular song, *The Little Old Sod Shanty on the Claim* proved two things—that the American pioneer had learned to build with something besides timber, and that the Homestead Law had come into effect. What Magnus and I were doing, all the settlers on the Monterey County farms were doing—raising sod corn and potatoes and buckwheat and turnips, preparing shelter for the winter, and wondering what they would do for fuel. Magnus helped me and I helped him.

A lot is said nowadays about the Americanization of the foreigner; but the only thing that will do the thing is to work with the foreigner, as I worked with Magnus —let him help me, and be active in helping him. The Americanization motto is, "Look upon the foreigner as an equal. Help him. Let him help you. Make each other's problems mutual problems and then he is no longer a foreigner." When Magnus Thorkelson came back on foot across the prairie from Monterey Centre, to lay his hand on the head of that weeping boy alone on the prairie, and to offer to live with him and help him, his English was good enough for me, and to me he was as fully naturalized as if all the judges in the world had made him lift his hand while he swore to support the Constitution of the United States and of the State of Iowa. He was a good enough American for Jacobus Teunis Vandemark.

CHAPTER XIII

THE PLOW WEDS THE SOD

THE next day was a wedding-day—the marriage morning of the plow and the sod. It marked the beginning of the subdual of that wonderful wild prairie of Vandemark Township and the Vandemark farm. No more fruitful espousal ever took place than that—when the polished steel of my new breaking plow was embraced by the black soil with its lovely fell of greenery. Up to that fateful moment, the prairie of the farm and of the township had been virgin sod; but now it bowed its neck to the yoke of wedlock. Nothing like it takes place any more; for the sod of the meadows and pastures is quite a different thing from the untouched skin of the original earth. Breaking prairie was the most beautiful, the most epochal, and most hopeful, and as I look back at it, in one way the most pathetic thing man ever did, for in it, one of the loveliest things ever created began to come to its predestined end.

The plow itself was long, low, and yacht-like in form; a curved blade of polished steel. The plowman walked behind it in a clean new path, sheared as smooth as a concrete pavement, with not a lump of crumbled earth under his feet—a cool, moist, black path of richness. The furrow-slice was a long, almost unbroken ribbon of

228

turf, each one laid smoothly against the former strand, and under it lay crumpled and crushed the layer of grass and flowers. The plow-point was long and tapering, like the prow of a clipper, and ran far out under the beam, and above it was the rolling colter, a circular blade of steel, which cut the edge of the furrow as cleanly as cheese. The lay of the plow, filed sharp at every round, lay flat, and clove the slice neatly from the bosom of earth where it had lain from the beginning of time. As the team steadily pulled the machine along, I heard a curious thrilling sound as the knife went through the roots, a sort of murmuring as of protest at this violation—and once in a while, the whole engine, and the arms of the plowman also, felt a jar, like that of a ship striking a hidden rock, as the share cut through a red-root—a stout root of wood, like red cedar or mahogany, sometimes as large as one's arm, topped with a clump of tough twigs with clusters of pretty whitish blossoms.

As I looked back at the results of my day's work, my spirits rose; for in the East, a man might have worked all summer long to clear as much land as I had prepared for a crop on that first day. This morning it had been wilderness; now it was a field—a field in which Magnus Thorkelson had planted corn, by the simple process of cutting through the sods with an ax, and dropping in each opening thus made three kernels of corn. Surely this was a new world! Surely, this was a world in which a man with the will to do might make something of himself. No waiting for the long processes by which the forests were reclaimed; but a new world with new processes, new neighbors, new ideas, new opportunities, new victories easily gained.

Not so easy, Jacobus! In the first place, we Iowa pioneers so ignorant of our opportunities that we hauled timber a hundred miles with which to build our houses, when that black sod would have made us better ones, were also so foolish as to waste a whole year of the time of that land which panted to produce. To be sure, we grew some sod-corn, and some sod-potatoes, and sowed some turnips and buckwheat on the new breaking; but after my hair was gray, I found out, for the first time as we all did, that a fine crop of flax might have been grown that first year. Dakota taught us that. But the farmer of old was inured to waiting—and so we waited until another spring for the sod to rot, and in the meantime, it grew great crops of tumble-weeds, which in the fall raced over the plain like scurrying scared wolves, piling up in brown mountains against every obstacle, and in every hole. If we had only known these simple things, what would it have saved us! But skill grows slowly. We were the first prairie generation bred of a line of foresters, and were a little like the fools that came to Virginia and Plymouth Colony, who starved in a country filled with food. How many fool things are we doing now, I wonder, to cause posterity to laugh, as foolish as the dying of Sir John Franklin in a land where Stefansson grew fat; many, I guess, as foolish as we did when Magnus Thorkelson and I were Vandemark Township.

The sod grew too mature for breaking after the first of June, and not enough time was left for it to rot during the summer; and my cows left with Mr. Westervelt were on my mind; so I stopped the plow and after Magnus and I had built my house and made a lot of hay in the marsh, I began to think of going back after my live stock.

I planned to travel light with one span to Westervelt's, pick up another yoke of cows, go on to Dubuque for a load of freight for Monterey Centre, and come back, bringing the rest of my herd with me on the return. When I went to "the Centre," as we called it, I waited until I saw Grandma Thorndyke go down to the store, and then tapped at their door. I thought they might want me to bring them something. They were living in a little house by the public square, where the great sugar maples stand now. These trees were then little bean-poles with tufts of twigs at the tops.

2

Virginia Royall came to the door, as I sort of sus-pected she might. At first she started back as if she hardly knew me. Maybe she didn't; for Magnus Thor-kelson had got me to shaving, and with all that gosling's down off my face, I suppose I looked older and more man-like than before. So she took a long look at me, and then ran to me and took both my hands in hers and pressed them—pressed them so that I remembered it always.

"Why, Teunis," she cried, "is it you? I thought I was never going to see you again!"

"Yes," I said, "it's me—it's me. I came——" and then I stopped, bogged down.

"You came to see me," she said, "and I think you've waited long enough. Only three friends in the world, you, and Mrs. Thorndyke, and Mr. Thorndyke—and you off there on the prairie all these weeks and never came to see me—or us! Tell me about the farm, and the cows, and the new house—I've heard of it—and your foreigner friend, and all about it. Have you any little calves?"

I was able to report that Spot, the heifer that we had such a time driving, had a little calf that was going to look just like its mother; and then I described to her the section of land—all but a little of it down in Hell Slew; and how I hoped to buy a piece across the line so as to have a real farm. Pretty soon we were talking just as we used to talk back there east of Waterloo.

"I came to see you and Elder Thorndyke and his wife," I said, "because I'm going back to Dubuque to get a load of freight, and I thought I might bring something for you."

"Oh," said she, "take me with you, Teunis, take me with you!"

"Could you go?" I asked, my heart in my mouth.

"No, oh, no!" she said. "There's nobody in Kentucky for me to go to; and I haven't any money to pay my way with anyhow. I am alone in the world, Teunis, except for you and my new father and mother—and I'm afraid they are pretty poor, Teunis, to feed and clothe a big girl like me!"

"How much money would it take?" I asked. "I guess I could raise it for you, Virginia."

"You're a nice boy, Teunis," she said, with tears in her eyes, "and I know how well you like money, too; but there's nobody left there. I'm very lonely—but I'm as well off here as anywhere. I'd just like to go with you, though, for when I'm with you I feel so—so safe."

"Safe?" said I. "Why aren't you safe here? Is any one threatening you? Has Buckner Gowdy been

around here? Just tell me if he bothers you, and I'll—
I'll——"

"Well," said she, "he came here and claimed me from
Mr. Thorndyke. He said I was an infant—what do you
think of that?—an infant—in law; and that he is my
guardian. And a lawyer named Creede, came and talked
about his right, not he said by consanguinity, but affinity,
whatever that is——"

"I know Mr. Creede," said I. "He rode with me for
two or three days. I don't believe he'll wrong any one."

"Mrs. Thorndyke told them to try their affinity plan
if they dared, and she'd show them that they couldn't
drag a poor orphan away from her friends against her
will. And I hung to her, and I cried, and said I'd kill
myself before I'd go with him; and that man"—meaning
Gowdy—"tried to talk sweet and affectionate and
brotherly to me, and I hid my face in Mrs. Thorndyke's
bosom—and Mr. Creede looked as if he were sick of his
case, and told that man that he would like further con-
sultation with him before proceeding further—and they
went away. But every time I see that man he acts as if
he wanted to talk with me, and smiles at me—but I
won't look at him. Oh, why can't they all be good like
you, Teunis?"

Then she told me that I looked a lot better when I
shaved—at which I blushed like everything, and this
seemed to tickle her very much. Then she asked if I
wasn't surprised when she called me Teunis. She had
thought a good deal over it, she said, and she couldn't,
couldn't like the name of Jacob, or Jake; but Teunis was
a quality name. Didn't I think I'd like it if I changed
my way of writing my name to J. Teunis Vandemark?

"I like to have you call me Teunis," I said; "but I wouldn't like to have any one else do it. I like to have you have a name to call me by that nobody else uses."

"That's a very gallant speech," she said, blushing— and I vow, I didn't know what gallant meant, and was a little flustered for fear her blushes were called out by something shady.

"Besides," I said, "I have always heard that nobody but a dandy ever parts his name or his hair in the middle!"

"Rubbish!" said she. "My father's name was A. Fletcher Royall, and he was a big strong man, every inch of him. I reckon, though, that the customs are different in the North. Then you won't take me with you, and go back by way of our grove, and——"

And just then Elder Thorndyke came in, and we wished that Mrs. Thorndyke would come to tell what I should bring from Dubuque. He told me in the meantime, about his plans for building a church, and how he was teaching Virginia, so that she could be a teacher herself when she was old enough.

"We'll be filling this country with schools, soon," he said, "and they'll want nice teachers like Virginia."

"Won't that be fine?" asked Virginia. "I just love children. I play with dolls now—a little. And then I can do something to repay my new father and mother for all they are doing for me. And you must come to church, Teunis."

"Virginia says," said the elder, "that you have a good voice. I wish you'd come and help out with the singing."

"Oh, I can't sing," I demurred; "but I'd like to come. I will come, when I get back."

"Yes, you can sing," said Virginia. "Here's a song he taught me back on the prairie:

" 'Down the river, O down the river, O down the river
    we go-o-o;
Down the river, O down the river, O down the Ohio-o-o!

" 'The river was up, the channel was deep, the wind was
    steady and strong,
The waves they dashed from shore to shore as we went
    sailing along——

" 'Down the river, O down the river, O down the river
    we go-o-o;
Down the river, O down the river, O down the
    Ohio-o-o!' "

"I think you learned a good deal—for one day," said Mrs. Thorndyke, coming in. "How do you do, Jacob? I'm glad to see you."

Thus she again put forth her theory that Virginia and I had been together only one day. It is what N. V. Creede called, when I told him of it years afterward, "a legal fiction which for purposes of pleading was incontrovertible."

The river of immigration was still flowing west over the Ridge Road, quite as strong as earlier in the season, and swollen by the stream of traffic setting to and from the settlements for freight. People I met told me that the railroad was building into Dubuque—or at least to the river at Dunlieth. I met loads of lumber which were going out for Buck Gowdy's big house away out in the middle of his great estate; and other loads for Lithopolis, where Judge Stone was making his struggle to build up a rival to Monterey Centre. I reached Dubuque on the seventeenth of July, and put up at a tavern down near the river, where they had room for my stock; and learned that the next day the first train would arrive at Dunlieth, and there was to be a great celebration.

It was the greatest day Dubuque had ever seen, they told me, with cannon fired from the bluff at sunrise, a long parade, much speech-making, and a lot of wild drunkenness. The boatmen from the river boats started in to lick every railroad man they met, and as far as I could see, did so in ninety per cent. of the cases; but in the midst of a fight in which all my canal experiences were in a fair way to be outdone, a woman came into the crowd leading four little crying children. She asked our attention while she explained that their father had had his hand blown off when the salute was fired in the morning, and asked us if we felt like giving something to him to enable him to keep a roof over these little ones. The fight stopped, and we all threw money on the ground in the ring.

There were bridges connecting the main island with the business part of the city, and lines of hacks and carts running from the main part of the town to deep water. There were from four to six boats a day on the river. Lead was the main item of freight, although the first tricklings of the great flood of Iowa and Illinois wheat were beginning to run the metal a close second. To show what an event it was, I need only say that there were delegates at the celebration from as far east as Cleveland; and folks said that a ferry was to be built to bring the railway trains into Dubuque. And the best of all these dreams was, that they came true; and we were before many years freed of the great burden of coming so far to market.

During the next winter the word came to us that the railroad—another one—had crept as far out into the state as Iowa City, and when the freighting season of 1856 opened up, we swung off to the railhead there. Soon, however, the road was at Manchester, then at Waterloo, then at Cedar Falls, and before many years the Iowa Central came up from the south clear to Mason City, and the days of long-distance freighting were over for most of the state; which is now better provided with railways, I suppose, than any other agricultural region in the world.

I couldn't then foresee any such thing, however. They talk of the far-sighted pioneers; but as far as I was concerned I didn't know B from a bull's foot in this business of the progress of the country. I whoa-hawed and gee-upped my way back to Monterey Centre, thinking how great a disadvantage it would be always to have to wagon it back and forth to the river—with the building of the railway into Dunlieth that year right before my face and eyes.

3

I found Magnus Thorkelson surrounded by a group of people arguing with him about something; and Magnus in a dreadful pucker to know what to do. In one group were Judge Horace Stone, N. V. Creede and Forrest Bushyager, then a middle-aged man, and an active young fellow of twenty-five or so named Dick McGill, afterward for many years the editor of the Monterey Centre *Journal*. These had a petition asking that the county-seat be located at Lithopolis, Judge Stone's new town, and they wanted Magnus to sign it. I suppose he would have done so, if it had not been for the other delegation, consisting of Henderson L. Burns and Doctor Bliven, who had another petition asking for the establishment of the county-seat permanently "at its present site," Monterey Centre. They took me into the confabulation as soon as I weighed anchor in front of the house; and just as they had begun to pour their arguments into me they were joined by another man, who drove up in a two-seated democrat wagon drawn by a fine team of black horses, and in the back seat I saw a man and woman sitting. I thought the man looked like Elder Thorndyke; but the woman's face was turned away from me, and I did not recognize her at first. She had on a new calico dress that I hadn't seen before. It was Virginia.

The man who got out and joined the group was a red-faced, hard-visaged man of about fifty, dressed in black broadcloth, and wearing a beaver hat. He had a black silk cravat tied about a standing collar, with high points that rolled out in front, and he looked rich and domineering. He was ever afterward a big man in Monterey County, and always went by the name of Governor Wade, because he was a candidate for governor two or three times. He was the owner of a big tract of land over to the southwest, next to the Gowdy farm the largest in the county. He came striding over to us as if whatever he said was the end of the law. With him and Henderson L. and N. V. Creede pitching into a leatherhead like me, no wonder I did not recognize Virginia in her new dress; I was in such a stew that I hardly knew which end my head was on.

Each side seemed to want to impress me with the fact that in signing one or the other of those petitions I had come to the parting of the ways. They did not say much about what was best for the county, but bore down on the fact that the way I lined up on that great question would make all the difference in the world with me. Each tried to make me think that I should always be an outsider and a maverick if I didn't stand with his crowd.

"Why," said N. V., "I feel sure that it won't take you long to make up your mind. This little group of men we have here," pointing to Henderson L. and Governor Wade, "are the County Ring that's trying to get this new county in their clutches—the County Ring!"

This made a little grain of an impression on me; and it was the first time I had ever heard the expression so common in local history "the County Ring." I looked at Governor Wade to see what he would say to it. His face grew redder, and he laughed as if Creede were not worth noticing; but he noticed him for all that.

"Young man," said he, "or young men, I should say, both of you want to be somebody in this new community. Monterey Centre represents already, the brains——"

"Like a dollar sign," said Dick McGill, "it represents it, but it hasn't any."

"——the brains," went on Governor Wade, glaring at him, "the culture, the progress and the wealth——"

"That they hope to steal," put in Dick McGill.

"——the wealth," went on the Governor, who hated to be interrupted, "of this Gem of the Prairies, Monterey County. Don't make the mistake, which you can never correct, of taking sides with this little gang of town-site sharks led by my good friend Judge Stone."

Here was another word which I was to hear pretty often in county politics—Gang. One crowd was called a Ring; the other a Gang. I looked at N. V. to see how wrathy he must be, but he only smiled sarcastically, as I have often seen him do in court; and shaking his head at me waved his hand as if putting Governor Wade quite off the map. Just then my team began acting up—they had not been unhitched and were thirsty and hungry; and I went over to straighten them out, leaving the Ring and the Gang laboring with Magnus, who was sweating freely—and then I went over to speak with the elder.

"How do you do, Teunis?" said Virginia very sweetly. "You'll sign our petition, won't you?"

"We don't want to influence your judgment," said the elder, "but I wanted to say to you that if the county-seat remains at Monterey Centre, it will be a great thing for the religious work which under God I hope to do. It will give me a parish. I should like to urge that upon you."

"Do you want me to sign it?" I asked him, looking at Virginia.

"Yes," said he, "if you have no objection."

"Please do!" said Virginia. "I know you can't have any objection."

I turned on my heel, went back to Governor Wade, and signed the petition for Monterey Centre; and then Magnus Thorkelson did the same. Then we both signed another petition carried by both parties, asking that an election be called by the judge of the county south which had jurisdiction over us, for the election of officers. And just as I had expected one side to begin crowing over the other, and I had decided that there would be a fight, both crowds jumped into their rigs and went off over the prairie, very good naturedly it seemed to me, after the next settler.

"Jake," said N. V., as they turned their buggy around, "you'll make some woman a damned good husband, some day!" and he took off his hat very politely to Virginia, who blushed as red as the reddest rose then blooming on the prairie.

That was the way counties were organized in Iowa. It is worth remembering because it was the birth of self-government. The people made their counties and their villages and their townships as they made their farms and houses and granaries. Everybody was invited to take part—and it was not until long afterward that I confessed to Magnus that I had never once thought when I signed those petitions that I was not yet a voter; and then he was frightened to realize that he was not either. He had not yet been naturalized. The only man in the county known to me who took no interest in the contest was Buck Gowdy. When Judge Stone asked him why, he said he didn't give a damn. There was too much government for him there already, he said.

We did get the election called, and after we had elected our officers there was no county-seat for them to dwell in; so that county judge off to the south appointed a commission to locate the county-seat, which after driving over the country a good deal and drinking a lot of whisky, according to Dick McGill, made Monterey Centre the county town, which it still remains. The Lithopolis people gained one victory—they elected Judge Horace Stone County Treasurer. Within a month N. V. Creede had opened a law office in Monterey Centre, Dick McGill had begun the publication of the Monterey Centre *Journal* of fragrant memory, Lithopolis began to advertise its stone quarries, and Grizzly Reed, an old California prospector, who had had his ear torn off by a bear out in the mountains, began prospecting for gold along the creek, and talking mysteriously. The sale of lots in Lithopolis went on faster than ever.

CHAPTER XIV

I BECOME A BANDIT AND A TERROR

WHEN General Weaver was running for governor, a Populist worker called on my friend Wilbur Wheelock, who was then as now a stock buyer at our little town of Ploverdale, and asked him if he were a Populist.

"No," said Wilbur, "but I have all the qualifications, sir!"

"What do you regard as the qualifications?" asked the organizer.

"I've run for county office and got beat," said Wilbur: "and that takes you in, too, don't it, Jake?" he asked, turning to me.

Wilbur, like most of our older people, has a good memory. Most of the folks hereabouts had already forgotten that I was a candidate on Judge Stone's Reform and Anti-Monopoly ticket, for County Supervisor, in 1874, and that I was defeated with the rest. This was the only time I ever had anything to do with politics, more than to be a delegate to the county convention two or three times. I mention it here, because of the chance it gave Dick McGill to rake me over the coals in his scurrilous paper, the Monterey Centre *Journal*, that most people have always said was never fit to enter a decent home, but which they always subscribed for and read as quick as it came.

Within fifteen minutes after McGill got his paper to Monterey Centre he and what he had called the County Ring were as thick as thieves, and always stayed so as long as Dick had the county printing. So when I was put on the independent ticket to turn this ring out of office, Dick went after me as if I had been a horse-thief, and made a great to-do about what he called "Cow Vandemark's criminal record." Now that I have a chance to put the matter before the world in print, I shall take advantage of it; for that "criminal record" is a part of this history of Vandemark Township.

The story grew out of my joining the Settlers' Club in 1856. The rage for land speculation was sweeping over Iowa like a prairie fire, getting things all ready for the great panic of 1857 that I have read of since, but of which I never heard until long after it was over. All I knew was that there was a great fever for buying and selling land and laying out and booming town-sites—the sites, not the towns—and that afterward times were very hard. The speculators had bought up a good part of Monterey County by the end of 1856, and had run the price up as high as three dollars and a half an acre.

This made it hard for poor men who came in expecting to get it for a dollar and a quarter; and a number of settlers in the township, as they did all over the state, went on their land relying on the right to buy it when they could get the money—what was called the preemption right. I could see the houses of William Trickey, Ebenezer Junkins and Absalom Frost from my house; and I knew that Peter and Amos Bemisdarfer and Flavius Bohn, Dunkards from Pennsylvania, had located farther south. All these settlers were located south of

Hell Slew, which was coming to be known now, and was afterward put down on the map, as "Vandemark's Folly Marsh."

And now there came into the county and state a class of men called "claim-jumpers," who pushed in on the claims of the first comers, and stood ready to buy their new homes right out from under them. It was pretty hard on us who had pushed on ahead of the railways, and soaked in the rain and frozen in the blizzards, and lived on moldy bacon and hulled corn, to lose our chance to get title to the lands we had broken up and built on. It did not take long for a settler to see in his land a home for him and his dear ones, and the generations to follow; and we felt a great bitterness toward these claim-jumpers, who were no better off than we were.

My land was paid for, such as it was; but when the people who, like me, had drailed out across the prairies with the last year's rush, came and asked me to join the Settlers' Club to run these intruders off, it appeared to me that it was only a man's part in me to stand to it and take hold and do. I felt the old urge of all landowners to stand together against the landless, I suppose. What is title to land anyhow, but the right of those who have it to hold on to it? No man ever made land—except my ancestors, the Dutch, perhaps. All men do is to get possession of it, and run everybody else off, either with clubs, guns, or the sheriff.

I did not look forward to all the doings of the Settlers' Club, but I joined it, and I have never been ashamed of it, even when Dick McGill was slangwhanging me about what we did. I never knew, and I don't know now, just what the law was, but I thought then, and

I think now, that the Settlers' Club had the right of it. I thought so the night we went over to run the claim-jumper off Absalom Frost's land, within a week of my joining.

It was over on Section Twenty-seven, that the claim-jumper had built a hut about where the schoolhouse now is, with a stable in one end of it, and a den in which to live in the other. He was a young man, with no dependents, and we felt no compunctions of conscience, that dark night, when two wagon-loads of us, one of which came from the direction of Monterey Centre, drove quietly up and knocked at the door.

"Who's there?" he said, with a quiver in his voice.

"Open up, and find out!" said a man in the Monterey Centre crowd, who seemed to take command as a matter of course. "Kick the door open, Dutchy!"

As he said this he stepped aside, and pushed me up to the door. I gave it a push with my knee, and the leader jerked me aside, just in time to let a charge of shot pass my head.

"It's only a single-barrel gun," said he. "Grab him!"

I was scared by the report of the gun, scared and mad, too, as I clinched with the fellow, and threw him; then I pitched him out of the door, when the rest of them threw him down and began stripping him. At the same time, some one kindled a fire under a kettle filled with tar, and in a few minutes, they were smearing him with it. This looked like going too far, to me, and I stepped back—I couldn't stand it to see the tar smeared over his face, even if it did look like a map of the devil's wild land, as he kicked and scratched and tried to bite, swearing all the time like a pirate. It seemed a degrading kind

of thing to defile a human being in that way. The leader
came up to me and said, "That was good work, Dutchy.
Lucky I was right about its being a single-barrel, ain't
it? Help get his team hitched up. We want to see him
well started."

"All right, Mr. McGill," I said; for that was his name,
now first told in all the history of the county.

"Shut up!" he said. "My name's Smith, you lunkhead!"

Well, we let the claim jumper put on his clothes over
the tar and feathers, and loaded his things into his wagon,
hitched up his team, and whipped them up to a run and
let them go over the prairie. All the time he was swearing that he would have blood for this, but he never stopped
going until he was out of sight and hearing.

2

("What a disgraceful affair!" says my granddaughter
Gertrude, as she finishes reading that page. "I'm
ashamed of you, grandpa; but I'm glad he didn't shoot
you. Where would I have been?" Well, it does seem
like rather a shady transaction for me to have been mixed
up in. The side of it that impresses me, however, is the
lapse of time as measured in conditions and institutions.
That was barbarism; and it was Iowa! And it was in my
lifetime. It was in a region now as completely developed
as England, and it goes back to things as raw and primitive as King Arthur's time. I wonder if his knights
were not in the main, pretty shabby rascals, as bad as
Dick McGill—or Cow Vandemark? But Gertrude has
not yet heard all about that night's work.)

"Now," said McGill, "for the others! Load up, and come on. This fellow will never look behind him!"

But he did!

The next and the last stop, was away down on Section Thirty-five—two miles farther. I was feeling rather wamble-cropped, because of the memory of that poor fellow with the tar in his eyes—but I went all the same.

There was a little streak of light in the east when we got to the place, but we could not at first locate the claim-jumpers. They had gone down into a hollow, right in the very corner of the section, as if trying barely to trespass on the land, so as to be able almost to deny that they were on it at all, and were seemingly trying to hide. We could scarcely see their outfit after we found it, for they were camped in tall grass, and their little shanty was not much larger than a dry-goods box. Their one horse was staked out a little way off, their one-horse wagon was standing with its cover on beside a mound of earth which marked where a shallow well had been dug for water. I heard a rustling in the wagon as we passed it, like that of a bird stirring in the branches of a tree.

McGill pounded on the door.

"Come out," he shouted. "You've got company!"

There was a scrabbling and hustling around in the shanty, and low talking, and some one asked who was there; to which McGill replied for them to come out and see. Pretty soon, a little doddering figure of a man came to the door, pulling on his breeches with trembling hands as he stepped, barefooted, on the bare ground which came right up to the door-sill.

"What's wanted, gentlemen?" he quavered. "I cain't ask you to come in—jist yit. What's wanted?"

He had not said two words when I knew him for Old Man Fewkes, whom I had last seen back on the road west of Dyersville, on his way to "Negosha." Where was Ma Fewkes, and where were Celebrate Fourth and Surajah Dowlah? And where, most emphatically, where was Rowena? I stepped forward at McGill's side. Surely, I thought, they were not going to tar and feather these harmless, good-for-nothing waifs of the frontier; and even as I thought it, I saw the glimmering of the fire they were kindling under the tar-kettle.

"We want you, you infernal claim-jumper!" said McGill. "We'll show you that you can't steal the land from us hard-working settlers, you set of sneaks! Take off your clothes, and we'll give you a coat that will make you look more like buzzards than you do now."

"There's some of 'em runnin' away!" yelled one of the crowd. "Catch 'em!"

There was a flight through the grass from the back of the shanty, a rush of pursuit, some feeble yells jerked into bits by rough handling; and presently, Celebrate and Surajah were dragged into the circle of light, just as poor Ma Fewkes, with her shoulder-blades drawn almost together came forward and tried to tear from her poor old husband's arm the hand of an old neighbor of mine whose name I won't mention even at this late day. I will not turn state's evidence notwithstanding the Statute of Limitations has run, as N. V. Creede advises me, against any one but Dick McGill—and the reason for my exposing him is merely tit for tat. Ma Fewkes could not unclasp the hands; but she produced an effect just the same.

"Say," said a man who had all the time sat in one of

the wagons, holding the horses. "You'd better leave out the stripping, boys!"

They began dragging the boys and the old man toward the tar-kettle, and McGill, with his hat drawn down over his eyes, went to the slimy mass and dipped into it a wooden paddle with which they had been stirring it. Taking as much on it as it would carry, he made as if to smear it over the old man's head and beard. I could not stand this—the poor harmless old coot!—and I ran up and struck McGill's arm.

"What in hell," he yelled, for some of the tar went on him, "do you mean!"

"Don't tar and feather 'em," I begged. "I know these folks. They are a poor wandering family, without money enough to buy land away from any one."

"We jist thought we'd kind o' settle down," said Old Man Fewkes whimperingly; "and I've got the money promised me to buy this land. So it's all right and straight!"

The silly old leatherhead didn't know he was doing anything against public sentiment; and told the very thing that made a case against him. I have found out since who the man was that promised him the money and was going to take the land; but that was just one circumstance in the land craze, and the man himself was wounded at Fort Donelson, and died in hospital—so I won't tell his name. The point is, that the old man had turned the jury against me just as I had finished my plea.

"You have got the money promised you, have you?" repeated McGill. "Grab him, boys!"

All this time I was wondering where Rowena could be. I recollected how she had always seemed to be mortified by her slack-twisted family, and I could see her as she meeched off across the prairie back along the Old Ridge Road, as if she belonged to another outfit; and yet, I knew how much of a Fewkes she was, as she joined in the conversation when they planned their great estates in the mythical state of Negosha, or in Texas, or even in California. I grew hot with anger as I began to realize what a humiliation this tarring and feathering would be to her —and I kept wondering, as I have said, where she could be, even as I felt the thrill a man experiences when he sees that he must fight: and just as I felt this thrill, one of our men closed with the old fellow from behind, and wrenching his bird's-claw hands behind his back, thrust the wizened old bearded face forward for its coat of tar.

I clinched with our man, and getting a rolling hip-lock on him, I whirled him over my head, as I had done with so many wrestling opponents, and letting him go in mid-air, he went head over heels, and struck ten feet away on the ground. Then I turned on McGill, and with the flat of my hand, I slapped him over against the shanty, with his ears ringing. They were coming at me in an undecided way: for my onset had been both sudden and unexpected; when I saw Rowena running from the rear with a shotgun in her hand, which she had picked up as it leaned against a wagon wheel where one of our crowd had left it.

"Stand back!" she screamed. "Stand back, or I'll blow somebody's head off!"

I heard a chuckling laugh from a man sitting in one of the wagons, and a word or two from him that sounded like, "Good girl!" Our little mob fell back, the man I had thrown limping, and Dick McGill rubbing the side of his head. The dawn was now broadening in the east, and it was getting almost light enough so that faces might be recognized; and one or two of the crowd began to retreat toward the wagons.

"I'll see to it," said I, "that these people will leave this land, and give up their settlement on it."

"No we won't," said Rowena. "We'll stay here if we're killed."

"Now, Rowena," said her father, "don't be so sot. We'll leave right off. Boys, hitch up the horse. We'll leave, gentlemen. I was gittin' tired of this country anyway. It's so tarnal cold in the winter. The trees is in constant varder in Texas, an' that's where we'll go."

By this time the mob had retreated to their wagons, their courage giving way before the light of day, rather than our resistance; though I could see that the settlers had no desire to get into a row with one of their neighbors: so shouting warnings to the Fewkeses to get out of the country while they could, they drove off, leaving me with the claim-jumpers. I turned and saw poor Rowena throw herself on the ground and burst into a most frightful fit of hysterical weeping. She would not allow her father or her brothers to touch her, and when her mother tried to comfort her, she said "Go away, ma. Don't touch me!" Finally I went to her, and she caught my hand in hers and pressed it, and after I had got her to her feet—the poor ragged waif, as limpsey as a rag, and wearing the patched remnants of the calico dress I had bought for her on the way into Iowa the spring before—she broke down and cried on my shoulder. She sobbed out that I was the only man she had ever known. She wished to God she were a man like me. The only

way I could stop her was to tell her that her face ought
to be washed; when I said that to her, she stopped her
sitheing and soon began making herself pretty: and
she was quite gay on the road to my place, where I took
them because I couldn't think of anything else to do with
them, though I knew that the whole family, not counting
Rowena, couldn't or wouldn't do enough work to pay the
board of their horse.

3

They hadn't more than got there and eaten a solid
meal, than Surajah asked me for tools so he could work
on a patent mouse-trap he was inventing, and when I
came in from work that evening, he was explaining it to
Magnus Thorkelson, who had come over to borrow some
sugar from me. Magnus was pretending to listen, but
he was asking his questions of Rowena, who stood by
more than half convinced that Surrager had finally hit
upon his great idea—which was a mouse-trap that
would always be baited, and with two compartments, one
to catch the mice, and one to hold them after they were
caught. When they went into the second compartment,
they tripped a little lever which opened the door for a
new captive, and at the same time baited the trap again.

It seemed as if Magnus could not understand what
Surajah said, but that Rowena's speech was quite plain
to him. After that, he came over every evening and
Rowena taught him to read in McGuffey's *Second
Reader*. I knew that Magnus had read this through time
and again; but he said he could learn to speak the words
better when Rowena taught him. The fact was, though,
that he was teaching her more than she him; but she
never had a suspicion of this. That evening Magnus

came over and brought his fiddle. Pa Fewkes was quite disappointed when Magnus said he could not play the *Money Musk* nor *Turkey in the Straw,* nor the *Devil's Dream,* but when he went into one of his musical trances and played things with no tune to them but with a great deal of harmony, and some songs that almost made you cry, Rowena sat looking so lost to the world and dreamy that Magnus was moist about the eyes himself. He shook hands with all of us when he went away, so as to get the chance to hold Rowena's hand I guess.

Every day while they were there, Magnus came to see us; but did not act a bit like a boy who came sparking. He did not ask Rowena to sit up with him, though I think she expected him to do so; but he talked with her about Norway, and his folks there, and how lonely it was on his farm, and of his hopes that one day he would be a well-to-do farmer.

After one got used to her poor clothes, and when she got tamed down a little on acquaintance and gave a person a chance to look at her, and especially into her eyes, she was a very pretty girl. She had grown since I had seen her the summer before, and was fuller of figure. Her hair was still of that rich dark brown, just the color of her eyes and eyebrows. She had been a wild girl last summer, but now she was a woman, with spells of dreaming and times when her feelings were easily hurt. She still was ready to flare up and fight at the drop of the hat—because, I suppose, she felt that everybody looked down on her and her family; but to Magnus and me she was always gentle and sometimes I thought she was going to talk confidentially to me.

After she had had one of her lessons one evening she

said to me, "I wish I wa'n't so darned infarnal ignorant. I wish I could learn enough to teach school!"

"We're all ignorant here," I said.

"Magnus ain't," said she. "He went to a big school in the old country. He showed me the picture of it, and of his father's house. It's got four stone chimneys."

"I wonder," said I, "if what they learn over there is real learning."

And that ended our confidential talk.

About the time I began wondering how long they were to stay with me, Buck Gowdy came careering over the prairie, driving his own horse, just as I was taking my nooning and was looking at the gun which Rowena had used to drive back the Settlers' Club, and which we had brought along with us. I thought I remembered where I had seen that gun, and when Buck came up I handed it to him.

"Here's your shotgun," I said. "It's the one you shot the geese with back toward the Mississippi."

"Good goose gun," said he. "Thank you for keeping it for me. I see you have caught me out getting acquainted with Iowa customs. If you had needed any help that night, you'd have got it."

"I came pretty near needing it," I said; "and I had help."

"I see you brought your help home with you," he said. "I think I recognize that wagon, don't I?" I nodded. "I wonder if they could come and help me on the farm. I'd like to see them. I need help, inside the house and out."

I left him talking with the whole Fewkes family, except Rowena, who kept herself out of sight somewhere, and went out to the stable to work. Gowdy was talking

to them in that low-voiced, smiling way of his, with the
little sympathetic tremor in his voice like that in the tone
of an organ. He had already told Surajah that his idea
for a mouse-trap looked like something the world had
been waiting for, and that there might be a fortune in the
scheme. Ma Fewkes was looking up at him, as if what
he said must be the law and gospel. He had them all
hypnotized, or as we called it then, mesmerized—so I
thought as I went out of sight of them. After a while,
Rowena came around the end of a haystack, and spoke
to me.

"Mr. Gowdy wants us all to go to work for him," she
said. "He wants pa and the boys to work around the
place, and he says he thinks some of Surrager's machines
are worth money. He'll give me work in the house."

"It looks like a good chance," said I.

"You know I don't know much about housework,"
said she; "poor as we've always been."

"You showed me how to make good bread," I replied.

"I could do well for a poor man," said Rowena, looking at me rather sadly. Then she waited quite a while
for me to say something.

"Shall I go, Jake?" she asked, looking up into my
face.

"It looks like a good chance for all of you,"
I answered.

"I don't want to," said she, "I couldn't stay here,
could I?......No, of course not!"

So away went the Fewkeses with Buck Gowdy. That
is, Rowena went away with him in his buggy, and the
rest of the family followed in a day or so with the cross
old horse—now refreshed by my hay and grain, and the

rest we had given him,—in their rickety one-horse wagon. I remember how Rowena looked back at us, her hair blowing about her face which looked, just a thought, pale and big-eyed, as the Gowdy buggy went off like the wind, with Buck's arm behind the girl to keep her from bouncing out.

This day's work was not to cease in its influence on Iowa affairs for half a century, if ever. State politics, the very government of the commonwealth, the history of Monterey County and of Vandemark Township, were all changed when Buck Gowdy went off over the prairie that day, holding Rowena Fewkes in the buggy seat with that big brawny arm of his. Ma Fewkes seemed delighted to see Mr. Gowdy holding her daughter in the buggy.

"Nobody can tell what great things may come of this!" she cried, as they went out of sight over a knoll.

She never said a truer thing. To be sure, it was only the hiring by a very rich man, as rich men went in those days, of three worthless hands and a hired girl; but it tore the state's affairs in pieces. Whenever I think of it I remember some verses in the *Fifth Reader* that my children used in school:

> "Somewhere yet that atom's force
> Moves the light-poised universe."*

It was a great deal more important then, though, that on that afternoon I was arrested for a great many things —assault with intent to commit great bodily injury,

*See *Gowdy vs. Buckner*, et al, Ia. Rep. Also accounts of relations of the so-called Gowdy Estate litigation to "The Inside of Iowa Politics" by the editor of these MSS.—in press.— G. v. d. M.

assault with intent to kill, just simple assault, unlawful
assembly, rioting, and I don't know but treason.   Dick
McGill, I am sure it was, told the first claim-jumper we
visited that I was at the head of the mob, and he had me
arrested.   I was taken to Monterey Centre by Jim Boyd,
the blacksmith, who was deputy sheriff; but he did the
fair thing and allowed me 'to get Magnus Thorkelson to
attend to my stock while I was gone.

I think that that passage in the Scriptures which tells
us to visit those who are in prison as well as the sick, is a
thing that shows the Bible to be an inspired work; but
this belief has come to me through my remembrance of
my sufferings when I was arrested.   Not that I went to
prison.   In fact, I do not believe there was anything like
a jail nearer than Iowa City or Dubuque; but Jim told me
that he understood that I was a terrible ruffian and would
have to be looked after very closely.   He made me help
him about the blacksmith shop, and I learned so much
about blacksmithing that I finally set up a nice little
forge on the farm and did a good deal of my own work.
At last Jim said I was stealing his trade, and when Virginia Royall came down to the post-office the day the mail
came in, which was a Friday in those days, and came to
the shop to see me, he told her what a fearful criminal
I was.   She laughed and told Jim to stop his fooling, not
knowing what a very serious thing it was for me.

When she asked me to come up to see the Elder
and Grandma Thorndyke, and I told her I was a
prisoner, Jim paroled me to her, and made her give him
a receipt for me which he wrote out on the anvil on the
leaf of his pass-book, and had her sign it.   He said he was
glad to get rid of me for two reasons: one was that I

was stealing his trade, and the other that I was likely to
bu'st forth at any time and kill some one, especially a
claim-jumper if there were any left in the county, which
he doubted.

So I went with Virginia and spent the night at the
elder's. Grandma Thorndyke took my part, though she
made a great many inquiries about Rowena Fewkes; but
the elder warned me solemnly against lawlessness, though
when we were alone together he made me tell him all
about the affair, and seemed to enjoy the more violent
parts of it as if it had been a novel; but when he asked
me who were in the "mob" I refused to tell him, and he
said maybe I was right—that my honor might be involved.
Grandma Thorndyke seemed to have entirely got over her
fear of having me and Virginia together, and let us talk
alone as much as we pleased.

I told them about the quantity of wild strawberries I
had out in Vandemark's Folly, and when Virginia asked
the sheriff if the elder and his wife and herself might go
out there with me for a strawberry-and-cream feast, he
said his duty made it incumbent upon him to insist that
he and his wife go along, and that they would furnish
the sugar if I would pony up the cream—of which I had
a plenty. So we had quite a banquet out on the farm.
Once in a while I would forget about the assaults and
the treason and be quite jolly—and then it would all come
back upon me, and I would break out in a cold sweat.
Out of this grew the first strawberry and cream festival
ever held in any church in Monterey Centre, the fruit
being furnished, according to the next issue of the
Journal "by the malefactors confined in the county Bas-
tille"—in other words by me.

4

Virginia and I gathered the berries, and she was as happy as she could be, apparently; but once in a while she would say, "Poor Teunis! Can't a Dutchman see a joke?"

After that, the elder and his wife used to come out to see me, bringing Virginia with them, almost every week, and I prided myself greatly on my fried chicken, my nice salt-rising bread, my garden vegetables, my green corn, my butter, milk and cream. I had about forgotten about being arrested, when the grand jury indicted me, and Amos Bemisdarfer and Flavius Bohn went bail for me. When the trial came on I was fined twenty dollars, and before I could produce the money, it was paid by William Trickey, Ebenezer Junkins and Absalom Frost, who told me that they got me into it, and it wasn't fair for a boy to suffer through doing what was necessary for the protection of the settlers, and what a lot of older men had egged him on to do. So I came out of it all straight, and was not much the less thought of. In fact, I seemed to have ten friends after the affair to one before. But Dick McGill, whose connection with it I have felt justified in exposing, still hounded me through his paper. I have before me the copy of the *Journal*— a little four-page sheet yellowed with time, with the account of it which follows:

"A desperado named Vandemark, well known to the annals of local crime as 'Cow Vandemark,' was arrested last Wednesday for leading the riots which have cleaned out those industrious citizens who have been jumping claims in this county. A reporter of the *Journal,* which finds out everything before it happens, attended the ceremonies of giving some of these people a coat of tar and feathers, and can speak from personal observation as to the ferocity of this ruffian Vandemark—also from slight personal contact.

"This hardened wretch is in every feature a villain—except that he has a rosy complexion, downy whiskers, and buttermilk eyes, instead of the black flashing orbs of fiction. Sheriff Boyd decoyed him into town, skilfully avoiding an rousing of his tigerish disposition, and is now making a blacksmith of him—or was until yesterday, when he paroled him to Miss Virginia Royall, the ward of the Reverend Thorndyke.

"This is a very questionable policy. If followed up it will result in a saturnalia of crime in this community. Already several of our young men are reading dime novels and taking lessons in banditry; but the sheriff has stated that this parole will not be considered a precedent. The affair has resulted in some good, however. In addition to placing the young man under Christian influences, and others, it has unearthed a patch of the biggest, best, ripest and sweetest wild strawberries in Monterey County on the ancestral estate of the criminal, known as Vandemark's Folly, and by the use of prison labor, and through the generosity and public spirit of our rising young fellow-citizen, Jacob T. Vandemark—whom we hereby salute—we are promised another strawberry festival before the crop is gone.

"In the meantime, it is worthy of mention that the industry of claim-jumping has suffered a sudden slump, and that the splendid pioneers who have opened up this Garden of Eden will not be robbed of the fruits of their enterprise."

When I came to run for county supervisor, he rehashed the matter without giving any hint that after all what I did was approved of by the people of the county in 1856 when these things took place or that he himself was in it up to the neck! But enough of that: the historical fact is that Settlers' Clubs did work of this sort all over Iowa in those times, and right or wrong, the pioneers held to the lands they took up when the great tide of the Republic broke over the Mississippi and inundated Iowa. The history of Vandemark Township was the history of the state.

CHAPTER XV

IN the month of May, 1857, I went to a party.
This was a new thing for me; for parties had been
something of which I had heard as of many things outside of the experience of a common fellow like me, but
always had thought about as a thing only to be read of,
like *porte cochères* and riding to hounds, and butlers and
books of poems. Stuff for story-books, and not for Vandemark Township; though when I saw the thing, it
was not so very different from the dances and "sings"
we used to have on the boats of the Grand Canal, as the
Erie Ditch was then called when you wanted to put on a
little style.

The party was at the "great Gothic house" of Governor Wade, just finished, over in Benton Township, The
Governor was not even a citizen of Vandemark Township, but he had some land in it. Buck Gowdy's great
estate lapped over on one corner of the township, Governor Wade's on the other, and Hell Slew, nicknamed
Vandemark's Folly Marsh cut it through the middle, and
made it hard for us to get out a full vote on anything
after we got the township organized.

The control shifted from the north side of the slew to
the south side according to the weather; for you couldn't

cross Vandemark's Folly in wet weather. Once what was called the Cow Vandemark crowd got control and kept it for years by calling the township meetings always on our own side of the slew; and then Foster Blake sneaked in a full attendance on us when we weren't looking by piling a couple of my haystacks in the trail to drive on, and it was five years before we got it back. But in the meantime we had voted taxes on them to build some schoolhouses and roads. That was local politics in Iowa when Ring was a pup.

But Governor Wade's party was not local politics, or so N. V. Creede tells me. He says that this was one of the moves by which the governor made Monterey County Republican. It had always been Democratic. The governor had always been a Democrat, and had named his township after Thomas H. Benton; but now he was the big gun of the new Republican Party in our neck of the woods, and he invited all the people who he thought would be good wheel-horses.

You will wonder how I came to be invited. Well, it was this way. I called on Judge Stone at the new courthouse, the building of which created such a scandal. He was county treasurer. He had been elected the fall before. I wanted to see him about a cattle deal. He was talking with Henderson L. Burns when I went in.

"I don't see how I can go," said he. "I've got to watch the county's money. If there was a safe in this county-seat any stronger than a cheese box, I'd lock it up and go; but I guess my bondsmen are sitting up nights worrying about their responsibility now. I'll have to decline, I reckon."

"Oh, darn the money!" said Henderson L. "You

can't be expected to set up with it like it had typhoid fever, can you? Take it with you, and put it in Wade's big safe."

"I might do that," said Judge Stone, "if I had a body-guard."

"I'd make a good guard," said Henderson L. "Let me take care of it."

"I'd have to win it back in a euchre game if I ever saw it again," said the judge. "I hate to miss that party. There'll be some medicine made there. I might go with a body-guard, eh?"

"So if the Bunker gang gets after you," suggested H. L., "there'd be somebody paid to take the load of buck-shot. Well, here's Jake. He's our local desperado. Ask Dick McGill, eh, Jake? He dared the shotgun the night they run that claim-jumper off. I know a feller that was there, and seen it—when he wa'n't scared blind. Take Jake."

2

The Bunker gang was a group of bandits that had their headquarters in the timber along the Iowa River near Eldora. They were afterward caught—some of them—and treated very badly by the officers who started to Iowa City with them. The officers, making quite a little posse, stopped at a tavern down in Tama County, I think it was at Fifteen Mile Grove, and took a drink or two too much. They had Old Man Bunker and one of the boys in the wagon tied or handcuffed, I never knew which; and while the posse was in the tavern getting their drinks the boy worked himself loose, and lay there under the buffalo robe when the men came back to take them on their journey to jail.

When they had got well started again, it was decided by the sheriff or deputy in charge that they would make Old Man Bunker tell who the other members were of their gang. So they took him out of the wagon and hung him to a tree to make him confess. When they let him down he stuck it out and refused. They strung him up again, and just as they got him hauled up they noticed that the boy—he wasn't over my age—was running away. They ran after the boy and, numbed as he was lying in the wagon in the winter's cold, he could not run fast, and they caught him. Then they remembered that they had left Old Man Bunker hanging when they chased off after the boy; and when they cut him down he was dead.

They were scared, drunk as they were, and after holding a council of war, they decided that they would make a clean sweep and hang the boy too—I forgot this boy's name. This they did, and came back telling the story that the prisoners had escaped, or been shot while escaping. I do not recall which. It was kind of pitiful; but nothing was ever done about it, though the story leaked out—being too horrible to stay a secret.

There was a great deal of sympathy with the Bunkers all over the country. I know where one of the men who did the deed lives now, out in Western Iowa, near Cherokee. He was always looked upon as a murderer here—and so, of course, he was, if he consented.

At the time when this conversation took place in Judge Stone's office, the Bunkers were in the hey-day of their bad eminence, and while they were operating a good

way off, there was some terror at the mention of their
name. The judge looked me over for a minute when
Henderson L. suggested me for the second time as a
good man for his body-guard.

"Will you go, Jake?" he asked. "Or are you scared
of the Bunkers?"

Now, as a general rule, I should have had to take
half an hour or so to decide a thing like that; but when
he asked me if I was scared of the Bunkers, it nettled me;
and after looking from him to Henderson L. for about
five minutes, I said I'd go. I was not invited to the
party, of course; for it was an affair of the big bugs;
but I never thought that an invitation was called for. I
felt just as good as any one, but I was a little wamble-
cropped when I thought that I shouldn't know how to
behave.

"How you going, Judge?" asked Henderson L.

"In my family carriage," said the judge.

"The only family carriage I ever saw you have,"
said Henderson L., "is that old buckboard."

"I traded that off," answered the judge, "to a fellow
driving through to the Fort Dodge country. I got a
two-seated covered carriage. When it was new it was
about such a rig as Buck Gowdy's."

"That's style," said Burns. "Who's going with you
—of course there's you and your wife and now you have
Jake; but you've got room for one more."

"My wife," said the judge, "is going to take the
preacher's adopted daughter. The preacher's wife
thought there might be worldly doings that it might be
better for her and the elder to steer clear of, but the girl
is going with us."

"Well, Jake," said Henderson L., "you're in luck. You'll ride to the party with your old flame, in a carriage. My wife and I are going on a load of hay. Jim Boyd is the only other man here that's got a rig with springs under it. The aristocracy of Monterey County, a lot of it, will ride plugs or shank's mares. You're getting up among 'em, Jakey, my boy. Never thought of this when you were in jail, did you?"

Nobody can realize how this talk made me suffer; and yet I kind of liked it. I suffered more than ever, because I had not seen Virginia for a long time for several reasons. I quit singing in the choir in the fall, when it was hard getting back and forth with no horses, and the heavy snow of the winter of 1855-6 began coming down.

It was a terrible winter. The deer were all killed in their stamping grounds in the timber, where they trod down the snow and struggled to get at the brush and twigs for forage. The settlers went in on snowshoes and killed them with clubs and axes. We never could have preserved the deer in a country like this, where almost every acre was destined to go under plow—but they ought to have been given a chance for their lives. I remember once when I was cussing* the men who butchered the pretty little things while Magnus Thorkelson was staying all night with me to help me get my stock through a bad storm—it was a blizzard, but we had never heard the word then—and as I got hot in my blast-

---

*"Cussing" and "cursing" are quite different things, insists the author. He would never have cursed any one, he protests; but a man is always justified in cussing when a proper case for it is presented.—G. v. d. M.

ing and bedarning of them (though they needed the venison) he got up and grasped my hand, and made as if to kiss me.

"It is murder," said he, and backed off.

I felt warmed toward him for wanting to kiss me, though I should have knocked him down if he had. He told me it was customary for men to kiss each other sometimes, in Norway. The Dunkards—like the Bohns and Bemisdarfers—were the only Americans I ever knew anything about (if they really were Americans, talking Pennsylvania Dutch as they did) who ever practised it. They greeted each other with a "holy kiss" and washed each other's feet at their great communion meeting every year. I never went but once. The men kissed the men and the women the women. So I never went but once; though they "fed the multitude" as a religious function—and if there are any women who can cook bread and meat so it will melt in your mouth, it is the Pennsylvania Dutch women. And the Bohn and Bemisdarfer women seem to me the best cooks among them, they and the Stricklers. They taught most of our wives the best cookery they know.

I was disappointed when we started from Monterey Centre, with Judge Horace Stone and me in the front seat, and Virginia in the back. As I started to say a while back, I had not been singing in the choir during the winter. The storms kept me looking out for my stock until the snow went off in the February thaw that covered Vandemark's Folly with water from bluff to bluff; and by that time I had stayed out so long that I thought I ought to be coaxed back into the choir by Virginia or Grandma Thorndyke in order to preserve my self-respect. But neither of them said anything about it. In fact, I thought that Grandma Thorndyke was not so friendly in the spring as she had been in the fall—and, of course, I could not put myself forward. I had the pure lunkhead pride.

So I had not seen Virginia for months. We early Iowa settlers, the men and women who opened up the country to its great career of development, shivered through that winter and many like it, in hovels that only broke the force of the tempest but could not keep it back. The storms swept across without a break in their fury as we cowered there, with no such shelters as now make our winters seemingly so much milder. Now it is hard to convince a man from the East that our state was once bare prairie.

"It's funny," said the young doctor that married a niece of mine last summer, "that all your groves of trees seem to be in rows. Left them that way, I suppose, when you cut down the forest."

The country looks as well wooded as the farming regions of Ohio or Indiana. Trees grew like weeds when we set them out; and we set them out as the years passed, by the million. I never went to the timber when the sap was down, without bringing home one or more elms, lindens, maples, hickories or even oaks—though the latter usually died. Most of the lofty trees we see in every direction now, however, are cottonwoods, willows and Lombardy poplars that were planted by the mere sticking in the ground of a wand of the green tree. They hauled these "slips" into Monterey County by the wagon-load after the settlers began their great rush for the prairies; and how they grew! It was no bad symbol of the state itself—a forest on four wheels.

What I began to write a few moments ago, though concerned the difference between our winter climate then and now. Then the snow drifted before our northwest winds in a moving ocean unbroken by corn-field, grove, or farmstead. It smothered and overwhelmed you when caught out in it; and after a drifting storm, the first groves we could see cast a shadow in the blizzard; and there lay to the southeast of every block of trees a long, pointed drift, diminishing to nothing at the point where ended the influence of the grove—this new foe to the tempest which civilization was planting. Our groves were yet too small of course to show themselves in this fight against the elements that first winter, and there I had hung like a leaf caught on a root in a freshet, an eighteen-year-old boy, lonely, without older people to whom I could go for advice or comfort, and filled with dreams, visions and doubts, and with no bright spot in my frosty days and frostier nights but my visions and dreams.

And I suppose my loneliness, my hardships, my lack of the fireplaces of York State and the warm rooms that we were used to in a country where fuel was plentiful, made my visions and dreams more to me than they otherwise would have been. It is the hermit who loses the world in his thoughts. And I dreamed of two things— my mother, and Virginia. Of my mother I found myself thinking with less and less of that keenness of grief which I had felt at Madison the winter before, and on my road west; so I used to get out the old worn shoe and the rain-stained letter she had left for me in the old apple-tree and try to renew my grief so as to lose the guilty feeling of which I was conscious at the waning sense of my loss of her. This was a strife against the inevitable; at eighteen—or at almost any other age, to the healthy mind—it is the living which calls, not the dead.

In spite of myself, it was Virginia Royall to whom my dreams turned all the time. Whether in the keen cold of the still nights when the howl of the wolves came to me like the cries of torment, or in the howling tempests which roared across my puny hovel like trampling hosts of wild things, sifting the snow in at my window, powdering the floor, and making my cattle in their sheds as white as sheep, I went to sleep every night thinking of her, and thinking I should dream of her—but never doing so; for I slept like the dead. I held her in my arms again as I had done the night Ann Gowdy had died back there near Dubuque, all senseless in her faint; or as I had when I scared the wolves away from her back along the Old Ridge Road; or as when I had carried her across the creek back in our Grove of Destiny—and she always, in my dreams, was willing, and conscious that I held her so tight because I loved her.

I saw her again as she played with her doll under the trees. Again I rode by her side into Waterloo; and again she ran back to me to bid me her sweet good-by after I had given her up. Often I did not give her up, but brought her to my new home, built my house with her to cheer me; and often I imagined that she was beside me, sheltered from the storm and happy while she could be by my side and in my arms. Oh, I lived whole lives over and over again with Virginia that lonely winter. She had been such a dear little creature. I had been able to do so much for her in getting her away from what she thought a great danger. She had done so much for me, too. Had not she and I cried together over the memory of my mother? Had she not been my intimate companion for weeks, cooked for me, planned for me, advised me, dreamed with me? It was not nearly so lonely as you might think, in one sense of the word.

And now I had not seen her for such a long time that I wondered if she were not forgetting me. No wonder that I was a little flighty, as I crowded myself into my poor best suit which I was so rapidly outgrowing, and walked into Monterey Centre in time to be Judge Horace Stone's body-guard the night of the party—I heard it called a reception—at Governor DeWitt Clinton Wade's new Gothic house, over in Benton Township that was to be.

I was proportionately miserable when I called at Elder Thorndyke's, to find that Virginia was not ready to see me, and that Grandma Thorndyke seemed cool and somehow different toward me. When she left me, I slipped out and went to Stone's.

"Thought you wasn't coming, Jake," said he. "Almost give you up. Just time for you to get a bite to eat before we start."

3

When we did start, his wife came out in a new black silk dress—for the Stones were quality—and was helped into the back seat, and the judge came out of the house carrying a satchel which when he handed it to me I found to be very heavy. I should say, as I have often stated, that it weighed about fifty to sixty pounds, and when he shoved it back under the seat before sitting down, it gave as I seemed to remember afterward a sort of muffled jingle.

"The treasures of Golconda, or Goldarnit," said he, "or some of those foreign places. Hear 'em jingle? Protect them with your life, Jake."

"All right," I said, as glum as you please; for he had left the only vacant place in the carriage back with Mrs. Stone. This was no way to treat me! But I was almost glad when Virginia came out to the carriage wearing a pink silk dress, and looking so fearful to the eyes of her obscure adorer that he could scarcely speak to her—she was so unutterably lovely and angelic-looking.

"How do you do, Teunis!" said she, and paused for some one to help her in. Judge Stone waited a moment, and gave her a boost at the elbow as she skipped up the step. I could have bitten myself. I was the person who should have helped her in. I was a lummox, a lunkhead, a lubber, a fool, a saphead—I was everything that was awkward and clumsy and thumb-hand-sided! To let an old married man get ahead of me in that way was a crime. I slouched down into the seat, and the judge drove off, after handing me a revolver. I slipped it into my pocket.

"Jake's my body-guard to-night, Miss Royall," said the judge. "We've got the county's money here. Did you hear it jingle?"

"No, Judge, I didn't," said she, and she never could remember any jingle afterward.

"Aren't you afraid, Teunis?"

"What of?" I inquired, looking around at her, just as she was spreading a beautiful Paisley shawl about her shoulders. I dared now take a long look at her. A silk dress and a Paisley shawl, even to my eyes, and I knew nothing about their value or rarity at that time and place, struck me all of a heap with their gorgeousness. They reminded me of the fine ladies I had seen in Albany and Buffalo.

"Of the Bunker boys," said she. "If they knew that we were out with all this money, don't you suppose they would be after it? And what could you and Mr. Stone do against such robbers?"

"I've seen rougher customers than they are," said I; and then I wondered if the man I had seen with the Bushyagers back in our Grove of Destiny had not been one of the Bunker boys. They certainly had had a bunch of stolen horses. If he was a member of the Bunker gang, weren't the Bushyagers members of it also? And was it not likely that they, being neighbors of ours, and acquainted with everything that went on in Monterey Centre, would know that we were out with the money, and be ready to pounce upon us? I secretly drew my Colt from my pocket and looked to see that each of the five chambers was loaded, and that each tube had its percussion cap. I wished, too, that I had had a little more practise in pistol shooting.

"What do you think of Virginia's dress and shawl?" asked Mrs. Stone, as we drove along the trail which wound over the prairie, in disregard of section lines, as all roads did then. The judge and I both looked at Virginia again.

"They're old persimmons," commented the judge. "You'll be the belle of the ball, Virginia."

"They're awful purty," said I, "especially the dress. Where did you get 'em, Virginia?"

"They were found in Miss Royall's bedroom," said Mrs. Stone emphasizing the "Miss"—for my benefit, I suppose; but it never touched me. "But I guess she knows where they come from."

"They were Ann's," said Virginia, a little sadly, and yet blushing and smiling a little at our open admiration, "my sister's, you know."

I scarcely said another word during all that trip. I was furious at the thought of Buck Gowdy's smuggling those clothes into Virginia's room, so she could have a good costume for the party. How did he know she was invited, or going? To be sure, her sister Ann's things ought to have been given to the poor orphan girl—that was all right; but back there along the road she would never speak his name. Had it come to pass in all these weeks and months in which I had not seen her that they had come to be on speaking terms again? Had that scoundrel who had killed her sister, after a way of speaking, and driven Virginia herself to run away from him, and come to me, got back into her good graces so that she was allowing him to draw his wing around her again? It was gall and wormwood to think of it. But why were the dress and shawl smuggled into her room, instead of being brought openly? Maybe they were not really on terms of association after all. I wished I knew, or that I had the right to ask. I forgot all about the Bunkers, until the judge whipped up the horses as we turned into the Wade place, and brought us up standing at the door.

"Well," said he, with a kind of nervous laugh, "the Bunkers didn't get us after all!"

I was out before him this time, and helped Virginia and Mrs. Stone to get down. The judge was wrestling with the heavy bag. The governor came out to welcome us, and he and Judge Stone carried it in. Mrs. Wade, a scared-looking little woman, stood in the hall and gave me her hand as I went in.

"Good evening, Mr. ——," said she.

"Mr. Vandemark," said the judge. "My body-guard, Mrs. Wade."

The good lady looked at my worn, tight-fitting corduroys, at my clean boiled shirt which I had done up myself, at my heavy boots, newly greased for the occasion, and at my bright blue and red silk neckerchief, and turned to other guests. After all I was dressed as well as some of the rest of them. There are many who may read this account of the way the Boyds, the Burnses, the Flemings, the Creedes, the Stones and others of our county aristocracy, came to this party in alpacas, delaines, figured lawns, and even calicoes, riding on loads of hay and in lumber wagons with spring seats, who may be a little nettled when a plain old farmer tells it; but they should never mind this: the time will come when their descendants will be proud of it. For they were the John Aldens, the Priscillas, the Miles Standishes and the Dorothy Q's of as great a society as the Pilgrim Fathers and Pilgrim Mothers set a-going: the society of the great commonwealth of Iowa.

The big supper—I guess they would call it a dinner now—served in the large room on a long table and some smaller ones, was the great event of the party. The Wades were very strict church-members. Such a thing as card playing was not to be thought of, and dancing was just as bad. Both were worldly amusements whose feet took hold on hell. We have lost this strictness now, and sometimes I wonder if we have not lost our religion too.

The Wades were certainly religious—that is the Governor and Mrs. Wade. Jack Wade, the John P. Wade who was afterward one of the national bosses of the Republican party, and Bob, the Robert S. Wade who became so prominent in the financial circles of the state, were a little worldly. A hired hand I once had was with the Wades for a while, and said that when he and the Wade boys were out in the field at work (for they worked as hard as any of the hands, and Bob was the first man in our part of the country who ever husked a hundred bushels of corn in a day) the Wade boys and the hired men cussed and swore habitually. But this scamp, when they were having family worship, used to fill in with "Amen!" and "God grant it!" and the like pious exclamations when the governor was offering up his morning prayer. But one morning Bob Wade brought a breast-strap from off the harness, and took care to kneel within easy reach of the kneeling hired man's pants. When he began with his responses that morning, a loud slap, and a smothered yell disturbed the governor—but he only paused, and went on.

"What in hell," asked the hired man when they got outside, "did you hit me for with that blasted strap?"

"To show you how to behave," said Bob. "When the governor is talking to the Lord, you keep your mouth shut."

I tell this, because it shows how even our richest and most aristocratic family lived, and how we were sup-

posed to defend religion against trespass. I am told
that in some countries the wickedest person is likely to
be a praying one. It seems, however, that in this country the church-members are expected to protect their
monopoly of the ear of God. Anyhow, Bob Wade felt
that he was doing a fitting if not a very seemly thing in
giving this physical rebuke to a man who was pretending
to be more religious than he was. The question is a little complex; but the circumstance shows that there could
be no cards or dancing at the Wade's party.

Neither could there be any drinking. The Wades
had a vineyard and made wine. The Flemings lived in
the next farm-house down the road, and when our party
took place, the families were on fairly good terms; though
the governor and his wife regarded the Flemings as beneath them, and this idea influenced the situation
between the families when Bob Wade began showing attentions to Kittie Fleming, a nice girl a year or so older
than I. Charlie Fleming, the oldest of the boys, was very
sick one fall, and they thought he was going to die.
Doctor Bliven prescribed wine, and the only wine in the
neighborhood was in the cellar of Governor Wade; so,
even though the families were very much at the outs, owing to the fuss about Bob and Kittie going together, Mrs.
Fleming went over to the Wades' to get some wine for
her sick boy.

"We can't allow you to have it," said the governor,
with his jaws set a little closer than usual. "We keep
wine for sacramental purposes only."

This proves how straight they were about violating
their temperance vows, and how pious. Though there
are some lines of poetry in the *Fifth Reader* which seem

to show that the governor missed a real sacrament. They read:

"Who gives himself with his alms feeds thee—
Himself, his hungering neighbor, and Me;"

but Governor Wade was a practical man who made his religion fit what he wanted to do, and what he felt was the proper thing. Bob and Jack were worldly, like the rest of us. The governor got the reputation of being a hard man, and the wine incident did a good deal to add to it. The point is that there had to be some other way of entertaining the company at the party, besides drinking, card-playing, or dancing. Of course the older people could discuss the price of land, the county organization and the like; but even the important things of the country were mostly in the hands of young people—and young folks will be young folks.

4

Kittie Fleming was a pretty black-eyed girl, who afterward made the trouble between Bob Wade and his father. At this party the thing which made it a sad affair to me was the attentions paid to Virginia by Bob. I might have been comforted by the nice way Kittie Fleming treated me, if I had had eyes for any one but Virginia; but when Kittie smiled on me, I always thought how much sweeter was Virginia's smile. But *her* smiles that evening were all for Bob Wade. In fact, he gave nobody else a chance. It really seemed as if the governor and his wife were pleased to see him deserting Kittie Fleming, but whether or not this was because they thought the poor orphan Virginia a better

match, or for the reason that any new flame would wean
him from Kittie I could not say. And I suppose they
thought Kittie's encouraging behavior to me was not
only a proof of her low tastes, or rather her lack of
ambition, but a sure sign to Bob that she was not in his
class. So far as I was concerned I was wretched, especially when the younger people began turning the
gathering into a "play party."

Now there was a difference between a play party and
a kissing party or kissing bee, as we used to call it. The
play party was quite respectable, and could be indulged
in by church-members. In it the people taking part sang
airs each with its own words, and moved about in step to
the music. The absence of the fiddle and the "calling
off" and the name of dancing took the curse off. They
went through figures a lot like dances; swung partners
by one hand or both; advanced and retreated, "balanced
to partners" bowing and saluting; clasping hands, right
and left alternately with those they met; and balanced to
places, and the like. Sometimes they had a couple to
lead them, as in the dance called the German, of which
my granddaughter tells me; but usually they were all supposed to know the way the play went, and the words
were always such as to help. Here is the one they started
off with that night:

> "We come here to bounce around,
> We come here to bounce around,
> We come here to bounce around,
>   Tra, la, la!
>   Ladies, do si do,
>   Gents, you know,
>   Swing to the right,
>   And then to the left,
>   And all promenade!"

Oh, yes! I have seen Wades and Flemings and Holbrooks and all the rest singing and hopping about to the tune of *We Come Here to Bounce Around;* and also *We'll All Go Down to Rowser;* and *Hey, Jim Along, Jim Along Josie;* and *Angelina Do Go Home;* and *Good-by Susan Jane;* and *Shoot the Buffalo;* and *Weevilly Wheat;* and *Sandy He Belonged to the Mill;* and *I've Been to the East, I've Been to the West, I've Been to the Jay-Bird's Altar;* and *Skip-to-My-Lou;* and *The Juniper Tree;* and *Go In and Out the Window;* and *The Jolly Old Miller;* and *Captain Jinks;* and lots more of them. Boyds and Burnses and Smythes tripping the light fantastic with them, and not half a dozen dresses better than alpacas in the crowd, and the men many of them in drilling trousers—and half of them with hayseed in their hair from the load on which they rode to the party! So, ye Iowa aristocracy, put that in your pipes and smoke it, as ye bowl over the country in your automobiles—or your airships, as I suppose it may be before you read this!

I went round with the rest of them, for I had seen all these plays on the canal boats, and had once or twice taken part in them. Kittie Fleming, very graceful and gracious as she bowed to me, and as I swung her around, was my partner. Bob Wade still devoted himself to Virginia, who was like a fairy in her fine pink silk dress.

"This is enough of these plays," shouted Bob at last, after looking about to see that his father and mother were not in the room. "Let's have the 'Needle's Eye'!"

"The 'Needle's Eye'!" was the cry, then.

"I won't play kissing games!" said one or two of the girls.

"Le's have 'The Gay Balonza Man'!" shouted Doctor

Bliven, who was in the midst of the gaieties, while his wife too, plunged in as if to outdo him.

"Oh, yes!" she said, smiling up into the face of Frank Finster, with whom she had been playing. "Let's have 'The Gay Balonza Man!' It's such fun!"*

"The Needle's Eye" won, and we formed in a long line of couples—Wades, Finsters, Flemings, Boyds and the rest of the roll of present-day aristocrats, and marched, singing, between a boy and a girl standing on chairs with their hands joined. Here is the song—I can sing the tune to-day:

> "The needle's eye,
> Which doth supply
> The thread which runs so true;
> {And many a lass
> {Have I let pass
> or

---

*One here discovers a curious link between our recent past and olden times in our Old Home, England. This game has like most of the kissing or play-party games of our fathers (and mothers) more than one version. By some it was called "The Gay Galoney Man," by others "The Gay Balonza Man." It is a last vestige of the customs of the sixteenth century and earlier in England. It was brought over by our ancestors, and survived in Iowa at the time of its settlement, and probably persists still in remote localities settled by British immigrants. The "Gay Balonza Man" must be the character—the traveling beggar, pedler or tinker,—who was the hero of country-side people, and of the poem attributed to James V. called *The Gaberlunzie-Man* (1512-1542) in which the event is summed up in two lines relating to a peasant girl, "She's aff wi the gaberlunzie-man." The words of the play run in part as follows:

"See the gay balonza-man, the charming gay balonza-man;
We'll do all that ever we can,
To cheat the gay balonza-man!"

The things he was to be cheated of seemed to be osculations.
—G. v. d. M.

{And many a beau
{Have I let go
Because I wanted you!"

At the word "you," the two on the chairs—they were
Lizzie Finster and Charley McKim at first—brought
their arms down and caught a couple—they caught Kittie and me—who were at that moment passing through
between the chairs—which were the needle's eye; and
then they sang, giving us room to execute:

"And they bow so neat!
And they kiss so sweet!
We do intend before we end, to have this couple meet!"

Crimson of face, awkward as a calf, I bowed to Kittie
and she to me; and then she threw her arms about me
and kissed me on the lips. And then I saw her wink
slyly at Bob Wade. Then Kittie and I became the
needle's eye and she worked it so we caught Bob Wade
and Virginia, even though it was necessary to wait a
moment after the word "you"—she meant to do it! As
Bob's lips met Virginia's I groaned, and turning my
back on Kittie Fleming, I rushed out of the room. Judge
Stone tried to stop me.

5

"Jake, Jake!" Judge Stone whispered in my ear, looking anxiously around, "have you seen the governor in the
last half or three-quarters of an hour?"

"He hain't been in here," I said, jerking away from
him.

"Sure?" he persisted. "I've looked everywhere except in his office where he put the money—and that's
locked."

I broke away from him and went out. I had no desire to see Governor Wade or any one else. I wanted to
be alone. I had seen Virginia kissed by Bob Wade—
and they were still singing that sickish play in there.
They would be kissing and kissing all the rest of the
night. She to be kissed in this way, and I had been so
careful of her, when I was all alone with her for days,
and would have given my right hand for a kiss! It was
terrible. I walked back and forth in the yard, and then
came up on the porch and sat down on a bench, so as to
hear the play-singing. They were singing *The Gay Balonza-Man,* now. I started up once to walk home, but I
thought that Judge Stone was paying me wages for
guarding the county's money, and turned to go back
where I could watch the games, lured by a sort of fas-
cination to see how many times Virginia would allow
herself to be kissed. A woman came out of the house,
and in passing saw and recognized me. It was Mrs.
Bliven. She dropped down on the bench.

"My God!" she sobbed. "I'll go crazy! I'll kill myself!"

I sat down again on the bench. She had been so happy a few minutes ago, to all appearances, that I was astonished; but after waiting quite a while I could think
of nothing to say to her. So I turned my face away for
fear that she might see what I felt must show in it.

"You're in trouble, too," she said. "You babies!
My God, how I'd like to change places with you! Did
you see him kissing them?"

"Who?" I asked.

"My man," she cried. "Bliven. You know how it is
with us. You're the only one that knows about me—

about us—Jake. I've been scared to death for fear you'd tell ever since I found you were coming here to live; and I dasn't tell him—he don't know you know. And now I almost wish you would tell—put it in Dick McGill's paper. He wants somebody else already. A woman that's done as I have—he can throw me away like an old shoe! But I want you to promise me that if he ever shelves me you'll let the world know. Did you see him hugging them girls? He's getting ready to shelve me, I tell you!"

I sat for some time thinking this matter over. Finally I spoke, and she seemed surprised, as if she had forgotten I was there.

"I'll tell you what I'll do," said I. "I won't tell on you just because you think you want me to. What would happen if everything in the lives of us folks out here was to be told, especially as it would be told in Dick McGill's paper? But if you ever find out for sure that he is going to—going to—to shelve you, why, come to me, and I'll go to him. I think he would be a skunk to—to shelve you. And I don't see that—that—that he—was any more fairce to hug and kiss than—than some others. Than you!"

"Or you," said she, sort of snickering through her tears.

"I hated it!" I said.

"So did I," said she.

"Maybe Doc did, too," I suggested.

"No," she replied, after a while. "I'll tell you, Jake, I'll hold you to your promise. Sometime I may come to you or send for you. May I?"

"Any time," I answered, and she went in, seeming quite cheered up. I suppose she needed that blow-off, like an engine too full of steam. I wonder if it was wrong to feel for her? But it must be remembered that I had very little religious bringing up.

Well, the party came to an end presently, and Judge Stone came out and hollo'd for me to bring the team. When I drove up to the door he asked me in a low tone to come and help carry the money out. The governor unlocked his office, and then the safe, and took out the bag, which he handed to Judge Stone.

"Heavy as ever," said the judge. "Catch hold here, Jake, and help me carry it."

"A heavy responsibility at least," said the governor.

The governor's hired people of whom he had always a large force had not taken part in the proceedings of the party, but most of them were gathered about as we took our departure. They were to a great extent the younger men among the settlers, and the governor in later times never got tired of saying how much he had done for the early settlers in giving them employment.

N. V. Creede in answering him in campaigns always said that if he gave the boys work, they gave the governor labor in return, and at a dollar a day it seemed to him that the governor was the one who was under obligations to them. It is a curious thing that people who receive money are supposed to be under obligations to those who pay it, no matter what the deal may be. We say "thank you" to the man who pays us for a day's wages; but why, if the work is worth the money?

Well, as I looked about among the governor's working people, as I have said, I saw a head taller than the rest, the big form of Pitt Bushyager. He was looking at me with that daredevil smile of his, the handsomest man there, with his curling brown mustache and goatee; and nodded at me as the judge got into the carriage in the back seat with Mrs. Stone, and Virginia came up in her pretty pink silk, with the Paisley shawl around her shoulders, to be helped up into the front seat with me. The satchel of money was placed under the seat where the judge could feel it with his feet.

We drove off in that silence which comes with the drowsiness that follows excitement, especially along toward morning. The night was dark and still. Virginia's presence reminded me of those days of happiness when we drove into Iowa alone together; but I was not happy. I had lived with this girl in my dreams ever since, and now I faced the wrench of giving her up; for I repeated in my own mind over and over again that she would never think of me with such big bugs as Bob Wade shining around her.

The Judge and Mrs. Stone were talking together now, and I heard references to the money. Then I began to turn over in my slow mind the fact, known to me alone, that there was a man at the Wade farm who was one of a band of thieves, and who knew about our having the money. If he really was connected with the Bunker boys, what was more likely than that he had ways of passing the word along to some of them who might be waiting to rob us on our way home? But the crime that I was sure had been committed back along the road the spring before had been horse-stealing. I wondered whether or not the business of outlawry was not specialized, so that some stole horses, others robbed banks, others were highwaymen, and the like.

All this time Virginia seemed to be snuggling up a little closer. Maybe Pitt Bushyager and his brothers were just plain horse-thieves, and nothing else. Perhaps they were just hired to help drive in the horses; but why, then, did Pitt have two animals in Monterey Centre when I saw him there the morning I arrived?

6

Jim Boyd's light buggy had got far ahead of us, out of hearing, and the lumber wagons, with the bulk of the crowd, were far in the rear. We were alone. As we came to a road which wound off to the south toward where there was a settlement of Hoosiers who had made a trail to the Wade place, I turned off and followed it, knowing that when I got to the Hoosier settlement, I should find a road into the Centre. It was a mistake made a-purpose, done on that instinct which protects the man who feels that he may be trailed. I was on an unexpected path to any one waiting for us. Finally Virginia spoke to me.

"How is our farm?" she asked.

Now I had not forgotten how she had been kissed by Bob Wade, and probably, while I was outside sulking, by a dozen others. By instinct again—the instinct of a jealous boy—I started in to punish her.

"All right," I said surlily.

"What crops have you planted?" she went on.

"About ten acres of wheat," I said, "and the rest of my breaking in corn and oats. You see, I have to put in all the time I can in breaking."

"How is the white heifer?" she asked, inquiring as to one of my cattle that she had petted a lot.

"She has a calf," said I.

"Oh, has she? How I wish I could see it! What color is it?"

"Spotted."

There followed a long silence, during which we went farther and farther off the road.

"Jake," said the judge, "whose house is that we just passed?"

"It's that new Irishman's," said I. "Mike Cosgrove, ain't that his name?"

"Well, then," said the judge, "we're off the road. Stop!"

"Yes," I said, "I made the wrong turn back there. It's only a little farther."

The judge was plainly put out about this. He even wanted to go back to the regular road again, and when I explained that we would soon reach a trail which would lead right into the Centre, he still persisted.

"If we were to be robbed on this out-of-the-way road," said he, "it would look funny."

"It would look funnier," I said, "if we were to go back and then get robbed. Any one waiting to rob us would be on the regular road, wouldn't they?"

So I stubbornly drove on, the judge grumbling all the while for a mile or so. Then he and Mrs. Stone began talking in a low tone, under the cover of which Virginia resumed her conversation with me.

"You are a stubborn Dutchman," said she. To which I saw no need of making any reply.

"You seemed to have a good time," she said, presently.

"I didn't," said I. "I'm nobody by the side of such people as Bob Wade. I wasn't even invited. I'm just paid to come along with the judge to protect the county's money. You'll never see me again at any of your grand kissing parties."

"It was the first I ever went to," said she; "but you seemed to know what to do pretty well—you and Kittie Fleming."

This stumped me for a while, and we drove on in silence.

"I didn't kiss her," I said.

"It looked like it," said Virginia.

"She kissed me," I protested.

"You seemed to like it," she insisted.

"I didn't!" I said, mad all over. "And I quit just as soon as the kissing began."

"You ought to have stayed," she said stiffly. "The fun was just beginning when you flounced out."

And then came one of the interesting events of this eventful night. We turned into the main road to Monterey Centre, just where Duncan McAlpine's barn now stands, and I thought I saw down in the hollow where it was still dark, though the light was beginning to dawn in the east, a clump of dark objects like cattle or horses—or horsemen. As I looked, they moved into the road as if to stop us. I drew my pistol, fired it over their heads, and they scattered. Then, I was scared still more, by a sound as of a cavalry or a battery of artillery coming behind us. It was three loads of people on the hayracks, who had overtaken us on account of our having gone by the roundabout way; coming at a keen gallop down the hill to have the credit of passing a fancy carriage. They passed us like a tornado; shouting as they went by, asking what I had shot at, and telling us to hurry up so as to get home by breakfast time. The horsemen ahead, whatever might have been their plans, did not seem to care to argue matters with so large a force, and rode off in several directions, while I pressed close to the rear of the last hayrack. Thus we drove into Monterey Centre.

"What did you shoot for?" asked the judge as we stopped at his house.

"I wanted to warn a lot of men on horseback that were heading us off, that there'd be trouble if they tried to stop us," I answered.

"Damned foolishness," said the judge. "Well, come in and let's have a bite to eat."

7

Virginia was staying with them the rest of the night; but as I helped her out, feeling in her stiffness that she was offended with me, I insisted that I would go on home. The judge, who had been ready to abuse me a moment before, now took hold of me and forced me into the house. As we went in carrying the satchel, he lifted it up on the table.

"We may as well take a look at it," said he.

Mrs. Stone and Virginia and I all stood by the table as he unsnapped the catch and opened the bag. It was full almost to the top.

"That ain't the way I packed that money!" said the judge.

His hands trembled as he pulled the contents out. It was full of the bags and wrappers in which the money had been packed, according to the judge's tell; but there was no money in the wrappers, and the bags were full, not of coins, but of common salt. That was what made it so heavy; and that was what always made it such a mystery: for all the salt used in Monterey County then was common barrel salt. It was the same kind, whether it was got from the barrel from which the farmer salted his cattle, or from the supply in the kitchen of the dweller in the town. There was no clue in it. It was just salt! We all cried out in surprise, not understanding that we were looking at the thing which was to be fought over until either Judge Stone or Governor Wade was destroyed.

"I am ruined!" Judge Stone fell back into a chair groaning. Then he jumped to his feet. "They've taken it out while we were at the party!" he shouted. "The damned, canting, sniveling old thief! No wonder he's got money! He probably stole it where he came from! Jake, we've got to go back and make him give this money back—come on!"

"Make who give it back?" I asked.

"Who?" said he. "Why old DeWitt Clinton Wade, the old thief! Who else had the key to the office or knew how to open that safe? Come on, Jake, and bring your pistol!"

I handed him the pistol.

"I agreed to guard you and the county's money," I said, "and that's all. You hain't got the county's money, it seems, and my job's over. I've got to break prairie to-day, and I guess I'd better be going!"

I passed out of the door, and as I went I heard them —the judge and his wife, and I thought Virginia joined in—condemning me for deserting them. But I needed to think this thing over before I could see into it. It looked pretty dark for some one then, and I saw it was a matter to see N. V. about before taking any further part.

I never have seen through it. There it was: The money in the treasury, and supposed to be in the bag, and placed in Governor Wade's safe. There were the two men, both supposed to be rich. There was the time, when the kissing games were going on, when the governor was not seen by any of his guests. The governor was rich always afterward, while the judge struggled along with adversity and finally went away from the county poor as a church mouse. Then there was the jingle I seemed to remember at starting, and Judge Stone's twice speaking of it—the jingle Virginia did not hear. Salt does not jingle.

For a long time it appeared to me that these things seemed to prove that the governor got the money; but lately, since both the men have passed away, I have had my doubts. Judge Stone was a much nicer man than the governor to meet up with, but—well, what's the use? It is long past. It was past for me, too, as I walked out to my farm that morning as the dawn broadened into day, with the prairie-chickens singing their wonderful morning song, and the blue-joint grass soaking me with dew to my knees.

At that moment, or soon after, in a stormy encounter at the Wade farm, with witnesses that the judge took with him, began the great Wade-Stone feud of Monterey County, Iowa. It lasted until the flood of new settlers floated it away in a freshet of new issues during and after the great Civil War.

I took the story to N. V. as soon as I went to

town. He sat looking at me with a mysterious grin on his face, as I told him of the loss of the county funds.

"Well," said he, "this will make history. I venture the assertion that the case will be compromised. I can't see this close corporation of a county government making Stone's bondsmen pay the loss. Or Stone either. And I can't see any one getting that amount of money out of old Wade, whether it was in the bag when it went into his safe or not. Your testimony on the jingle feature ain't worth a cuss. The Bunker boys had that bag marked for their own; for we know now that they were out on a raid that night and cleaned up several good horses. I must say, Jake, that you are a hell of a hired man. If you had kept the main road, this trouble which will raise blazes with things in this county till you and I are gray-headed, never would have happened. The Bunkers would have had that salt, and everybody else would have had an alibi. Maybe it was Judge Stone's instinct for party harmony that made him cross at you for dodging the Bunkers by driving down by the Hoosier settlement. He was cross, wasn't he? Instinct is a great matter, says Falstaff. He was mad on instinct, I reckon! And you drove off the road on instinct. 'Beware instinct,' say I on the authority aforesaid. It would have smoothed matters all out if the Bunker boys had got that salt!"

CHAPTER XVI

THE FEWKESES IN CLOVER AT BLUE-GRASS MANOR

IOWA lived in the future in those days. It was a land of poverty and privations and small things, but a land of dreams. We shivered in the winter storms, and dreamed; we plowed and sowed and garnered in; but the great things, the happy things, were our dreams and visions. We felt that we were plowing the field of destiny and sowing for the harvest of history; but we scarcely thought it. The power that went out of us as we scored that wonderful prairie sod and built those puny towns was the same power that nerved the heart of those who planted Massachusetts and Rhode Island and Virginia, the power that has thrilled the world whenever the white man has gone forth to put a realm under his feet.

Our harvest of that day seems pitifully small as I sit on my veranda and look at my barns and silos, and see the straight rows of corn leaning like the characters of God's handwriting across the broad intervale of Vandemark's Folly flat, sloping to the loving pressure of the steady warm west wind of Iowa, and clapping a million dark green hands in acclamation of the full tide of life sucked up from the richest breast that Mother Earth in all her bountiful curves turns to the lips of her offspring. But all our children for all future generations shall help to put the harvests of those days into the barns and silos of the future state. God save it from the mildews of monopoly and tyranny, and the Red rot of insurrection and from repression's explosions!

We were children, most of those of whom I have been writing. It was a baby county, a baby state, and Vandemark Township was still struggling up toward birth. "The thoughts of youth are long, long thoughts": but after all they are only the stirrings of the event in the womb of life. I would not have married Virginia on the day after the party at Judge Stone's if she had in some way conveyed to me that she wanted me. I should not have dared; for I was a child. I suppose that Magnus would have taken Rowena Fewkes in a minute, for he was older; but I don't know. It takes a Norwegian or a Swede a long time to get ripe.

The destinies of the county and state were in the hands of youth, dreaming of the future: and when the untamed prairie turned and bit us, as it did in frosts and blizzards and floods and locusts and tornadoes, we said to each other, like the boy in the story when the dog bit his father, "Grin and bear it, Dad! It'll be the makin' o' the pup!" Even the older men like Judge Stone and Governor Wade and Elder Thorndyke and heads of families like the Bemisdarfers, were dreamers: and as for such ne'er-do-weels as the Fewkeses, they, with Celebrate's schemes for making money, and Surrager's inventions, and their plans for palaces and estates, were only a little more absurd in their visions than the rest of us. The actual life of to-day is to the dreams of that day as the wheat plant to the lily. It starts to be a lily, but the finger and thumb of destiny—mainly in the form of heredity—turn it into the wheat, and then into the prosaic flour and bran in the bins.

As I came driving into Monterey County, every day had its event, different from that of the day before; but now comes a period when I must count by years, not days, and a lot of time passes without much to record. As for the awful to-do about the county's lost money, I heard nothing of it, except when, once in a while, somebody, nosing into the matter for one reason or another, would come prying around to ask me about it. I began by telling them the whole story whenever they asked, and Henderson L. Burns once took down what I said and made me swear to it. Whenever I came to the jingle of the money in the bag as we put it in the carriage on starting for the Wades', they cross-examined me till I said I sort of seemed to kind of remember that it jingled, and anyhow I recollected that Judge Stone had said "Hear it jingle, Jake!" This proved either that the money was there and jingled, or that it wasn't there and that the judge was, as N. V. said, "As guilty as hell."

Dick McGill didn't know which way the cat would jump, and kept pretty still about it in his paper; but he printed a story on me that made everybody laugh. "There was once a Swede," said the paper, "that was running away from the minions of the law, and took refuge in a cabin where they covered him with a gunny sack. When the Hawkshaws came they asked for the Swede. No information forthcoming. 'What's in that bag?' asked the minions. 'Sleighbells,' replied the accomplices. The minion kicked the bag, and there came forth from under it the cry, 'Yingle! Yingle!' We know a Dutchman who is addicted to the same sort of ventriloquism." (Monterey *Journal*, September 3, 1857.)

In 1856 we cut our grain with cradles. In 1857 Magnus and I bought a Seymour & Morgan hand-rake reaper. I drove two yoke of cows to this machine, and Magnus raked off. I don't think we gained much over cradling, except that we could work nights with the cows, and bind day-times, or the other way around when the straw in the gavels got dry and harsh so that heads would pull off as we cinched up the sheaves. At that very moment, the Marsh brothers back in De Kalb County, Illinois, were working on the greatest invention ever given to agriculture since the making of the first steel plow, the Marsh Harvester.

Every year we broke some prairie, and our cultivated land increased. By the fall of 1857, my little cottonwood trees showed up in a pretty grove of green for a distance of two or three miles, and were ten to fifteen feet high: so I could lie in the shade of the trees I had planted.

But if the trees flourished, the community did not. The panic of 1857 came on in the summer and fall; but we knew nothing, out in our little cabins, of the excitement in the cities, the throngs on Wall Street and in Philadelphia, the closing banks, the almost universal bankruptcy of the country. It all came from land speculation. According to what they said, there was more land then laid out in town-sites in Kansas than in all the cities and towns of the settled parts of the country. In Iowa there were town-sites along all the streams and scattered all over the prairies. Everybody was in debt, in the business world, and when land stopped growing in value, sales stopped, and then the day of reckoning came. All financial panics come from land speculation. Show me a way to keep land from advancing in value, and I will tell you how to prevent financial panics.*

But, though we knew nothing about this general wreck and ruin back east, we knew that we were miserably poor. In the winter of 1857-8 Magnus and I were beggarly ragged and so short of fuel and bedding that he came over and stayed with me, so that we could get along with one bed and one fire. My buffalo robes were the things that kept us warm, those howling nights, or when it was so still that we could hear the ice crack in the creek eighty rods off. My wife has always said that Magnus and I holed up in our den like wild animals, and sometimes like a certain domestic one. But what with Magnus and the fiddle and his stories of Norway and mine of the canal we amused ourselves pretty well and got along without baths. My cows, and the chickens, and our vegetables and potatoes, and our white and buckwheat flour and the corn-meal mush and johnny-cake kept us fat, and I entirely outgrew my best suit, so that I put it on for every day, and burst it at most of the seams in a week.

2

I was sorry for the people in the towns, and sold most of my eggs, fowls, butter, cream and milk on credit: and though Virginia and I were not on good terms and I never went to see her any more; and though Grandma

---

*The author, when his attention is called to the Mississippi Bubble, insists that it was nothing more nor less than betting on the land development of a great new region. As to the "Tulipomania" which once created a small panic in Holland, he insists that such a fool notion can not often occur, and never can have wide-spread results like a genuine financial panic. In which the editor is inclined to believe the best economists will agree with him.—G. v. d. M.

Thorndyke was, I felt sure, trying to get Virginia's mind fixed on a better match, like Bob Wade or Paul Holbrook, I used to take eggs, butter, milk or flour to the elder's family almost every time I went to town: and when the weather was warm enough so that they would not freeze, I took potatoes, turnips, and sometimes some cabbage for a boiled dinner, with a piece of pork to go with it.

When the elder found out who was sending it he tried to thank me, but I made him promise not to tell his family where these things came from, on pain of not getting any more. I said I had as good right to contribute to the church as any one, and just because I had no money it was tough to have the little I could give made public. By this time I had worked up quite a case, and was looking like a man injured in his finest feelings and twitted of his poverty. The elder looked bewildered, and promised that he wouldn't tell.

"But I'm sure, Jake, that the Lord won't let your goodness go unrewarded, in the next world, anyhow, and I don't think in this."

I don't think he actually told, but I have reason to believe he hinted. In fact, Kittie Fleming told me when I went down to their place after some seed oats, that Grandma Thorndyke had said at the Flemings' dinner table that I was an exemplary boy, in my way, and when I grew up I would make some girl a husband who would be kind and a good provider.

"I was awful interested," she said.

"Why?" I asked; for I couldn't see for the life of me how it interested her.

"I'm a girl," said she, "and I feel interested in—in—

in such things—husbands, and good providers." Here I grew hot all over, and twisted around like a worm on a hot griddle. "I didn't think, when you were playing the needle's eye with me, that you acted as if you would be a very good husband!"

I peeked up at her through my eyebrows, and saw she was grinning at me, and sort of blushing, herself. But I had only one word for her.

"Why?"

"You didn't seem to—to— kiss back very much," she giggled; and as I was struggling to think of something to say (for it seemed a dreadful indictment as I looked at her, so winning to a boy who hadn't seen a girl for weeks) she ran off; and it was not till I was sitting by the stove at home after washing up the dishes that evening that I thought what a fine retort it would have been if I had offered to pay back then, with interest, all I owed her in the way of response. I spent much of the evening making up nice little speeches which I wished I had had the sprawl to get off on the spur of the moment. I grew fiery hot at the thought of how badly I had come off in this little exchange of compliments with Kittie. Poor Kittie! She supped sorrow with a big spoon before many years; and then had a long and happy life. I forgave her, even at the time, for making fun of the Hell Slew Dutch boy. All the girls made fun of me but Virginia, and she did sometimes—Virginia and Rowena Fewkes.

Thinking of Rowena reminded me of the fact that I had not seen any of the Fewkeses for nearly two years. This brought up the thought of Buck Gowdy, who had carried them off to his great farmstead which he called Blue-grass Manor. Whenever I was in conversation with

him I was under a kind of strain, for all the fact that he
was as friendly with me as he was with any one else. I
remembered how I had smuggled Virginia away from
him; and wondered whether or not he had got intimate
enough by this time at Elder Thorndyke's so that she had
given him any inkling as to my share in that matter.

This brought me back to Virginia—and then the whole
series of Virginia dreams recurred. She sat in the chair
which I had bought for her, in the warm corner next the
window. She was sewing. She was reading to me. She
was coming over to my chair to sit in my lap while we
talked over our adventures. She looked at my chapped
and cracked hands and told me I must wear my mittens
every minute. She—but every boy can go on with the
series: every boy who has been in the hopeless but bliss-
ful state in which I then was: a state which out of hope-
lessness generates hope as a dynamo generates current.

This was followed by days of dark despondency.
Magnus Thorkelson and I were working together plowing
for oats, for we did not work our oats on the corn ground
of last year then as we do now, and he tried to cheer me
up. I had been wishing that I had never left the canal;
tor there I always had good clothes and money in my
pocket. We couldn't stay in this country, I said. Nobody had any money except a few money sharks, and
they robbed every one that borrowed of them with their
two per cent. a month. I was getting raggeder and raggeder every day. I wished I had not bought this other
eighty. I wished I had done anything rather than what
I had done. I wished I knew where I could get work at
fair wages, and I would let the farm go—I would that!

I would be gosh-blasted if I wouldn't, by Golding's bow-key!*

"Oh!" exclaimed Magnus, "you shouldn't talk so! Ve got plenty to eat. Dere bane lots people in Norvay would yump at de shance to yange places wit' us. What nice land here in Iovay! Some day you bane rich man. All dis slew bane some day dry for plow. I see it in Norvay and Sveden. And now dat ve got ralroad, dere bane t'ousan's an' t'ousan's people in Norvay, and Denmark, and Sveden and Yermany come here to Iovay, an' you an' your vife an' shildern bane big bugs. Yust vait, Yake. Maybe you see your sons in county offices an' your girls married vit bankers, an' your vife vare new calico dress every day. Yust vait, Yake. And to-night I pop some corn if you furnish butter, hey?"

To hear the pop-corn going off in the skillet, like the volleys of musketry we were so soon to hear at Shiloh; to see Magnus with his coat off, stirring it round and round in the sizzling butter until one or two big white kernels popped out as a warning that the whole regiment was about to fire; to see him, with his red hair all over his freckled face, lift the hissing skillet and shake it until the volleys died down to sharpshooting across the lines; and then to hear him laugh when he turned the vegetable snowdrift out into the wooden butter-bowl a little too soon, and a last shot or two blew the fluffy kernels all over the room—all this was the very acme of success in

---

*"By Golding's bow-key" was a very solemn objurgation. It could be used by professors of religion, but under great provocation only. It harks back to the time when every man who had oxen named them Buck and Golding, and the bow-key held the yoke on. Ah, those far-off, Arcadian days, and the blessing of knowing those who lived in them!—G. v. d. M.

making a pleasant evening. All the time I was thinking of Magnus's prediction.

"County officer!" I snorted. "Banker! Me!"

"Ay dank so," said Magnus. "Or maybe lawyers and yudges."

"Any girl I would have," I said, "wouldn't have me; and any girl that would have me, the devil wouldn't have!"

"Anybody else say dat to me, I lick him," he stated.

"There ain't any farm girls out in this prairie," I said; "and no town girl would come in here," and I spread my hands out to show that I thought my house the worst place in the world, though I was really a little proud of it—for wasn't it mine? made with my own hands, mainly?

"Girls come where dey want to come," said he, "in spite of——"

"Of hell and high water," I supplied, as he hesitated.

"So!" he answered, adopting my words, and afterward using them at a church social with some effect. "In spite of Hell Slew and high water. An' if dey bane too soft in de hand to come, I bring you out a fine farm girl from Norvay."

3

This idea furnished us meat for much joking, and then it grew almost earnest, as jokes will. We finally settled down to a cousin of his, Christina Quale. And whenever I bought anything for the house, which I did from time to time as I got money, we discussed the matter as to whether or not Christina would like it. The first thing I bought was a fine silver-plated castor, with six bottles in it, to put in the middle of the table so that it could be turned around as the company helped themselves to salt, mustard, vinegar, red or black pepper; and the sixth thing I never could figure out until Grandma Thorndyke told me it was oil. A castor was a sort of title of nobility, and this one always lifted me in the opinions of every one that sat down at my table. Magnus said he was sure Christina would be tickled yust plumb to death with it. Ah! Christina was a wonderful legal fiction, as N. V. calls it. How many times Virginia's ears must have burned as we tenderly discussed the poor yellow-haired peasant girl far off there by the foaming fjords.

One trouble with all of us Vandemark Township settlers was that we had no money. I had long since stopped going to church or to see anybody, because I was so beggarly-looking. Going away from our farms to earn wages put back the development of the farms, and made the job of getting started so much slower. It is so to-day in the new parts of the country, and something ought to be done about it. With us it was hard to get work, even when we were forced to look for it. I hated to work for Buck Gowdy, because there was that thing between us, whether he knew it or not; but when Magnus came to me one day after we had got our oats sowed, and said that Mr. Gowdy wanted hands, I decided that I would go over with Magnus and work out a while.

4

I was astonished, after we had walked the nine miles between the edge of the Gowdy tract and the headquarters, to see how much he had done. There were square miles of land under plow, and the yards, barns, granaries and houses looked almost as much like a town as Monterey Centre. We went straight to Gowdy's office. His overseer was talking with us, when Gowdy came in.

"Hello, Thorkelson," said he; "you're quite a stranger. Haven't seen you for a week."

Magnus stole a look at me and blushed so that his face was as red as his hair. I was taken aback by this for he had never said a word to me about the frequent visits to the Gowdy ranch which Buck's talk seemed to show had taken place. What had he been coming over for? I wondered, as I heard Gowdy greeting me.

"Glad to see you, Mr. Vandemark," said he. "What can I do for you-all?"

"We heard you wanted a couple of hands," said I, "and we thought——"

"I need a couple of hundred," said he. "Put 'em to work, Mobley," turning to the overseer; and then he went off into a lot of questions and orders about the work, after which he jumped into the buckboard buggy, in which Pinck Johnson sat with the whip in his hands, and they went off at a keen run, with Pinck urging the team to a faster pace, and Gowdy holding to the seat as they went careering along like the wind.

We lived in a great barracks with his other men, and ate our meals in a long room like a company of soldiers. It was a most interesting business experiment which he was trying; and he was going behind every day. Where land is free nobody will work for any one else for less than he can make working for himself; and land was pretty nearly free in Monterey County then. All a man needed was a team, and he could get tools on credit; and I know plenty of cases of people breaking speculator's land and working it for years without paying rent or being molested. The rent wasn't worth quarreling about. But Gowdy couldn't get, on the average, as much out of his hired men in the way of work as they would do for themselves.

Most of the aristocrats who came early to Iowa to build up estates, lost everything they had, and became poor; for they did not work with their own hands, and the work of others' hands was inefficient and cost, anyhow, as much as it produced or more. Gowdy would have gone broke long before the cheap land was gone, if it had not been for the money he got from Kentucky. The poor men like me, the peasants from Europe like Magnus—we were the ones who made good, while the gentility went bankrupt.

After a few years the land began to take on what the economists call "unearned increment," or community value, and the Gowdy lands began the work which finally made him a millionaire; but it was not his work. It was mine, and Magnus Thorkelson's, and the work of the neighbors generally, on the farms and in the towns. It was the railroads and school and churches. He would have made property faster to let his land lie bare until in the 'seventies. I could see that his labor was bringing him a loss, every day's work of it; and at breakfast I was studying out ways to organize it better,—when a small hand pushed a cup of coffee past my cheek, and gave my nose a little pinch as it was drawn back. I looked up, and there was Rowena, waiting on our table!

"Hello, Jake!" said she. "I heared you was dead."

"Hello, Rowena," I answered. "I'm just breathin' my last!"

All the hands began yelling at us.

"No sparkin' here!"

"None o' them love pinches, Rowena!"

"I swan to man if that Dutchman ain't cuttin' us all out!"

"Quit courtin' an' pass them molasses, sweetness!"

"Mo' po'k an' less honey, thar!"—this from a Missourian.

"Magnus, your pardner's cuttin' you out!"

I do not need to say that all this hectoring from a lot of men who were most of them strangers, almost put me under the table; but Rowena, tossing her head, sent them back their change, with smiles for everybody. She was as pretty a twenty-year-old lass as you would see in a day's travel. No longer was she the ragged waif to whom I had given the dress pattern back toward Dubuque. She was rosy, she was plump, her new calico dress was as pretty as it could be, and her brown skin and browner hair made with her dark eyes a study in brown and pink, as the artists say.

It was two or three days before I had a chance to talk with her. She had changed a good deal, I sensed, as she told me all about her folks. Old Man Fewkes was working in the vegetable garden. Celebrate was running a team. Surajah was working on the machinery. Ma Fewkes was keeping house for the family in a little cottage in the corner of the garden. I went over and had a talk with them. Ma Fewkes, with her shoulder-blades almost touching, assured me that they were in clover.

"I feel sure," said she, "that Celebrate Fourth will soon git something better to do than make a hand in the field. He has idees of makin' all kinds of money, if he could git Mr. Gowdy to lis'en to him. But Surrager Dowler is right where he orto be. He has got a patent corn-planter all worked out, and I guess Mr. Gowdy'll help him make and sell it. Mr. Gowdy is awful good to us—ain't he, Rowena."

Rowena busied herself with her work; and when Mrs. Fewkes repeated her appeal, the girl looked out of the window and paused a long time before she answered.

"Good enough," she finally said. "But I guess he ain't strainin' himself any to make something of us."

There was something strange and covered up in what she said, and in the way she said it. She shot a quick glance at me, and then looked down at her work again.

"Well, Rowena Fewkes!" exclaimed her mother, with her hands thrown up as if in astonishment or protest. "In all my born days, I never expected to hear a child of mine——"

Old Man Fewkes came in just then, and cut into the talk by his surprised exclamation at seeing me there. He had supposed that I had gone out of his ken forever. He had thought that one winter in this climate would be all that a young man like me, free as I was to go and come as I pleased, would stand. As he spoke about my being free, he looked at his wife and sighed, combing his whiskers with his skinny bird's claws, and showing the biggest freckles on the backs of his hands that I think I ever saw. He was still more stooped and frail-looking than when I saw him last; and when I told him I had settled down for life on my farm, I could see that I had lost caste with him. He was pining for the open road.

"Negosha," he said, "is the place for a young man. You can be a baron out there with ten thousan' head o' cattle. But the place for me is Texas. Trees is in constant varder!"

"But," said Ma Fewkes, repeating her speech of three years ago, "it's so fur, Fewkes!" ·

"Fur!" he scornfully shouted, just as he had before. "Fur!" this time letting his voice fall in contempt for the distance, for any one that spoke of the distance, and for things in general in Iowa. "Why, Lord-heavens, womern, it hain't more'n fifteen hundred mile!"

"Fewkes," she retorted, drawing her shoulders back almost as far as she had had them forward a moment before, "I've been drailed around the country, fifteen hundred miles here, and fifteen hundred miles there, with old Tom takin' mad fits every little whip-stitch, about as much as I'm a-going to!"

"I don't," said Rowena, "see why you've got so sot on goin' into your hole here, an' pullin' the hole in after you. You hook up ol' Tom, pa, an' me an' you'll go to Texas. I'll start to-morrow morning, pa!"

"I never seen sich a girl," said her mother; "to talk of movin' when prospects is as good f'r you as they be now!"

"Wal, le's stop jourin' at each other," said Rowena, hastily, as if to change the subject. "It ain't the way to treat company."

I discovered that Rowena was about to change her situation in the Blue-grass Manor establishment. She was going into "the Big House" to work under Mrs. Mobley, the wife of the superintendent, or as we called him, the overseer.

"Well, that'll be nice," said I.

"I don't want to," she said. "I like to wait on table better."

"Then why do you change?" said I.

"Mr. Gowdy——," began Ma Fewkes, but was interrupted by her daughter, who talked on until her mother was switched off from her explanation.

"I wun't work with niggers!" said Rowena. "That Pinck has brought a yellow girl here from Dubuque, and she's goin' to wait on the table as she did in Dubuque. They claim they was married the last time he was back there, an' he brought her here. I wun't work with her. I wun't demean myself into a black slave——. But tell me, Jake," coming over and sitting by me, "how you're gittin' along. Off here we don't hear no news from folks over to the Centre at all. We go to the new railroad, an' never see any one from over there——."

"Exceptin' Magnus," said Ma Fewkes.

"You ain't married, yet, be you?" Rowena asked.

"I should say not! Me married!"

We sat then for quite a while without saying anything. Rowena sat smoothing out a calico apron she had on. Finally she said: "Am I wearin' anything you ever seen before, Jake?"

Looking her over carefully I saw nothing I could remember. I told her so at last, and said she was dressed awful nice now and looked lots better than I had ever seen her looking. My own rags were sorely on my mind just then.

"This apern," said she, spreading it out for me to see, "is the back breadth of that dress you give me back along the road. I'm goin' to keep it always. I hain't goin' to wear it ever only when you come to see me!"

This was getting embarrassing; but her next remark made it even more so.

"How old be you, Jake?" she asked.

"I'll be twenty," said I, "the twenty-seventh day of next July."

"We're jest of an age," she ventured—and after a long pause, "I should think it would be awful hard work to keep the house and do your work ou'-doors."

I told her that it was, and spread the grief on very thick, thinking all the time of the very precious way in which I hoped sometime to end my loneliness, and give myself a house companion: in the very back of my head even going over the plans I had made for an "upright" to the house, with a bedroom, a spare room, a dining-room and a sitting-room in it.

"Well," said she, "for a smart, nice-lookin' young man like you, it's your own fault——"

5

And then there was a tap on the door. Rowena started, turned toward the door, made as if to get up to open it, and then sat down again, her face first flushed and then pale. Her mother opened the door, and there stood Buckner Gowdy. He came in, with his easy politeness and sat down among us like an old friend.

"I didn't know you had company," said he; "but I now remember that Mr. Vandemark is an old friend."

He always called me Mr. Vandemark, because, I guess, I owned seven hundred and twenty acres of land, and was not all mortgaged up. Virginia told me afterward, that where they came from people who owned so much land were the quality, and were treated more respectfully than the poor whites.

"Yes, sir," said Old Man Fewkes, "Jake is the onliest real old friend we got hereabouts."

Gowdy took me into the conversation, but he sat where he could look at Rowena. He seemed to be carrying on a silent conversation with her with his eyes, while he talked to me, looking into my eyes a good deal too, and stooping toward me in that intimate, confidential way of his. When I told him that I thought he was not getting as much done as he ought to with all the hands he had, he said nobody knew it better than he; but could I suggest any remedy? Now on the canal, we had to organize our work, and I had seen a lot of public labor done between Albany and Buffalo; so I had my ideas as to people's getting in one another's way. I told him that his men were working in too large gangs, as I looked at it. Where he had twenty breaking-teams following one another, if one broke his plow, or ran on a boulder and had to file it, the whole gang had to stop for him, or run around him and make a balk in the work. I thought it would be better to have not more than two or three breaking on the same "land," and then they would not be so much in one another's way, and wouldn't have so good an excuse for stopping and having jumping matches and boxing bouts and story-tellings. Then their work could be compared, they could be made to work against one another in a kind of competition, and the bad ones could be weeded out. It would be the same with corn-plowing, and some other work.

"There's sense in that, sir," he said, after thinking it over. "You see, Mr. Vandemark, my days of honest industry are of very recent date. Thank you for the suggestion, sir."

I got up to leave. Rowena's father was pulling off his boots. which with us then, was the signal that he was going to bed. If I stayed after that alone with Rowena, it was a sign that we were to "sit up"—and that was courtship. I was slowly getting it through my wool that it looked as if Buckner Gowdy and Rowena were going to sit up, when I heard her giving me back my good evening, and at the same time, behind his back, motioning me to my chair, and shaking her head. And while I was backing and filling, the door opened and a woman appeared on the step.

"Ah, Mrs. Mobley," said Buck, "anything for me?"

She was very nicely dressed for a woman busy about her own home, but the thing that I remembered was her pallor. Her hair was light brown and curled about her forehead, and her eyes were very blue, like china. And there was a quiver in her like that which you see in the little quaking-asps in the slews—something pitiful, and sort of forsaken. Her face was not so fresh as it had been a few years before, and on her cheeks were little red spots, like those you see in the cheeks of people with consumption—or a pot of face-paint. She was tall and strong-looking, and somewhat portly, and quite masterful in her ways as a general rule; but that night she seemed to be in a sort of pleading mood, not a bit like herself when dealing with ordinary people. She was not ordinary, as could be sensed by even an ignorant bumpkin like me. She had more education than most, and had been taught better manners and brought up with more style.

"Mr. Mobley requested me to say," she said, her voice low and quivery, bowing to all of us in a very polite and elegant way, "that he has something of importance to say to you, Mr. Buckner."

"I'm greatly obliged to you, Miss Flora," said he. "Let me go to him with you. Good evening, Rowena. Good evening, Mr. Vandemark. I shall certainly think over what you have been so kind as to suggest."

He bowed to Rowena, nodded to me, and we all three left together. As we separated I heard him talking to her in what in any other man I should have called a loving tone; but there was a sort of warm note in the way he spoke to me, too; and still more of that vital vibration I have mentioned before, when he spoke to Rowena. But he did not take my arm, as he did that of the imposing "Miss Flora" as he called Mrs. Mobley, to whom he was "Mr. Buckner." I could see them walking very, very close together, even in the darkness.

6

When I found that Mr. Mobley was over at the barracks, and had been there playing euchre with the boys since supper, I wondered. I wondered why Mrs. Mobley had come with an excuse to get Mr. Gowdy away from me—or after a couple of weeks' thinking, was it from Rowena? Yet Mr. Gowdy did see Mr. Mobley that evening; for the next morning Mobley put me over a gang of eight breaking-teams, "To handle the way you told Mr. Gowdy last night," he said.

He was a tall, limber-jointed, whipped-looking man with a red nose and a long stringy mustache, and always wore his vest open clear down to the lower button which was fastened, and thus his whole waistcoat was thrown open so as to show a tobacco-stained shirt bosom. The

Missourian whom I had noticed at table said that this
was done so that the wearer of the vest could reach his
dirk handily. But Mobley was the last man I should
have suspected of carrying a dirk, or if he did packing
the gumption to use it.

I made good with my gang, and did a third more than
any other eight teams on the place. Before I went away,
Gowdy talked around as if he wanted me for overseer;
but I couldn't decide without studying a long time, to
take a step so far from what I had been thinking of, and
he dropped the subject. I did not like the way things
were going there. The men were out of control. They
despised Mobley, and said sly things about his using his
wife to keep him in a job. One day I told Magnus Thorkelson about Mrs. Mobley's coming and taking Gowdy
away from the little cabin of the Fewkes family.

"She do dat," said he, "a dozen times ven Ay bane
dar. She alvays bane chasing Buck Gowdy."

"Well," I said, "who be you chasing, coming over
here a dozen times when I didn't know it? That's why
you bought that mustang pony, eh?"

"I yust go over," said he, squirming, " to help Surajah
fix up his machines—his inwentions. Sometimes I take
over de wyolin to play for Rowena. Dat bane all, Yake."

When we went home, I with money enough for some
new clothes, with what I had by me, we caught a ride
with one of Judge Stone's teams to a point two-thirds of
the way to Monterey Centre, and came into our own
places from the south. We were both glad to see long
black streaks of new breaking in the section of which my
eighty was a part, and two new shanties belonging to
new neighbors. This would bring cultivated land up to

my south line, and I afterward found out, take the whole half of the section into the new farms. The Zenas Smith family had moved on to the southwest quarter, and the J. P. Roebuck family on the southeast.

The Smiths and Roebucks still live in the township—as good neighbors as a man need ask for; except that I never could agree with Zenas Smith about line fences, when the time came for them. Once we almost came to the spite-fence stage; but our children were such friends that they kept us from that disgrace. But Mrs. Smith was as good a woman in sickness as I ever saw.

George Story was working for the Smiths, and was almost one of the family. He finally took the northeast quarter of the section, and lives there yet. David Roebuck, J. P.'s son, when he came of age acquired the eighty next to me, and thus completed the settlement of the section. Most of the Roebuck girls and boys became school-teachers, and they had the biggest mail of anybody in the neighborhood. I never saw Dave Roebuck spelled down but once, and that was by his sister Theodosia, called "Dose" for short.

We went to both houses and called as we went home, so as to begin neighboring with them. Magnus stopped at his own place, and I went on, wondering if the Frost boy I had engaged to look out for my stock while I was gone had been true to his trust. I saw that there had been a lot of redding up done; and as I came around the corner of the house I heard sounds within as of some one at the housework. The door was open, and as I peeped in, there, of all people, was Grandma Thorndyke, putting the last touches to a general house-cleaning.

The floor was newly scrubbed, the dishes set away in

order, and all clean. The churn was always clean inwardly, but she had scoured it on the outside. There was a geranium in bloom in the window, which was as clear as glass could be made. The bed was made up on a different plan from mine, and the place where I hung my clothes had a flowered cotton curtain in front of it, run on cords. It looked very beautiful to me; and my pride in it rose as I gazed upon it. Grandma Thorndyke had not heard me coming, and gave way to her feelings as she looked at her handiwork in her manner of talking to herself.

"That's more like a human habitation!" she ejaculated, standing with her hands on her hips. "I snum! It looked like a hooraw's nest!"

"It looks a lot better," I agreed.

She was startled at seeing me, for she expected to get away, with Henderson L. Burns as he came back from his shooting of golden plover, all unknown to me. But we had quite a visit all by ourselves. She said quite pointedly, that somebody had been keeping her family in milk and butter and vegetables and chickens and eggs all winter, and she was doing a mighty little in repayment. Her eyes were full of tears as she said this.

"He who gives to the poor," said she, "lends to the Lord; and I don't know any place where the Lord's credit has been lower than in Monterey Centre for the past winter. Now le'me show you where things are, Jacob."

I got all the news of the town from her. Several people had moved in; but others had gone back east to live with their own or their wives' folks. Elder Thorndyke, encouraged by the favor of "their two rich men," had laid plans for building a church, and she believed their fellowship would be blessed with greater growth if they had a consecrated building instead of the hall where the secret societies met. On asking who their two richest men were she mentioned Governor Wade, of course, and Mr. Gowdy.

"Mr. Gowdy," she ventured, "is in a very hopeful frame of mind. He is, I fervently hope and believe, under conviction of sin. We pray for him without ceasing. He would be a tower of strength, with his ability and his wealth, if he should, under God, turn to the right and seek salvation. If you and he could both come into the fold, Jacob, it would be a wonderful thing for the elder and me."

"I guess I'd ruther come in alone!" I said.

"You mustn't be uncharitable," said she. "Mr. Gowdy is still hopeful of getting that property for Virginia Royall. He is working on that all the time. He came to get her signature to a paper this week. He is a changed man, Jacob—a changed man."

I can't tell how thunderstruck I was by this bit of news. Somehow, I could not see Buck Gowdy as a member of the congregation of the saints—I had seen too much of him lately: and yet, I could not now remember any of the old hardness he had shown in every action back along the Ridge Road in 1855. But Virginia must have changed toward him, or she would not have allowed him to approach her with any kind of paper, not even a patent of nobility.

But I rallied from my daze and took Grandma Thorndyke to see my live stock—birds and beasts. I discovered that she had been a farmer's daughter in New England, and I began to suspect that it relieved her to drop into

New England farm talk, like "I snum!" and "Hooraw's nest." I never saw a hooraw's nest, but she seemed to think it a very disorderly place.

"This ain't the last time, Jacob," said she, as she climbed into Jim Boyd's buggy that Henderson L. had borrowed. "You may expect to find your house red up any time when I can get a ride out."

I was in a daze for some time trying to study out developments. Buck Gowdy and Mrs. Mobley; Rowena and Magnus Thorkelson; Gowdy's calls on Rowena, or at least at her home; Rowena's going to live in his house as a hired girl; her warmth to me; her nervousness, or fright, at Gowdy; Gowdy's religious tendency in the midst of his entanglements with the fair sex; his seeming reconciliation with Virginia; his pulling of the wool over the eyes of Mrs. Thorndyke, and probably the elder's——. Out of this maze I came to a sudden resolution. I would go to Waterloo and get me a new outfit of clothes, even to gloves and a pair of "fine boots."

CHAPTER XVII

DOGS and cats get more credit, I feel sure, for being animals of fine feeling and intelligence, than in justice they are entitled to; because they have so many ways of showing forth what they feel. A dog can growl or bark in several ways, and show his teeth in at least two, to tell how he feels. He can wag his tail, or let it droop, or curl it over his back, or stick it straight out like a flag, or hold it in a bowed shape with the curve upward, and frisk about, and run in circles, or sit up silently or with howls; or stand with one foot lifted; or cock his head on one side: and as for his eyes and his ears, he can almost talk with them.

As for a cat, she has no such rich language as a dog; but see what she can do: purring, rubbing against things, arching her back, glaring out of her eyes, setting her hair on end, swelling out her tail, sticking out her claws and scratching at posts, sneaking along as if ready to pounce, pouncing either in earnest or in fun, mewing in many voices, catching at things with nails drawn back or just a little protruded, or drawing the blood with them, laying back her ears, looking up pleadingly and asking for milk—why a cat can say almost anything she wants to say.

Now contrast these domestic animals with a much

more necessary and useful one, the cow. Any stockman knows that a cow is a beast of very high nervous organization, but she has no very large number of ways of telling us how she feels: just a few tones to her lowing, a few changes of expression to her eye, a small number of shades of uneasiness, a little manner with her eyes, showing the whites when troubled or letting the lids droop in satisfaction—these things exhausted, and poor bossy's tale is told. You can get nothing more out of her, except in some spasm of madness. She is driven to extremes by her dumbness.

I am brought to this sermon by two things: what happened to me when Rowena Fewkes came over to see me in the early summer of 1859, a year almost to a day from the time when Magnus and I left Blue-grass Manor after our spell of work there: and what our best cow, Spot, did yesterday.

We were trying to lead Spot behind a wagon, and he did not like it. She had no way of telling us how much she hated it, and how panicky she was, as a dog or a cat could have done; and so she just hung back and acted dumb and stubborn for a minute or two, and then she gave an awful bellow, ran against the wagon as if she wanted to upset it, and when she found she could not affect it, in as pathetic a despair and mental agony as any man ever felt who has killed himself, she thrust one horn into the ground, broke it off flush with her head, and threw herself down with her neck doubled under her shoulder, as if trying to commit suicide, as I verily believe she was. And yet dogs and cats get credit for being creatures of finer feelings than cows, merely because cows have no tricks of barking, purring, and the like.

It is the same as between other people and a Dutchman. He has the same poverty of expression that cows are cursed with. To wear his feelings like an overcoat where everybody can see them is for him impossible. He is the bovine of the human species. This is the reason why I used to have such fearful crises once in a while in my dumb life, as when I was treated so kindly by Captain Sproule just after my stepfather whipped me; or when I nearly killed Ace, my fellow-driver, on the canal in my first and successful rebellion; or when I used to grow white, and cry like a baby in my fights with rival drivers. I am thought by my children, I guess, an unfeeling person, because the surface of my nature is ice, and does not ripple in every breeze; but when ice breaks up, it rips and tears—and the thicker the ice, the worse the ravage. The only reason for saying anything about this is that I am an old man, and I have always wanted to say it: and there are some things I have said, and some I shall now have to say, that will seem inconsistent unless the truths just stated are taken into account.

But there are some things to be told about before this crisis can be understood. Life dragged along for all of us from one year to another in the slow movement of a new country in hard times: only I was at bottom better off than most of my neighbors because I had cattle, though I could not see how they then did me much good. They grew in numbers, and keeping them was just a matter of labor. My stock was the only thing I had except land which was almost worthless; for I could use the land of others for pasture and hay without paying rent.

Town life went backward in most ways. My interest in it centered in Virginia and through her in Elder Thorndyke's family; but of this family I saw little except for my visits from Grandma Thorndyke. She came out and red up the house as often as she could catch a ride, and I kept up my now well-known secret policy of supplying the Thorndyke family with my farm, dairy and poultry surplus. Why not? I lay in bed of nights thinking that Virginia had been that day fed on what I grew, and in the morning would eat buckwheat cakes from grain that I worked to grow, flour from my wheat that I had taken to mill, spread with butter which I had made with my own hands, from the cows she used to pet and that had hauled her in my wagon back along the Ridge Road, and with nice sorghum molasses from cane that I had grown and hauled to the sorghum mill. That she would have meat that I had prepared for her, with eggs from the descendants of the very hens to which she had fed our table scraps when we were together. That maybe she would think of me when she made bread for Grandma Thorndyke from my flour. It was sometimes almost like being married to Virginia, this feeling of standing between her and hunger. The very roses in her cheeks, and the curves in her developing form, seemed of my making. But she never came with grandma to help red up.

2

Grandma often told me that now I was getting pretty nearly old enough to be married, or would be when I was twenty-one, which would be in July—"Though," she always said, "I don't believe in folks's being married under the spell of puppy love. Thirty is soon enough; but yet, you might do well to marry when you are a little younger, because you need a wife to keep you clean and tidy, and you can support a wife." She began bringing girls with her to help fix my house up; and she would always show them the castor and my other things.

"Dat bane for Christina," said Magnus one time, when she was showing my castor and a nice white china dinner set, to Kittie Fleming or Rose Roebuck, both of whom were among her samples of girls shown me. "An' dat patent churn—dat bane for Christina, too, eh, Yake?"

"Christina who?" asked Grandma Thorndyke sharply.

"Christina Quale," said Magnus, "my cousin in Norvay."

This was nuts and apples for Grandma Thorndyke and the girls who came. Magnus showed them Christina's picture, and told them that I had a copy of it, and all about what a nice girl Christina was. Now grandma made a serious thing of this and soon I had the reputation of being engaged to Magnus's cousin, who was the daughter of a rich farmer, and could write English; and even that I had received a letter from her. This seemed unjust to me, though I was a little mite proud of it; for the letter was only one page written in English in one of Magnus's. All the time grandma was bringing girls with her to help, and making me work with them when I helped. They were nice girls, too—Kittie, and Dose, Lizzie Finster, and Zeruiah Strickler, and Amy Smith—all farmer girls. Grandma was always talking about the wisdom of my marrying a farmer girl.

"The best thing about Christina," said she, "is that she is the daughter of a farmer."

I struggled with this Christina idea, and tried to make

it clear that she was nothing to me, that it was just a joke. Grandma Thorndyke smiled.

"Of course you'd say that," said she.

But the Christina myth grew wonderfully, and it made me more interesting to the other girls.

> "You look too high
> For things close by,
> And slight the things around you!"

So sang Zeruiah Stricker as she scrubbed my kitchen, and in pauses of her cheerful and encouraging song told of the helplessness of men without their women. I really believed her, in spite of my success in getting along by myself.

"Why don't you bring Virginia out some day?" I asked on one of these occasions, when it seemed to me that Grandma Thorndyke was making herself just a little too frequent a visitor at my place.

"Miss Royall," said she, as if she had been speaking of the Queen of Sheba, "is busy with her own circle of friends. She is now visiting at Governor Wade's. She is almost a member of the family there. And her law matters take up a good deal of her time, too. Mr. Gowdy says he thinks he may be able to get her property for her soon. She can hardly be expected to come out for this."

And grandma swept her hands about to cast down into nothingness my house, my affairs, and me. This plunged me into the depths of misery.

So, when I furnished the cream for the donation picnic at Crabapple Grove in strawberry time, I went prepared to see myself discarded by my love. She was there,

and I had not overestimated her coldness toward me.
Buck Gowdy came for only a few minutes, and these he
spent eating ice-cream with Elder Thorndyke, with Virginia across the table from him, looking at her in
that old way of his. Before he left, she went over and sat
with Bob Wade and Kittie Fleming; but he joined them
pretty soon, and I saw him bending down in that intimate
way of his, first speaking to Kittie, and then for a longer
time, to Virginia—and I thought of the time when she
would not even speak his name!

Once she walked off by herself in the trees, and
looked back at me as she went; but I was done with
her, I said to myself, and hung back. She soon
returned to the company, and began flirting with
Matthias Trickey, who was no older than I, and just
as much of a country bumpkin. I found out afterward
that right off after that, Matthias began going to see her,
with his pockets full of candy with mottoes on it. I called
this sparking, and the sun of my hopes set in a black bank
of clouds. I do not remember that I was ever so unhappy,
not even when John Rucker was in power over me and
my mother, not even when I was seeking my mother up
and down the canal and the Lakes, not even when I found
that she had gone away on her last long journey that
bleak winter day in Madison. I now devoted myself to
the memory of my old dreams for my mother, and blamed
myself for treason to her memory, getting out that old
letter and the poor work-worn shoe, and weeping over
them in my lonely nights in the cabin on the prairie. I
can not now think of this without pity for myself; and
though Grandma Thorndyke was one of the best women
that ever lived on this footstool, and was much to me in

my after life, I can not think of her happiness at my despair without blaming her memory a little. But she meant well. She had better plans, as she thought, for Virginia, than any which she thought I could have.

3

It was not more than a week after this donation picnic, when I came home for my nooning one day, and found a covered wagon in the yard, and two strange horses in the stable. When I went to the house, there were Old Man Fewkes and Mrs. Fewkes, and Surajah Dowah and Celebrate Fourth. I welcomed them heartily. I was so lonesome that I would have welcomed a stray dog, and that is pretty nearly what I was doing.

"I guess," ventured the old man, after we had finished our dinner, "that you are wondering where we're goin', Jake."

"A long ways," I said, "by the looks of your rig."

"You see us now," he went on, "takin' steps that I've wanted to take ever sen' I found out what a den of inikerty we throwed ourselves into when we went out yon'," pointing in the general direction of the Blue-grass Manor.

"What steps are you takin'?" I asked.

"We are makin'," said he, "our big move for riches. Gold! Gold! Jake, you must go with us! We are goin' out to the Speak."

I had never heard of any place called the Speak, but I finally got it through my head that he meant Pike's Peak. We were in the midst of the Pike's Peak excitement for two or three years; and this was the earliest sign of it that I had seen, though I had heard Pike's Peak mentioned.

"Jake," said Old Man Fewkes, "it's a richer spot than the Arabian Knights ever discovered. The streams are rollin' gold sand. Come along of us to the Speak, an' we'll make you rich. Eh, ma?"

"I have been drailed around," said ma, as she saw me looking at her, "about as much as I expect to be; but this is like goin' home. It's the last move; and as pa has said ag'in an' ag'in, it ain't but six or eight hundred mile from Omaha, an' with the team an' wagin we've got, that's nothin' if we find the gold, an' I calculate there ain't no doubt of that. The Speak looks like the best place we ever started fur, and we all hope you'll leave this Land o' Desolation, an' come with us. We like you, an' we want you to be rich with us."

"Where's Rowena?" I asked.

Silence for quite a while. Then Ma Fewkes spoke.

"Rowena," she said, her voice trembling, "Rowena ain't goin' with us."

"Why," I said, "last summer, she seemed to want to start for Texas. She ain't goin' with you? I want to know!"

"She ain't no longer," said Old Man Fewkes, "a member o' my family. I shall will my proputty away from her. I've made up my mind, Jake: an' now le's talk about the Speak. Our plans was never better laid. Celebrate, tell Jake how we make our money a-goin', and you, Surrager, denote to him your machine f'r gittin' out the gold."

I was too absorbed in thinking about Rowena to take in what Surajah and Celebrate said. I have a dim recollection that Celebrate's plan for making money was to fill the wagon box with white beans which were scarce in

Denver City, as we then called Denver, and could be sold for big money when they got there. I have no remembrance of Surajah Dowlah's plan for mining. I declined to go with them, and they went away toward Monterey Centre, saying that they would stay there a few days, "to kind of recuperate up," and they hoped I would join them.

What about Rowena? They had been so mysterious about her, that I had a new subject of thought now, and, for I was very fond of the poor girl, of anxiety. Not that she would be the worse for losing her family. In fact, she would be the better for it, one might think. Her older brothers and sisters, I remembered, had been bound out back east, and this seemed to show a lack of family affection; but the tremor in Ma Fewkes's voice, and the agitation in which Old Man Fewkes had delivered what in books would be his parental curse, led me to think that they were in deep trouble on account of their breach with Rowena. Poor girl! After all, they were her parents and brothers, and as long as she was with them, she had not been quite alone in the world. My idea of what had taken place may be judged by the fact that when I next saw Magnus I asked him if he knew that Rowena and her people had had a fuss. I looked upon the case as that of a family fuss, and that only. Magnus looked very solemn, and said that he had seen none of the family since we had finished our work for Gowdy—a year ago.

"What said the old man, Yake?" he asked anxiously.

"He said he was going to will his property away from her!" I replied, laughing heartily at the idea: but Magnus did not laugh. "He said that she ain't no longer a member of his family, Magnus. Don't that beat you!"

"Yes," said Magnus gravely, "dat beat me, Yake."

He bowed his head in thought for a while, and then looked up.

"Ay can't go to her, Yake. Ay can't go to her. But you go, Yake; you go. An' you tal her—dat Magnus Thorkelson—Norsky Thorkelson—bane ready to do what he can for her. All he can do. Tal her Magnus ready to live or die for her. You tal her dat, Yake!"

I had to think over this a few days before I could begin to guess what it meant; and three days after, she came to see me. It was a Sunday right after harvest. I had put on my new clothes thinking to go to hear Elder Thorndyke preach, but when I thought that I had no longer any pleasure in the thought of Virginia, no chance ever to have her for my wife, no dreams of her for the future even, I sat in a sort of stupor until it was too late to go, and then I walked out to look at things.

The upland phlox, we called them pinks, were gone; the roses had fallen and were represented by green haws, turning to red; the upland scarlet lilies were vanished; but the tall lilies of the moist places were flaming like yellow stars over the tall grass, each with its six dusty anthers whirling like little windmills about its red stigma; and beside these lilies, with their spotted petals turned back to their roots, stood the clumps of purple marsh phlox; while towering over them all were the tall rosin-weeds with their yellow blossoms like sun-flowers, and the Indian medicine plant waving purple plumes. There was a sense of autumn in the air. Far off across the marsh I saw that the settlers had their wheat in symmetrical beehive-shaped stacks while mine stood in the shock, my sloping hillside slanting down to the marsh freckled with the shocks until it looked dark—the almost sure sign of a bountiful crop. And as I looked at this scene of plenty, I sickened at it. What use to me were wheat in the shock, hay in the stack, cattle on the prairie, corn already hiding the ground? Nothing! Less than nothing: for I had lost the thing for which I had worked—lost it before I had claimed it. I sat down and saw the opposite side of the marsh swim in my tears.

4

And then Rowena came into my view as she passed the house. I hastily dried my eyes, and went to meet her, astonished, for she was alone. She was riding one of Gowdy's horses, and had that badge of distinction in those days, a side-saddle and a riding habit. She looked very distinguished, as she rode slowly toward me, her long skirt hanging below her feet, one knee crooked about the saddle horn, the other in the stirrup. I had not seen a woman riding thus since the time I had watched them sweeping along in all their style in Albany or Buffalo. She came up to me and stopped, looking at me without a word.

"Why of all things!" I said. "Rowena, is this you!"

"What's left of me," said she.

I stood looking at her for a minute, thinking of what her father and mother had said, and finally trying to figure out what seemed to be a great change in her. There was something new in her voice, and her manner of looking at me as she spoke; and something strange in the way she looked out of her eyes. Her face was a little paler than it used to be, as if she had been indoors more; but there was a pink flush in her cheeks that made her look prettier than I had ever seen her. Her eyes were bright as if with tears just trembling to fall, rather than with the old glint of defiance or high spirits; but she smiled and laughed more than ever I had seen her do. She acted as if she was in high spirits, as I have seen even very quiet girls in the height of the fun and frolic of a dance or sleigh-ride. When she was silent for a moment, though, her mouth drooped as if in some sort of misery; and it was not until our eyes met that the laughing expression came over her face, as if she was gay only when she knew she was watched. She seemed older—much older.

Somehow, all at once there came into my mind the memory of the woman away back there in Buffalo, who had taken me, a sleepy, lonely, neglected little boy, to her room, put me to bed, and been driven from the fearful place in which she lived, because of it. I have finally thought of the word to describe what I felt in both these cases—desperation; desperation, and the feeling of pursuit and flight. I did not even feel all this as I stood looking at Rowena, sitting on her horse so prettily that summer day at my farm; I only felt puzzled and a little pitiful for her—all the more, I guess, because of her nice clothes and her side-saddle.

"Well, Mr. Vandemark," said she, finally, "I don't hear the perprietor of the estate say anything about 'lighting and stayin' a while.' Help me down, Jake!"

I swung her from the saddle and tied her horse. I stopped to put a halter on him, unsaddle him, and give him hay. I wanted time to think; but I do not remember that I had done much if any thinking when I got back to the house, and found that she had taken off her long skirt and was sitting on the little stoop in front of my door. She wore the old apron, and as I came up to her, she spread it out with her hands to call my attention to it.

"You see, Jake, I've come to work. Show me the morning's dishes, an' I'll wash 'em. Or maybe you want bread baked? It wouldn't be breakin' the Sabbath to mix up a bakin' for a poor ol' bach like you, would it? I'm huntin' work. Show it to me."

I showed her how clean everything was, taking pride in my housekeeping; and when she seemed not over-pleased with this, I had in all honesty to tell her how much I was indebted to Mrs. Thorndyke for it.

"The preacher's wife?" she asked sharply. "An' that adopted daughter o' theirn, Buck Gowdy's sister-in-law, eh?"

I wished I could have admitted this; but I had to explain that Virginia had not been there. For some reason she seemed in better spirits when she learned this. When it came time for dinner, which on Sunday was at one o'clock, she insisted on getting the meal; and seemed to be terribly anxious for fear everything might not be good. It was a delicious meal, and to see her preparing it, and then clearing up the table and washing the dishes gave me quite a thrill. It was so much like what I had seen in my visions—and so different.

"Now," said she, coming and sitting down by me, and laying her hand on mine, "ain't this more like it? Don't that beat doing everything yourself? If you'd only try havin' me here a week, nobody could hire you to go back to bachin' it ag'in. Think how nice it would be jest to go out an' do your chores in the morning, an' when you come in with the milk, find a nice breakfast all ready to set down to. Wouldn't that be more like livin'?"

"Yes," I said, "it—it would."

"That come hard," said she, squeezing my hand, "like makin' a little boy own up he likes a girl. I guess I won't ask you the next thing."

"What was the next thing, Rowena?"

"W'y, if it wouldn't be kind o' nice to have some one around, even if she wa'n't very pretty, and was ignorant, if she was willin' to learn, an' would always be good to you, to have things kind o' cheerful at night—your supper ready; a light lit; dry boots warmed by the stove; your bed made up nice, and maybe warmed when it was cold: even if she happened to be wearin' an old apern like this— if you knowed she was thinkin' in her thankful heart of the bashful boy that give it to her back along the road when she was ragged and ashamed of herself every time a stranger looked at her!"

Dumbhead as I was I sat mute, and looked as blank as an idiot. In all this description of hers I was struck by the resemblance between her vision and mine; but I was dreaming of some one else. She looked at me a moment, and took her hand away. She seemed hurt, and I thought I saw her wiping her eyes. I could not believe that she was almost asking me to marry her, it seemed so beyond belief—and I was joked so much about the girls, and about getting me a wife that it seemed this must be just banter, too. And yet, there was something a little pitiful in it, especially when she spoke again about my little gift to her so long ago.

"I never looked your place over," said she at last. "That's what I come over fur. Show it to me, Jacob?"

This delighted me. We looked first at the wheat, and the corn, and some of my cattle were near enough so that we went and looked at them, too. I told her where I had got every one of them. We looked at the chickens and the ducks; and the first brood of young turkeys I ever had. I showed her all my elms, maples, basswoods, and other forest trees which I had brought from the timber, and even the two pines I had made live, then not over a foot high.

I just now came in from looking at them, and find them forty feet high as I write this, with their branches resting on the ground in a great brown ring carpeted with needles as they are in the pineries.

We sat down on the blue-grass under what is now the big cottonwood in front of the house. I had stuck this in the sod a little twig not two feet long, and now it was ten or twelve feet high, and made a very little shade, to be sure, but wasn't I proud of my own shade trees! Oh, you can't understand it; for you can not realize the beauty of shade on that great sun-bathed prairie, or the promise in the changing shadows under that little tree!

Rowena leaned back against the gray-green trunk, and patted the turf beside her for me to be seated.

Every circumstance of this strange day comes back to me as I think of it, and of what followed. I remember just how the poor girl looked as she sat leaning against the tree, her cheeks flushed by the heat of the summer afternoon, that look of distress in her eyes as she looked around so brightly and with so gay an air over my little kingdom. As she sat there she loosened her belt and took a long breath as if relieved in her weariness at the long ramble we had taken.

"I never have had a home," she said. "I never had no idee how folk that have got things lived—till I went over —over to that—that hell-hole there!" And she waved her hand over toward Blue-grass Manor. I was startled at her fierce manner and words.

"Your folks come along here the other day," I said, to turn the subject, I guess.

"Did they?" she asked, with a little gasp. "What did they say?"

"They said they were headed for Pike's Peak."

"The old story," she said. "Huntin' f'r the place where the hawgs run around ready baked, with knives an' forks stuck in 'em. I wish to God I was with 'em!"

Here she stopped for a while and sat with her hands twisted together in her lap. Finally, "Did they say anything about me, Jacob?"

"I thought," said I, "that they talked as if you'd had a fuss."

"Yes," she said. "They're all I've got. They hain't much, I reckon, but they're as good as I be, I s'pose. Yes, a lot better. They're my father an' my mother, an' my brothers. In their way—in our way—they was always as good to me as they knowed how. I remember when ma used to kiss me, and pa held me on his lap. Do you remember he's got one finger off? I used to play with his fingers, an' try to build 'em up into a house, while he set an' told about new places he was goin' to to git rich. I wonder if the time'll ever come ag'in when I can set on any one's lap an' be kissed without any harm in it!"

There was no false gaiety in her face now, as she sat

and looked off over the marsh from the brow of the hill-slope. A feeling of coming evil swept over me as I looked at her, like that which goes through the nerves of the cattle when a tornado is coming. I remembered now the silence of her brothers when her father and mother had said that she was no longer a member of their family, and was not going with them to "the Speak."

The comical threat of the old man that he would will his property away from her did not sound so funny now; for there must have been something more than an ordinary family disagreement to have made them feel thus. I recalled the pained look in Ma Fewkes's face, as she sat with her shoulder-blades drawn together and cast Rowena out from the strange family circle. What could it be? I turned my back to her as I sat on the ground; and she took me by the shoulders, pulled me down so that my head was lying in her lap, and began smoothing my hair back from my forehead with a very caressing touch.

"Well," said she, "we wun't spoil our day by talkin' of my troubles. This place here is heaven, to me, so quiet, so clean, so good! Le's not spoil it."

And before I knew what she meant to do, she stooped down and kissed me on the lips—kissed me several times. I can not claim that I was offended, she was so pretty, so rosy, so young and attractive; but at the same time, I was a little scared. I wanted to end this situation; so, pretty soon, I proposed that we go down to see where I kept my milk. I felt like calling her attention to the fact that it was getting well along in the afternoon, and that she would be late home if she did not start soon; but that would not be very friendly, and I did not want to hurt

her feelings. So we went down to the spring at the foot
of the hill, where the secret lay of my nice, firm, sweet
butter. She did not seem very much interested, even
when I showed her the tank in which the pans of milk
stood in the cool water. She soon went over to a big
granite boulder left there by the glaciers ages ago when
the hill was made by the melting ice dropping its earth
and gravel, and sat down as if to rest. So I went and
sat beside her.

"Jacob," said she, with a sort of gasp, "you wonder
why I kissed you up there, don't you?"

I should not have confessed this when I was young,
for it is not the man's part I played; but I blushed, and
turned my face away.

"I love you, Jacob!" she took my hand as she said
this, and with her other hand turned my face toward
her. "I want you to marry me. Will you, Jacob? I—I—
I need you. I'll be good to you, Jake. Don't say no!
Don't say no, for God's sake!"

Then the tragic truth seemed to dawn on me, or rather
it came like a flash; and I turned and looked at her as
I had not done before. I am slow, or I should have
known when her father and mother had spoken as they
did; but now I could see. I could see why she needed
me. As an unsophisticated boy, I had been blind in my
failure to see something new and unexpected to me in
human relations; but once it came to me, it was plain. I
was a stockman, as well as a boy; and my life was closely
related to the mysterious processes by which the world
is filled with successive generations of living beings. I
was like a family physician to my animals; and wise in
their days and generations. Rowena was explained to me

in a flash of lightning by my every-day experiences; she was swept within the current of my knowledge.

"Rowena," said I, "you are in trouble."

She knew what I meant.

I hope never again to see any one in such agony. Her face flamed, and then turned as white as a sheet. She looked at me with that distressful expression in her eyes, rose as if to go away, and then came back and sitting down again on the stone, she buried her head on my breast and wept so terribly that I was afraid. I tried to dry her tears, but they burst out afresh whenever I looked in her face. The poor thing was ashamed to look in my eyes; but she clung to me, sobbing, and crying out, and then drawing long quivering breaths which seemed to be worse than sobs. When she spoke, it was in short, broken sentences, sometimes unfinished, as her agony returned upon her and would not let her go on.

I could not feel any scorn or contempt for her; I could as soon have looked down on a martyr burning at the stake for an act in which I did not believe. She was like a dumb beast tied in a burning stall, only able to moan and cry out and endure.

I have often thought that to any one who had not seen and heard it, the first thing she said might seem comic.

"Jacob," she said, with her face buried in my breast, "they've got it worked around so—I'm goin' to have a baby!"

But when you think of the circumstances; the poor, pretty, inexperienced girl; of that poor slack-twisted family; of her defenselessness in that great house; of the experienced and practised and conscienceless seducer into whose hands she had fallen—when you think of all this, I do not see how you can fail to see how the words were wrung from her as a statement of the truth. "They" meant all the forces which had been too strong for her, not the least, her own weakness—for weakness is one of the most powerful forces in our affairs. "They had got it worked around"—as if the very stars in their courses had conspired to destroy her. I had no impulse to laugh at her strange way of stating it, as if she had had nothing to do with it herself: instead, I felt the tears of sympathy roll down my face upon her hair of rich brown.

"That's why my folks have throwed me off," she went on. "But I ain't bad, Jacob. I ain't bad. Take me, and save me! I'll always be good to you, Jake; I'll wash your feet with my hair! I'll kiss them! I'll eat the crusts from the table an' be glad, for I love you, Jacob. I've loved you ever since I saw you. If I have been untrue to you, it was because I was overcome, and you never looked twice at me, and I thought I was to be a great lady. Now I'll be mud, trod on by every beast that walks, an' rooted over by the hawgs, unless you save me. I'll work my fingers to the bone f'r you, Jacob, to the bone. You're my only hope. For Christ's sake let me hope a little longer!"

The thought that she was coming to me to save her from the results of her own sin never came into my mind. I only saw her as a lost woman, cast off even by her miserable family, whose only claim to respectability was their having kept themselves from the one depth into which she had fallen. I thought again of that wretch who had been kind to me in Buffalo, and of poor Rowena, in poverty and want, stripped of every defense against wrongs piled on wrongs, rooted over, as she said, by the very swine, until she should come to some end so dreadful that I could not imagine it; and not of her alone. There would be another life to be thought of. I knew that Buckner Gowdy, for she had told me of his blame in the matter, of her appeal to him, of his light-hearted cruelty to her, of how now at last, after months of losing rivalry between her and that other of his victims, the wife of Mobley the overseer, she had come to me in desperation —I knew there was nothing in that cold heart to which Rowena could make any appeal that had not been made unsuccessfully by others in the same desperate case.

I had no feeling that she should have told me all in the first place, instead of trying to win me in my ignorance: for I felt that she was driven by a thousand whips to things which might not be honest, but were as free from blame as the doublings of a hunted deer. I felt no blame for her then, and I have never felt any. I passed that by, and tried to look in the face what I should have to give up if I took this girl for my wife. That sacrifice rolled over me like a black cloud, as clear as if I had had a month in which to realize it.

I pushed her hands from my shoulders, and rose to my feet; and she knelt down and clasped her arms around my knees.

"I must think!" I said. "Let me be! Let me think!"

I took a step backward, and as I turned I saw her kneeling there, her hair all about her face, with her hands stretched out to me: and then I walked blindly away into the long grass of the marsh.

I finally found myself running as if to get away from the whole thing, with the tall grass tangling about my feet. All my plans for my life with Virginia came back to me: I lived over again every one of those beautiful days I had spent with her. I remembered how she had come back to bid me good-by when I left her at Waterloo, and turned her over again to Grandma Thorndyke; but especially, I lived over again our days in the grove. I remembered that for months, now, she had seemed lost to me, and that all the hope I had had appeared to be that of living alone and dreaming of her. I was not asked by poor Rowena to give up much; and yet how much it was to me! But how little for me to lose to save her from the fate in store for her!

I can not hope to make clear to any one the tearing and rending in my breast as these things passed through my mind while I went on and on, through water and mud, blindly stumbling, dazed by the sufferings I endured. I caught my feet in the long grass, fell—and it did not seem worth while to rise again.

The sun went down, and the dusk came on as I lay there with my hands twisted in the grass which drooped over me. Then I thought of Rowena, and I got upon my feet and started in search of her, but soon forgot her in my thoughts of the life I should live if I did what she wanted of me. I was in such a daze that I went within a rod of her as she sat on the stone, without seeing her, though the summer twilight was still a filtered radiance, when suddenly all went dark before my eyes, and I fell again. Rowena saw me fall, and came to me.

"Jacob," she cried, as she helped me to my feet, "Jacob, what's the matter!"

"Rowena," said I, trying to stand alone, "I've made up my mind. I had other plans—but I'll do what you want me to!"

CHAPTER XVIII

THE collapse of mind and body which I underwent in deciding the question of marrying Rowena Fewkes or of keeping unstained and pure the great love of my life, refusing her pitiful plea and passing by on the other side, leaving her desolate and fordone, is a thing to which I hate to confess; for it was a weakness. Yet, it was the directing fact of that turning-point not only in my own life, but in the lives of many others—of the life of Vandemark Township, of Monterey County, and of the State of Iowa, to some extent. The excuse for it lies, as I have said, in the way I am organized; in the bovine dumbness of my life, bursting forth in a few crises in storms of the deepest bodily and spiritual tempest. I could not and can not help it. I was weak as a child, as she clasped me in her arms in gratitude when I told her I would do as she wanted me to; and would have fallen again if she had not held me up.

"What's the matter, Jacob?" she said, in sudden fright at my strange behavior.

"I don't know," I gasped. "I wish I could lay down."

She was mystified. She helped me up the hill, telling me all the time how she meant to live so as to repay me for all I had promised to do for her. She was stronger

345

than I, then, and helped me into the house, which was dark, now, and lighted the lamp; but when she came to me, lying on the bed, she gave a great scream.

"Jake, Jake!" she cried. "What's the matter! Are you dying, my darling?"

"Who, me dying?" I said, not quite understanding her. "No—I'm all right—I'll be all right, Rowena!"

She was holding her hands up in the light. They were stained crimson where she had pressed them to my bosom.

"What's the matter of your hands?" I asked, though I was getting drowsy, as if I had been long broken of my sleep.

"It's blood, Jacob! You've hurt yourself!"

I drew my hand across my mouth, and it came away stained red. She gave a cry of horror; but did not lose her presence of mind. She sponged the blood from my clothes, wiping my mouth every little while, until there was no more blood coming from it. Presently I dropped off to sleep with my hand in hers. She awoke me after a while and gave me some warm milk. As I was drowsing off again, she spoke very gently to me.

"Can you understand what I'm saying?" she asked; and I nodded a yes. "Do you love her like that?" she asked.

"Yes," I said, "I love her like that."

Presently she lifted my hand to her lips and kissed it. She was quite calm, now, as if new light had come to her in her darkness; and I thought that it was my consent which had quieted her spirits: but I did not understand her.

"I can't let you do it, Jacob," said she, finally. "It's

too much to ask.............I've thought of another
way, my dear........Don't think of me or my troubles
any more............I'll be all right......You go on
loving her, an' bein' true to her........and if God is
good as they say, He'll make you happy with her sometime. Do you understand, Jacob?"

"Yes," I said, "but what will you........"

"Never mind about me," said she soothingly. "I've
thought of another way out. You go to sleep, now, and
don't think of me or my troubles any more."

I lay looking at her for a while, and wondering how
she could suddenly be so quiet after her agitation of the
day; and after a while, the scene swam before my eyes,
and I went off into the refreshing sleep of a tired boy.

The sun was up when I awoke. Rowena was gone. I
went out and found that she had saddled her horse and
left sometime in the night; afterward I found out
that it was in the gray of the morning. She had watched
by my bedside all night, and left only after it was plain
that I was breathing naturally and that my spasm had
passed. She had come into my life that day like a tornado, but had left it much as it had been before, except
that I wondered what was to become of her. I was comforted by the thought that she had "thought of another
way." And it was a long time before the nobility of her
action was plain to me; but when I realized it, I never
forgot it. I had offered her all I had when she begged
for it, she had taken it, and then restored it, as the dying
soldier gave the draught of water to his comrade, saying, "Thy necessity is greater than mine."

Once or twice I made an effort to tell Magnus Thorkelson about this, as we worked at our after-harvest hay-

ing together that week; but it was a hard thing to do. Perhaps it would not be a secret much longer; but as yet it was Rowena's secret, not mine. I knew, too, that Magnus had been haunting Rowena for two years; that he had been making visits to Blue-grass Manor often when she was there, without taking me into his confidence; that his excuse that he went to help Surajah Fewkes with his inventions was not the real reason for his going. I remembered, too, that Rowena had always spoken well of Magnus, and seemed to see what most of us did not, that Magnus was better educated in the way foreigners are taught than the rest of us; and she did not look down on him the way we did then on folks from other countries. I had no way of knowing how they stood toward each other, though Magnus had looked sad and stopped talking lately whenever I had mentioned her. I knew it would be a shock to him to learn of her present and coming trouble; and, strange as it may seem, I began to put it back into the dark places in my brain as if it had not happened; and when it came to mind clearly as it kept doing, I tried to comfort myself with the thought that Rowena had said that she had thought of another way out.

We had frost early that year—a hard white frost sometime about the tenth of September. Neither Magnus nor I had any sound corn, though our wheat, oats and barley were heavy and fine; and we had oceans of hay. The frost killed the grass early, and early in October we had a heavy rain followed by another freeze, and then a long, calm, warm Indian summer. The prairie was covered with a dense mat of dry grass which rustled in the wind but furnished no feed for our stock. It was a splendid fall for plowing, and I began to feel hope return to me as I followed my plow around and around the lands I laid off, and watched the black ribbon of new plowing widen and widen as the day advanced toward night.

Nothing is so good a soil for hope as new plowing. The act of making it is inspired by hope. The emblem of hope should be the plow; not the plow of the Great Seal, but a plow buried to the top of the mold-board in the soil, with the black furrow-slice falling away from it —and for heaven's sake, let it fall to the right, as it does where they do real farming, and not to the left as most artists depict it! I know some plows are so made that the nigh horse walks in the furrow, but I have mighty little respect for such plows or the farms on which they are used.

My cattle strayed off in the latter part of October; being tolled off in this time between hay and grass by the green spears that grew up in the wet places in the marsh and along the creek. I got uneasy about them on the twentieth, and went hunting them on one of Magnus Thorkelson's horses. Magnus was away from home working, and had left his team with me. I made up my mind that I would scout along on my own side of the marsh until I could cross below it, and then work west, looking from every high place until I found the cattle, coming in away off toward the Gowdy tract, and crossing the creek above the marsh on my way home. This would take me east and west nearly twice across Vandemark Township as it was finally established.

I expected to get back before night, but when I struck the trail of the stock it took me away back into the region in the north part of the township back of Vandemark's Folly, as we used to say, where it was not settled, on account of the slew and the distance from town, until in the 'seventies. Foster Blake had it to himself all this time, and ran a herd of the neighbors' stock there until about 1877, when the Germans came in and hemmed him in with their improvements, making the second great impulse in the settlement of the township.

2

There was a stiff, dry, west wind blowing, and a blue haze in the air. As the afternoon advanced, the sun grew red as if looked at through smoked glass, burning like a great coal of fire or a broad disk of red-hot iron.

There was a scent of burning grass in the air when I found my herd over on Section Eight, about where the cooperative creamery and store now stand. The cattle seemed to be uneasy, and when I started them toward home, they walked fast, snuffing the air, and giving once in a while an uneasy, anxious falsetto bellow; and now and then they would break into a trot as they drew nearer to the places they knew. The smell of smoke grew stronger, and I knew there was a prairie fire burning to the westward. The sun was a deeper red, now, and once in a while almost disappeared in clouds of vaporous smoke which rolled higher and higher into the sky. Prairie chickens, plover and curlew, with once in a while a bittern, went hurriedly along to the eastward, and several wolves crossed our path, trotting along and paying no attention to me or the cows; but stopping from time to time and looking back as if pursued from the west.

They were pursued. They were fleeing from the

great prairie fire of 1859, which swept Monterey County from side to side, and never stopped until it struck the river over in the next county. I felt a little uneasy as I hiked my cattle down into the marsh on my own land, and saw them picking their way across it toward my grove, which showed proudly a mile away across the flat. I had plowed firebreaks about my buildings and stacks, and burned off between the strips of plowing, but I felt that I ought to be at home. So I rode on at a good trot to make my circuit of the marsh to the west. The cattle could get through, but a horse with a man on his back might easily get mired in Vandemark's Folly anywhere along there; and my motto was, "The more hurry, the less speed."

As I topped the hill to get back to the high ground, I saw great clouds of smoke pouring into the valley at the west passage into the big flat, and the country to the south was hidden by the smoke, except where, away off in the southwest in the changing of the wind, I could see the line of fire as it came over the high ground west of the old Bill Trickey farm. It was a broad belt of red flames, from which there crept along the ground a great blanket of smoke, black at first, and then turning to blue as it rose and thinned. I began making haste; for it now looked as if the fire might reach the head of the slew before I could, and thus cut me off. I felt in my pocket for matches; for in case of need, the only way to fight fire is with fire.

I was not scared, for I knew what to do; but not a mile from where I saw the fire on the hilltop, a family of Indiana movers were at that moment smothering and burning to death in the storm of flames—six people, old and young, of the score or more lost in that fire; and the first deaths of white people in Vandemark Township. Their name was Davis, and they came from near Vincennes, we found out.

And within five minutes, as I looked off to the northwest, I saw a woman walking calmly toward the marsh. She was a long way off, and much nearer the fire than I was. I looked for the wagon to which she might belong, but saw none, and it took only one more glance at her to show me that she was in mortal danger. For she was walking slowly and laboriously along like a person carrying a heavy burden. The smoke was getting so thick that it hid her from time to time, and I felt, even at my distance from the fire, an occasional hot blast on my cheek—a startling proof of the rapid march of the great oncoming army of flames.

I kicked my heels into the horse's flanks and pushed him to a gallop. I must reach her soon, or she would be lost, for it was plain that she was paying no attention to her danger. I went down into a hollow, pounded up the opposite hill, and over on the next rise of ground I saw her. She was standing still, now, with her face turned to the fire: then she walked deliberately toward it. I urged my horse to a faster gait, swung my hat, and yelled at her, but she seemed not to hear.

The smoke swept down upon her, and when I next could see, she was stooped with her shawl drawn around her head; or was she on her knees? Then she rose, and turning from the fire, ran as fast as she could, until I wheeled my horse across her path, jumped to the ground and stopped her with my arm about her waist. I looked at her. It was Rowena Fewkes.

"Rowena," I shouted, "what you doin' here? Don't you know you'll get burnt up?"

"I couldn't go any closer," she said, as if excusing herself. "Would it hurt much? I got scared, Jake. Oh, don't let me burn!"

There was no chance to make the circuit of the slew now, even if I had not been hampered with her. I told her to do as she was told, and not bother me. Then I gave her the horse to hold, and sternly ordered her not to let loose of him no matter what he did.

I gathered a little armful of dry grass, and lighted it with a match to the leeward of us. It spread fast, though I lighted it where the grass was thin so as to avoid a hot fire; but on the side toward the wind, where the blaze was feeble, I carefully whipped it out with my slouch hat. In a minute, or so, I had a line two or three rods long, of little blazes, each a circle of fire burning more and more fiercely on the leeward side, and more feebly on the side where the blaze was fanned away from its fuel. This side of each circle I whipped out with my hat, some of them with difficulty. Soon, we had a fierce fire raging, leaving in front of us a growing area of black ashes.

We were now between two fires; the great conflagration from which we were trying to protect ourselves came on from the west like a roaring tornado, its ashes falling all about us, its hot breath beginning to scorch us, its snapping and crackling now reaching the ear along with its roar; while on the east was the fire of my own kindling, growing in speed, racing off away from us, leaving behind it our haven of refuge, a tract swept clean of food for the flames, but hot and smoking, and as yet all too small to be safe, for the heat and smoke might kill where the flames could not reach. Between the two fires was the fast narrowing strip of dry grass from which we must soon move. Our safety lay in the following of one fire to escape the other.

The main army of the flames coming on from the west, with its power of suction, fanned itself to a faster pace than our new line could attain, and the heat increased, both from the racing crimson line to the west, and the slower-moving back-fire on the other side. We sweltered and almost suffocated. Rowena buried her face in her shawl, and swayed as if falling. I took her by the arm, and leading the excited horse, we moved over into our zone of safety. She was trembling like a leaf.

I was a little anxious for a few minutes for fear I had not started my back-fire soon enough; but the fear soon passed. The fire came on with a swelling roar. We followed our back-fire so close as to be almost blistered by it, coughing, gasping, covering our mouths and nostrils in such a heat and smother that I could scarcely support Rowena and keep my own footing. Suddenly the heat and smoke grew less; I looked around, and saw that the fire had reached our burnt area, and the line was cut for lack of fuel. It divided as a wave is split by a rock, and went in two great moving spouting fountains of red down the line of our back-fire, and swept on, leaving us scorched, blackened, bloodshot of eye and sore of lips, but safe. We turned, with great relief to me at least, and made for the open country behind the lines. Then for the first time, I looked at Rowena.

If I had been surprised at the way in which, considering her trouble, she had kept her prettiness and gay actions when I had last seen her, I was shocked at the change in her now. The poor girl seemed to have given up all attempt to conceal her condition or to care for her looks. All her rosy bloom was gone. Her cheeks were pale and puffy, even though emaciated. Her limbs looked thin through her disordered and torn clothes. She wore a dark-colored hood over her snarled hair, in which there was chaff mixed with the tangles as if she had been sleeping in straw. She was black with smoke and ashes. Her skirts were draggled as if with repeated soaking with dew and rain. Her shoes were worn through at the toes, and through the holes the bare toes stuck out of openings in her stockings. While her clothes were really better than when I had first seen her, she had a beggarly appearance that, coupled with her look of dejection and misery, went to my heart—she was naturally so bright and saucy. She looked like a girl who had gone out into the weather and lived exposed to it until she had tanned and bleached and weathered and worn like a storm-beaten and discouraged bird with its plumage soiled and soaked and its spirit broken. And over it all hung the cloud of impending maternity—a cloud which should display the rainbow of hope. But with her there was only a lurid light which is more awful than darkness.

I could not talk with her. I could only give her directions and lend her aid. I tried putting her on the horse behind me, but he would not carry double; so I put her in the saddle and walked by or ahead of the horse, over the blackened and ashy prairie, lit up by the red glare of the fire, and dotted here and there with little smokes which marked where there were coals, the remains of vegetable matter which burned more slowly than the dry grass. She said nothing; but two or three times she gave a distressed little moan as if she were in pain; but this she checked as if by an effort.

When we reached the end of the slew, we turned south and crossed the creek just above the pond which we called Plum Pudd'n' Pond, from the number of bitterns that lived there. It disappeared when I drained the marsh in the 'eighties. Then, though, it spread over several acres of ground, the largest body of water in Monterey County. We splashed through the west end of it, and Rowena looked out over it as it lay shining in the glare of the great prairie fire, which had now swept half-way down the marsh, roaring like a tornado and sending its flames fifty feet into the air. I could not help thinking what my condition would have been if I had tried to cross it and been mired in the bog, and like any good stockman, I was hoping that my cattle had got safe across in their rush for home and safety.

"What water is that?" asked Rowena as we crossed.

"Plum Pudd'n' Pond," I told her.

"Is it deep?" she said.

"Pretty deep in the middle."

"Over your head?"

"Oh, yes!"

"I reckoned it was," said she. "I was huntin' fur it when you found me."

"That was after you saw the fire," I said.

"No," said she. "It was before."

In my slow way I pondered on why she had been hunting water over her head, and sooner than is apt to be the case with me I understood. The despair in her face as she turned and looked at the shining water told me. She had refused to accept my offer to be her protector, because she saw how it hurt me; but she was now ready to balance the books—if it ever does that—by taking shelter in the depths of the pool! And this all for the pleasure of that smiling scoundrel!

"I hope God will damn him," I said; and am ashamed of it now.

"What good would that do?" said she wearily. "This world's hard enough, Jake!"

3

We got to my house, and I helped her in. I told her to wait while I went to look at the fire to see whether my stacks were in danger, and to put out and feed the horse. Then I went back, and found her sitting where I had left her, and as I went in I heard again that little moan of pain.

The house was as light as day, without a lamp. The light from the fire shone against the western wall of the room almost as strong as sunlight, and as we sat there we could hear the roar of the fire rising in the gusts of the wind, dying down, but with a steady undertone, like the wind in the rigging of a ship. I got some supper, and after saying that she couldn't eat, Rowena ate ravenously.

She had gone away from Blue-grass Manor, whipped forth by Mrs. Mobley's abuse, days and days before, living on what she had carried with her until it was gone, drinking from the brooks and runs of the prairie, and then starving on rose-haws, and sleeping in stacks until I had found her looking for the pool. If people could only have known! Presently she moaned again, and I made her lie down on the bed.

"What will you do with me, Jacob?" she asked.

"We'll think about that in the morning," said I.

"Maybe you can bury me in the morning," she said after a while. "Oh, Jake, I'm scared, I'm scared. My trouble is comin' on! My time is up, Jake. Oh, what shall I do! What shall I do?"

I went out and sat on the stoop and thought about this. Finally I made up my mind what she really meant by "her trouble," and I went back to her side. I found her moaning louder and more agonizingly, now: and in my turn I had my moment of panic.

"Rowena," I said, "I'm goin' out to do something that has to be done. Will you stay here, and not move out of this room till I come back?"

"I'll have to," she said. "I guess I've walked my last."

So I went out and saddled the fresh horse, and started through that fiery night for Monterey Centre. The fire had burned clear past the town, and when I got there I saw what was left of one or two barns or houses which had caught fire from the burning prairie, still blazing in heaps of embers. The village had had a narrower escape from the rain of ashes and sparks which had swept to the very edges of the little cluster of dwellings. I rode to Doctor Bliven's drug store, climbed the outside stairway which led to his living-room above, and knocked. Mrs. Bliven came to the door. I explained that I wanted the doctor at once to come out to my farm.

"He's not here," said she. "He is dressing some

burns from the fire; but he must be nearly through. I'll go after him."

I refused to go in and sit until she came back, but stood at the foot of the stair on the sidewalk. The time of waiting seemed long, but I suppose he came at once.

"Who's sick, Jake?" he asked.

"A girl," I said. "A woman."

"At your house?" asked he. "What is it?"

"It's Rowena Fewkes," said I.

"I thought they had gone to Colorado," said the doctor.

"They said they were leaving her behind," said Mrs. Bliven. "They said.............Do you say she's at your house? Who's with her?"

"No one," said I. "She's alone. Hurry, Doctor: she needs you bad."

"Just a minute," said he. "What seems to be the matter? Is she very bad?"

"It's a confinement case," said I. I had been thinking of the proper word all the way.

"And she alone!" exclaimed Mrs. Bliven. "Hurry, Doctor! I'll get your instruments and medicine-case, and you can hitch up. You stay here, Jake. I want to speak to you."

She ran up-stairs, and down again in a few seconds, with the cases, and wearing her bonnet and cloak. I could hear the doctor running his buggy out of the shed, and speaking to his horses. She set the cases down on the sidewalk, came up to me, put her hand on my arm and spoke.

"Jake," said she, "are you and Rowena married?"

"Us married!" I exclaimed. "Why, no!"

"This is bad business," said she. "I am surprised, and there's no woman out there with the poor little thing?"

"No," I said; "as soon as I could I started for the doctor because I thought he was needed first. But she needs a woman—a woman that won't look down on her. I wish—I wish I knew where there was one!"

"Jake," said she, "you've done the fair thing by me, and I'll stand by you, and by her. I'll go to her in her trouble. I'll go now with the doctor. And when I do the fair thing, see that you do the same. I'm not the one to throw the first stone, and I won't. I'm going with you, Doctor."

"What for?" said he.

"Just for the ride," she said. "I'll tell you more as we go."

They outstripped me on the return trip, for my horse was winded, and I felt that there was no place for me in what was going on at the farm, though what that must be was very dim in my mind.

I let my horse walk. The fire was farther off, now; but the sky, now flecked with drifting clouds, was red with its light, and the sight was one which I shall never see again: which I suppose nobody will ever see again; for I do not believe there will ever be seen such an expanse of grass as that of Iowa at that time. I have seen prairie fires in Montana and Western Canada; but they do not compare to the prairie fires of old Iowa. None of these countries bears such a coating of grass as came up from the black soil of Iowa; for their climate is drier. I can see that sight as if it were before my eyes now. The roaring came no longer to my ears

as I rode on through the night, except faintly when
the breeze, which had died down, sprang up as the fire
reached some swale covered with its ten-foot high saw-
grass. Then, I could see from the top of some rising
ground the flames leap up, reach over, catch in front
of the line, kindle a new fire, and again be overleaped
by a new tongue of fire, so that the whole line became
a belt of flames, and appeared to be rolling along
in a huge billow of fire, three or four rods across, and
miles in length.

The advance was not in a straight line. In some
places for one reason or another, the thickness or thin-
ness of the grass, the slope of the land, or the varying
strength of the wind, the fire gained or lost ground. In
some places great patches of land were cut off as islands
by the joining of advanced columns ahead of them, and
lay burning in triangles and circles and hollow squares
of fire, like bodies of soldiers falling behind and formed
to defend themselves against pursuers. All this
unevenness of line, with the varying surface of the lovely
Iowa prairie, threw the fire into separate lines and columns and detachments more and more like burning
armies as they receded from view.

Sometimes a whole mile or so of the line disappeared
as the fire burned down into lower ground; and then
with a swirl of flame and smoke, the smoke luminous
in the glare, it moved magnificently up into sight, rolling
like a breaker of fire bursting on a reef of land, buried
the hillside in flame, and then whirled on over the top, its
streamers flapping against the horizon, snapping off
shreds of flame into the air, as triumphantly as a human
army taking an enemy fort. Never again, never again!

We went through some hardships, we suffered some ills to be pioneers in Iowa; but I would rather have my grandsons see what I saw and feel what I felt in the conquest of these prairies, than to get up by their radiators, step into their baths, whirl themselves away in their cars, and go to universities. I am glad I had my share in those old, sweet, grand, beautiful things—the things which never can be again.

An old man looks back on things passed through as sufferings, and feels a thrill when he identifies them as among the splendors of life. Can anything more clearly prove the vanity of human experiences? But look at the wonders which have come out of those days. My youth has already passed into a period as legendary as the days when King Alfred hid in the swamp and was reproved by the peasant's wife for burning the cakes. I have lived on my Iowa farm from times of bleak wastes, robber bands, and savage primitiveness, to this day, when my state is almost as completely developed as Holland. If I have a pride in it, if I look back to those days as worthy of record, remember that I have some excuse. There will be no other generation of human beings with a life so rich in change and growth. And there never was such a thing in all the history of the world before.

I knew then, dimly, that what I saw was magnificent; but I was more pleased with the safety of my farmstead and my stacks than with the grim glory of the scene; and even as to my own good fortune in coming through undamaged, I was less concerned than with the tragedy being enacted in my house. I could not see into the future for Rowena, but I felt that it would be terrible. The words "lost," "ruined," "outcast," which were always ap-

plied to such as she had become, ran through my mind all
the time; and yet, she seemed a better girl when I talked
with her than when she was running over the prairie
like a plover following old Tom and the little clittering
wagon. Now she seemed to have grown, to have taken
on a sort of greatness, something which commanded my
respect, and almost my awe.

It was the sacredness of martyrdom. I know this
now: but then I seemed to feel that I was disgracing myself for not loathing her as something unclean.

"It's a boy!" said Doctor Bliven, as I came to the
house. "The mother ain't in very good shape. Seems
exhausted—exhausted. She'll pull through, though—
she'll pull through; but the baby is fat and lusty.
Strange, how the mother will give everything to the offspring, and bring it forth fat when she's as thin as a rail
—thin as a rail. Mystery of nature, you know—perpet-
uation of the race. Instinct, you know, instinct. This
girl, now—had an outfit of baby clothes in that bundle
of hers—instinct—instinct. My wife's going to stay a
day or so. I'll take her back next time I come out."

"You must 'tend to her, Doc," said I. "I'll guarantee
you your pay."

"Very well, Jake. Of course you would—of course,
of course," said he. "But between you and me there
wouldn't be any trouble about pay. Old friends, you
know; old friends. Favors in the past. You've done
things for me—my wife, too. Fellow travelers, you
know. Never call on us for anything and be refused.
Be out to-morrow. Ought to have a woman here when
I go. Probably be milk for the child when it needs it;
but needs woman. Can get you a mover's wife's sister—

widow—experienced with her own. Want her? Bring her out for you—bring her out to-morrow. Eh?"

I told him to bring the widow out, and was greatly relieved. I went to Magnus's cabin that night to sleep, leaving Mrs. Bliven with Rowena. I hoped I might not have to see Rowena before she went away; for the very thought of seeing the girl with the child embarrassed me; but on the third day the widow—they afterward moved on to the Fort Dodge country—came to me, and standing afar off as if I was infected with something malignant, told me that Mrs. Vandemark wanted to see me.

"She ain't Mrs. Vandemark," I corrected. "Her name is Rowena Fewkes."

"I make it a habit," said the widow, whose name was Mrs. Williams, "to speak in the present tense."

Whatever she may have meant was a problem to me; but I went in. Rowena lay in my bed, and beside her was a little bundle wrapped in a blanket made of one of my flannel sheets. The women were making free of my property as a matter of course.

"What are you goin' to do with me, Jake?" she asked again, looking up at me pleadingly.

"I'm goin' to keep you here till you're able to do for yourself," I said. "Time enough to think of that after a while."

She took my hand and pressed it, and turned her face to the pillow. Pretty soon she turned the blanket back, and there lay the baby, red and ugly and wrinkled.

"Ain't he purty?" said she, her face glowing with love. "Oh, Jake, I thank God I didn't find the pond before you found me. I didn't know very well what I was doin'. I'll have something to love an' work fur, now. I wonder if they'll let me be a good womern. I will be, in spite of hell an' high water—f'r his sake, Jake."

4

As I lay in Magnus's bed that night, I could see no way out for her. She could get work, I knew, for there was always work for a woman in our pioneer houses. The hired girl who went from place to place could find employment most of the time; but the baby would be an incumbrance. It would be a thing that the eye of censure could not ignore, like the scarlet "A" on the breast of the girl in Nathaniel Hawthorne's story. I could not foresee how the thing would work out, and lay awake pondering on it until after midnight, and I had hardly fallen asleep, it seemed to me, when the door was opened, and in came Magnus. He had finished his job and come back.

"You hare, Yake?" he said, in his quiet and unmoved way. "I'm glad. Your house bane burn up in fire?"

I told him the startling news, and as the story of poor Rowena slowly made its way into his mind, I was startled and astonished at its effect on him; for he has always been to me a man who would be calm in a tornado, and who would meet shipwreck or earthquake without a tremor. I have seen him standing in his place in the ranks with his comrades falling all about loading and firing his musket, with no more change in his expression than a cold light of battle in his mild buttermilk eyes. I have seen him wipe from his face the blood of a fellow-soldier spattered on him by a fragment of shell, as if it had been a splash of water from a puddle. But now, he trembled. He turned pale. He raged up and down the little room with his hands doubled into fists and beating the air. He bit down upon his Norwegian words with clenched teeth. I was afraid to talk to him at last. Finally, he turned to me and said:

"Ay know de man! So it vas in de ol' country! Rich fallar bane t'inking poor girl notting but like fresh fruit for him to eat; a cup of vine for him to drink; an' he drink it! He eat de fruit. But dis bane different country. Ay keel dis damned Gowdy! You hare, Yake? Ay keel him!"

Of course I told him that this would never do, and talked the way we all do when it is our duty to keep a friend from ruining himself. He sat down while I was talking, and as far as I could see heard never a word of what I said. Finally I talked myself out, and still he sat there as silent as a statue.

"Ay—tank—Ay—take—a—valk," he said at last, in the jerky way of the Norwegian; and he went out into the night.

I lay back expecting that he would come in pretty soon, when I had more of which I had thought to talk to him about; but I went to sleep, and having been a good deal broken of my rest, I slept late. He was still absent when I woke up. When I got to my place, the widow told me that he had been there and had a long talk with Rowena, and had hitched up his team and driven away.

Rowena was asleep when I looked in, and I went out to plow. If Magnus had gone to kill Buck Gowdy, there was nothing I could do to prevent it. As a matter of fact, I approved of his impulse. I had felt it myself, though not with any such wrathful bitterness. I had known for a long time that Magnus had a tenderness toward Rowena; but he was such a gentle fellow, and seemed to be so slow in approaching her, with his fooling with Surajah's inventions and the like, that I set down his feeling as a sort of sheepish drawing toward her which never would amount to anything. But now I saw that his rage against Gowdy was of the kind that overpowered him, stolid as he had always seemed. It rose above mine in proportion to the passion he must have felt for her, when she was a girl that a man could take for a wife. I pitied him; and I did not envy Buck Gowdy, if it chanced that they should come together while Magnus's white-hot anger was burning; but I rather hoped they would meet. I did not believe that in any just court Magnus would be punished if he supplied the lack in the law.

When I turned out at noon, I saw Magnus's team, and a horse hitched to a buggy tied to my corn-crib; and when I went into the house, I half expected to find Jim Boyd, the sheriff, there to arrest Magnus Thorkelson for murder, at the bedside of Magnus's lady-love. I could imagine how N. V. Creede, whom I had already resolved I would retain to defend Magnus, would thrill the jury in his closing speech for the prisoner as the bar.

What I found was Elder Thorndyke and grandma and the widow, all standing by Rowena's bed. The widow was holding the baby in her arms, but as I came in she laid it in a chair and covered it up, as much as to indicate that on this occasion the less seen of the infant the better. Magnus was holding Rowena's hand, and the elder was standing on the other side of the bed holding a book. Grandma Thorndyke stood at the bed's foot looking severely at a *Hostetter's Almanac* I had hanging on the head-board. The widow was twittering around from place to place. When I came in, Magnus motioned me to stand beside him, and as I took my place handed me a gold ring. Rowena looked up at me piteously, as if to ask forgiveness. Sometime during the ceremony we had the usual hitch over the ring, for I had put it in my trousers pocket and had to find it so that Magnus could put it on Rowena's finger. I had never seen a marriage ceremony, and was at my wit's end to know what we were doing, thinking sometimes that it was a wedding, and sometimes that it might be something like extreme unction; when at last the elder said, "I pronounce you man and wife!"

CHAPTER XIX

NOW I leave it to the reader—if I ever have one besides my granddaughter Gertrude—whether in this case of the trouble of Rowena Fewkes and her marriage to Magnus Thorkelson, I did anything by which I ought to have forfeited the esteem of my neighbors, of the Reverend and Mrs. Thorndyke, or of Virginia Royall. I never in all my life acted in a manner which was more in accordance to the dictates of my conscience. You have seen how badly I behaved, or tended to behave in the past, and lost no friends by it. In a long life of dealing in various kinds of property, including horse-trading, very few people have ever got the best of me, and everybody knows that this is less a boast than a confession; and yet, this one good act of standing by this poor girl in her dreadful plight degraded me more in the minds of the community than all the spavins, thorough-pins, poll-evils and the like I ever concealed or glossed over. We are all schoolboys who usually suffer our whippings for things that should be overlooked; and the fact that we get off scot free when we should have our jackets tanned does not seem to make the injustice any easier to bear.

Dick McGill, the editor of the scurrilous Monterey *Journal* was, as usual, the chief imp of this as of any other deviltry his sensational paper could take a part in. Of course, he would be on Buck Gowdy's side; for what rights had such people as Magnus and Rowena and I?

"A wedding took place out on the wild shores of Hell Slew last week," said this paper. "It was not a case, exactly, of the funeral baked meats coldly furnishing forth the marriage supper; but the economy was quite as striking. The celebration of the arrival of the heir of the Manor (though let us hope not of the manner) was merged in the wedding festivities. We make our usual announcements: Married at the residence of J. T. Vandemark, Miss Rowena Fewkes to Mr. Magnus Thorkelson. It's a boy, standard weight. The ceremonies were presided over by Doctor Bliven, our genial disciple of Esculapias, and by Elder Thorndyke, each in his respective sphere of action. Great harmony marked the carrying out of these usually separate functions. The amalgamation of peoples goes on apace. Here we have Yankee, Scandinavian and Dutch so intertwined that it will take no common 'glance of eye, thought of man, wing of angel' to separate the sheep from the goats in the sequel. *Nuff ced.*"

He little knew the sequel!

I did not read this paper. In fact, I did not read anything in those days; and I do not believe that Magnus and Rowena knew for some time anything more about this vile and slanderous item than I did. It was only by the way we were treated that we felt that the cold shoulder of the little world of Vandemark Township and Monterey County was turned toward us. Of course Magnus and Rowena expected this; but I was hurt more deeply by this injustice than by anything in my whole life. Grandma Thorndyke came out no more to red up my house, and exhibit her samples of prospective wives to me. The neighbors called no more. I began driving over to the new railroad to do my marketing, though it was twice as close to go to Monterey Centre. When Elder Thorndyke, largely through the contributions of Governor Wade and Buckner Gowdy, succeeded in getting his church built, I was not asked to go to the doings of laying the corner-stone or shingling the steeple. I was an outsider.

I quit trying to neighbor with the Roebucks, Smiths, and George Story, my new neighbors on the south; and took up with some French who moved in on the east, the families of Pierre Lacroix and Napoleon B. Bouchard. We called the one "Pete Lackwire" and the other "Poly Busher." They were the only French people who came into the township. They were good neighbors, and fair farmers, and their daughters made some of the best wives the sons of the rest of us got. One of my grandsons married the prettiest girl among their grandchildren—a Lacroix on one side and a Bouchard on the other.

It may well be understood that I now took no part in the township history, which gets more complex with the coming in of more settlers; but it was about this time that what is now Vandemark Township began agitating for a separate township organization. We were attached to Centre Township, in which was situated the town of Monterey Centre. This town, dominated by the County Ring, clung to all the territory it could control, so as to spend the taxes in building up the town. A great four-room schoolhouse was finished in the summer of

1860; most of it built by taxes paid by the speculators who still owned the bulk of the land.

The Vandemark Township people made a great outcry about the shape of Centre Township, and called it "The Great Crane," with our township as the neck, and a lot of other territory back of us for the body, and Monterey Centre for the head. I took no part in this agitation, for I was burning with a sense of indignation at the way people treated me; but the County Ring compromised by building us a schoolhouse on my southwest corner, now known as the Vandemark School. But I cared nothing about this. I had no children to go to school, and while I never ceased to dream of a future with Virginia as my wife, I kept saying to myself that I never should have a family. Consistency is the least of the necessaries of our visions and dreams. I never tried to see Virginia. I avoided the elder and Grandma Thorndyke. I knew that she was disgusted with me for even an innocent connection with the Thorkelson matter, and I supposed that Virginia felt the same way. So I went on trying to be as near to a hermit as I could.

2

I know now that things began to change for me in the minds of the people when Rowena's baby was christened. This took place early in the winter. Magnus asked me to go to the church; so I was present when Magnus and Rowena stood before the altar in a ceremony which Rowena would have given anything to escape, and Magnus, too, but he believed that the child's soul could not be saved if it died unchristened, and she yielded to his urgings in the matter. He held his head high as he stood by her, as he always stood in every relation in life, witnessing before God and man that he believed her a victim, and that whatever guilt she may have incurred, she had paid for it in full. After the responses had been made, Elder Thorndyke unfolded a paper which had been handed him with the name of the child on it; then he went on with his part of the ceremony: "In the name of the Father, the Son, and the Holy Ghost, I baptize thee——" And then he carried on a whispered conversation with the mother, gave the loudest honk I ever heard him utter, and went on: "I baptize thee, Owen Lovejoy Gowdy."

They said that Gowdy swore when he heard of this, and exclaimed, "I don't care about her picking me out; but I hate to be joined with that damned Black Abolitionist."

The elder seemed dazed after he had done the deed, and looked around at the new church building as if wondering whether he had not committed some sort of crime in thus offending a man who had put so much money in it. He had not, however; for in advertising in this way Gowdy's wrong to one girl, he ended forever his sly approaches, under the excuses of getting her some fictitious property, saving his soul, and the like, to another.

I think it was the word of what Gowdy said about the christening that finally wrought Magnus up to the act he had all along resolved upon, the attempt on Gowdy's life. He armed himself and went over to the Blue-grass Manor looking for Buck; but found that his man had gone to Kentucky. Magnus left word for Gowdy to go armed and be prepared to protect himself, and went home. He said nothing to me about this; but the next spring when

Gowdy came back, Magnus started after him again with a gun loaded with buckshot, and Gowdy, who, I suppose, looked upon Magnus as beneath him, had him arrested. I went to Monterey Centre and put my name on Magnus's bond when he was bound over to keep the peace.

I hinted to Magnus that he needn't mind about the bond if he still believed in his heart that Gowdy needed killing; but Rowena pleaded with him not to ruin himself, me and her by pursuing his plan of executing what both he and I believed to be justice on a man who had forfeited his life by every rule of right. This lapse into lawlessness on his part and mine can not be justified, of course. It is set forth here as a part of the history of the place and the time.

I am not equipped to write the history of the celebrated Gowdy Case, which grew out of these obscure circumstances in the lives of a group of pioneers in an Iowa township. Probably the writers of history will never set it down. Yet, it swayed the destiny of the county and the state in after years, when Gowdy had died and left his millions to be fought over in courts, in caucuses, in conventions, state and county. If it does not go into the histories, the histories will not tell the truth. If great law firms, governors, judges, congressmen and senators, lobbyists and manipulators, are not judged in the light of the secret as well as the surface influence of the Gowdy Case, they will not be rightly judged.

The same thing is true of the influence of the loss of the county funds by Judge Stone. Who was guilty? Was the plan to have the bag of "treasure" stolen from us by the Bunker gang a part of the scheme of whoever took the money? Did the Bushyagers know about the satchel? Did they know it was full of salt instead of money? Of course not, if they were in the thing.

Did some one mean to fix it so the Bunkers would rob us of the satchel and thus let everybody off? And if so, what about me? I should have had to fight for the money, for that was what I was hired for. Was I to be killed to save Judge Stone, or Governor Wade, and if so, which?

My part in the affair was never much spoken of in the hot newspaper and stump-speech quarrels over the matter; but after a while, when I had had time to figure it all out, I began to think I had not been treated quite right; but what was I anyhow? This was another thing that made me sore at all the Monterey Centre crowd, including the elder and grandma, with their truckling to Gowdy and Wade and Stone and the rest who helped the elder build his church. I suppose that the stolen money, some of it, went to pay for that church; but if every church had remained unbuilt that has stolen money in it, there would be fewer temples pointing, as the old song says, with taper spire to heaven, wouldn't there?

Of course these scandalous matters were soon lost sight of in the excitement of the Civil War. This thing which changed all our lives the way war does, came upon me like a clap of thunder. I was living like a hermit, and working like a horse, not trying to make any splurge, as I might have done, even having given up the idea of getting me a team of horses, which I had been thinking of for a while back with the notion of maybe getting a buggy and beginning to take Virginia out buggy-riding, and thus working up in a year or two to popping the question to her. But now I sulked in my cabin.

3

I guess the war surprised the people who read about it as much as it did me. I often thought of the poor slaves, and liked Dunlap and Thatcher, the men I had run into back in Wisconsin on the road in 1855, for going down into Kansas to fight for Free Soil; but as for fighting in which I should have any interest; bless you, it never occurred to any of us, either North or South. The trouble was always going to be off somewhere else. I guess that's the way with the oncoming of wars. If we knew they would come to us, we'd be less blood-thirsty.

I heard of the Dred Scott Decision, and thought J. P. Roebuck was talking foolishness when he came to me one day over in my back field to borrow a chew of tobacco— he was always doing that—and said that this decision made slavery a general thing all over the Union. I didn't see any slavery around Vandemark Township, and no signs of any. I heard of Old John Brown, and had a hazy idea that he was some kind of traitor who ought to have been hanged, or the government wouldn't have hanged him. You see how inconsistent I was. But wars are fought by inconsistent men who suffer and die for other people's ideas: don't you think so? Abraham Lincoln was nominated about corn-planting time; but I was not thrilled. I had never heard of him. The nation was drifting down the rapids to the falls; and for all the deafening roar that came to our ears, we did not know or think of the cataract we were to be swept over.

I was a voter now, and so was Magnus; but he was for Lincoln, and I was not. It seemed to me that the Republican Party was too new. And yet I was not satisfied with Douglas. Why? It was merely because I had got it into my mind that he had been beaten in a debate by Lincoln, and it seemed that this defeat ought to put him out of the running for president. I sat down a few rods from the polls and thought over the matter of choosing between Edward Everett and John C. Breckenridge, pestered by Governor Wade and H. L. Burns and N. V. and the rest, until finally they left me and when I had made my decision, I found that the polls had closed. I was a good deal relieved.

I am giving you a glimpse into the mind of a conscientious and ignorant voter. If I had read more, my mind would have been made up beforehand, but by some one else. I was not a fool; I was just slow and bewildered. The average voter shoots at the flock and gets it over with. He has had his mind made up for him by some one—and maybe it's just as well: for when he tries, as I did, to make it up for himself, he is apt to find that he has no basis for judgment. That is why all governments, free and the other kind, have always been minority governments, and always will be. And I reckon that's just as well, too.

Lincoln's first call for volunteers took only a few men out of the county, and none from Vandemark Township, except George Story. I had not begun to take much interest in the matter; and when in the summer of 1861 there began to be war meetings to spur up young men to enlistment the speakers all shouted to us that the war was not to free the slaves, but to save the Union. Now this was a new slant on the question, and I had to think over it for a while.

Sitting in the wagon of history with my feet dangling down and facing the rear, as we all ride, I can now see that the thing was as broad as it was long. The Union could not be preserved without freeing the slaves, for all of what Lincoln said when he stated that he would save the Union by freeing the slaves if he could do that, or by keeping them slaves if he could do that, or by freeing some of them and leaving the rest in servitude if he could do that; but that save the Union he would. Now in my narrow way, I could see some point in freeing the slaves, but as for the Union, I hardly knew whether it was important or not. I needed to think it over. It might be just as well not to fight to preserve the Union; and when I had heard men say, "I enlisted to save the Union, and not to free niggers," as a lot of them did, I scratched my head and wondered why I could not feel so devoted to the Union as they did. Looking back from the tail-end of the wagon, I now see what Lincoln meant by the importance of keeping us all under one flag; but I didn't know then, and I don't believe one man in a hundred who shouted for the Union knew why the Union was so important. There never was a better cause than the one we sung for in "The Union, the Union forever!" but thousands and thousands sang and shouted it, and died for it—how bravely and wonderfully they died for it!—who knew as little what it meant as I did. And the rebels—how gallantly they died for their cause, too. Not for slavery, as we blindly thought, misjudging them as we must always misjudge our foes (or we should not have the hate in our hearts to fight them); but for the very thing we were fighting for—liberty, as they believed.

Both sides are always right in war.

I finally began to see light when I thought one night of my old life on the canal, and asked myself how it would affect us in Iowa if York State and the East should secede, as the South was trying to do. It would put them in shape to starve us of the West by levying duties on our crops when going to market. But, said I to myself, we could then ship down the Mississippi; but the river was already closed and would always be controlled by the Confederacy. This was serious; but when I said to myself that the East would never secede, the question, Why not? could not be answered if the principle of secession could once be set up as correct and made good by victory. Then, it came into my mind after a month or two of thinking, that any state or group of states could secede whenever they liked; that others would go to war with them to keep such unions as were left; and we should never be at peace long: so after all, the Union *was* important, and must be preserved.

The question must be settled now in this war.

But I don't know how long I should have studied this matter over in my lonely benightedness, if I had not seen Virginia one night at a war meeting that I sneaked into in the Centre, with a young man dressed in store clothes whom I afterward knew as Will Lockwood, the principal of the Monterey Centre school, who seemingly was going forward to put his name down as enlisted. I jumped in ahead of him, so as to show Virginia that her fellow was not the only patriot, and beat him to it.

"So you are going to fight Kaintucky?" said she to me as if I had engaged to ruin everything she held dear.

"We must save the Union," I said. "I didn't think of you being on the other side!"

"Mr. Lockwood," said she, "this is Teunis Vandemark, an old friend of mine. He's going to fight my friends, too."

In two or three minutes I found that he was from Herkimer County, had lived along the Erie Canal, and was actually the son of my old teacher Lockwood, to whom I had gone when I was wintering with Mrs. Fogg in the old canalling days. He was my best friend during all my service as a soldier—which you will soon see was not long. We left him on the field at Shiloh.

4

The recruiting officer got us uniforms—or somebody did; and during the nice weather—it was October when I enlisted—our company did some drilling. We had no arms, but used shotguns, squirrel rifles, and even sticks. Will Lockwood tried to drill us, but made a bad mess of it. Then one day Buckner Gowdy, who had also enlisted, took charge of a squad of men and in ten minutes showed that he knew more about drill than any one else in the county. He had been educated at a military school in Virginia.

All the skill in drill that we ever got, we owed to him. The sharp word of command; the quick swing to the proper position; the snappy step; everything that we knew more than a lot of yokels might be expected to know, we got from Buck Gowdy. Magnus admitted it, even; but he turned pale whenever he was in a squad under Gowdy's command. It was gall and wormwood for me, and worse for him; but when it came to electing a captain of our company, I voted for Gowdy, and under the same conditions would do it again. It was better to have a real captain who was a scoundrel, than a man who knew nothing but kept the Commandments. War is hell in more than one respect. I felt that Gowdy would be more likely to bring us safe out of any bad hole in which we might find ourselves, than any one else. But I was glad, sometimes, when he was rawhiding us into shape, that Magnus Thorkelson was drilling with a wooden gun. I wondered how the new captain himself felt about this.

Governor Wade gave us a great entertainment at his farm just before we marched—still without guns—to the railroad to take the cars for Dubuque, where boats were supposed to be waiting to take us down the river—if we could make it before navigation was closed by the ice. His great barns were cleared out for tables, and the house was open, and there were flags and transparencies expressing the heroism of those who were willing to do anything to get us into the fight.

Everybody was there—except Judge Stone. I remember looking through the open door at the great iron safe into which he had put the county satchel—I am careful not to commit myself as to the money part of it—and all the events of the previous visit came back through my mind ; but mainly how angry I had been with Virginia for being kissed by Bob Wade. And Bob was there, too, all spick and span in his new lieutenant's uniform with Kittie Fleming hanging on his arm, her eyes drinking him in with every glance. The governor was in no position to make a row about this. The occasion had caused an armistice to be signed as to all our neighborhood quarrels, and Bob Wade was emancipated from the stern paternal control, as Jack had been when he went off with the first flight in the original seventy-five thousand—emancipated by the uniform. Bob and Kittie sailed along in the face and eyes of the governor and his wife in spite of the fact that such association was forbidden—and sailed down to Waterloo where they were married before we went off hurrahing for the cause.

Virginia was there with the elder and grandma. The old preacher and his wife looked more shabby than I had ever seen them, grandma's gloves more extensively darned, the elder's clothes shinier, his cuffs in all their whiteness more frayed, and there were beautifully darned places in the stiff starched bosom of his shirt. He pressed my hand warmly as he said, "God bless you, Jacob, and bring you safe back to us, my boy!" Grandma's eyes glistened as she echoed his sentiments and began asking me about my underwear and especially my socks. Virginia looked the other way; but when I went off my myself, Will Lockwood came and drew me away into a corner to talk with me about old times along the canal; and suddenly we found Virginia there, and Will all at once thought of some one he wanted to speak to and left us together.

"I didn't mean that I thought you ought not to go to the war, Teunis," said she. "You must go, of course."

"Maybe your friends," I said after standing dumb for a while, "will be on the Union side."

"No," said she. "I have no relations—and few friends there; but all I have will be on the other side, I reckon. It makes no difference. They've forgotten me by this time. Everybody has forgotten me that once liked me—everybody but Elder Thorndyke and Mrs. Thorndyke. They love me, but nobody else does."

"I thought some others acted as if they did," I said.

"You thought a lot about it!" she scoffed. Then we sat quite a while silent. "I shall think every day," said she at last, "about the only happy time I have had since Ann took sick—and long before that. The only happy time, and the happiest, I reckon, that I ever'll have. I'll think of it every day while you're at the front. I want you to know when you are suffering and in danger that some one thinks of the kindest thing you ever did—and maybe the kindest thing any boy ever did. You don't care about it now, maybe; but the time may come when you will."

"What time was that?" I asked.

"You know, Teunis," the tears were falling in her lap now. "Those days when we were together alone on the wide prairie—when you took me in and was so good to me—and saved me from going wild, if not from anything else bad. I remember that for the first few days, I was not quite easy in my feelings—I reckon your goodness hadn't come to me yet; but one day, after you had been away for a while, there in the grove where we stayed so long, you looked so pale and sorry that I began talking to you more intimately, you remember, and we suddenly drew close to each other, and for the first time, I felt so safe, so safe! Something has come between us lately, Teunis. I partly know what; and partly I don't; but something——"

She stopped in the middle of what she seemed to be saying. At first I thought she had choked up with grief, but when I looked her in the face, except for her eyes shining very bright, I could not see that she was at all worked up in her feelings. She spoke quite calmly to some one that passed by. I was abashed by the thought that she was giving me credit for something I was not entitled to. She spoke of the day when I was in my heart the meanest: but how could I explain? So I said nothing, much, but hummed and hawed, with "I——" and "Yes, I——," and nothing to the point. Finally, I bogged down, and quit.

"We are very poor," said she, nodding toward the elder and grandma. "So, ignorant as I am, I kept a school last summer—did you know that?"

"Yes," I said, "I knew about it. Over in the Hoosier settlement."

"I ain't a good teacher," she said, "only with the little children; but sometimes we shouldn't have had the necessaries of life, if it hadn't been for what I earned. I can't do too much for them. They have been father and mother to me, and I shall be a daughter to them. If—if they want me to go with—with—in circles which I—I—don't care half so much about as for—for the birds, and flowers—and the people back in our grove—and for people who don't care for me any more—why, I don't think I ought to disobey Mrs. Thorndyke. But I don't believe as she does—or did—about things that have happened to you since—since we parted and got to be strangers, Teunis. And neither does any one else, nor she herself any more. People respect you, Teunis. I wanted to say that to you, too, before you go away—maybe forever, Teunis!"

She touched on so many things—sore things and sacred things—in this speech, that I only looked at her with tears in my eyes; and she saw them. It was the only answer I could make, and before she could say any more, the elder and his wife came and took her home. I had got half-way to Cairo, Illinois, before I worked it out that by "the people back in our grove," she must have meant me; for the only others there had been that gang of horse-thieves: and if so she must have meant me when she spoke of "people who don't care for me any more"—but it was too late to do anything in the way of correcting this mistake then. All I could pride myself on was having a good memory as to what she said. I guess this proves my relationship to that other Dutchman who took so long to build the church. Remember, though, that he finally built it.

5

The Civil War is no part of the history of Vandemark Township; and I had small part in the Civil War. But one thing that took place on the field of Shiloh does belong in this history. Most of the members of my company enlisted in October, 1861, but we did not get to the front until the very day of the Battle of Shiloh. I was in one of the two regiments whose part in the battle has caused so much controversy. I gave Senator Cummins an affidavit about it only the other day to settle something about a monument on the field.

We came up the Tennessee River the night of the day before the battle, and landed at Pittsburgh Landing at daybreak of the first day's fight. We had not had our guns issued to us yet. Some have thought it a little hard on us to be shoved into a great battle without ever having loaded or fired our muskets. When we were landed the guns were issued to my company, and we were given about half an hour's instruction in the way they were worked. Of course most of us had done shooting, and were a little better than green hands; but Will

Lockwood during the fight loaded his gun until it was full of unfired loads, and forgot to put a cap on. Then he discovered his mistake, and put on a cap, and would have blown off his own head by firing all the stuff out at once, when Captain Gowdy saw what he was doing and snatched the gun away from him calling him a damned fool, and broke the stock off the musket on the ground. There were plenty of guns for Will to select from by that time which were not in use, so he picked up another and made a new start; but not for long.

After the guns were issued to us, we stood there on the bank, and lounged about on the landing, waiting for the issue of cartridges. An orderly came to me with Magnus following him, and gave me the captain's order to report to him in the cabin of the transport which lay tied up at the river bank. We looked at each other in wonder, but followed the orderly into the cabin, where we stood at attention. The captain returned our salutes, dismissed the orderly, and after his footsteps had gone out of hearing, turned to us.

"Thorkelson and Vandemark," said he, "I have a few words to say to you. I don't find anything in the books covering the case, and am speaking as man to man."

"Yes, sir," said I.

"Ay hare," said Magnus.

"Thorkelson," Gowdy went on, "you have had an ambition to put an end to me. Well, now's your chance, or will be when we get out there where the shooting is going on. You've had a poor chance to practise marksmanship; but maybe you can shoot well enough to hit a man of my size from the rear—for my men will be to the rear of me in a fight."

He stopped and looked straight in Magnus's eyes; and Magnus stared straight back. At last, Gowdy's eyes swept around toward me, and then back again.

"Well," said he, "what do you and your friend say? The bond to keep the peace doesn't run in Tennessee."

"I think," said I, "as man to man, that you deserve shooting; but maybe this ain't the place for it. I voted for you for captain because you seem to know your business—and I don't b'lieve we've got another that does. That's how I feel."

Gowdy laughed, that friendly, warm, musical laugh of his, just as he would have laughed in a horse trade, or over the bar, or while helping the church at a donation party.

"Well," said he, "I called you in here—especially you, Thorkelson—to say that if you feel bound by any vow you've made, to shoot me, why, you may shoot and be damned. I shan't pay any attention to the matter. From the way it sounds out there at the front, it will be only one bullet added to a basketful. That's all, Thorkelson."

"Captain Gowdy," said Magnus.

"Go on, Thorkelson," said Gowdy.

"Van Ay bane svorn in," said Magnus, "Ay take you for captain. You bane a dam good-for-nothing rascal, but you bane best man for captain. Ay bane tied up. You bane necessary to maybe save lives of a hundred dam sight better men dan you. Ay not shoot. You insult me ven you talk about it."

"In spite of the somewhat uncomplimentary and insubordinate language in which you express yourself," said Gowdy, "which I overlook under the peculiar circumstances, I reckon I must admit that I did assume an

attitude on your part of which you are incapable, and
that such an assumption was insulting—if a private can
be insulted by a commissioned officer. This being man to
man, I apologize. You may go, Thorkelson."

Magnus clicked his heels together in the way he had
learned in the old country, and saluted; Captain Gowdy
returned the salute, and Magnus marched out with his
head high, and his stomach drawn in.

"Devilish good soldier!" said Gowdy as he went out.
"Well, that clears the atmosphere a little! So, Vandemark, you think I need killing, eh?"

"Yes, sir."

"Well, it's all in the point of view," said he, leaning
toward me and smiling that ingratiating smile of his.
"Sometimes I think so, too; but there's only one policy
for me—lose 'em and forget 'em. I sometimes think that
the time may come when I shall wish I had married that
girl. Have you seen the baby lately?"

"I used to see it every few days," said I. "It's runnin' all over the place."

"Look like me?"

"It will when it gits older."

"When you go back," said he, "if I don't, will you do
me and this little offspring of mine—and its mother—a
favor?"

"I'll have to wait and see what it is," said I.

"Same old cautious Vandemark!" said he, laughing.
"Well, that's why I picked you to do this, if you will be
so good. You can look the matter over in case it comes to
anything, and act if you think best; but I think you will
decide to act. Please go to Lusch in Waterloo and ask
for a packet of papers I left there, to be opened in your

presence and at your request if I wink out in this irrepressible conflict.   Remember, I shall be on the other side of Jordan or some other stream.   Inside of the outer envelope will be a letter to Rowena, which please deliver. There will also be one for you, with some securities and other things to be held in trust for the benefit of Rowena's boy—and mine.   I hate that 'Owen Lovejoy' part of his name; but he is entitled to the name of Gowdy, and in view of the fact that he has it, I want him to have a good chance—as good as he can have in view of the irregularity of his birth.   To tell you the plain truth, as my affairs are now situated, I'm giving him more than he could take as my son if he were legitimate—for as neighbor to neighbor, I'm practically bu'sted.   All I'm doing is hanging on for land to rise.   Now this isn't much to do, and you won't have to act unless you want to. Will you have the papers opened, and act for the dead scoundrel if it seems the proper thing to do?   You see, there's hardly anybody else who is satisfactory to me, and at the same time a friend to the other parties."

"I'll have the papers opened," said I; "but remember, this don't take back what I said a few minutes ago.   I think you ought to be killed."

"Thank you," said he.   "Private Vandemark!   You may go!"

Now I have told this story over and over again in court, to commissioners taking testimony, to lawyers in their offices, to lawyers out at my farm.   It has been printed in court records, including the Reports of the Supreme Court of Iowa.   Judges of the Supreme Court of Iowa have been nominated or refused nomination because of their views, or their lack of views, or their refusal to state in advance off in some hole and corner, what their views would be on the legal effect of this conversation between me and Buckner Gowdy in the cabin of the transport on the morning of the first day's battle of Shiloh—so N. V. says—but this is the first time I have had a chance to tell it as it was, without some squirt of a lawyer pointing his finger at me and trying to make me change the story; or some other limb of the law interrupting me with objections that it was incompetent, irrelevant and immaterial, not the best evidence, hearsay, a privileged communication, and a lot of other balderdash. This is what took place, just as I have stated it; and this is all the Vandemark Township, Monterey County, or Iowa history there was in the battle so far as I know—except that Iowa had more men in that fight than any other state in proportion to her population.

Just to show you that I didn't run away, I must tell you that we had ammunition issued to us after a while, and were told how to use it. We got forty rounds of cartridges at first and ten rounds right afterward. Then we formed and marched, part of the time at the double, out into a cotton-field. In front of us a few hundred yards off, was a line of forest trees, and under the trees were tents, that I guess some of our other men were driven out of that morning. Here we were at once under a hot fire and lost a lot of men. We went into action about half-past nine or ten o'clock in the forenoon, and two regiments of us stood the enemy off along that line until about noon. Then they rushed us, and such of us as could went away from there. Those that didn't are most of them there yet. I stayed, because of a shot through my leg which splintered the bone. The enemy trampled over me as they drove our men off the field, and a horse stepped on my shoulder, breaking the collar-bone. Then, when the Johnnies were driven back, I was mauled around again, but don't remember much except that I was thirsty. And then, for months and months, I was in one hospital or another; and finally I was discharged as unfit for service, because I was too lame to march. I can feel it in frosty weather yet; but it never amounted to much except to the dealers in riding plows and the like. So ended my military life. I had borne arms for my country for about three hours!

It was the eighth of January, 1863, when I got home. I rode from the railroad to Foster Blake's in his sleigh, looked over my herd which he was running on shares for me, and crossed Vandemark's Folly Marsh on the hard snow which was over the tall grass and reeds everywhere. How my grove had grown that past summer! I began to feel at home, as I warmed the little house up with a fire in the stove, and rolling up in my blankets, which for a long time were more comfortable to me than a bed, went to sleep on the floor. I never felt the sense of home more delightfully than that night. I would set things to rights, and maybe go over to Monterey Centre and see Virginia next day. I could see smoke at Magnus's down the road. I felt a pleasure in thus sneaking in without any one's knowing it.

I had not gone to see Mr. Lusch in Waterloo, for I had learned that so far from being killed, Captain Gowdy had come through Shiloh without a scratch, and that he had soon afterward resigned and gone back to Monterey County. It has always been believed, but I don't know why, that he was allowed to resign either because of his relationship to the great Confederate families of Kentucky, or because of his record there before he went to Iowa. Anyhow, he never joined the G. A. R. or fellowshipped with the soldiers after the war. I always hated him; but I do him the justice to say here that he was a brave man, and except for his one great weakness—the weakness that I am told Lord Byron was destroyed by— he would have been a good man. I feel certain that if he had been given a chance to make a career in either army, he would have been a general before the war was over.

That afternoon, J. P. Roebuck, who had seen my smoke, came over to welcome me home and to talk politics with me. We must have a township for ourselves, he said. Now look at the situation in the school. We had a big school in the Vandemark schoolhouse, thirteen scholars being enrolled. We had a good teacher, too, Virginia Royall. But there wasn't enough fuel to last two days, and those Monterey Centre folks were dead on their feet and nobody seemed to care if the school closed down. He went on with his argument for a separate township organization; I all the time thinking with my mind in a whirl that Virginia was near, and I could see her next day. When he said that we would have to get the vote of Doc Bliven, who was a member of the Board of Supervisors, I began to take notice.

"Bliven always seemed to like you," said Roebuck. "We all kind of wish you'd see what you can do for us with him."

"I think I can get his vote," I said, after thinking it over for a while—and as I thought of it, the Dubuque ferry in 1855, the arrest of Bliven in the queue of people waiting at the post-office, my smuggled passenger, and the uplift I felt as the Iowa prairie opened to my view as we drew out of the ravines to the top of the hills—all this rolled over my memory. Roebuck looked at me like a person facing a medium in a trance.

"Yes," I said, "I believe I can get his vote. I'll try."

CHAPTER XX

I WAS surprised next morning to note the change which had taken place in the weather. It had been cold and raw when I was crossing the prairies to my farm, with the wind in the southeast, and filled with a bitter chill. In the night the wind had gone down, and it was as still as death in the morning. For the first time in my life, and it has happened but twice since, I heard the whistles of the engines on the railroad twelve miles away to the north. There was a little beard of hoar frost along the side of every spear of grass and weed; which, as the sun rose higher, dropped off and lay under every twig and bent, in a little heap if it stood up straight, or in a wind-row if it slanted; for so still was the air that the frost went straight down, and lay as it fell. I could hear the bawling of the cattle in every barnyard for miles around, and the crowing of roosters as the fowls strutted about in the warm sun. It was thawing by ten o'clock. The temperature had run up as the wind dropped; and as I now know, with the lowering of the pressure of the barometer, if we had had one.

"This is a weather-breeder!"

This was my way of telling to myself what a scientist would have described as marked low barometer; and he would have predicted from his maps that we should

394

soon find ourselves in the northwest quadrant of the "low" with high winds and falling temperature. It all comes to the same thing.

Instead of going to see Virginia before her school opened in the morning, I went to work banking up my house, fixing my sheds, and reefing things down for a gale as I learned to say on the Lakes. I made up my mind that I would go to the schoolhouse just before four and surprise Virginia, and hoped it would be a little stormy so I could have an excuse to take her home. I need not have worried about the storm. It came.

At noon the northwestern sky, a third of the way to a point overhead, was of an indigo-blue color; but it still seemed to be clear sky—though I looked at it with suspicion, it was such an unusual thing for January. As I stood gazing at it, Narcisse Lacroix, Pierre's twelve-year-old boy, came by with his little sister. I asked him if school was out, and he said the teacher had sent them home because there was no more fuel for the stove; but it was so warm that the teacher was going to stay and sweep out, and write up her register.

As the children went out of sight, a strange and awful change came over the face of nature. The bright sun was blotted out as it touched the edge of that rising belt of indigo blue. This blanket of cloud, like a curtain with puckering strings to bring it together in the southeast, drew fast across the sky—very, very fast, considering that there was not a breath of wind stirring. It was a fearful thing to see, the blue-black cloud hurrying up the sky, over the sky, and far down until there was no bright spot except a narrowing oval near the southeastern horizon; and not a breath of wind. The storm was like a leaning wall, that bent far over us while its foot dragged along the ground, miles and miles behind its top. Everything had a tinge of strange, ghastly greenish blue like the face of a corpse, and it was growing suddenly dark as if the day had all at once shut down into dusk.

I knew what it meant, though I had never seen the change from calm warmth to cold wind come with such marked symptoms of suddenness and violence. It meant a blizzard—though we never heard or adopted the word until in the late 'seventies. I thought I had plenty of time, however, and I went into the house and changed my clothes; for I wanted to look my best when I saw my girl. I put on new and warm underwear, for I foresaw that it might be bad before I could get home. I put on an extra pair of drawers under my blue trousers, and a buckskin undervest under my shirt. I thanked God for this forethought before the night was over.

As I stood naked in making this change of clothes, suddenly the house staggered as if it had been cuffed by a great hand. I peeped out of the window, and against the dark sky I could see the young grove of trees bowing before the great gusts which had struck them from the northwest. The wall of wind and frost and death had moved against them.

2

The thought in my mind was, Hurry! Hurry! For what if Virginia, in the schoolhouse without fuel, should try to reach the place where she boarded, or any inhabited house, in that storm? As yet there was no snow in the air except the few flakes which were driven horizontally out of the fierce squall; but I knew that this could not last; for the crust on the blanket of snow already on the ground would soon be ground through wherever exposed to the sand-blast of particles already driven along the surface of the earth in a creeping sheet of white. As I hurriedly finished my dressing, I heard the rattle of a shower of missiles as they struck the house; and looking out I saw that the crust was already being cut through by this grinding process; and as the wind got a purchase under the crust, it was torn up in great flakes as if blown up by a thousand explosions from underneath. In an instant, almost, for these bursts of snow took place nearly all at once, the air was filled with such a smother of snow that the landscape went out of sight in a great cloud of deep-shaded whiteness. The blizzard was upon us. I should have my work cut out for me in getting to the schoolhouse.

I wonder if the people who have been born in or moved to Iowa in the past thirty to forty years can be made to understand that we can not possibly have such winter storms of this sort as we had then. The groves themselves prevent it. The standing corn-stalks prevent it. Every object that civilization and development have placed in the way of the wind prevents it. Then, the snow, once lifted on the wings of the blast, became a part of the air, and remained in it. The atmosphere for hundreds of feet, for thousands of feet from the grassy surface of the prairie, was a moving cloud of snow, which fell only as the very tempest itself became over-burdened with it. As the storm continued, it always grew cold; for it was the North emptying itself into the South. I knew what the blizzard was; and my breath caught as I thought of Virginia, in what I knew must be a losing struggle with it.

Even to the strongest man, there was terror in this storm, the breath of which came with a roar and struck with a shiver, as the trees creaked and groaned, and the paths and roads were obliterated. As the tumult grows hills are leveled, and hollows rise into hills. Every shed-roof is the edge of an oblique Niagara of snow; every angle the center of a whirlpool. If you are caught out in it, the Spirit of the Storm flies at you and loads your eyebrows and eyelashes and hair and beard with icicles and snow. As you look out into the white, the light through your bloodshot eyelids turns everything to crimson. Your feet lag, as the feathery whiteness comes almost to your knees. Your breath comes choked as with water. If you are out far away from shelter, God help you! You struggle along for a time, all the while fearing to believe that the storm which did not seem so very dangerous, is growing more violent, and that the daylight, which you thought would last for hours yet, seems to be fading, and that night appears to be setting in earlier than usual. It is! For there are two miles of snow between you and the sun. But in a swiftly moving maze of snow, partly spit out of the lowering clouds, and partly torn and swept up from the gray and cloud-like earth, in a roar of rising wind, and oppressed by growing anxiety, you stubbornly press on.

Night shuts down darker. You can not tell, when you try to look about you, what is sky and what is earth; for all is storm. You feel more and more tired. All at once, you find that the wind which was at your side a while ago, as you kept beating into it on your course toward help and shelter, is now at your back. Has the wind changed? No; it will blow for hours from the same quarter—perhaps for days! No; you have changed your course, and are beating off with the storm! This will never do: you rally, and again turn your cheek to the cutting blast: but you know that you are off your path; yet you wonder if you may not be going right—if the wind *has* changed; or if you have not turned to the left when you should have gone to the right.

Loneliness, anxiety, weariness, uncertainty. An awful sense of helplessness takes possession of you. If it were daylight, you could pass around the deep drifts, even in this chaos; but now a drift looks the same as the prairie grass swept bare. You plunge headlong into it, flounder through it, creeping on hands and knees, with your face sometimes buried in the snow, get on your feet again, and struggle on.

You know that the snow, finer than flour, is beating through your clothing. You are chilled, and shiver. Sometimes you stop for a while and with your hands over your eyes stand stooped with your back to the wind. You try to stamp your feet to warm them, but the snow, soft and yielding, forbids this. You are so tired that you stop to rest in the midst of a great drift—you turn your face from the driving storm and wait. It seems so much easier than stumbling wearily on. Then comes the in-rushing consciousness that to rest thus is to die. You rush on in a frenzy. You have long since ceased to think of what is your proper course,—you only know that you must struggle on. You attempt a shout;—ah, it seems so faint and distant even to yourself! No one else could hear it a rod in this raging, howling, shrieking storm, in which awful sounds come out of the air itself, and not alone from the things against which it beats. And there is no one else to hear.

You gaze about with snow-smitten eyeballs for some possible light from a friendly window. Why, the sun itself could not pierce this moving earth-cloud of snow! Your feet are not so cold as they were. You can not feel them as you walk. You come to a hollow filled with soft snow. Perhaps there is the bed of a stream deep down below. You plunge into this hollow, and as you fall, turn your face from the storm. A strange and delicious sense of warmth and drowsiness steals over you; you sink lower, and feel the cold soft whiteness sifting over neck and cheek and forehead: but you do not care. The struggle is over; and—in the morning the sun glints coldly over a new landscape of gently undulating alabaster. Yonder is a little hillock which marks the place where the blizzard overtook its prey. Sometime, when the warm March winds have thawed the snow, some gaunt wolf will snuff about this spot, and send up the long howl that calls the pack to the banquet.

Such thoughts as these were a part of our lives then; and with such thoughts my mind was filled as I stepped out into the storm, my trousers tied down over my boots with bag-strings; my fur cap drawn down over my eyes; my blue military overcoat flapping about my legs; the cape of it wrapped about my head, and tied with a woolen comforter.

3

Through these wrappings, a strange sound came to my ears—the sound of sleigh-bells; and in a moment, so close were they, there emerged from the whirl of snow, a team of horses drawing a swell-body cutter, in which sat a man driving, wrapped up in buffalo robes and blankets until the box of the sleigh was filled. The

horses came to a stop in the lee of my house. There had
been so such rig in the county before I had gone to the
war.

"Is this the Vandemark schoolhouse?" came from
the man in the cutter.

"No, Captain," said I; for discipline is strong, "this
is my farm."

"Ah, it's you, Mr. Vandemark, is it?" said he. "Can
you tell me the way to the schoolhouse?"

Discipline flew off into the storm. I never for a moment harbored the idea that I was to allow Buck Gowdy
to rescue Virginia from the blizzard, and carry her off
into either danger or safety. There was none of my
Dutch hesitation here. This was battle; and I behaved
with as much prompt decision as I did on the field of
Shiloh, where, I have the captain's word for it in writing, I behaved with a good deal of it.

"Never mind about the schoolhouse," I said. "I'll attend to that!'

"The hell you will!" said he, in that calm way of his.
"Let me see. Your house faces the north. These trees
are on the section line.... The schoolhouse is........I
have it, now. Sorry to cut in ahead of you; but——
get up, Susie—Winnie, go on!"

But I had Susie and Winnie by the bits.

"Vandemark," he said, and as he shouted this to make
me hear I could feel the authority I had grown to recognize in drill, "you forget yourself! Let go those
horses!"

"Not by a damned sight!"

I found myself swearing as if I were in the habit of it.
Now the man in any kind of rig with another holding

his horses' bits is in an embarrassing fix. He can't do anything so long as he remains in the vehicle; and neither can his horses. He must carry the fight to the other man, or be made a fool of.

Buck Gowdy was not a man to hesitate in such a case. He carried the fight to me—and I was glad to see him coming. I had waited for this a long time. I have no skill in describing fights, and I was too much engaged in this to remember the details. How many blows were exchanged; what sort of blows they were; how much damage they did until the last, more than a cut lip on my part, I can not tell. Why no more damage was done is clearer—we were both so wrapped up as to be unable to do much. I only know that at the last, I had Gowdy down in the snow right by my well-curb; and that without taking time to make any plan, I wrapped the well-rope around him so as to make it necessary for him to take a little time in getting loose; I wrote him a receipt for the team and rig, which N. V. Creede tells me would not have done me any good; and I went out, very much winded, shut the door behind me, and getting into the cutter, drove off into the blizzard with Gowdy's team and sleigh, leaving him rolling around on the floor unwinding the well-rope, swearing like a trooper, and in a warm room where there was plenty to eat.

"And in my opinion," said N. V., "no matter how much girl there was at stake, the man that chose to go out into that storm when he could have let the job out was the fool in the case."

It was less than a mile to the schoolhouse, which I was lucky to find at all. I could not see it twenty feet away; but I was almost upset by a snow fort which the children had built, and taking this as the sure sign of a playground, I guessed my way the fifty or sixty feet that more by luck than judgment brought me to the back end of the house, instead of the front. I made my way around on the windward side of the building, hoping that the jingle of the bells might be heard as I passed the windows—for I dared not leave the horses again, as I had done during my contest with Gowdy. Nothing but the shelter in which they then found themselves had kept them from bolting—that and their bewilderment.

I pulled up before the door and shouted Virginia's name with all my might, over and over again. But I suppose I sat there ten or fifteen minutes before Virginia came to the door; and then, while she had all her wraps on, she was in her anxiety just taking a look at the weather, debating in her mind whether to try for the safety of the fireside, or risk the stay in the schoolhouse with no fuel. She had not heard the bells, or the trampling, or my holloing. More by my motions than anything else, she saw that I was inviting her to get in; but she knew no more than her heels who I was. She went back into the schoolhouse and got her dinner-basket—lucky or providential act!—and in she climbed. If I had been Buck Gowdy or Asher Bushyager or the Devil himself, she would have done the same. She would have thought, of course, that it was one of the neighbors come for her; and, anyhow, there was nothing else to do.

As I turned back the rich robes and the jingle of the bells came to her ears, she started; but I drew her down into the seat, and pulled the flannel-lined coonskin robe which was under us, up over our laps; I wrapped the army blanket and the thick buffalo-robe over and under us; and as I did so, a little black-and-tan terrier came shivering out from under the coonskin robe and jumped into her lap. I started to put it down again, but she held it—and as she did she looked at my blue sleeve, and then up at the mass of wrappings I had over my face. I thought she snuggled up against me a little closer, then.

4

I turned the horses toward her boarding-place, which was with a new family who had moved in at the head of the slew, near the pond for which poor Rowena was making the day of the prairie fire; and in doing so, set their faces right into the teeth of the gale. It seemed as if it would strip the scalps from our heads, in spite of all our capes and comforters and veils. Virginia pulled the robe up over her head. I had to face the storm and manage my team; but before I had gone forty rods, I saw that I was asking too much of them; and I let them turn to beat off with it. At that moment I really abandoned control, and gave it over to the wind and snow. But I thought myself steering for my own house. I was not much worried; having the confidence of youth and strength. The cutter was low and would not tip over easily. The horses were active and powerful and resolute. We were nested down in the deep box, wrapped in the warmest of robes; and it was not yet so very cold—not that cold which draws down into the lungs; seals the nostrils and mouth; and paralyzes the strength. That cold was coming—coming like an army with banners; but it was not yet here. I was not much worried until I had driven before the wind, beating up as much as I could to the east, without finding my house, or anything in the way of grove or fence to tell me where it was. I now remembered that I had not mounted the hill on which my house stood. In fact, I had missed my farm, and was lost, so far as knowing my locality was concerned: and the wind was growing fiercer and the cold more bitter.

For a moment I quailed inwardly; but I felt Virginia snuggled down by me in what seemed to be perfect trust; and I brushed the snow from my eye-opening and pushed on—hoping that I might by pure accident strike shelter in that wild waste of prairie, and determined to make the fight of my life for it if I failed.

It was getting dusk. The horses were tiring. We plunged through a deep drift under the lee of a knoll; and I stopped a few moments to let them breathe. I knew that stopping was a bad symptom, unless one had a good reason for it—but I gave myself a good reason. I felt Virginia pulling at my sleeve; and I turned back the robes and looked at her. She pulled my ear down to her lips.

"I know you now," she shouted. "It's Teunis!"

I nodded; and she squeezed my arm with her two hands. Give up! Not for all the winds and snows of the whole of the Iowa prairie! I disarranged the robes while I put my arm around her for a moment; while she patted my shoulder. Then, putting tendernesses aside, when they must be indulged in at the expense of snow in the sleigh, I put my horses into it again. A few minutes ago, I gave you the thoughts that ran through my mind as I conjured up the image of one lost in such a storm; but now I thought of nothing—only for a few minutes after that pressure on my arm—but getting on from moment to moment, keeping my sleigh from upsetting, encouraging those brave mares, and peering around for anything that might promise shelter. Virginia has always told of this to the children, when I was not present, to prove that I am brave, even if I am mortal slow; and if just facing danger from minute to minute without looking further, is bravery, I suppose I am—and there is plenty of good courage in the world which is nothing more, look at it how you will.

So far, the cutter and team of which I had robbed Buck Gowdy, had been a benefit to us. They gave us transportation, and the warm sleigh in which to nest down. I began to wonder, now, as it began to grow dark, as the tempest greatened, as my horses disappeared in the smother, and as the frost began to penetrate to our bodies, whether I should not have done better to have stayed in the schoolhouse, and burned up the partitions for fuel; but the thought came too late; though it troubled me much. Two or three times, one of the mares fell in the drifts, and nothing but the courage bred into them in the blue-grass fields of Kentucky saved us from stalling out in that fearful moving flood of wind and frost and snow. Two or three times we narrowly escaped being thrown out into it by the overturn of the sleigh; and then I foresaw a struggle, in which there would be no hope; for in a storm in which a strong man is helpless, how could he expect to come out safe with a weak girl on his hands?

At last, the inevitable happened: the off mare dove into a great drift; the nigh one pulled on: and they came to a staggering halt, one of them was kept from falling partly by her own efforts, and partly by the snow about her legs against which she braced herself. As they stood there, they turned their heads and looked back as if to say that so far as they were concerned, the fight was over. They had done all they could.

I sat a moment thinking. I looked about, and saw, between gusts, that we were almost against a huge straw-pile, where some neighbor had threshed a setting of wheat. This might mean that we were close to a house, or it might not. I handed the lines to Virginia under the robes, got out, and struggled forward to look at my team. Their blood-shot eyes and quivering flanks told me that they could help us no longer; so I unhitched them, so as to keep the cutter as a possible shelter, and turned them loose. They floundered off into the drifts, and left us alone. Cuffed and mauled by the storm, I made a cir-cuit of the stack, and stumbled over the tumbling-rod of the threshing-machine, which was still standing where it had been used. Leaning against the wheel was a shovel, carried for use in setting the separator. This I took with me, with some notion of building a snow-house for us; for I somehow felt that if there was any hope for us, it lay in the shelter of that straw. As I passed the side of the stack, just where the ground was scraped bare by the wind, I saw what seemed to be a hole under and into the great loose pile of dry straw. It looked ex-actly like one of those burrows which the children used to make in play in such places.

Virginia was safe for the moment, sitting covered up snugly with her hands warmed by the little dog; but the cold was beginning to penetrate the robes. I could leave her for the moment while I investigated the burrow with the shovel. As I gained a little advantage over the snow which was drifted in almost as fast as I could shovel it out, my heart leaped as I found the hole opening out into the middle of the stack; and I plunged in on my hands and knees, found it dry and free from snow within ten feet of the mouth, and after enlarging it by humping up my back under it where the settling had made it too small, I emerged and went to Virginia; whom I took out with her dog, wrapped her in the robes so as to keep them from getting snowy inside, and backing into the burrow, hauled the pile of robes, girl and dog in after me, like a gigantic mouse engaged in saving her young. I think no mouse ever yearned over her treasures in such case more than I did.

And then I went back to get the dinner-basket, which was already buried under the snow which had filled the cutter; for I knew that there was likely to be something left over of one of the bountiful dinners which a farmer's wife puts up for the teacher. Then I went back into the little chamber of straw in which we had found shelter, stopping up the mouth with snow and straw as I went in. I drew a long breath. This was far better than I had dared hope for. There is a warmth generated in such a pile, from the slow fermentation of the straw juices; even when seemingly dry as this was: and far in the middle of the stack, vegetables might have been stored without freezing. The sound of the tempest did not reach us here; it was still as death, and dark as tar. I wondered that Virginia did not say anything; but she kept still because she did not understand where she was, or what I had done with her.

Finally, when she spoke it was to say, "Unwrap me, Teunis! I am smothering with the heat!"

I laughed a long loud laugh. I guess I was almost

hysterical. The change was so sudden, so complete. Virginia was actually complaining of the heat!

I unwrapped her carefully, and kissed her. Did ever any peril turn to any one a face so full of clemency and tenderness as this blizzard to me?

"It takes," says she, "a storm to move *you* to any speed faster than a walk."

The darkness in the burrow was now full of light for me. I made it soft as a mouse-nest, by pulling down the clean straw, and spreading it in the bottom, with the coonskin under her, and the buffalo-robe for a coverlid. There was scarcely room for two there, but we made it do, and found room for the little dog also. There was an inexpressible happiness in our safety from the awful storm, which we knew raged all about our nest; but to be together, and to feel that the things that stood between us had all been swept away at once—even the chaff that fell down our necks only gave us cause for laughter.

"Your coat is all wet!" she exclaimed.

"It was the snow, shoveling the way in," I said. "It's nothing."

But she began right there to take care of me. She made me take off the overcoat, and wrap myself in the blanket. The dampness went out into the dry straw; but when drowsiness came upon us, she would not let me take the chance of getting chilled, but made me wrap myself in the robes with her; and we lay there talking until finally, tired by my labors, I went to sleep with her arms about me, and her lips close to mine; and when I awoke, she was asleep, and I lay there listening to her soft breathing for hours.

We were both hungry when she awoke, and in the

total darkness we felt about for the dinner-basket, in which were the dinners of the children of the McConkey family with whom she had boarded, and who had gone home at noon, because the fuel was gone. We ate frozen pie, and frozen boiled eggs, and frozen bread and butter; and then lay talking and caressing each other for hours. We talked about the poor horses, for which Virginia felt a deep pity, out there in the fierce storm and the awful cold. We talked of the beautiful cutter; and finally, I explained the way in which I had robbed Gowdy of horses and robes and sleigh, and dog.

"He can never have the dog back," said she. "And to think that I am hiding out in a strawstack with a robber and a horse-thief!"

Then she said she reckoned we'd have to join the Bunker gang, if we could find any of it to join. Certainly we should be fugitives from justice when the storm was over; but she for herself would rather be a fugitive always with me than to be rescued by "that man"—and it was lucky for him, too, she said, that I had licked him and shut him up in a house where he would be warm and fed; because he never would have been able to save himself in this awful storm as I had done. Nobody could have done so well as I had done. I had snatched her from the very jaws of death.

"Then," said I, "you're mine."

"Of course I am," said she. "I've been yours ever since we lived together so beautifully on the road, and in our Grove of Destiny. Of course I'm yours—and you are mine, Teunis—ain't you?"

"Then," said I, "just as soon as we get out of here, we'll be married."

It took argument to establish this point, but the jury was with me from the start; and finally nothing stood between me and a verdict but the fact that she must finish her term of school. I urged upon her that my house was nearer the school than was McConkey's, and she could finish it if she chose. Then she said she didn't believe it would be legal for Virginia Vandemark to finish a contract signed by Virginia Royall—and pretty soon I realized that she was making fun of me, and I hugged her and kissed her until she begged my pardon.

And all the time the storm raged. We finished the food in the dinner pail, and began wondering how long we had been imprisoned, and how hungry we ought to be by this time. I was not in the least hungry myself; but I began to feel panicky for fear Virginia might be starving to death. She had a watch, of course, as a teacher; but it had run down long ago, and even if it had not, we could not have lit a match in that place by which to look at it. Becoming really frightened as the thought of starvation and death from thirst came oftener and oftener into my mind, I dug my way to the opening of the burrow, and found it black night, and the snow still sweeping over the land; but there was hope in the fact that I could see one or two bright stars overhead. The gale was abating; and I went back with this word, and a basket of snow in lieu of water.

Whether it was the first night out or the second, I did not know, and this offered ground for argument. Virginia said that we had lived through so much that it had probably made the time seem longer than it was; but I argued that the time of holding her in my arms, kissing her, telling her how much I loved her, and persuading her to marry me as soon as we could get to Elder Thorndyke's, made it seem shorter—and this led to more efforts to make the time pass away. Finally, I dug out again, just as we both were really and truly hungry, and went back after Virginia. I made her wrap up warmly, and we crawled out, covered with chaff, rumpled, mussed up, but safe and happy; and found the sun shining over a landscape of sparkling frost, with sundogs in the sky and spiracles of frost in the air, and a light breeze still blowing from the northwest, so bitingly cold that a finger or cheek was nipped by it in a moment's exposure. And within forty rods of us was the farmstead of Amos Bemisdarfer; who stood looking at us in amazement as we came across the rippled surface of the snow to his back door.

"I kess," said Amos, "it mus' have peen your team I put in de parn lass night. Come in. Preckfuss is retty."

I left it to Virginia—she had been so sensible and wise in all her words since we had agreed to be married at once—to tell the elder and Grandma Thorndyke about it. But she went to pieces when she tried it. She ran into their little front room where the elder was working on a sermon, pulling grandma out of the kitchen by the hand.

"Teunis and I," she gasped, "have been lost in the storm, and nearly froze to death, and he tied that man up with the well-rope, and maybe he's starved to death in Teunis's house, and Teunis and I slept in a straw-stack, and Teunis is just as brave as he can be, and we're going to be married awful soon, and I'm going to board with him then, and that'll be nicer than with the McConkeys'

and nearer the schoolhouse, and cheaper, and Teunis
will build fires for me, and we'll be just as happy as we
can be, and when you quit this stingy church you'll both
of you live with us forever and ever, and I want you to
kiss Teunis and call him your son right now, and if you
don't we'll both be mad at you always—no we won't, no
we won't, you dear things, but you will marry us, won't
you?"

And then she cried hysterically and kissed us all.

"What Virginia says," said I, "is all true—especially
the getting married right now, and your living with us.
We'll both be awful sorry if we can't have you right off."

"I snum!" exclaimed Grandma Thorndyke. "Just as
I expected!"

Grandma outlived the elder by many years; and it was
not very long before she came, a widow, to live with
us "until she could hear from her folks in Massachusetts."
She finally heard from them, but she lived with us, and is
buried in our lot in the Monterey Centre burying-ground.
She always expected everything that happened. I have
given some hints of her character; but she had one weakness; she always, when she was a little down, spoke of
herself as being a burden to us, especially in the hard
times in the 'seventies. There was never a better woman,
or one that did more for a family than she did for Virginia
and me and our children—and our chickens and our
calves and our lambs and goslings and ducks and young
turkeys. Of course, she wanted Virginia to do better than
to marry me; and that was all right with me after I understood it: but grandma made that good, by always taking
my side of every little difference in the family. Peace to
her ashes!

5

Now I have reached the point in this history where things get beyond me. I can't tell the history of Monterey County; and the unsettled matters like the Wade-Stone controversy, the outcome of the betrayal of Rowena Fewkes by Buckner Gowdy, and other beginnings of things like the doings of the Bushyager bandits; for some of them run out into the history of the state as well as the county. And as for the township history, it is now approaching the point where there is nothing to it but more settlers, roads, schools, and the drainage of the slew —of which, so far as the reader is concerned if he is not posted, he may post himself up by getting that Excelsior County History, which he can do cheaply from almost any one who was swindled by their slick agent. What remains to be told here is a short horse and soon curried. Vandemark Township was set off as a separate township within six weeks of the day we crawled out of the strawstack—and on that day we had been married a month, and Virginia was boarding with me as she predicted. Doctor Bliven as a member of the County Board voted for the new township just as his wife said he would after I talked with her about it.

N. V. Creede says that at this time I was threatened with political ability; but happily recovered. One reason for this joke he finds in the fact that I was elected justice of the peace in the township at the first election of officers; and got some reputation out of the fact that they named the township after me when it was fashionable to name them after Lincoln, Colfax, Grant, Sherman, Sheridan and the rest of the Civil War heroes. The second is the way I handled Dick McGill. N. V. says this was very subtle. I knew that if he wrote up my dragging Virginia into a straw-pile and keeping her there two nights and a day, while he would make folks laugh all over the county, he would make us ashamed; for he never failed to give everything a tint of his own color. So I went to him and told him that if he said a word about it, I should maul him into a slop and feed him to the hogs. This was my way of being "subtle."

"Why, Jake," he said, "I never would say anything to take the shine off the greatest thing ever done in these parts. I've got it all written up, and I'm sending a copy of it to the Chicago *Tribune*. It's an epic of prairie life. Read it, and if you don't want it printed, why, it's me for the swine; for it's already gone to Chicago."

Of course it seemed all right to me, but I was afraid of it, and was thinking of pounding him up right then, when in came Elder Thorndyke to put in the paper something about his next Sunday's services, and McGill asked him to read the story and act as umpire. And after he had gone over it, he grasped my hand and said that Virginia and I had not told them half of the strange story of our living through the blizzard out on the prairie, and that it was a great drama of resolution, resource and bravery on my part, and seemed almost like a miracle.

"Will this hurt Virginia's feelings if it is printed?" I asked.

"No, no," he said. "It will make her fiancé a hero. It will tickle her," said he, "half to death."

Then I told Dick he might go on with it if he would leave it just as it was. The joke was on him, after all, for there was nothing in it about my fight with Buck

Gowdy, or of my robbing him of the team and sleigh and harness and robes and Nick, the little dog.

The third thing that N. V. thought might have sent me down through the greased tin horn of politics, which has ruined more good men than any other form of gambling, was my management of the business of getting the township set off, against the opposition of the whole Monterey Centre Ring. But he did not know of that day in Dubuque, and of my smuggling of Mrs. Bliven into Iowa, as I have told it in this history. It hurt Bliven politically, but he kept on boosting me, and it was his electioneering, that I knew nothing about, that elected me justice of the peace; and it was Mrs. Bliven's urging that caused me to qualify by being sworn in—though I couldn't see what she meant by her interest.

6

On my next birthday, the twenty-seventh of July, however, something happened that after a few months of figuring made me think that they knew what they were about all the time; for on that day they (the Blivens) got up a surprise party on us, and came in such rigs as they had (there were more light rigs than at the Governor Wade reception, a fact of historical interest as showing progress); though Virginia did not seem to be much surprised. In the course of the evening Doc Bliven started in making fun of me as a justice of the peace.

"I helped a little to elect you, Jake," said he, "but I'll bet you couldn't make out a mittimus if you had to send a criminal to jail to-night."

"I won't bet," I said. "I know I couldn't!"

"I'll bet the oysters for the crowd, Squire Vandemark," he went on deviling me, "that you couldn't perform the marriage ceremony."

Now here he came closer to my abilities, for I had been through a marriage ceremony lately, and I have a good memory—and oysters were a novelty in Iowa, coming in tin cans and called cove oysters, put up in Baltimore. It looked like a chance to stick Doc Bliven, and while I was hesitating, Mrs. Bliven whispered that there was a form for the ceremony in the instruction book.

"I'll bet you the oysters for the crowd I can," I said. "You furnish the happy couple—and I'll see that you furnish the oyster supper, too."

"Any couple will do," said the doctor. "Come, Mollie, we may as well go through it again."

The word "again" seemed suspicious. I began to wonder: and before the ceremony was over, I reading from the book of instructions, and people interrupting with their jokes, I saw that this meant a good deal to the Blivens. Mollie's voice trembled as she said "I do!"; and the doctor's hand was not steady as he took hers. I asked myself what had become of the man who had made the attack on Bliven as he stood in line for his mail at the Dubuque post-office away back there in 1855.

"Don't forget my certificate, Jake," said Mrs. Bliven, as they sat down; and I had to write it out and give it to her.

"And remember the report of it to the county clerk," said Henderson L. Burns, who held that office himself. "The Doc will kick out of the supper unless you do everything."

I did not forget the report, and I suppose it is there in the old records to this day.

"We got word," whispered Mrs. Bliven to me as she went away, "that I have been a widow for more than a year. You've been a good friend to me, Jake!"*

I shall not close this history, without clearing up my record as to the mares, Susie and Winnie, and the cutter, and Nick, the black-and-tan, that saved Virginia's fingers from freezing, and the robes. First, I kept the property, and every horse on the farm is descended from Susie and Winnie. Second, I paid Buck Gowdy all the outfit was worth, though he never knew it, and never would have taken pay: I drove a bunch of cattle over into his corn-field the next fall and left them just before day one morning, and he took them up, advertised them as estrays, and finally, as N. V. says, reduced them to possession. And third, they were legally mine, anyhow; for when I got home, I found this paper lying on the bed, where he had slept those two nights when we were nesting in the straw-pile:

BILL OF SALE

In consideration of one lesson in the manly art of self-defense, of two days' board and lodging, and of one dollar ($1.00) to me in hand by J. T. Vandemark, the receipt of which is hereby acknowledged, I hereby sell

---

*There is no record of this marriage in the clerk's office; where it was regarded, of course, as a joke. This was probably a unique case of a secret marriage made in public; but there is no doubt as to its validity. The editor remembers the Blivens as respected citizens. They are dead long since, and left no descendants. Otherwise the historian would not have told their story—which is not illustrative of anything usual in our early history; but shows that in Iowa as in other new countries there were those who were escaping from their past.—G. v. d. M.

and transfer to said J. T. Vandemark, possession having already been given, the following described personal property, to wit:

1 Bay Mare called Susie, weight 1150 lbs., with star in forehead, and white left hind foot, five years old;

1 Bay Mare called Winnie, weight 1175 lbs., with star in forehead, and two white hind feet, six years old;

1 one-seated, swell-body cutter, one fine army blanket, one coonskin robe lined with flannel, one large buffalo robe.

It is hereby understood that if any of said animals are ever returned to me at Blue-grass Manor or elsewhere they will be hamstrung by the undersigned and turned out to die.   Signed, J. Buckner Gowdy.

One of my grandsons, Frank McConkey, has just read over this chapter, and remarks, "He was a dead game sport!" But he had also read what Captain Gowdy had interlined, or rather written on the margin to go in after the description of the property conveyed: "Also one blue-blooded black-and-tan terrier name 'Nicodemus.' The tail goes with the hide, Jacob!" Since his death, I have grown to liking the man much better; in fact ever since I whaled him.

Here ends the story, so far as I can tell it. It is not my story. There are some fifteen hundred townships in Iowa; and each of them had its history like this; and so had every township in all the great, wonderful West of the prairie. The thing in my mind has been to tell the truth; not the truth of statistics; not just information: but the living truth as we lived it. Every one of these townships has a history beginning in the East, or in Scandinavia, or Germany, or the South. We are a result of lines of effect which draw together into our story; and we are a cause of a future of which no man can form a conjecture.

The prairies took me, an ignorant, orphaned canal hand, and made me something much better. How much better it is not for me to say. The best prayer I can utter now is that it may do as well with my children and grandchildren, with the tenants on these rich farms, and the farm-hands that help till them, and with the owners who find that expensive land is just like expensive clothes:—merely something you must have, and must pay heavily for.

THE END

DATE DUE

AG 2'91			
AG13'91			
AG19'91			
SEP 9 '91			
SE20'91 A			
SEP 30'91			
OC 8'91			
DE 6'91			
DE 1 '92			

Keep 5/98

F
QUI   40966

Quick, Herbert

Vandemark's Folly

F
QUI

Glenwood Public Library
109 North Vine Street
Glenwood, Iowa 51534

40966

DEMCO